Resounding Praise for
HOLLY LISLE
and
THE WORLD GATES

"A delightful yarn of shared lives, shared universes, and shared magic . . . [that] grips from the opening paragraph, snagging the reader on a fast and furious tale that is at times heroic, at times poignant, and at all times entertaining."
Elizabeth Haydon

"A literal walk through the looking glass into worlds of adventure and romance."
Susan Sizemore

"Lisle seems to be an author unlikely to write a sloppy or stupid book."
Chicago Sun-Times

"Holly Lisle at her best . . . It's always a delight to read [her] books."
S.L. Viehl

"Holly Lisle's work has grown beyond my wildest expectations."
Mercedes Lackey

Also by Holly Lisle

MEMORY OF FIRE
Book One of The World Gates

THE WRECK OF HEAVEN
Book Two of The World Gates

HOLLY LISLE

Gods Old and Dark

BOOK THREE OF THE WORLD GATES

An Imprint of HarperCollinsPublishers

EOS
An Imprint of HarperCollins*Publishers*
10 East 53rd Street
New York, New York 10022-5299

Copyright © 2004 by Holly Lisle
ISBN: 0-380-81839-6
www.eosbooks.com

First Eos paperback printing: April 2004

HarperCollins® and Eos® are trademarks of HarperCollins Publishers Inc.

Printed in the U.S.A.

10 9 8 7 6 5 4 3 2 1

For the real Sentinels, the real heroes:
the men and women all around us who
move quietly from day to day but,
when disaster and terror descend,
run up the stairs, not down;
run to the front of the plane, not the back,
and move forward when forward is
the worst place to be.

With love and gratitude.

Acknowledgments

My thanks to:

The fast turnaround crew, who bug-hunted with both vim AND vigor, and with lightning speed found an astonishing array of typos, spellos, and continuity errors—Sheila Kelly, Kay House, James Milton, Jim & Valerie Mills, Linda Sprinkle, and Lazette & Russ Gifford. Between them, they dug out 497 mistakes that I missed, and got these errors back to me in typed, line-separated, database-sortable form in three days from the day they received a manuscript they'd never seen—and in some cases got them back in hours rather than days. Your comments were brilliant, your eyes were keen, and I am deeply grateful. You were wonderful.

The slow turnaround crew, who read long and deeply, sought out theme and story and the places where those two failed to meet, and brought the news back to me clearly and kindly, asking incisive questions and offering useful suggestions—Sheila Kelly again, BJ Steeves, Joshua Johnston, Krista Heiser, Jinx Kimmer, and David Stone. You pushed me to think harder about the story, the theme, what I wanted to do with this story and how I wanted to get there, and if, after all the revising and reworking, I have not answered your questions, the fault is mine alone. Thank you so much for your help; it made a world of difference.

Gods Old and Dark

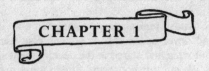

CHAPTER 1

Siren, Wisconsin

HEYR THORRSON, pounding roofing nails into shingles on the hottest August afternoon Wisconsin had seen in ten years, suddenly smelled spring in the air. He slid his hammer into his tool belt, closed his eyes, and inhaled deeply.

The scent that he caught this time wasn't spring, but it had the same feel to it. Newness, and life, and goodness—but fragile. Fragile.

"Hmmm," he said. And, "Well. By damn."

He yelled to his fellow roofer, "Hey, Lars, I'm on break." Lars, sweating and shirtless and looking like he'd been run through a wringer, just grunted. Heyr took the time to go down the ladder, though it would have been easier just to jump. He kept breathing deeply, making sure all the time that this wasn't just his imagination, just wishful thinking, because jobs were hard enough to come by anymore and he didn't want to do anything stupid.

The smell was still in his nose when he went to the foreman, who gave him a little smile when he walked up and said, "You could have the decency to pretend to be as exhausted as the rest of us. Doesn't this heat bother you?"

Heyr shrugged. Extremes of weather had never bothered him. "Just lucky," he said. And then, one more quick breath. Still there. "I hate to do this to you in the middle of a job, Colly, but I've got someplace I need to be."

Colly shrugged. "Don't worry about it. You never miss a

day, never ask for time off. You need to go someplace this afternoon, go ahead."

"I don't mean this afternoon. I mean I have to leave now. I quit."

Colly, whose real name was something so dreadful that Heyr had never heard him or anyone else use it, held his hands out wide and stared at the development springing out of dirt. "We got this house and fifteen more just like it. You know you got a job until this is done, and for anything else I get when this project is finished. You're my best guy. You quit, I'm going to have to hire three other people to replace you. You can't just walk out on me like this, man. In the middle of the day. In the middle of a roof. . . . Jesus wept, your nail box is still up there, and half a flat of shingles."

"Told you when I signed on I'd stay as long as I could. Well—this is as long as I could."

Colly looked at him, exasperated. "You said that six years ago. I figured by now you'd made up your mind."

"Doesn't have anything to do with me," Heyr said. "I like you, liked working with you. You treated me right, and the rest of your men, too, and I appreciate it. I just got my call. Have to go now. *Right* now." He turned and left.

Colly was yelling after him, but Heyr walked across the site, climbed into his white pickup truck, and pulled out. He had a cell phone in the truck. Soon as he was out on the street, he picked up the phone and hit "1" on the quick dial.

He heard two rings. Then a voice one degree too sexy for professional use said, "First National Savings and Loan, Nancy Soderlund speaking. How may I help you?"

Heyr had his window rolled down. He took another deep breath. Yep, it was still there. "Have to go, Nancy," he said.

There was a moment's silence, in which Heyr had time to wish he'd stuck to his guns about keeping his relationships uncomplicated.

"Go? Where?"

"I'm not sure. I just have to go."

Another silence. "Well . . . for how long?"

Make it clean, he told himself. Make it quick.

"This is what I told you about when we moved in together, Nancy—that one day I was going to have to leave."

A very, very long silence followed this announcement, while she tried to figure out what he was talking about. Then, in the silence, she screamed into his ear, *"That was FOUR YEARS ago!"*

"I know." He was going to have to let her get this out of her system. Let her yell at him. If things were different, he'd go home one last time and let her scream at him in person and punch him and maybe break things and throw them at him, but he didn't have the time. What he smelled was pure live magic, too fragile and too tentative to be left untended. He needed to track it down fast, before someone else got to it first and destroyed the source. "I'm sorry."

"Sorry? You're *sorry?* I have put four years of my life into *us*, into taking care of you and loving you and . . . We don't even *fight* much, you son of a bitch, and now you're telling me that you're *leaving* me, and I get no warning? What, am I supposed to just go away now and pretend you never existed? Find someplace new to live, and someone else to love, and act like the last four years never happened?"

"You don't have to go anywhere," he said. He stopped the truck at an intersection, closed his eyes, and sniffed. Trying to get a sense of the direction of the smell's origin. East, he thought. East, and maybe south, too, though at the moment east was strongest.

"I don't? How do you figure that? I'm living in your house, unless you forgot."

"It's *your* house," he said. "I bought it for you. It's all in your name, and paid for. I didn't want you to not have anything when I had to go."

Suddenly she was crying. "What happened? Did you kill somebody? Have you been in hiding? Have the police or something tracked you down?"

"Nancy, I just have to go. I didn't do anything wrong, but I knew eventually I was going to find what I was looking for, and when I found it, I was going to have to leave."

Weeping on the other end of the phone. He could just

imagine the looks Nancy was getting from the patrons in
First National. She had one of those pitiful glass-walled offices that let everyone look in; he thought her job would
have to be like working in a fishbowl or being on display at
a zoo. He wouldn't have been a banker for any amount of
money, but banking was regular work, and the bank was
warm in the winter and cool in the summer, and that mattered a lot to Nancy.

"Who is she?" Nancy whispered. "What's her name?"

He was going to war, and her mind was jumping to other
women. Well, of course she'd think that. What did she know
of war?

Heyr, following the road, heading east, smelled the scent
of new life, of fresh beginnings, of rebirth, and the thought
occurred to him that maybe it would be easier for Nancy if
he *was* leaving her for another woman—if she could tell her
friends what a dog he'd been, how sneaky for having a long-
distance affair under her nose, and if she could hate him and
bad-mouth him and feel justified.

"Her name's . . . Hope," Heyr said. "You don't know her.
She lives out east."

More sobbing, some words Heyr didn't even know that
Nancy knew, and then she seemed to pull herself together.
"We have four good years behind us, and I thought we had a
lot of good years ahead of us. I'm leaving work now, and I'll
see you when you get home, and we're going to talk about
this. You and I—we're worth fighting for."

He sighed. "I'm not coming home. I . . . won't see you
again. I'm sorry. You can throw out all my things if you
want. Or sell them. Or keep them." He'd reached the edge of
town, and wild Wisconsin spread before him, hills and fields
and forest. The road curled eastward, black and smooth and
narrow, rolling up at the horizon into a copse of trees. "I
have to go now, Nancy. You'll find the deed to the house and
some money I left for you and some other things in the red
box under my side of the bed. The key for the box is in our
safety-deposit box, taped to the back. It's labeled 'Spare
House Key.' " He took a deep breath and gave her the lie, be-

cause lies were sometimes better than the truth. "I loved you more than I ever loved anyone, but I don't love you anymore. I'm sorry, Nancy. I really am. I wish you well, and hope that you'll someday find someone who's good enough for you."

She was yelling, but he cut her off.

Then, because he didn't want her to be able to call him again, he threw the cell phone out the window. He'd gotten the phone for her, so she could call him when she needed him, and now there was no more her.

Keep it clean. Let her hate him. Give her a reason to say "Good riddance" and move on with her life.

Heyr studied those trees at the top of the rise. Probably not, he decided after a moment. He was still too close to town. He drove past them, rolled onward. Fine countryside surrounded him—a land dotted with glacial lakes, scoured by an ancient ice age, grown back tough and fierce. He'd spent a long time in Wisconsin, and he'd grown comfortable there. The place fit him, fit him as well as any place he'd ever lived.

He sighed. Sooner or later, it had always been time to move on. This time, it had been sooner.

He let the road hum beneath his tires for a while, until he found a good spot to pull off the pavement. He drove the truck down a two-rut road, listening to the hiss of tall grasses dragging against the truck sides, smelling the green of late summer so rich in his nose it was almost a feeling, sensing the weight of the heat, liking the taste of dust billowing up from the track. This newest smell—this spring-blown thread of life—curled his toes, arched his back, made him hungry and sharp and tight as a new bowstring. Took some of the edge off of pain so overwhelming he'd stopped fighting it, pain so old that he'd forgotten until just now that pain sometimes lessened, instead of always getting worse.

Good stand of trees up ahead, fronted by some low understory growth that formed a natural arch over the road. Yes. He was far enough; this place would do. He pulled up close, left the truck running, and from his glove compartment, pulled out a length of twine. He measured out four arm's lengths, frowned thoughtfully and added another two arm's lengths, and snapped the twine in two with one sharp movement. He hopped out of the truck and jogged to the two closest saplings that could be formed into an arch—two pliable young white oaks that grew directly across the road from each other, with single trunks and few side branches.

Heyr pulled the flexible tops together and bound them with a knot that would untie with one hard tug of the string. He eased the arch he'd formed out of his hands and watched it for a moment. It held, though the trees strained against the twine.

Then he studied the long tail of string now dragging on the ground and realized he'd still left it a bit too short, so he pulled the truck up until its front bumper rested only a couple of feet from the arch. He tied the string to the back bumper. Patted the hood of the truck as he walked by and said, "Going on a little trip, boys."

And then he stood before the tree arch. He stared into it, letting his eyes unfocus, so that the shadowed greens and browns of the woods beyond seemed to form a flat, mottled canvas for the arch. He let the image of a surface grow in his mind, and did not stare directly at the little green lights that began to zip and streak across that surface. They began to connect, and then, like spilled ink spreading out across a blank page, radiant green fire filled in the arch, making a doorway big enough for Heyr and the truck. Heyr stared into that sheet of light that hummed with life and promise and energy. In it, he sought the source of the tender, sweet scent that had first caught his attention—and when he located the scent, he found a deceptive web, one that wandered from world to world, universe to universe, that popped up in unexpected places from seemingly random connections in other universes. He found, in short, an intentionally tangled, confusing mess. That was good. But the mess had a center, a strong core to which every single thread could eventually be traced. And that was bad, because if he could find that center, others could, too.

That core was a single house in a small southern town. He

marked the house with a tiny magical tracer and set his vision roaming. A sign outside the town, with badges for the Lions, the Rotarians, the Masons, and the Jaycees, said, "Welcome to Cat Creek, North Carolina, Home of the Fighting Tigers."

He directed his vision out of town, keeping careful watch on the road. He hated being lost, or wandering around looking for things. Just comfortably distant from the town he found a good patch of woods that bordered on fields white with cotton, with a dirt road running straight out to the road that would carry him back to town. That would do.

He turned to the truck. "Let's go."

The door opened for him as he approached, and the motor growled.

He jumped in and put his hands on the steering wheel, but it was shifting beneath his fingers, becoming hard leather reins. The truck changed as it slid into the green light, and for one brief, wondrous span that was no time and all time as he slid into one of Yggdrasil's branches, he could feel his old friends Tanngrísnir and Tanngnjóstr leaping forward, while at his hip Mjollnir sang, wearing its true seeming. He roared his pleasure, and the green fire enveloped him, and in his ears the Valkyries sang songs of heroes and feasting and mighty battles, and the world tree spun him forward, embracing him, welcoming him, and as quickly and as slowly as that, it spat him out, taking thunder and lightning, sheeting rain and towering black clouds with him.

Heyr sat in the truck, window still down, while the rain pounded the windshield and sluiced away the dust and grime, while lightning crashed all around him and thunder roared like a choir of giants in his ears, and he threw back his head and laughed. He bellowed into the storm, "*I'm here now, you slinking cowards, serpents, you hiders in darkness and weak-kneed back-biters. I'm here, and I brought my hammer. Come play with me . . . if you DARE!*"

Night Watch Control Hub, Barâd Island, Oria

Rekkathav, personal servant of Aril, keth dark god and Master of the Night Watch, trotted along beside the Master of the Night Watch as the Master glided through the corridors of the ancient Barâd palace, heading for the control hub hidden at its core. Aril was typical of the keth; he was twice as tall as Rekkathav—tall enough to look a rrôn in the eye—and slender as cattail reeds, with huge, black almond eyes, a tiny rosebud mouth, and almost no nose, and an androgynous beauty that added a taste of awe and lust to the terror that he inspired. His silk robes, light as air, floated around him, and the thousands of braids of his pale gold hair swirled as if alive. The aura of power that poured from him terrified Rekkathav, even though he had survived more than two years already as Aril's closest assistant, something of a record.

In the Hub, the true center of all the universes, where the dark gods watched and controlled and commanded the fates of worlds, mere assistants were as disposable as mayflies, and warranted as much interest. Rekkathav had spent the last two years balanced on the sharp edge of a knife, with fear his constant companion. The Night Watch was almost ready to harvest Earth and drink its death, and Rekkathav, if he survived to that point, would partake of the feast and get his first taste of the dark power created from the slaughter of a world and all its inhabitants. And he would move up in rank; Rekkathav would become a dark god, and no longer just a pretender. Surviving long enough to feast, though, was his great challenge.

The hyatvit, dozen legs scrambling and twin hearts racing, kept up with the Master. "You've returned in such a state, Master. Your inspection did not go well?" He instantly regretted that question—clearly things had not gone well. The question was whether they had gone badly in a way that could be blamed on Rekkathav. "What may I do to assist you?" he asked.

Aril stared down at him. *Summon the off-duty fieldmasters. Bring them to the Hub.*

The hyatvit—his mind touched by the coldness of Aril's thoughts and the depth of Aril's anger—nodded, terror-stricken, and fled.

Rekkathav sent messages to each of the fieldmasters via the emergency communication gates, then raced back to Aril's side to await his next orders. No new orders were forthcoming, however; instead, the Master of the Night Watch beckoned him to follow, and floated at terrible speed to the enormous main doors of the Hub, the central nervous system of the Night Watch's reality-spanning organization.

The Master approached the doors of the Hub, stared at them for just an instant, then blew them open with the force of his thoughts. They exploded off their hinges and buried themselves in the marble floor, the metal twisted and ribboned like fruit peels. Everyone within the Hub dove for cover.

"Not me," Rekkathav whispered. He wore a resurrection ring driven through the skin fold behind his right front powerleg, but he had not yet passed through his first death. He clung to life, an old god but not yet a dark god, not yet fed by the power of death, and every time he was faced with the possibility of his own first death he had second thoughts.

To command the powers of the universe, to hold eternity in his hand—he wanted this for himself. He wanted some day to become what Aril was: the Master of the Night Watch, the true owner of worlds.

But to rise through the ranks to the Mastery, first he had to survive. He did not have to avoid death, of course. A Master had died a hundred times or more by the time he reached the pinnacle of dark godhood. But Rekkathav had to keep resurrecting, and the moments between death and rebirth were when a dark god was most vulnerable. Aril knew of his ambition, and though at the moment the Master of the Night Watch was amused by it—that Rekkathav dared dream so high who had not yet tasted a single death, even his own—Aril's amusement had a nasty way of vanishing like smoke in the first stiff breeze.

Aril glided to the center of the Hub, with Rekkathav hurrying behind him.

Heads began popping up from behind the tall consoles that powered the Hub's observation and intervention gates. The head fieldmaster, Vanak, who was in charge of tracking activity on the worlds in which the Night Watch worked, was on duty at the time. When the Master beckoned, he came cringing up to Aril like a whipped cur. Rekkathav watched the Master, ever silent, point a finger at Vanak.

It seemed nothing but a gesture. No lightning crackled; no thunder rolled. Yet the fieldmaster's spine arced and his fingers clenched into fists and his arms went rigid at his sides, and for a moment he made a strangling noise in the back of his throat. He stared at the Master, his mouth opening and closing as if he were a fish torn from the water and tossed into the tall grass to die.

Then Vanak's eyes rolled back in his head and he fell to the floor, twitching. He pissed himself, flopped and spasmed, vomited, lost control of his bowels. Watching this display, Rekkathav felt terror digging inside his gut as if it were full of fighting reptiles, cold and clawed and sharp of tooth and spine.

Fieldmasters' live log, Aril whispered in Rekkathav's skull, and Rekkathav leapt as if stabbed and raced for the log, skittering back to place it with trembling fingers in the Master's outstretched hand.

Aril did not look at the log, though. He simply stood, waiting, sniffing the air as if he smelled the fear that rose in the room like heat off of stones after a blazing summer day.

Nine gates in the staff gatewall at the far rim of the Hub shimmered to life, and nine fieldmasters—dark gods of the Night Watch all, with positions of tremendous power and privilege—stepped through almost simultaneously. Their eyes first found Aril, and then Vanak at his feet, still flopping, no shred of awareness or dignity left to him.

The fieldmasters had endured thousands of their own deaths among them. Any aspects of their living selves had long ago been stripped away, leaving them creatures of keen intelligence, ravenous dark appetites, and little else. But they were still capable of fear. Not an emotion, fear—it was

a simple survival instinct. Creatures with no capacity for
fear could not recognize danger to their existence and avoid
it; most creatures so made didn't last long in a universe well
endowed with teeth. The dark gods of the Night Watch were
survivors. They stared at the grotesque remains of their still-
living but destroyed colleague, and they recoiled.

Come, Aril told them in a thought-voice that everyone
within the Hub could hear, and the fieldmasters stepped toward him, their horror clear in every reluctant step.

In the whole of the Hub, the only sound Rekkathav heard
was ragged breathing.

When the fieldmasters stood before him, Aril held the log-
book out. *Find an example of your signature, one at a time,
and show it to me.* This, too, he broadcast into the minds of
everyone present.

He handed the log to the first fieldmaster to his left, and
Rekkathav watched the fieldmaster flip to a page, point to his
initials, and pass the book to the next. The log went down the
line, each fieldmaster finding an example of his or her initials
and pointing it out, and the last fieldmaster demonstrating the
presence of his own signature and returning the log to Aril.

Thank you, Aril said. In the whisper in Rekkathav's mind,
no trace of gratitude echoed.

For a moment the Master did nothing else. Then he turned
to walk away, and Rekkathav, watching the fieldmasters,
saw each of them relax.

Around the room, Rekkathav saw echoing relief on the
faces of the lesser staffers. Whatever had happened was
over—it had been Vanak's sin alone. And they had survived it.

What happened next, Rekkathav would never be able to
expunge from his memory.

Aril made a tiny gesture with his left hand. All nine fieldmasters, plus the twitching hulk that had been Vanak, exploded in green fire and crumbled to dust.

One of them had been so close to Rekkathav that he could
feel the backwash of magic curling against his skin, could
smell dust that was all that remained of flesh and bone and
blood. Rekkathav heard screams of shock and dread

throughout the Hub. He did not scream, though; he could not even breathe. His throat locked shut, his many knees gave way, and he dropped to the floor in a shivering, chittering pile.

The Master seemed uninterested in Rekkathav or the rest of the room's survivors. His attention fixed on the senior field assistant like the rays of the sun focused through a lens. Rekkathav would have felt pity for the senior assistant had he not been so relieved not to *be* him.

Gather their rings, Aril told the assistant. *Place them in the terminal box.*

The fear in the room grew deeper, sharper—until that moment, the punishment of the fieldmasters had seemed simply that, a punishment, something that they would return from once their resurrection rings re-created them. Until that instant, Rekkathav had believed the Master of the Night Watch had been making a dramatic gesture of his displeasure.

Instead, clearly, Aril intended to overturn the universe as Rekkathav had known it.

The terminal box changed everything. The terminal box was designed to destroy resurrection rings—to grind the gold to powder, to strip away the magic that powered them, and to wash the resultant slurry into the sea, from whence not even the Master himself would be able to gather all the bits back up again.

The Master was choosing to exercise his right to pass capital sentence on immortals. Rekkathav knew of the terminal box's being used through the history of the Night Watch, though its use had always been rare. He was certain it had never been used to dispose of every chief officer in the most important branch of service in the Night Watch.

The senior assistant looked like he was about to be sick. He dropped the resurrection rings into the terminal box, one after the other. Two trips, twenty-seven rings ranging from small finger-rings to heavy bracelets to thick, massive chains. Each fieldmaster had clearly been hedging his bets, augmenting his main resurrection ring with backup rings.

When the last of the rings dropped into the ancient, bejeweled box, the senior assistant looked to the Master, waiting for a sign that he should remove the rings—that the object lesson for all those present was done.

Close the lid, the master said so that all could hear.

Not just a display, then; Aril intended the destruction of the entire field command of the Night Watch in an instant.

The senior assistant closed the lid, and tortured screams of metal against metal and magic against magic filled the Hub. Everyone stood frozen, knowing they were witnessing something unprecedented, something both huge and terrible, none of them daring to move in case whatever had happened was not over, and moving might bring them to the attention of the Master.

The moments in which the terminal box destroyed all twenty-seven resurrection rings were the longest Rekkathav had ever experienced. When the box finished its work, the Master of the Night Watch pointed to the assistant. *You are the new head fieldmaster. Choose nine associates today. Your mutual survival depends on your mutual competence, so choose carefully.*

Aril then told them something so ludicrous that, had Rekkathav not seen the destruction of the fieldmasters, he would have thought the Master of the Night Watch lied.

New, live magic has reappeared on Earth. The planet has, under the watch of those now destroyed, begun to heal itself in spite of our working against it. The new fieldmasters' primary duties will be to determine how this has been accomplished and to eliminate whomever and whatever is responsible. The new fieldmasters will have limited time to reverse the damage done and set the world back upon our chosen course to its destruction.

You have seen the price for failure or carelessness. Make sure you succeed.

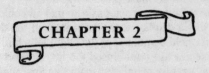

CHAPTER 2

Cat Creek, North Carolina

ERIC MACAVERY, Cat Creek's sheriff and the leader of the Cat Creek Sentinels, had the watch. He'd been sitting half in and half out of the official watch gate in the Daisies and Dahlias Florist, now run by round, sweet Betty Kay Nye, taking a restful day shift. The green fire of the gate surrounded him, the energy of the universe flowed through him, and he could feel the smooth workings of the region. His watch area had no major traffic at the moment—Lauren Dane and her son, Jake, had been in and out of her home gate a couple of times. Eric currently showed both of them at Lauren's parents' old cabin in Oria, Earth's closest downworld. He didn't know why she was there, but Lauren, as the Sentinels' gateweaver, had a lot of things to keep track of. Lauren Dane's relationship with the Sentinels had been uncomfortable for a while after her dead husband's parents kidnapped him; Lauren returned from the ordeal of getting him back gaunt and strange-eyed and with her hair whacked off and not a word to say to anybody except Pete. She didn't even seem to have much to say to *Pete* after the first few days.

Lauren was not a happy lady—she kept her child within arm's reach always, and vanished without warning for hours at a time. She didn't trust anyone anymore, Eric had finally realized. And he guessed she had a reason.

He'd finally realized, as well, that he couldn't demand a minute-by-minute accounting from her and still expect her to accomplish anything, though, so in the last few months he'd backed off a bit from his close watch.

That day, aside from Lauren, Eric had tracked a couple of little natural gates that had blinked in and out of existence in the uninhabited parts of the area. This once-rare event was becoming a more frequent occurrence, and Eric would have been happier had he known why that was so. And he'd caught Pete Stark, his deputy, friend, and fellow Sentinel, using a gate to get something from Pete's refrigerator at home while he was on duty at the station. As long as Pete hadn't been snagging some of that British beer he liked, Eric was inclined not to notice the little misuse of magic.

He could hear Betty Kay downstairs taking an FTD order. She'd turned out to be a perfect replacement for Nancine Tubbs, the Sentinel who had previously owned the Daisies and Dahlias, but who had died in the line of duty. Betty Kay was cheerful and friendly, and people in the town liked her, even if she was a Yankee. She dated the local boys, she knew to eat grits with butter and salt and pepper—not, for God's sake, milk and sugar—and she worked hard. She talked too much, and every time he saw her she had her nose in one Jude Devereaux novel or another, and Terry Mayhew's frequent pursuit aside, Eric guessed she was still a virgin, but there were worse things you could say about a person.

He heard her hang up the phone and come to the stairs. She yelled, "You want any lunch? Or a . . . rest room break . . . or anything?"

"I'm good," he said.

And then he wasn't.

A pulse that felt like an atom bomb going off tore through the fabric of the universes and slammed waves of energy at Eric, pounding him with the wake of something huge that had moved past. The last, hardest wave physically picked him up and threw him out of the gate-mirror and sent him crashing into the wall on the opposite side of the room. He hit his head and saw stars and toppled to the floor, dazed, while thunder erupted from the middle of a tranquil, sunny afternoon, shaking the foundations of the old house that held the florist shop and the Sentinels' gate, and lightning ripped into a tree next to the building, cracking limbs and sending them flying. Downstairs he heard glass shatter and Betty Kay scream—and then rain blasted the windows like it had been shot out of a pressure nozzle.

Eric rolled over, getting hands and knees under him. He tried to stand, but he couldn't. He was too dizzy. He looked up long enough to see that the gate was closed and the mirror had a crack running through it from top to bottom. He hung his head and found himself staring at the floor between his hands, where a little puddle was forming. Bright red. Shiny. Funny—the roof didn't usually leak red.

The red puddle seemed to expand, or maybe it was just that everything else got smaller, fuzzed in grey. And he seemed to be falling forward . . .

Natta Cottage, Ballahara, Oria

"I don't know if I can do this anymore." Molly McColl, who had once seemed as human as her half sister, Lauren Dane, stood beside the fireplace in the cottage in a world that less than a year earlier neither of them had known existed.

"I know it's awful for you. But we can't quit," Lauren said. "If we quit, the Night Watch wins. Everything dies." Lauren's short, dark hair swung as she struggled to hang on to her son, Jake, three years old, bright-eyed and blond and squirming to get down. Jake was alive because Molly had died to save him—her first death, and the only one she could have prevented.

"You don't know *how* awful," Molly told her. "I've died five times since this started. I'm weary, I'm scared all the time, and"—Molly turned away—"and I'm losing *me*," she said. "It's all just slipping out of my fingers—my memory of what it was to be alive, to be real. It's like I can hold what's left of the person I used to be up to the light and see nothing there but a few threads and tatters. Rags. And the funny thing is, it doesn't even hurt much anymore."

Lauren put Jake down, crouched, and said, "Play in here. Quietly." She handed him his toys, a stuffed duck and a teddy bear and a bag of blocks, then came over to Molly's side. With the two women standing side by side, the difference in their heights, which only a year before had been identical, became impossible to overlook. Lauren was still about five-foot-six; Molly had topped out at six feet.

An observer looking at the two of them would never have guessed how much they had looked alike before the events that had changed Molly. Lauren, in her mid-thirties, looked like the girl next door all grown up, with scruffy jeans and dark eyes and a lean prettiness that was holding up well as she got older. Molly's change following her death had brought out the veyâr in her blood and mixed it with the human; her hair was copper with a metallic sheen, braided to her waist, her eyes were enormous and the color of emeralds, and she had become thin to the point of attenuation, her body reshaping itself along alien lines until by human standards she looked like she might blow away in a good spring breeze. By veyâr standards she was still short and solid, but Molly didn't think in veyâr standards. Her body had been purely human for a quarter of a century, and sometimes the reshaping and the differences it made in the way she moved still caught her off guard.

"I'm so sorry," Lauren said, and hugged Molly. "I hate what you have to go through. What we *both* have to go through. But there isn't anyone else who can do what I do, and there sure isn't anyone else who can do what you do. You can find them, Molly. You can feel them. And you can destroy them. The Night Watch can't hide from you the way it can from everyone else." She paused and cocked her head to one side. "And I only knew about four times that you'd died."

"I just made it back from this last one. I took out a major cell of the Night Watch over on the other side of Oria. Managed to locate their resurrection rings. The damn things hide themselves if you don't get to them fast enough. They actually burrow into the ground or anything else that's soft." She tried not to feel the living gold knotting tight in her belly as she said that, and tried not to compare herself to the monsters she hunted. "I had to rip the last ring out of a mattress. I destroyed the members of the cell, and then the rings, and as I was leaving I tripped a deadfall." She shrugged off the memories of pain, of fear, of waking up again when it was over, naked on cold earth, in darkness, hungry for something she couldn't describe. "I'm changing, Lauren. There's less of me, and more of them. I know the monsters of the Night Watch better, and none of them but Baanraak can hide from me, but now I can feel the same hunger they feel. It's all the time, Laurie, and it's getting stronger, and it's horrible. As what I remember of life washes away, I'm filling up with death, and all death wants is more death." She closed her eyes. "The magic pouring down from Earth into Oria—that poison of war and genocide and hatred and destruction—is starting to . . . God, how do I put this? . . . It's starting to smell like Thanksgiving, and I haven't eaten. Ever."

Molly turned and looked at her sister and saw the fear in Lauren's eyes. But it wasn't fear of her, though Molly thought perhaps it should have been. It was fear *for* her.

"You can't give in to it," Lauren said. "You have a chance to create a new soul for yourself. To be alive again for real, not because of that damned necklace."

The Vodi necklace, its clasp broken during one of Molly's previous deaths, now coiled inside Molly like a snake. It was malevolence made solid, a thing of gold and gems and poisonous magic that had crawled beneath her skin during one resurrection and that lay within her, exuding its parasitic evil, giving her a hellish sort of immortality that came without invulnerability, and that, death by death, was ripping everything she valued in her life from her.

"You say that, but I'm on the inside and I can't *feel* any chance. Or any hope. I can't see or feel anything except the darkness closing in on me. And how would someone whose whole reason for being is to destroy going to earn a soul? I'm the Grim Reaper, Laurie. You're the Angel of Light, and I'm Death on the hoof."

"I know what . . . what . . . I don't know what to call it. God? The universal mind?" Lauren blew out a breath and spread her hands wide. "You know where I went. You felt the River of the Dead. You saw. I touched whatever it is on the other side. And I know this, as sure as I know I'm breathing. You have a chance, and you have a choice. You'll know the right thing; you'll know the wrong thing." She laced her fingers together and bit her lower lip. "You have the hard path. But you can do the right thing. Just do the right thing, Molly, and you can win this."

Molly smiled a little. She played with the pommel of the dagger Seolar had given her shortly after the nearly successful attempt on Lauren's life, and noted that Lauren still wore hers, too. They weren't innocent anymore, either of them. They'd lost their naïveté a while back, and some of their illusions, and most of their hope. And yet they soldiered on, both of them, through fear and pain and despair, because there was a rainbow at the end of the tunnel if they could avoid getting run over by all the damned trains.

They could save their world. They could save all the worlds. All they had to do to succeed was risk everything they'd ever loved and everything about themselves that had ever mattered.

Molly thought of Seolar, with whom she had discovered love for the first time in her life. She could remember in an academic way the breathless passion she had felt for him, the excitement at his touch, the joy she took in each glance from him, each smile. And now . . .

She still cared for Seo. She was still capable of love—at least in a limited fashion, at least for a while. For how long, she didn't know.

Molly understood losing everything. She didn't want to lose it for no reason. She studied Jake, building a pretty nice little block tower on the floor, and she said, "I have to know you're safe."

Lauren gave her a tiny smile. "There is no 'safe,' Molly. In place of safety, we have vigilance. And I'm vigilant."

"You can't be awake all the time; you can't be on guard

all the time. No one can. I *know* you can't be safe. But you can be safer. Please. *Please.* For me, bring Jake to Oria, stay at Copper House, let the guards watch over you both and allow me this one little bit of peace of mind."

"That's why you asked me to meet you here? To ask me that?"

Molly nodded. "I died again. No warning, no one who knew where I was. While I was dead, you were unguarded. And having me living on Oria most of the time and you living on Earth all of the time isn't helping matters."

"We both have our reasons, Molly. You don't want to be away from Seolar. I don't want to see magic change Jake into someone I can't raise. I have to be on Earth; you have to be here. But we're doing okay."

"Only because you haven't come into anyone's sights yet. That's all going to change when they track the live magic back to you."

"I'll deal with it when it happens," Lauren said.

Molly said nothing. She couldn't think of anything she hadn't said already. Instead, she hugged Lauren, hugged Jake, and walked out the front door, not sure where she would go or what she would do. Sure only that she had found no peace from Lauren, and peace was the thing she most needed.

Cat Creek

Lauren and Jake stepped through the mirror-gate into the foyer of Lauren's house in the middle of the worst storm Lauren had ever seen. A police car waited in the driveway out front, and in the flashes of lightning, she could see that Pete Stark was sitting in the car, waiting.

Burly, open-faced, sandy-haired, Pete looked tired and frustrated and worried. On his face, those expressions were out of character, but Lauren had been seeing them more and more in the last few months. Well, maybe this time his frustration wasn't about her, or because of her. Pete had been so sure, six months earlier, that the worst of the obstacles were behind them, and that the two of them were going to build a life together.

At first, Lauren had thought so, too.

But things had gotten in the way. A wariness had developed between the two of them as they tried to get to know each other better; Lauren kept running into places in Pete's life that he wouldn't talk about, and Pete was first awkward and then defensive as she tried to find out what he was hiding. But there was more to it than that, too. A lot more, and the biggest part of the problem Lauren could blame on no one but herself. Faced with the prospect of a real relationship with someone who wasn't Brian, she'd locked up inside. She stalled, and she was still stalling, torn between the living man she cared for and might even be able to love, and the dead one she knew she would love forever—and who she knew still loved her and always would.

And while she tried to find some way to make peace between her past and her present, Pete became more tense and more frustrated.

Thunder shook the floor beneath Lauren's feet, slamming her out of her reverie, and lightning crackled so close the thunder came only an instant after each strike. Tree branches and whole trees lay scattered in the street in front of the house, which had become a muddy river. Jake looked around, interested. "Wow," he said.

"Wow is right." Lauren considered taking both of them back through the gate into Oria until the storm was over, but if Pete was waiting for her in his official capacity, she probably needed to stick around. She went to the front door, opened it, and waved to him. He saw her, opened his car door, and shot from the black-and-white as if propelled by cannon fire.

He was soaked to the skin in the handful of steps it took him to get to the porch.

"Why didn't you just come inside to wait?" Lauren asked him, watching him drip on the foyer rug. She hurried to the downstairs bathroom and got him a towel.

"I was hoping this would slow down by the time you got home," he told her.

Lauren frowned. "How long have you been waiting out there?"

"Over an hour."

"It's been doing this for over an hour?"

He nodded. "No letup. I've never seen anything like it."

"We under a tornado watch?"

"No. Nobody else is even having rain. Well—Laurinburg and Bennettsville are both getting *some* rain, but they're on the outside edges of this. The rest of the state is experiencing a beautiful, sunny day."

"And this has just been sitting here?"

Pete nodded. "That's not the worst of it."

"It wouldn't be," Lauren muttered. She wanted to touch him as he stood there dripping. Just reach out with one finger and touch his lower lip as he was talking. She wanted so much to have that human touch again; she wanted arms around her at night and someone to whisper that everything was going to be all right, even if it wasn't true. She wanted more than that, too, and when she looked at Pete she could feel the hunger in her belly.

But twin ghosts walked beside her. Brian, dead and gone and waiting for her beyond life, had set her free. But her guilt, that she had outlived him and wanted someone else; and her fear, that if she ever let herself love again she would lose the second love as she had lost the first, held her back.

So she did not reach out that finger to touch Pete. She just stood there, her hands at her sides.

"All the gates in town are down."

Lauren stared at him. She was the Cat Creek Sentinels' gateweaver—one of the rare people capable of seeing connections between her Earth and the worlds that existed in the same space but remained separated by forces she could manipulate, even though she did not understand them. The gates permitted the Sentinels to track magic use, watch out for problems that could affect Earth's survival, and in emergencies walk the fire road between the worlds, though they did not take those paths lightly. Most of the time, keeping the gates in working order was a simple enough job—Cat Creek had a population of less than a thousand people, and not much happened there. Sparse population and little change from day to day were the key elements in keeping world gates stable.

Lauren had not been tending gates long, but she'd never experienced anything that had caused all of them to crash.

"What happened?" she asked him.

Pete gave her a worried look. "We don't know. *All* the gates are down—even the tiny ones like June Bug's viewing mirror and my pocket mirror. We're sitting here blind and deaf, while something huge is going on around us."

"So I have work to do."

"Lots of it. And fast. We have to know what's going on."

Lauren looked out into the storm. "God, I hate taking Jake out in this." She ran to the coat closet and got Jake's raincoat and her own. She put him into it, tied his hood to keep it in place, and shrugged into her own coat. "You have other things you have to do?" she asked.

"Haven't had any calls yet, but I could get one at any time. We should probably go in separate cars."

Lauren nodded. "I'm going to need your help for something later—once we get this all put away, I need to do some of *my* work." She started to give him the usual, intentionally vague code that she had to use when asking for his help with one of her special projects. But all the gates in town were down. None of the Sentinels would be listening. For once, she could just tell him what was on her mind. "I'm ready to create the siphon upworld to Kerras. Molly . . ." She faltered, and decided this time she *had* to lie. Pete was already wary of Molly—telling him that Molly was having doubts about what they were doing and that she was fighting off the call of the dark gods would not help matters at all. "She's after some of the Night Watch, and she can't come with me. So you'll be it. Can you help me?"

Pete looked uneasy. "I'm off duty at seven. Give me until seven-thirty to throw some food in my stomach, and meet me in front of my place with your kit."

Lauren nodded.

Pete leaned over and gave her a wary kiss. He looked like he wanted to ask her something—instead, she heard him sigh. "I'm glad you're back," he said.

"Me, too."

But she felt the guilt for that kiss deep in her gut.

Cat Creek

June Bug's house smelled like cigar smoke and English Red Oil, and it was big and elegant and faded around the edges. It had been in her family for generations, a tradition that would end with her. She and Louisa were the last of their line of Tates. She'd never even considered the end of their line until Bethellen, her youngest sister, and Bethellen's boy, Tom, died. Then, of course, it was too late.

In less than a year she went from knowing the family would go on to knowing that it wouldn't. That knowledge pained her in places she hadn't even known she had.

June Bug watched Lauren lugging her little boy up the stairs to her gate-mirror. Lauren looked a lot like her mother with quite a bit of her father thrown in, but June Bug closed her eyes and remembered Lauren's half sister Molly walking into the library one day and thinking that she was seeing a ghost. Molly had looked exactly like her mother, Marian. It had been so uncanny that for a moment June Bug hadn't been able to breathe.

And now Molly was dead, too. A few times, June Bug had walked out to Molly's gravesite at night, just to stand there wishing that she had been the sort of woman who, grown old, regretted the things she'd done and not the things she hadn't.

"Once the gate is up, I need you to fix my viewing mirror,

too," she said, shaking off her ghosts and her regrets. "The auxiliary gate in the library rest room can wait, I reckon."

"I reckon," Lauren agreed.

"Can I have that?" Jake asked, pointing to June Bug's cigar, and June Bug laughed.

"Not yet," she said. "But I'll give you a whole box of them when you turn twenty-one, all right?"

"No she won't," Lauren said to her son. "Those things smell like dirty sweat socks." Lauren looked sidelong at June Bug, and for just that moment, with that expression of mixed amusement and exasperation, she looked just like her mother. June Bug sat down in one of the old horsehair chairs, the weight of old loss and fresh loss and loss of any sort of future hitting her. She covered her eyes.

"June Bug?" A light step. Slender fingers on her shoulder, and a worried voice by her ear. "What's wrong?"

And that just made it worse—this taste of what she had denied herself her whole life, this faintest hint of what it would have been like to have someone with whom to share her life.

The lump in her throat choked her. "I . . . miss them," she said, and her voice broke. "Your mother, mostly, but others, too. Others that might have been . . . And seeing Molly, who looked just like her and sounded just like her and walked just like her. And knowing that I tried to save her but that I failed."

"Molly?"

"Your mother."

Lauren crouched down so their eyes were level and said, "You tried to save my parents. You're the only one who tried, and that matters."

"But I lost her . . . *them* . . . anyway. Not that I ever had her . . . but . . ." June Bug took a long drag on the cigar and gathered her composure. "It all falls away," she said after a while. "You start feeling worn around the edges and thin through the middle, as if the sun would shine right through you if you stood in it."

"That's what Molly says, too," Lauren said, pressing her fingers to the glass and summoning green fire from it.

"Who?"

"M——" Lauren stopped, and June Bug saw color rush to her cheeks. "Molly—what she said. Before she died. Damn!" she muttered, and the green fire flickered out. "Something still not right in there. Hold on."

Lauren made a production fixing the gate a second time, but June Bug wasn't fooled. The first statement had been the truth, the second a lie to cover it up, and the crash of the gate a manufactured diversion. Molly wasn't dead. No matter what June Bug had seen in the foyer that day, Molly had somehow managed to survive. She was alive somewhere—and Lauren was still in touch with her. Which was why Lauren kept disappearing—dropping downworld to Oria or completely out of reach.

The two of them were still working together.

June Bug watched Lauren finish the gate, and carefully close it, then take June Bug's hand mirror and turn that into a little gate as well.

"Don't despair," Lauren told June Bug when she finished. "Getting old, moving on, losing the people we love—we haven't lost them. We've just misplaced them for a while."

And June Bug showed her out the front door with a polite smile and a sincere "Thank you."

And then she turned to the stairs that led up to her room and the gates there. Molly, still alive. Both of Marian's daughters still alive. She went upstairs to get her little viewing gate; she needed to know what that meant.

Cat Creek

Lauren waited until eight before she dropped by to pick up Pete. The storm had finally blown over, and stars and the edge of a crescent moon threw shadows across his driveway; she turned in, gravel crunching beneath her tires, and killed the lights. Jake slept in his car seat in the back, buzzing softly with that little-guy snore that Lauren loved.

Pete had been watching for her. He jogged down the stairs before she even had a chance to turn the engine off, opened the passenger door, and slid into the seat. While he fastened his seat belt, he said, "I wish we had other backup. I don't feel like I'm enough to protect you and Jake while you're working. I can't do what Molly can do. And there's so much at stake. If we lose you, we lose everything."

"We aren't going to lose me. We go in quiet to a random point, do what we have to do, and get back here fast. We've done this before. It's always gone fine."

"It only takes one slip. Just one. If the rest of the Sentinels knew about you and Molly and your mission, they could provide a full backup; some of them are damned good in tight spots."

By that he mostly meant Eric. But Lauren could not forget, or forgive, that Eric had been glad to see Molly dead. She could not forget that Eric's father had taken part in the murder of her parents. The mission then—her parents' mission—had been the same as the mission now, and Lauren didn't think the Sentinels had gotten any more willing to tolerate dissension in the ranks, or independent initiatives.

They had their reasons.

But she had hers, too.

"No. I don't want Jake and me to have any unfortunate accidents."

"Neither do I." Pete sighed. "I still wish we had backup. But you're right. We can't count on the Sentinels' coming down on the right side in this." He shrugged. "Let's just go do it, then."

They drove out beyond the range of the Cat Creek Sentinels' territory and parked in a sort of no-man's-land in the Sandhills—a place remote enough that none of the Sentinel territories at the moment covered it. There, Lauren set up a big mirror, leaning it against a tree. While Pete unpacked the back of Lauren's old Dodge Caravan—a replacement for her previous car, which had died a few months earlier—and moved Jake into the little drag-behind Lauren had devised for taking him with her while he was sleeping, Lauren started building the gate.

Proximity to Pete distracted her. I want, she thought. I want, I want . . . and I'm ashamed of being weak enough to want.

She stared into the mirror, into her reflection's eyes, and she reached out for the energy that connected all the worlds to each other. After a moment, she got the green flash that signaled connection. She relaxed her mind and her body, and focused on a place that would be out of the way of all traffic—distant, far downworld, vibrantly alive. She needed a place that was already working to her advantage and the Night Watch's disadvantage, a live world untainted by their death magic that would serve as her best ally.

She didn't know which world she connected to, and she didn't care. Getting a world at random was part of her protection, part of what would keep her and Pete safe long enough to get in, do what they had to do, and get back out. In the green fire that shimmered in the depths of the mirror, images began to resolve. A broad, sunny plain, flowers and tall grasses blowing in a breeze. In the distance in one direction, low, rolling hills. As she turned the image, she caught more hills, more plain, and finally, forest. No sign of habitation, no indication of the presence of intelligent life anywhere nearby.

She was getting good at finding remote areas.

She told Pete, "Got it."

He brought the few tools and weapons the two of them would need, and dragged Jake and his little travois behind him.

They each slung a weapon by its strap over one shoulder. The weapons had been devised by Molly; they wouldn't work on Earth, but anywhere downworld they would be powerful and, because Molly had made them, would cause only limited magical repercussions. Lauren took the tool bag, slung it over her other shoulder, and then took Pete's hand, shivering at his touch. He led through the mirror, pressing into the green fire confidently, but with his weapon readied. Lauren, holding Pete's hand and dragging Jake behind her, came next. She had a hard time concentrating on what she needed to do on the other side of the gate—the path between the worlds vibrated through her blood and her bones and comforted her and sang to her of her own immortality. With that power and joy suffusing her, keeping her mind on preparing a magical shield to activate the second she stepped into the next world was as hard as balancing a deck of playing cards into a pyramid.

She kept her focus only by reminding herself that outside of the fire road she and Jake and Pete were still painfully mortal.

When she slipped into the other world, she felt, as always, a sharp pang of loss. But she recovered quickly, and focused her will, and created around herself and Jake and Pete a tight, hard shield—a faintly glowing sphere of magic that would keep out most attacks. She damped down the glow until it was invisible; no sense calling attention to the three of them. She didn't think anyone or anything was in the area, but she had to act as if enemies were all around her.

Pete crouched over the sleeping Jake, weapon still at ready, and said, "Go ahead. I've got us covered."

Lauren dropped to her hands and knees and closed her eyes. The tall grasses brushed her face and tickled her nose, the scent of crushed greenery rose up from the ground beneath her, and the sharp edges of the leaves and stems beneath her palms kept her from directly touching the rich, dark soil beneath. But she could feel the power of the place. She moved herself into a state of deep focus, probing with her mind for something solid deep within the earth.

Palms flat on the soft earth, mind focused on the bedrock that lay far beneath, she hollowed out a sphere, and within that sphere created another gate much like the one through which she had reached this world, but tiny, no bigger than a clenched fist. And through that gate, she fed her love for her world, for the people who inhabited it, for life. She fed her hope, her will to survive, her dreams of honor and peace and compassion. Only this time, she did not direct the other end of the gate back to Earth. Instead, she reached farther, up-world from Earth, into the poisoned, frozen death that had only half a century before been the living world of Kerras.

Stone was no rarity on Kerras; that and ice were all that remained. Nevertheless, she buried the other end of her gate deep. She could make no physical changes to the world of Kerras. It was upworld of Earth, her world of origin, and her sole power in Kerras lay in her ability to open gates there. She felt through the world for a natural stone foundation—a bubble in bedrock—and within the bubble she anchored the other end of her gate.

She created shields around both ends of the gate, little bits of deception that would hide them from those capable of seeing magic. Her shields could not protect the gates from those who already knew where to look, but they would be enough to hide them away from casual observation. That was the best she could do.

She rose out of her trance state to find Pete scanning the skies with a frantic expression on his face and his weapon braced against his shoulder.

"We have company," he said.

CHAPTER 3

Somewhere Downworld

PETE STARED THROUGH THE SKY at the dark winged shapes that dotted the sun. A dozen of them, he thought. Not more than that. But he knew the shapes, recognized what was coming from the chill of evil and the wet-leather flapping of massive wings.

Rrôn. Giant, intelligent, evil—they were the source of Earth legends about dragons, one of the motivating forces behind the Night Watch, and they had access to magic and power humans couldn't even imagine.

"Get us out of here fast," he told Lauren.

She didn't argue—she started putting a gate together and he started shooting. With the rrôn, a first strike would be the only strike he got.

He fired steadily into the cluster heading toward them, and had the satisfaction of seeing one fall from the sky in an uncontrolled plummet. The others split off, moving out of range and circling around. He could see that they would surround him and Lauren and the sleeping Jake in just a moment, and he would be helpless.

"Gate?" he said, still firing, hoping for a lucky shot."

"Problems," Lauren said. "Something on the other end is . . . looking at us. Blocking me."

"You can't make a gate?"

"Should have made it first."

"Yes."

Lauren didn't say anything.

Pete got another one, which left ten, still too many. Now they'd completed their circle, and Pete saw them turn inward.

"If you can't get the gate, get the gun," he said. He felt like throwing up.

"Got it," Lauren said, and pushed her back to his, and he heard the click as she flipped off the safety on her weapon. So. They were stuck. Committed to finish this.

"This isn't the way I wanted to die."

He could feel the recoil of her weapon through the steady slam of her right shoulder against his back. "Got one," she said, but there was no satisfaction in her voice. And she added, "This isn't the way I wanted to die, either. Keep shooting. Jake deserves better than this."

"Fuck. We all deserve better than this."

The rrôn had been spiraling just out of range—except, apparently, for the one Lauren had hit—but then one shrieked and all of them turned and started inward. Coming fast.

Pete sprayed the magic-edged bullets in an arc, willing them to hit all the rrôn, willing all the monsters to fall at once. But the rrôn had their own magic, and none were falling.

"God, get us out of this," he whispered.

"Shit! A gate!" Lauren said, and at the same instant that she said it, black thunderheads billowed out of nowhere, right over their heads, and ripped out from where he and Lauren stood as if they were speeding from the center of a dropped H-bomb. The rrôn kept coming, but they weren't gliding anymore with wings set. They were fighting whirlwinds. Lightning smashed the ground all around Lauren and Pete, and slammed into some of the rrôn, tearing them apart like rag dolls and dropping them from the sky, and thunder roared and raindrops the size of baseballs tore across the field, flattening the grasses and flowers.

But in the tiny circle where Lauren and Pete and Jake were, it stayed dry. Pete got in a good shot, and killed another of the rrôn, and a voice that sounded like more of the thunder, but with words, bellowed, "Good. Good. Kill them all, the miserable bastards."

Pete turned his head just enough to see a man who had to be nearly seven feet tall, with bright red hair, wearing a black T-shirt and jeans and a carpenter's belt, standing just behind him, grinning.

"You did okay, by damn," the stranger said. "But we'll get these motherless flying pigs in a hurry, and then we'll all go home."

And the big man turned his back on Pete and roared into the wind, a wordless bellow filled with fury and elation, and the lightning struck harder, and the thunder shook the world, and the rrôn dropped like shattered stones.

The storm did not abate.

The big man looked at them and said, "We should probably get out of here. If those found you, others might, too."

And he put a hand to the slender metal hoop that Lauren had brought through as part of her kit, and spun a gate through it. "Women and children first," he said, and picked up the travois that contained the still-sleeping Jake—how did kids *do* that?—and pushed Jake and Lauren through. "You next. I'll clean this up and follow behind."

"Who *are* you?" Pete asked.

"Later. Not here. We need to get away from this place before we draw more attention to what she's done here."

And he put a hand on Pete's back, and without being ready to leave, Pete was suddenly falling between the worlds, racing through the music of the universes, through the light and the joy and the comfort, and tripping out the mirror on the other side to sprawl on his face on the floor of Lauren's foyer.

It was still night in Cat Creek.

"Pete," Lauren whispered. Pete got to his feet, moving out of the way of the mirror so the big stranger wouldn't step on him as he came through. He put an arm around Lauren and waited, watching the mirror, but it stayed dark. The stranger didn't come through, and after a few minutes, Pete realized he wasn't going to.

He turned and wrapped his arms around Lauren. "We're still alive."

"How? Who was he? How did he find us?"

"I don't know. He said he'd tell us when he got here. But he isn't coming."

"No," she said.

In the distance, they heard thunder chuckle—a soft, almost comforting sound.

Pete buried his face in Lauren's hair and pulled her closer. "Doesn't matter. What matters is we're still alive." He was shaky from his near brush with death, and so was she. He could feel her trembling.

He kissed her once, lightly, and she responded, running her fingers through his hair, pressing her lips to his with a passion and a hunger that shook him. Tonight. Maybe tonight, at last, she'd put her ghosts behind her. Maybe tonight, finally, she could let go of her past and just hang on to the present, and to him.

He slid a hand down to the small of her back and pulled her body tight against his. She was lean, strong; she felt warm and vibrant, and his body said, "Yes. Now."

And then he felt her pull away. The same thing he felt every time, usually sooner rather than later, but there it was again. He let her go and stepped back.

"What?" he said, expecting to hear again, "I'm not ready for this" or "It's been too soon." It was going on three years, but she refused to see it that way.

Instead, she glanced over at Jake, asleep in the travois. "We're going to have to go get my van," she said. "It's out in the Sandhills somewhere. I'm not even exactly sure where."

Pete stared at her, not comprehending for a moment. And then swore softly. "We didn't leave from here."

"No, we didn't."

"Oh, shit. And *my* car is at my apartment. So is the squad car."

"Yes."

"And the only car seat for Jake is in the van."

"Yes, it is."

"Son of a *bitch*." This might have been the night. This time he might have been able to get past that barrier that she kept up all the time. Maybe their near brush with death would have let him get close enough to her that she could put the Sainted Dead Husband behind her and let herself love him—love the living man beside her and start living in the present again.

But he wasn't going to get to find out, because she was right. They did have to get the van back. Fast. They couldn't afford the questions that its absence would create. As long as Lauren had to hide what she was doing from the Sentinels— as long as she had reason to fear the people who were supposed to be her allies—keeping up appearances was going to be of paramount importance.

It was more important than the two of them and his possible shot at getting her into bed with him, at winning her over to his love for her and, no sense kidding himself, his lust.

"Yeah," he said. "I guess I'll run home and get my car. You'll have to strap Jake into the middle seat in the back. I hate doing that, but this hour of the night at least traffic will be light. Stay here. I'll be back in just a few minutes."

He started to walk out the front door and realized Lauren had a big white pickup truck sitting in her driveway.

"Lauren," he said, "where did that come from?"

A van was driving down the street from the edge of town. A bit faster than the speed limit would allow, Pete thought, but not dangerously fast. He watched it roll under a street-light, and thought that it looked just like Lauren's van: black, with wood sides, square headlights, some paint peeling off the hood. Same year, same model. And it slowed before it reached her house, and at the driveway stopped. And turned in.

It was too dark to make out the driver, but Pete was pretty sure he knew who it was. Was absolutely certain there was no way to get that van from out in the Sandhills where it had been to Lauren's house in Cat Creek in the few minutes that had passed, too, no matter how fast the driver had pushed the van.

"Our man of mystery is back," Pete said, his voice sounding flat and wary in his own ears. "Driving your van. So I guess we don't have to worry about how to get it back here."

Lauren came over to look. "White truck must be his."

"I guess," Pete said. "It'll certainly give your neighbors something to talk about."

Lauren sighed. Her neighbors on either side of her house were elderly and more than a little interested in her activities. Pity soap operas weren't on television twenty-four hours a day, Pete thought; that would give her some peace. "Oh, Lord. They'll be hanging over the fences for sure. Maybe I can tell people he's my cousin."

"Maybe," Pete said, doubtful. Lauren looked nothing like the big redheaded man. "Maybe you can tell them he's a *distant* cousin."

And maybe we'll be lucky and he'll get a lot more distant very soon. Pete had appreciated the rescue. He owed the stranger his life. But everything about the stranger struck Pete as . . . wrong. His great height, his booming voice, his bodybuilder muscles, the sheer redness of his hair. He was too intense, too big, too *there*. And of course things like the storm that followed him through the gate and the lightning that knocked the rrôn from the sky didn't help. The van, too, suddenly appearing where it needed to be.

Pete knew how all these things were done. Downworld of Earth, Pete could do them, too. The stranger was clearly a gateweaver like Lauren. Seemingly one of the good guys. Apparently a friend, or someone who could become a friend. Pretty hard to think of someone who'd just killed the better part of a dozen rrôn to save *your* ass as an enemy.

But unless the stranger had created a gate for the van and had driven it through that gate, between the worlds, and popped it back onto Earth just outside of town, he was doing magic on Earth.

And that meant that, whatever else he was, and whoever's side he was on, he wasn't human. Which, at least in Pete's eyes, made him a problem.

In spite of the fact that he didn't trust her, Pete would have preferred to have Molly at his back. She represented the familiar. Not the fully known, but the familiar.

So, with Lauren's continued survival being most of what stood between the Night Watch and Earth's destruction, what had been so important that Molly hadn't been with them?

Fael Faen Warrior Peak, Tinhaol, Oria

Molly hadn't gone after any Night Watch nest after her talk with Lauren. She hadn't gone home, either—she hadn't been ready to face Copper House and its boundaries, Seolar and his worries, the obsequious staff and the restrictions of being the Vodi. She especially hadn't been ready to face the hollowness she found at Copper House, where everything reminded her that once she had been passionately in love and that in the eternity that lay before her she would never know what love felt like again.

Instead of going home, she'd wandered—first slowly, and then faster, her path sped by magic, seeking isolation and the peace that came with solitude. And she'd found herself in the ruins of Tinhaol, once one of the great veyâr cities of Oria, at the burial mound of Fael Faen, where the bones of ten thousand veyâr warriors lay.

She stood atop the vast mound, the Warrior Peak, feeling the death that lay beneath her feet. The ghosts of the place pushed close to the surface for her; they stood before her as clear memories that resonated in her gut. One of the earlier Vodian had fought here and had died her first of many deaths here—the death that had cost that woman her soul. When Molly closed her eyes, she could see the flames of the falling city, could hear the screams, could smell the smoke—burning dreams, burning flesh. She could feel the pain of that earlier woman's death-wound, and no less painful, the ache of loss. It was as if this destruction had happened ten seconds before, not a thousand years.

Family and friends lay within this mound, lovers and enemies, neighbors. Not Molly's by fact, yet hers all the same, for she knew their names and remembered their faces and their shared pasts and their lost hopes.

Molly sat on the mound and stared down into the vague outlines of the lost city. Nothing remained but a few broken walls, mounds and ridges of ground that ran in suspiciously straight lines, and a tower at some distance only just beginning to crumble. With her eyes closed, she could see Fael Faen as it had been—an obsidian city, polished and gleaming in the sun, pennants flying, full of bustling crowds, markets and homes, children playing in the streets.

In a hundred years, or two hundred, she would have places of her own like this. Not borrowed memories of things lost, but bits of her own life ripped away and laid ruin. She would have to stand by Seolar's grave, perhaps, or look at rubble where Copper House had once stood. If she and Lauren failed, then she would know the ruin of Earth and everyone on it; she would see cinders and frozen wastelands where nothing survived, and remember the green of growing things, the blue of the sky, the roar of the ocean in a world with atmosphere and hope both blown away. And the hollowness inside her would expand, for that which was lost and could not be regained.

Her eye caught movement down in the ruins. She stilled herself, blanked her mind, slowed heart rate and breath, and released from the distractions of her body, but with magic ready to strike, she focused on the man who had wandered into her field of vision.

He walked along the line of what had once been a street, stopping from time to time to kneel, push tall grass out of his way, and feel around on the ground. From time to time he dug a bit with a little trowel he carried, and once he stood and put something in his pocket. Molly caught his thoughts as a low, steady hum that she found calming. He was looking for artifacts from the lost city. Touching his thoughts, she discovered that he did this from time to time, and that he had quite a collection of artifacts already. His family was a surviving branch from Tinhaol. Like many of the veyâr, he engaged in ancestor worship. Also like many of the veyâr, he yearned for days long gone, for times that had been safer and better. Days when the survival of the veyâr had not been in question.

For a while Molly let herself be lulled by the ordinariness and simplicity of his mind; his thoughts felt so much better than hers had. She could just amuse herself by watching him; he would not see her atop the peak. No one would unless she chose to be seen. But in that moment, she felt a bit of kinship to him, with his fascination for ruins and things lost. She felt like the ruin of the woman she had been, and had never felt more lost. She was darkness to his light, and suddenly she wanted a bit of that light to shine on her, if only for a moment. She rose, shook off the shields that hid her, and walked down the side of the peak toward him.

"Well met, stranger!" she called.

He jumped and turned. He was broader than the average veyâr, muscular where most were whippet-slender. And dark-skinned—the veyâr she knew were fair; they ran, both in skin and hair, to pale blues and ambers and pinks, but this man was a rich blue-black. His cobalt hair, braided simply instead of in the complex fashion of the court, shimmered with a butterfly iridescence. And his amber eyes studied her, startled and curious.

"Well met, indeed," he said, and his voice held the vibrancy and beauty of all veyâr voices. He had tattoos on his cheeks, as did all the veyâr she knew—his had been done in a very pale pigment that lightened the skin above just enough to make the marks readable. She could not read them. She had never been able to read any of the veyâr marks. "Though this place of ghosts is not, perhaps, the safest place for a lady of a faraway court, a mystery such as yourself."

She stopped a ways from him. "How do you know about me?"

"I know little enough of you, fair one. But what little I know, any who met you would know. You are not veyâr— your eyes and your unmarked cheeks and the color of your skin and hair announce this. Yet you wear the robes of the court at Copper House, with the mark of the Imallin Seolar on your belt and in your silks; you are held in high favor. Your face bears not the first mark, but you are too old not to have earned marks, so you are above veyâr society and veyâr laws, where we must wear our lives on our faces for all to see. Perhaps, from the look of you, you come from outside of this world altogether. The gods, they say, have unmarked cheeks."

He smiled at her a little, and added, "Are you a god, little one?"

She thought, *Yes, I am. Or a devil—I have not found the way to the truth of this new me just yet.* But she said, "Would it matter? I'm no threat to you. I just came down to see what you were doing."

"And I am no threat to you, or you would not have come down. Only gods have no need for fear. So you are even more of a mystery." His smile broadened, and from his pocket he pulled a pouch, and from the pouch, removed a little statuette no bigger than his thumb, worn and dirt-covered. "This is what I have been doing. I found a house god," he said. "Once I get him cleaned up I think I'll find that he's Podrin, the Water God. I can't really tell now; the dirt has covered all the defining marks."

He passed the statuette to her and their hands brushed, and at the touch of his skin, she almost jumped. He . . . resonated. He fit her, as if she'd just walked through the door of the childhood home of her wishes and dreams. Or as if he were comfortable shoes, she thought, puzzled. She stared into his eyes, and though veyâr faces were hard to read, she caught her own surprise echoed there.

She looked quickly to the statue she held, and used a corner of her belt to rub the dirt away. At another time she might have recoiled at the idea of using the beautiful, heavy silk as a cleaning rag, but at that moment she needed some distance.

The statuette cleaned up well enough. It turned out to be a

little ivory man in classic veyâr robes, with inscriptions running across his belt and down the shoulders of the robe. He had the classic veyâr build, the classic veyâr face. His eyes, though, were hollow sockets.

Molly ran a finger over them, and the stranger said, "They should have obsidian beads in them. Or . . ." He held out a hand and she laid the statuette in his palm, being careful not to touch him again. He turned the statuette in his hand and shook his head. "In this case, not obsidian. Emerald. This isn't Podrin after all. It's Allren, the God of the High Places. First time I've ever found an Allren here." He smiled at her again. "He wasn't a local god—didn't even have a temple. So this must have belonged to a foreigner. You're good luck." He was watching her closely as he said, "And fluent, too. You're the first person I've ever met from Ballahara who didn't speak Shenrin with a heavy accent."

And the language issue reared its head again. Molly didn't speak *any* of the veyâr languages, or any of the languages of the other peoples of Oria, for that matter. Yet she could converse with any of them, and they with her. The necklace she wore deep in her belly, the Vodi necklace that was both her curse and her blessing, carried with it a spell that let her hear alien words—and often alien thoughts—in her own language, and spun her own words into something comprehensible to her listener.

She shrugged, as if accent were of no import.

He watched her with a steady intensity that, strangely, she did not find unnerving. She studied him in return, frankly interested.

"Why don't you walk with me a while, and I will show you the sights of this place, which was once one of the grandest and most beautiful cities on Oria."

Molly knew she shouldn't accept his invitation—but something about him drew her. It was nothing sexual, nothing illicit, not even anything emotional. She analyzed her response to him and finally decided that what drew her to him was a simple feeling of kinship, as if the two of them might under-

stand each other. She did not let herself question too deeply
the presence of a man who could understand a thing such as
she was.

"I would enjoy that," she said. And followed him into the
ruins.

In the Ruins, Tinhaol, Oria

The wings were a problem. They kept wanting to re-form,
and the rrôn Baanraak, his body compressed for the moment
into veyâr form, found that every time he became too interested in Molly and her doings, his body tried to return to his
natural form. He was out of practice; he'd had more than a
thousand years of mostly basking on sun-warmed rocks in
the comfort of his natural form, and now, having reshaped
them by magic and sheer bloody-minded determination, his
bones hurt.

But she was walking with him. He had thought to lure
Molly within his reach so that he might capture her again—
and he had succeeded in luring her close.

But with her right there next to him, with her alive and
talking and with her very nearness singing in his blood and
in his shift-sore bones, suddenly he found that he did not
wish to kill her again. At least not at that moment. He could
let the destruction wait while he assessed the need. He found
himself interested in her, and interested in her reaction to
him. She was responding, not to his dull seeming—to the
soothing lies that he'd placed on the surface of his mind to
convince her that he was harmless—but to something
deeper, something that was not a lie at all. She was responding to *him*.

He could feel her being drawn to what he was, and she
was not repelled.

He found himself achingly curious; was she becoming
more like him, even without his intervention? Or was he becoming more like her?

They ambled along the ghosts of roads, over mounds

and shards, and through the bones of the city, and they talked. "What of that one?" she asked him, pointing to a heap of rubble. "Do you know what was there?" And he spun out for her a tale of what lay beneath the grass and the dirt. Or, "I cannot help but feel what this place must have been when it was full of people, full of life and color," and he would draw her a picture with words, trying to bring to life the city as he remembered it, as he had seen and experienced it, walking along the same roads, wearing this same form. She sounded so wistful, and she felt so beautiful.

The dead city still rang fresh in his memory—the place it had been before he led the rrôn and his hordes of prakka slaves against it; the place it became after. He'd never felt remorse for the attack. He'd had his reasons, and they had been valid. But seeing the place through her eyes, suddenly he felt a pang of regret that she had not shared it with him, that she had not walked these streets when they were whole, that he could not bring it back for her amusement.

He would do that if it were within his power, he realized. He would rebuild the city with a word, with a spell, and fill it once again with its stinking, crowded masses, so that she might wander through the streets and passageways, enjoying the bright colors and the babble of the markets, wandering through the libraries and the theaters.

She ached for the freedom to wander comfortably through the grand places of the world. He could feel that inside of her. He read her first life as dark and grim and lonely, where his had been wondrous. In all her existence on her homeworld—before she became the Vodi—she had never been free to move where people gathered. Among her own kind, she had suffered hellish physical pain: the absorbed pain of everyone she passed, the poisons and diseases of multitudes, all touching her, shaping her, devouring her until in self-defense she had to devour their sickness just to make the pain end. The pain of endlessly encroaching death had finally driven her into seclusion.

He had never had an experience with such a curse before.

His own first life had been blissful. He had been first-egg first-clutch of one of the great rrôn-mothers of his world's last age, and was rumored to have been conceived of a mating with a god or a demon in rrôn-skin, a mark of great portent. His hatching had been attended by the notables of his sky-clan; his childhood had been pampered and full of favorable omens and auguries and budding awareness of access to magic conferred by the blood of his mysterious father; his adulthood had been an unending series of fine hunts, fine feasts, and ever-expanding acclaim and admiration. He had earned his way into the little band of world-walkers, and he had seen the potential for expansion. For greater, magnificent magic for all the rrôn.

For him, the pain had come much later, when he was capable of dealing with it. When he was capable of inflicting some pain of his own.

"Please forgive my impertinence," Molly said suddenly, and the sound of her voice snapped him back to the present, to the dead city and his itching shoulder blades, "but I have never seen a veyâr who looked like you before."

Baanraak shrugged. "I'm a transplant. My people origi-nated far to the south and east of here. We're Tladi, also called Wanderers. I have traveled across much of Oria, seek-ing the scraps and whispers the past leaves behind; I washed up here some time back, and found enough of a treasure trove that I have not felt the call to wander further. I'm alone, but being alone doesn't bother me."

"Nor me. I'm used to it," Molly told him. She shrugged. "Sometimes I prefer it."

"Yes," he said. "Sometimes alone is best." He turned to face her and smiled suddenly. "We could be alone together, you and I." He laughed a little to show that he was joking. Except, of course, he wasn't.

She watched him, gaze steady and intent. "I feel I know you. Know you quite well," she said. "It's the oddest thing. I don't, of course, but that sense of recognition lies just below the skin."

His shoulder blades itched harder, and he could feel

weight gathering around them. He could feel his tailbone pressing, heavy along his spine. Could feel claws re-forming beneath his fingertips, could feel his face longing to stretch forward, could feel the mass of his true body, tucked tightly in on itself with molecules and atoms rearranged in denser, compact configurations, dragging outward in all directions as those folds of matter worked toward their natural states.

He was much more badly out of practice than he had realized.

He would be lucky to get out of her sight before he betrayed himself for what and who he was. If that happened, the two of them would have no choice but to attempt to kill each other.

"Perhaps we can meet here again sometime," he said, and smiled, hoping his smile had not grown bigger and toothier without his noticing. "But I must be going. I tire easily lately. I spent a time being so ill I thought I would not live, and some time after that recovering. And now I am better, but I must husband my strength."

She started to say something, but he held up a hand. "Meeting you has been a joy, little goddess. Should you venture in this direction on another day, perhaps you will be so kind as to walk with me again."

And then he hurried away from her, aware suddenly that his tracks across the ground and the thick grass pressed too deep, and that his veyâr seeming was beginning to take on the pebbled skin texture of his rrôn true-self.

He stilled his mind, sought calm, and prayed to the Egg that he would be out of view of her mind before he had to release his body from this tiny veyâr cage.

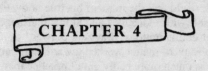

CHAPTER 4

Tinhaol, Oria

MOLLY STOOD WATCHING the place where the stranger had been long after he moved beyond her sight. The feeling that she knew him only grew stronger. She knew his eyes, she knew his voice, she knew the cadence of his speech, she knew the rhythm and shape of his mind.

He had not offered his own name, any more than she had offered hers, but had they exchanged names, she had no doubt that the names given would have both been equally false. The stranger was not who he claimed to be.

She studied this growing conviction of hers curiously.

Hmmmm. She drew her shields around herself again, making herself unnoticeable to anyone or anything passing by, and turned and walked slowly back up the Fael Faen Warrior Peak, thinking. By the time she'd reached the top, nothing useful had suggested itself, so she closed her eyes and let the sun beat down on her, and slowly erased everything about the stranger that she did not recognize. His face and body—gone. The language he spoke—gone. His claimed history, his interest in antiquities, his remarks about past illness—gone.

With her eyes still closed, she studied what remained. Eyes of deep, unblinking amber, eyes that sent a tiny shiver down her spine. Thoughts that moved slowly, deliberately, with force and focus, not as a stream ran over pebbles but as a river ran between deep, well-cut banks. The sense of kinship, of being kindred spirits. The darkness.

In the distance, Molly's ears caught a sound out of place. For a moment, she couldn't identify it; from so far away, at first all she could catch was the rhythm. Then, however, that rhythm, the eyes, the voice, the thoughts, the bond of empathy all clicked, and Molly's skin went goose bumped all over, and she become violently sick. She flung herself forward on hands and knees and threw up in the tall grass until her muscles ached.

What she'd heard had been a rrôn flying away. The man she'd walked with had been no man at all, but a rrôn disguised in veyâr form. And the feeling of déjà vu—that had been because the rrôn had been Baanraak, who had already killed her more than once. Who intended to kill her again and again, while he claimed her and possessed her and made her into a monster like himself.

She had walked with him. She had touched him. She had let herself *like* him, and had been so lulled by his form and the layer of thoughts he floated across the surface of his mind that she had actually planned to return to this place to meet with him again. To walk with him again. To see if perhaps the two of them might become friends, if such a thing as she could have friends. He could have killed her at any time, but instead he'd used their meeting to . . . what? Gather information? Set up some different approach? Amuse himself by getting past her defenses?

It didn't matter.

He'd proved that he could get close to her, that he could step inside her defenses, lure her into false security. If he could do it once, he could do it again. And the next time, she might be with Lauren and Jake. The next time could cost them everything.

She had to destroy him—she had to hunt him down, kill him, gather up his resurrection ring or rings, make sure she removed him from existence not just once but for all time. Baanraak had to die.

Cat Creek, North Carolina

In the kitchen, still in his travois, Jake sat up and pushed the dark blue sun canopy out of his way. Rubbing his eyes, he said, "Mama, is it time to get up?"

Lauren leaned down and stroked his forehead. "Not now, sweetheart. We'll talk quieter. Hush. Roll over and go back to sleep."

He nodded, not worried, and snuggled back into the sleeping bag on the travois, and went back to sleep.

"Maybe we *should* talk a little softer," Lauren said, watching him sleep. Round-cheeked, trusting, but less the baby than he had been, he looked more like his father every day.

Pete said, "We could turn out the lights down here and light a candle."

Heyr sat back from the table a bit, working his way through the second bottle of Pete's smuggled, prized Wychwood beer—this time Hobgoblin Strong Ale, though the last time Lauren had noticed, Pete had in a case of Hareraiser. She couldn't help but see Pete counting the stranger's swallows.

"It's all well and good to say you're a Sentinel from out of town, Heyr," Lauren said, "but if that's the case, why didn't we have some warning that you were coming? And what did you do that crashed all the gates in town?"

Pete added, "And what interest do the West Sweden Sentinels have in the business of the Cat Creek Sentinels?"

"I'm more from Siren," Heyr said. He took a long draw on the second beer, draining it to the dregs. "Fine stuff," he said. "Has a bit of hair on it. Have another?"

"No," Pete said, though Lauren knew that not to be true.

"Ah, well. Better than the local horse-piss by a long shot." Heyr sat forward. He seemed too big for the room—too big for the house, or for anything with walls. His hair was so red she could have thought he dyed it, except he didn't seem the type to resort to such vanity. He kept his beard neatly trimmed, his skin was browned by the sun, and his eyes were that October-sky blue that showed up in tinted contact lenses and not in real eyes. But he didn't seem the type for contacts, either. The black T-shirt draped across a set of muscles that were just . . . damn. They were lovely. He wasn't wearing tight clothes to show off that body. He was wearing loose, practical clothes to work in, and still had his tool belt hanging around his hips with his hammer in the hammer loop, and a pair of worn work gloves tucked beneath the belt. And, a little grubby, a little sweaty, he was still so damnably attractive Lauren felt shivers down her spine.

He said, "I came down here because the lot of us up there got hit by a flow of fresh magic. Healthy stuff—upflow from the downworlds. You know there hasn't been any of that on our world since Kerras fell and the Night Watch focused their top-level operations here."

Lauren nodded, nervous. The fact that Sentinels were picking up the magic already could prove to be a problem for her. The fact that one of them had tracked it all the way back to her was certainly a problem; it meant she and Molly hadn't done nearly as good a job of covering their tracks as they'd thought.

But those weren't the only problems she was looking at right at that moment.

Heyr's presence tingled all up and down her nerves, and the sensation was getting stronger the longer the two of them were in the room together. He was like . . . she couldn't think of a good human analogy, dammit. But looking at him, she felt like a cat with catnip, and that wasn't good. Further, it didn't make sense.

She cleared her throat and focused on her most pressing problem. "Pushing the live magic in from downworld isn't precisely an official project," she said.

Heyr looked straight into her eyes and said, "I didn't think it was. The Sentinels have a habit of dragging their feet when presented with possibilities. They like to do risk analysis. They like to talk themselves out of things."

Pete laughed, and for just a second Lauren could see him liking Heyr in spite of his first inclinations.

Heyr chuckled, and at the same instant that he did, thunder rumbled nearby. The coincidence of timing unnerved her a little. "So . . . how unofficial are you with this . . . initiative?" he asked.

"We're it," Lauren said, waving a hand to include Pete. "Him, me, and my sister, who is officially dead, and who stays downworld on Oria."

Heyr looked impressed. "You two must be really good if you've managed to fake a death well enough to fool Sentinels. I've seen it tried before, by people who wanted out. The Sentinels don't usually miss a trick."

"Probably helped that Molly was really dead when they buried her," Pete said.

Heyr sat there for a long moment while an uncomfortable silence grew in the room. He looked from Pete to Lauren, back to Pete, back to Lauren. Lauren could see the red hairs on his muscled forearms standing up, and goose bumps rising. "She was dead when they buried her. But. She isn't. Now."

Pete said, "She's what the veyâr call a Vodi. Half-human, half-veyâr. They kidnapped her into Oria, gave her a gold necklace, and when she got killed, the necklace brought her back to life."

Heyr stood, all the color drained out of his face. "No, it didn't," he said. "All hells, man, you've been keeping this a secret, communing with one of those things?" He turned away from them, and Lauren was more aware than she wanted to be of the muscles bunching in his back, of the way his fists clenched and unclenched.

"Your sister is *gone*," he said, turning back to face Lauren. "That thing that looks like her is a soulless monster. Deadly. The gold she wears may be preserving enough of her that you think you know her. But you *don't*. They turn on the people who trust them. Sooner or later, everything you know about her is going to wash away, and you're going to find yourself looking into the eyes of someone you love who is in the process of killing you. Or your little boy. Or . . ." He put his hands on the table and stared down at her and at Pete.

"You need to kill the thing, and once you kill it, you need to destroy the gold ring that brings it back. The veyâr . . . Odin's eye on all of them, that they see their madness before it's too late. They always were willing to meddle and tinker with toys that they should have destroyed." He stood straight, thinking. "I'll help you kill her," he said.

"No you won't." Now Lauren stood. "I know what Molly is, and as she is now, I don't trust her. I watch her all the time. But I have it on the highest authority that she has a chance to create a soul for this new body of hers. That she has a chance to matter, to come in on the side of good. She's fighting beside me to bring life back to Earth. I bring life back to the worlds, she hunts and destroys the Night Watch."

"She *is* the Night Watch," Heyr growled, and on the travois beside Lauren, Jake stirred. Heyr noticed and lowered his voice. "She just doesn't know it yet."

Lauren gave him a hard, cold look, and said, "I know how badly this could go. I also know how well it could turn out."

"You do, do you? Who was your higher authority? Some wishful veyâr who told you the dead things sometimes grow souls?"

Lauren watched him, not saying anything.

Heyr caught some whiff of her confidence—her certainty—and he paused. "Highest authority. Head of the Sentinels?"

She said nothing.

"Some meddling old god thinking about trying the metal magics himself, in spite of years of bad experiences with that kind of immortality?"

She shook her head.

"Beyond the old gods, there is no higher authority. Unless you're talking about the one who made the Tree, but he doesn't give direct answers."

"He does if you go to him," Lauren said.

"You'd have to travel Gjoll—the River of Souls—to get to him. And once there, you couldn't have left. Not even the gods leave He—— . . . that place."

"You might be surprised."

Heyr digested that implication with a long silence, never taking his eyes off her. "I am . . . and yet, seeing you . . . less so than I would have expected." He fell silent again, looking at her thoughtfully, and stood with his thumbs hooked into his work belt for a moment.

"I want you to understand this: Molly fights for us. There are less of the Night Watch today than there were yesterday because she is on our side. Without her, I cannot do what I must do."

"If you declare her your equal, then she is your equal. Nevertheless, if you're in company with one of the dead things, the Night Watch will use her to watch you. You'll be the next best thing to an open book for them. I have something in my truck that will help you."

He turned and walked out of the kitchen, and until they heard the front door open, then close quietly, neither Lauren nor Pete said anything.

As soon as the door shut, however, Pete stood up. "Eric is going to have to know about this guy," he said. "I'll tell him he needs to call a meeting tomorrow. Today. I hate late nights—I can't keep track of what day it is. I don't believe for a second that he's here with Sentinel permission."

"You think he's . . . working independently. Like us?"

"At the very least," Pete told her.

They heard the front door open again, and Lauren put her hand on the dagger at her waist. Heyr might be coming in, or something that had surprised Heyr out by his truck. Lauren preferred to assume the worst.

"It's just me," Heyr called. He walked to the back of the house and filled the kitchen doorway as he came through it. "Take this," he said, and handed Lauren a large knife in a sheath.

"Got one already," she said, not accepting the blade. Instead, she patted the pommel of the veyâr dagger.

"No, you don't. Not like this one, anyway. This is of up-worlder make."

Lauren, still not inclined to accept a gift from this unsettling man, shook her head. "I'll keep the one I have."

Heyr sighed. "You've heard the stories about old heroes and their magic swords and magic cups and flasks that filled themselves, haven't you?"

"Of course."

"The stories are, for the most part, true." He shook his head, and for a moment those fierce blue eyes were focused on something far away. Another time, another place. "The named weapons are almost all gone from Earth, moved downworld yet again, where the heroes who wield them hope to do some good. But there are other weapons, unnamed ones—"

"Rather like unregistered guns," Pete said, and Heyr frowned at him.

"A bit like that, I suppose. Weapons whose past has not been glorious enough to earn them a name and a pedigree, or weapons whose past has been lost in time. Or, like this blade, weapons that are small and unobtrusive, not meant to draw attention to themselves. This blade was created on this world by one of the old gods."

"If you tell me it glows blue when orcs are near, so help me God, I'll go get the poker from beside the fireplace and bash your head in with it," Lauren said.

"No glowing. No singing. Nothing so . . . showy. This blade will guide your hand to danger, even in the darkness, even when you are not watching. And when you wield it, it will give your blows strength."

"Why aren't *you* using it?"

"I have other tools and weapons. I . . . found this one, and carried it with me. I have not bound it to me; it has no owner, and at the moment no specific loyalty. But my belly told me I should someday have use for such an ownerless weapon, and clearly this is what I have been waiting for."

"I drive a twelve-year-old Dodge Caravan," Lauren said, taking the knife and removing it from its sheath. It was a pretty thing—silvered handle with a comfortable, hand-formed grip, double-edged blade, strong crosspiece. In her hand, it felt . . . at home, actually. As if it had been made just for her. "I'm a widow with a three-year-old kid." She tested the balance of it, and drew a couple of lines in the air. "I shouldn't have a magic blade."

"You hide behind the ordinary," Heyr said, his voice strangely intimate, "but you have never been ordinary."

She looked into his eyes, and her heart raced and her mouth went dry and in her belly, everything tightened, aching. Holy hell, how did he do that?

Heyr looked into her eyes and the world became a tunnel between the two of them, with nothing outside of it. "You bind it to yourself by giving it a name and a taste of your blood," Heyr told her.

Pete, looking from the knife to Lauren to Heyr, said, "That sounds like a nasty little ritual."

Heyr shook his head, and thank all the gods he looked away from her, because Lauren wasn't sure she could have looked away from him. "It's a . . . courtesy," Heyr said to Pete. "And an introduction. *It's not just a knife.*" He turned back to Lauren. "Be sure to remember that. Give it a unique name. Something short, something strong and good that you'll remember in tight places and times of need. You'll soon grow to know it well enough, but the first time—well, the first time your objective is to survive to the second time."

Lauren nodded. Curious or compelled—she would never after know which—she touched the point of one finger to the tip of the blade. It was the lightest of touches, but the point cut her finger nonetheless, and for just an instant her blood stained the blade's tip. Then the blood vanished, and the cut at the tip of her finger healed.

Heyr nodded. "It knows you, now. It will never again cut you. It cannot be used against you, and even in the hand of an enemy will fight in your defense, and the defense of those you consciously guard. Until you die or destroy it, it will be your blade."

Lauren could feel the truth of that, actually. In her blood and bones, she could feel the presence of the blade as if it were a warrior standing beside her, guarding her. She thought of heroes in movies and books, and tried to think of a name worthy of the hero-spirit that she felt. Nothing, no one, seemed to do it justice.

"The name will come to you," Heyr said. He glanced out the window. "As will the dawn, and too quickly at that. But you'll sleep better tonight, I think."

Cat Creek

One instant Lauren was sleeping soundly with Jake's back curled against her belly, and the next she was standing barefoot on the wood floor, a knife in her hand, with the absolute certainty that something moved toward her that had no business being there.

Night Watch, a sort of second voice in her head whispered. *Just about to come through your door.*

How did she know this? How had she woken up? Beneath a layer of alertness and ferocity, she was still a fuzzy-headed, bleary-eyed woman who had only had—she glanced at her clock—forty-five minutes of sleep.

She almost swore out loud, but self-preservation and the warrior-skin that she seemed to have slipped into moved her toward the door instead. As if on cue, something slipped into her bedroom. That something carried a wickedly curved knife and moved soundlessly. The hunter had about it a reptilian stink that shot clear through the base of Lauren's brain.

It wanted to kill her. And Jake.

The reflexes might have been augmented by the knife, but the rage was all hers. Lauren struck, driving into the thing's throat, feeling the knife slam into bone as a jolt through her hand and her arm and her shoulder, into her spine, all the way down to her tailbone. She yanked the knife free, feeling hot blood spurt against her hands, and with the blade blocked her hunter's parry. Her knife sliced through the tendons at his wrist, and he dropped his weapon. He made a weird, gurgling sound, soft and terrifying.

Belly, she thought, and drove the knife in low, gripping the handle with both hands, digging up through softer flesh.

Heavy liquid heat spilled across her hands, and an unbearable stink filled the room. Lauren leapt back, feeling her skin burning, and the thing that had come after her fell forward, swiping at her with talons that caught her left arm at the shoulder and dragged through her skin. The pain was blinding, and in the back of her head, the phrase *poisoned claws* echoed.

Poisoned claws.

She didn't know if her would-be killer was dead, but she knew she didn't have time to wait to find out. She grabbed Jake from the bed and dragged him, protesting the disturbance and the stink, into the bathroom down the hall. She did not turn on the light—just sat Jake on the toilet and jumped into the shower with her clothes on, with the knife still in her hand, not even closing the shower curtain. She turned the water on full blast, and the cold as it first came out of the showerhead jolted all the way to her back teeth.

"—shit, shit, shit, shit—"

Lauren realized suddenly that the monotonously swearing voice was her own. The pain in her left arm got less horrible. Water pounded the wound clean and sluiced blood and guts and digestive juices and excrement and she-did-not-want-to-know-what-else from her clothes, her face, her hair.

"Mama, I want to go back to sleep."

"In a minute, Jake."

"You are taking a shower with your clothes on."

"I know."

"You're silly."

"I know, Jake."

"I have to go to the potty."

"Okay. Your potty chair is right there. You can pull down your pants by yourself. But hurry, okay?"

"I'll hurry," he said.

Most of the time she was grateful that he was finally potty-trained. She didn't have to deal with diapers anymore, which was pleasant. But diapers did have that one advantage—that when things were going bad in a big hurry, you never had to come to a dead stop because your kid was peeing. You could do what you had to do, he could do what he had to do, and at a time convenient for both of you, you could clean everything up.

The pain was gone from her left arm, the stink from her body. She needed to go deal with the corpse on her bedroom floor, she thought, and tried to turn off the water with her left hand because the right one was still locked around the knife. And that was when she realized that her left arm didn't work anymore. At all. That the left side of her body was going numb. That when Jake said, "I'm all done. I hurried," and she tried to answer, the words came out thick and blurred because only half of her tongue was responding to her brain.

Lauren grabbed Jake with her good arm, with the knife still locked in her hand; she pointed the blade outward—away from him—but she hoped to hell Heyr knew what he was talking about when he said the knife would not hurt her or anyone she protected. She didn't let herself worry that Jake's pajamas and his Spiderman underpants were still around his ankles, though he yelled and started tugging them up in midair. She didn't let herself think. She ran toward the stairs, thankful that her legs still worked. Then the left one started to go numb halfway down, and the first thought into her head was, *My heart is on the left side of my body, too.*

The poison was spreading fast. When it hit her respiratory center or the nerve center that kept her heart beating, she was done for.

Her gate would be ready—she should be able to open it into Oria and her parents' old place with a thought. She should. But, stumbling down the last few stairs, making the turn toward the back of the foyer and the mirror, limping, and then hopping when her left leg gave up, she realized that she could very easily not make it.

She lost her balance and couldn't catch herself. She fell, Jake underneath her, only feet from the mirror. Jake shrieked, then ran to the huge old mirror and rested his fingertips on the glass. In an instant he had the gate open, with the cabin in Oria waiting on the other side.

He grabbed her and tried to pull her toward the gate, but three-year-old strength and fear couldn't overcome the disparity in their sizes. If she could push, though. . . .

She did, moving her good arm, her good leg, flopping into the gate.

Jake clung to her, dragging, a ferocious expression on his face. The green fire enveloped her and swallowed him, and for the time that she hung in the middle of nowhere and everywhere, suspended in the infinite, peace flowed through her, and with it, the awareness of the touch of her soul and the comforting sense of her nearness to the infinite. She had no body, no pain, no boundaries. She was, for that time, infinite and immortal and everything was okay.

Then she fell through the other side of the gate into the first pale light of dawn, into heat and humidity and the sound of rain hitting the roof, and she thought, *I have to heal myself.*

And darkness devoured her whole.

CHAPTER 5

Natta Cottage, Ballahara, Nuue, Oria

JAKE LEANED OVER HER, poking her face with one finger. "Wake up now," he said. "Wake up." And he smiled at her, that happy-without-shadows little-kid smile that Lauren so loved.

I'm not dead, she thought.

She sat up, surprised that she could. Her clothes were still soaked, so she hadn't been gone long. She moved her left hand. It worked. Wiggled her left foot. It worked, too. Her heart was still beating, lungs were still moving air.

"What happened?" she asked Jake.

"I fixded you," he said. "I fixded your arm and I made you all better."

Jake and magic and Oria. The concept scared her shitless, but she had to acknowledge that this time she would have been dead—and him an orphan—if he hadn't figured out how to do the right thing.

Lauren wrapped her arms around him and hugged him. "Thank you," she said. She blinked back her tears, swallowed against the lump in her throat. "I love you."

His arms were around her, his soft cheek pressed against her neck. "I love you, too," he said.

She took them home. Held tight to Jake with one hand and to the knife with the other, and stepped back through the gate into her own house, into the first faint light of Earth's morning. The house smelled *dreadful*.

"Eeeuwww!" Jake pulled the edge of his pajama shirt up over his face and said, "Gas-mask time."

That came from a silly game they played together, pulling shirt collars over their faces while taking out the trash, wiping poop, dealing with other bad smells. In this case, she had to agree. "Gas-mask time," she echoed, and took the two of them to the kitchen phone. She dialed Pete, who sounded worse than she felt when he picked up the phone. "I have a dead or mostly dead monster in my house," she told him. "One of the Night Watch. He almost killed me. I need a cleanup crew and some help."

"Not human?"

"Not even close. That knife came in handy—I would have been dead without it. Almost was anyway."

"I'll be right over."

"Bring our friends," she said.

The house was full of Sentinels in five minutes. They all looked at the dead thing on her bedroom floor and confessed complete ignorance of what it was. Lauren pointed out the gold ring embedded in the back of the monster's neck, and said, "We should burn the body, gather up the gold we find, and rasp it down to powder."

June Bug said, "Then pour the powder into the Pee Dee River."

Lauren nodded. Heard heavy footsteps in the hallway, and looked up to see Heyr. And waited for the fireworks.

"It's a Beithan," he said. "From way, way upworld."

Eric MacAvery turned and looked at the stranger with the shock he felt clear on his face. "Who the hell are you?"

Heyr held out a hand. "Heyr Thorrson. West Sweden Sentinels, up in Wisconsin. "I've been tracking this guy and a whole nest of others like him; we managed to rout them from our area, but they're Night Watch, and working on whatever the current Night Watch problem is. So far, it seems to be hunting gateweavers."

"That sounds about right," June Bug Tate said. She was puffing on a cigar, which Lauren didn't actually mind because it cut the smell of dead monster innards, and glaring at

Darlene, who hadn't seemed to be bothered by the corpse-and-crap stench, but clearly resented anyone smoking in her presence. "I'd ask why here and why now, but Lauren seems to have made sure we wouldn't get the answer to that." June Bug grinned a little and looked over at Lauren. "Nice work," she said. "You're lucky he didn't kill you."

"Luckier than you know." Lauren told them quickly about the thing's poisoned claws, about her rush for Oria, and about Jake's getting her through the gate and healing her.

They all looked shaken when she finished, Pete especially. He pulled her into his arms and hugged her, then released her quickly. "You're still all wet."

"Haven't had time to change. Or to sleep. Or anything. We got back, I called you, you all came, and here we are."

Eric and Pete rolled the body into a black tarp, and while they and Heyr and Terry "Mayhem" Mayhew hauled it down the back stairs toward the kitchen, Darlene and Louisa Tate and Betty Kay started scrubbing. George Mercer looked at the stains that wouldn't wash away. "You're going to have to run a drum sander to get rid of those bloodstains," he said. "The wood absorbed a lot." He glanced around the house. "You probably want to go over all the floors with a good floor varnish," he added. "You don't want any more messes like this."

And that, Lauren thought, was the hell of the thing. He was probably right. She needed better varnish on her floors because they were likely to end up having to repel even more blood and guts. She amused herself for just an instant by imagining walking into Pate's Hardware and asking which varnish they'd recommend for protecting her floor against stains from monster entrails. That image would have been funnier, of course, if the situation that spawned it hadn't been real.

She felt sick. She wondered if she did need to think about moving into Copper House in Oria—or someplace even farther from home.

Magic mattered. If the thing that had come at her had used magic instead of stealth, she would have had no defense. It was to her advantage that there wasn't much magic left on Earth—but that was exactly the thing she and Molly were working to change. They were bringing back magic. And the more successful they were, the more of an advantage her enemies would have against her.

Daisies and Dahlias Florist, Cat Creek

"Quiet, everyone. Sit down, and let's talk about this," Eric said.

The Cat Creek Sentinels were gathered in their room on the top floor of the Daisies and Dahlias Florist. They sat in their folding chairs, with Mayhem doing gate duty over in the corner, sitting half in and half out of the gate and winking at Betty Kay every time she looked over at him just to make her blush. Eric had let Heyr attend, which Pete protested vigorously—but Eric had overruled him. "He's the one who knows what these things are and how they managed to get rid of them in Wisconsin."

Everyone was there except for Lauren, who had begged off on account of having had no sleep in twenty-four hours. She'd assured everyone she'd be fine. Pete suspected that the minute they were gone she'd taken Jake and retreated to the little safe room she'd created inside of Copper House, but he wouldn't suggest anything of the sort to anyone else.

Eric leaned on the edge of the old oak worktable and looked at all of them. "Things have been bad, and they seem to be getting worse," he said. "We've had some suggestions from among you that we're in the end times, and I can't say that's wrong. I'd like to, but I can't. I reckon if we aren't in the end times, these are bad enough to get our attention, anyway." He shrugged. "According to our Yankee colleague over there, the Sentinels are getting hit by more trouble, no matter where they are. We have upworlders hunting gateweavers, old gods leaving Earth to flee downworld. And the Night Watch has come to town. I cannot think of a time when any of the dark gods have chosen to attack us in our homes, our town, the center of our stronghold. I cannot think of a time when they've felt the need. But we've got the body of a dark god cooking in a couple of vats of lime in the old tobacco warehouse on Railroad Street, and when the flesh is off the bone, we're going to have the grim task of destroying whatever gold jewelry we may find and dealing with the magic from that, so that the dark god doesn't come back."

He took a deep breath and stood up. "Someone changed the rules while we weren't looking. We've been trying to hold the line, but I do not think this line will hold. And this is a war we cannot lose, because if we lose, the whole world loses with us. We are going to have to take our fight to the enemy." His voice got softer, and Pete saw a sadness in his old friend's eyes that wrenched him. Eric said, "And I do *not* know how. I don't know where he is, or how to find him, or what to do with him once we do. In the War Between the States, our great-grandfathers fought against a side that was bigger and better-funded and better-armed. In spite of that, we nearly won—because we fought for what we believed in and for what we knew to be right. We fought for the sanctity of our homes and our land, and for the right of self-determination. Our leaders were men of integrity, men of honor, men with fire in their bellies and principles in their hearts."

Eric was staring down at the floor. "The South knows what it feels like to lose a war that means everything. To fight on our own land, to watch our own cities burn, to watch our people die. We know what it means to fight for home and family and faith, and to lose. And now we face an enemy that is bigger than us, who has better weapons and power we do not—and cannot—have. We *must* win. If we have any chance at all, we must have leaders—men of integrity and honor, with fire in their bellies and the charisma of gods, men whom the brave will follow into the mouth of Hell. Because in this war, that may be where we have to go." He looked up at the Sentinels, and the sadness in his eyes burned deeper. "I don't know where to find such men as that."

"I want to talk to you later," Heyr said. "Meantime, look in a mirror."

"I'm no hero. I'm a small-town sheriff who ended up with more power than was good for him, and who is just smart enough to know to be scared of it."

Heyr shook his head. "Heroes are made, not born. Heroes are the men who see a moment when they and they alone can make a difference, and who choose to make that difference even though doing so always has a price. I know heroes. They're sort of my stock-in-trade. And you have what it takes to make them—and to lead them. To be first among them."

"You boys are leaving out women," Betty Kay said.

June Bug Tate shook her head and leaned across Pete to tell Betty Kay—in a whisper that could have been heard from the back row of a large theater—"You're so young you still think that's something to get riled about. Don't. Those two are old-school, both of them. They use *men* to mean *human*. It's an orator's grace note—when you say 'men and women' every time, the ear tires and the mind says, 'I already know that, thank you very much, and must you keep pounding me with the obvious?' They haven't forgotten about us, though. If they did, we'd run their nuts through a pecan sheller before either of them could blink."

And *that*, Pete thought, was *true* old-school. June Bug and her I'm-old-and-hard-of-hearing whisper hadn't actually been meant for Betty Kay. It had been aimed straight at Eric and Heyr. She'd just demonstrated the art of chastising people while seeming to agree with them. No matter what they thought of women as heroes or warriors, neither Eric nor Heyr could disagree with her without looking like a complete ass.

Pete liked the whisper, too. Thought it was a nice touch. He happened to know that June Bug could hear a mouse fart in the next room, but no one could call her on it.

Heyr said, "You think anyone questions that women can be heroes when your Lauren and her sister are making the first effective stand ever against the dark gods . . ." His voice trailed off as the Sentinels turned to stare at him.

Pete's heart sank. Clearly he should have made sure Heyr

knew Molly and Lauren and their activities were a secret. That Molly's existence was a secret.

Everyone stared at Heyr. But then . . . then they turned to look at Pete. In most eyes, Pete saw shock or disbelief. Eric looked pissed. June Bug looked . . . amused, oddly. The silence was so heavy the weight of it damn near pushed all the air out of the room. This was the sort of slip that cost people their lives. And he couldn't fix it.

And then Eric said, "The last I heard, Molly was dead and buried out in the cemetery. Seems I've managed to fall a little out of the loop. But you're with Lauren all the time. So my guess is you knew about this."

Pete took a deep breath. "Yeah. I knew. Molly came back to life," he said. "Downworld. In Oria."

Eric raised an eyebrow, "Well, how convenient for her. And when did this little miracle happen?"

"Three—four months ago?"

"Mmmm. And in three, maybe four months, you've been so busy that you couldn't take the time to say, 'Oh, by the way, Eric, Molly McColl has come back from the dead, and she and Lauren are fooling around in Oria with God-only-knows-what, and *maybe* you *might* want to talk to the two of them. Maybe. You might." He glowered at Pete. "All those times when we're sitting in the office shooting the shit, it just never occurred to you that this might be an interesting topic of conversation. Or that I might have some thoughts on it. Or—Heaven forbid—an opinion."

"I know what they're doing," Pete said.

"Well. How very nice for you. Would you mind sharing this information with the rest of us—since apparently the dark gods aren't traipsing around inside Lauren's house with big knives and poisoned claws just because it seems like it might be fun. We've been thinking this was the dark gods' final push to end the world. If it isn't, and if we're going to get to fight and die for Lauren's and Molly's little project instead, I'd goddamn well like to know what we're dying for."

"It's the end of the world, all right," Heyr said from his place on the wall. "But the dark gods have suddenly run into a snag."

Eric glanced for just a second at Heyr, then turned back to Pete. He was furious. From the looks on their faces, so were the rest of the Sentinels—still excluding June Bug. Pete had told Lauren she ought to come clean with everyone and that it would have been better that way, or at least it wouldn't have been worse.

Now—well, now it was definitely worse.

"They're bringing magic back to Earth," Eric said.

"We can't use magic here," Pete said. "But the dark gods can. The old gods can, too."

Eric's face turned a dark, beefy red. "THE OLD GODS ALL LEFT!"

The shout shook all of them up. Pete had never seen Eric really lose his temper, and had never heard him roar like that. Ever.

And then Heyr stood up, and in a voice as fierce as Eric's, though more contained, he said, "The cowards among the old gods have fled, this is true. And the weak. But some among the Æsir still stand side by side with men, nor are the Æsir the last of the old gods still here. Not all have fled."

Eric wasn't cowed. "Well, maybe they're still hanging around in Wisconsin, but they packed their toothbrushes and left this part of the world three or four months"—he paused and stared at Pete—"ago. About the same time that Molly came back."

And then everyone was staring at Pete *again*.

"Healthy magic—live energy, the stuff that holds the universe together and that makes the gates—is what keeps this world alive, and you know it," Pete said. "You *know* it. Lauren is bringing healthy magic back. Molly is hunting down the Night Watch and killing them off. How can you be against that?"

Eric watched him, his distaste clear. "If they're doing such a good thing, why are they hiding it?"

"How about because you people murdered Lauren's parents for working toward this same goal?"

Heyr said, "That certainly would have to be considered. I had not thought to find myself among murderers."

"None of the people who killed Lauren's parents are still alive," June Bug said. She looked, at that moment, very old and painfully sad. "A couple of people here knew what was happening and did nothing to stop it. I let her parents know so that they could get away; by doing that, I actually got them killed. They fled at my recommendation—I didn't know their car had been tampered with." Pete saw the glimmer of tears sliding down her cheeks.

"Lauren wants to fulfill her destiny, but she doesn't want to be killed by some zealot among you, or to have her child killed," Pete said. He stood up and walked to the table at the front of the room. He crossed his arms over his chest and stared at Eric. "When she told me what she needed to do, I supported her. And Molly. They're doing what you can't, and what I can't. If they succeed, we get our world back."

Raymond Smetty, the transfer from Enigma, Georgia—whose future as a college football star had been destroyed by a knee injury during his last high school game—said, "The first thing you learn from your mentor is that you don't act outside the Sentinels. Oh . . . but you didn't *have* a mentor, Pete." He turned to Eric. "And this is why *well-run* Sentinel crews don't let outsiders in. If you kill trouble before it starts, you don't *have* trouble."

Everyone started shouting then, and Pete's head began throbbing. If only Heyr had kept his mouth shut.

And now the threads of the conversation were getting ugly—Raymond Smetty, that miserable bastard, pushing to have Eric removed as head of the group, pushing to send Lauren and Jake and Molly and him before a Sentinel tribunal with a recommendation to make all of them disappear, and June Bug about ready to kill Raymond, and Betty Kay sitting in the corner weeping, and Darlene siding with Raymond for the first time ever.

And then Heyr slammed his fist on something and bellowed "SILENCE!" and the room shook.

All conversation stopped. Pete would have taken odds
that his wasn't the only heart that had almost stopped, too.
Everyone looked at Heyr.

"I'm not here by accident," Heyr said. His voice had returned to a conversational level, but it didn't brook argument
or interruption. Pete had never seen anyone look more con-
vincingly terrifying. "I followed the trails of the first fresh
magic to reach this world since Kerras fell. The tracks were
very well hidden, but if I could follow them, so can others.
For the first time ever—*ever*—someone is doing something
that is reversing the damage done by the Night Watch. For
the first time ever, a world has a chance of coming back.
Your Lauren is the reason. She is doing something no one
else could do, and she is vulnerable.

"I've come to fight for her. To protect her. Others will follow the same trails I did, and they will get here as well—either soon or later, but they will arrive—and they will declare
themselves for the path of life or for the path of death. Because war is coming, you fools. War—and not a war of men,
but a war of gods. The Night Watch has seen its own demise
written in her work, and they are coming for her."

To Pete's astonishment, Raymond Smetty now stood,
glaring, and said to Heyr, "And I *still* say send them before a
tribunal, and eliminate all three of them. Lauren, Molly, and
the kid. Because in case you hadn't noticed, in a war between gods, *all the gods around here are playing on the
other team*."

Heyr glanced around the room and smiled, an unnerving,
cannibal-looking-over-the-menu smile that made Pete's skin
crawl. Heyr's eyes got bluer, though Pete would have
thought that impossible. His hair looked redder. He stood
taller, and his shoulders grew broader, and his muscles all
flexed. Outside, thunder exploded out of a clear blue sky and
lightning crashed all around the building, and rain poured
out of nowhere in sheets and buckets. Heyr began to glow,
and his voice took on a resonance that rattled the walls and
floor. *"Look at me, that you will know me. I do not concern
myself in the petty squabbles of men, but in a war between*

gods, I am still first, and greatest." Plaster dust rattled loose from the ceiling.

Pete almost couldn't tear his eyes away. But he looked at the others in the room, and on their faces he saw the same things that he was feeling. Wonder. Amazement. Awe. On their lips, one word, whispered.

Thor.

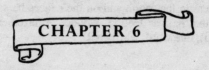

CHAPTER 6

The Wilds of Southern Oria

BAANRAAK WORRIED. This was foreign to him; he was not by nature a worrier. A thinker, a planner—yes. But he saw little benefit in endlessly looping through the details of things that could not be changed or corrected, and he did not like finding himself constantly returning to three threads.

He set his wings and spiraled upward in a good, strong thermal, letting the sun warm him and the wind cool him, trying to find some peace in the rush of air past his skin. But peace eluded him.

Three threads.

One. He had not killed Molly and claimed her, though she had been within his reach.

Two. Something inside of him was twisting him away from his true nature.

Three. Someone had sabotaged one of his resurrection rings, contaminating gold with silver, and he blamed that contamination for both one and two.

The silver had to have been there all along, didn't it? Barring his recent clashes with Molly, he had not died in thousands of years. If any of Molly's people had found his many rings, they would not have tampered with them, had such tampering even been possible; they would have destroyed them. At his last prior death, thousands of years ago, he had been the Master of the Night Watch—and again, anyone coming across his rings while he was temporarily dead would have destroyed them. Or had the contamination come from a ring he'd added later, one he'd taken as a trophy from a valiant opponent?

But those were all lesser rings. They served as an added layer of protection for him, in that if he were killed and his main ring destroyed, one of those he'd added later might still bring him back to life, if in lesser form. The secondary rings, though, had little power over him so long as the first, which held all of who he was, still existed.

So he thought the contamination had to be in that ring alone. And if that were true, then he was betrayed at the moment of its forging. So why? And by whom? The makers of his ring had known him. They'd created it for him alone. What benefit had they hoped to gain by introducing a thread of order into the essential chaos of the spell that would reanimate him?

Gold was the metal of chaos, silver the metal of order. Only gold could be used to bind a spell that would create a dark god—that could hold the memories and rebuild flesh once life and soul had fled a corpse. Such magic ran counter to the order of the universe. It drew its energy from the destruction of life to create a creature with an appearance of life, but animated by anti-life. It created a moving, breathing, thinking, soulless monster, eternally hungry for destruction, hungry to create more of the power that fed it by wreaking havoc, spreading death. For that reason, vast hoards of gold drew evil to themselves—they summoned chaos. Their gleam, their beauty, their attraction came from terrifying places, and gold became an obsession because of the energy that it drew to it and because of the power it could confer.

Silver was different. Silver channeled life energies, repelled anti-life, drank from the well of order, not chaos. Silver clung to passions and emotions the way gold clung to logic and fact.

The metals, mixed, became dangerous and unpredictable, with the energies they channeled flowing erratically. Silver . . . confused things.

Like his goal to capture Molly, slaughter and rebuild her repeatedly until all emotion washed out of her, until he could train her as his successor. His heir. She had been within his reach, and part of him was furious that he had let her slip from his grasp when he could have taken her and returned to the plan that her sister and an army of veyâr and the disruption of other dark gods had interrupted some months before.

The thermal he'd been riding petered out and Baanraak had to work to keep himself aloft, flapping his way to the airspace above a massive sun-warmed boulder that rose through the canopy of trees beneath him. He caught the updraft he knew he'd find there and set his wings again, spiraling, thinking.

Silver. It was the cause of his failure, why he felt as well as thought. It was why some confused emotion had moved him to spare Molly's life, had let him walk with her and talk with her and find some . . . some amusement in her company and then walk away. Silver was the poison killing his appetite, too—dulling his taste for the death of worlds and the magnificent power that flowed from drinking it in, devouring it, reveling in it.

Silver had to have had a part in his departure from the Night Watch; no one before him had willingly walked away from the Mastery. No one after him had, either. Masters of the Night Watch stepped down when their successors murdered them and destroyed their resurrection rings. Yet after being the most effective and most successful Master in the history of the Night Watch, *he* had one day handed rule over to his chosen successor and walked away. He thought at the time that he had simply lived too long—that he had grown bored and weary with the game. But boredom and weariness were both functions of life, not of anti-life. They were feelings, not thoughts.

Above all else, in the tens of thousands of years that he had existed as a dark god, Baanraak had been his own anchor in rough seas, his own shelter in storms, his own trusted advisor and sole confidant. He'd been sure that he knew

himself, every bit of himself, and that he understood who
and what he was, and always would.

In the last handful of months, in a space of time that was
the merest eyeblink of his existence, every bit of that assur-
ance had fallen away. He had discovered that he was not one
Baanraak, but two: a Baanraak born of gold and a Baanraak
born of silver. And the second Baanraak had secrets he was
hiding from the first. Now every decision, every thought,
every impulse became suspect.

Baanraak did not want to think anymore, at least not for a
while. The boulder below him looked pleasant and secure,
its peak inaccessible from the ground, all approaches clearly
visible from the air.

He dropped downward, backwinging the last bit of his
landing and dropping neatly to the warm sandstone surface.

He had not been to this place before. He looked around,
liking what he saw: sun-scoured, moss-dappled rock, a few
little bits and starts of plant life working their way from narrow crevasses, and below, a forest rich with the smell and
sound of life. He could stay here for a while, sleep, eat, fall
into stillness and let himself rest. Eventually he would have
to figure out what the betrayal of silver meant to him, but
that was not an exercise for the moment.

Sleep first.

Food second.

All else would follow.

Fael Faen Warrior Peak, Tinhaol, Oria

Molly had been at her task all day, patiently tracking Baanraak. She sprawled on her back atop the Fael Faen mound,
eyes closed, shielded from notice by delicate magic and her
utter stillness. Her stillness penetrated not just the movement of muscle and bone, but of breath and thought, so that
she would have seemed dead to any who came upon her who
had the capacity to see her in the first place. But she was

alive. And aware. Baanraak's thoughts flowed over her, multilayered, complex, as fascinating as a puzzlebox to her. Observing from the outside, she could see patterns to them that she doubted even Baanraak would be able to discern—the upper layer ran quickly back and forth over his worries. Fear of contamination by silver. Questions about his own judgment. Worries over his obsession with her, and questions about the origin of that obsession—whether he was drawn to her through gold or silver.

Beneath that upper layer, a watchful second layer. Baanraak the hunter, scanning outward in all directions with every sense. This was a part of him so ingrained by use it almost didn't feel like thought. He had no other blind spots that she could discover, except the one in which she lay. At the moment he was not looking inward. Had he been, and had something disturbed her, he would have found her watching. But the noise of his worries precluded his noticing a silent pool of otherness lying within his thoughts.

Finally, deeper sublayers—first and most powerful, a dark, cold river of hunger, death, destruction and chaos, heavy and terrifying, wide as the Mississippi. Lying within its currents, Molly could feel its pull, as irresistible as gravity. Her own echoing hungers grew keen and sharp. The capacity for chaos and the yearning to feed on destruction lay within her, deeper and stronger than she dared let anyone know, growing more fierce each time she died. In the river of Baanraak's dark currents, she saw her own reflection, and hated what she saw.

A second stream fed into that powerful river—a thin, bright trickle—a yearning toward order, toward light, toward . . .

Molly almost lost her focus, almost betrayed her presence to Baanraak. Despair would have given her away, and she lay so close to that edge.

The tiny trickle dripped into the raging current of Baanraak's darkness and was subsumed. She could find no trace of goodness in him beyond that first thread.

That. *That* was the effect of silver. That was her hope—
and she could see how futile a hope it was.

She should have known. She wasn't the first woman to
wear the Vodi necklace, or to face these changes in herself,
or to search for something to hang on to, for some little
thread of evidence that she might become more than what
she was rather than less.

Her sister, Lauren, had come back from her traverse of the
River of Souls with a message for Molly: Some people threw
away their souls, and some, soulless, could create a new soul
for themselves by focusing on the quality and the meaning
of the life they led. But no one had ever actually done it,
Lauren said. The possibility existed, but no past success stories were there to make it seem even remotely attainable.

Molly kept seeing threads that might give her something
to hang on to, but every time, those threads broke off as she
reached for them—they were nothing but illusions of hope.
In the end, the previous Vodian had all removed the Vodi
necklace of their own free will and walked into situations
that led to their final, irrevocable deaths. They did not regain
their souls; they did not find their way from anti-life to true
life. They just took what shreds of their humanity remained,
used that to gather the strength to remove the necklace that
had made them monsters, and before they turned the final
corner and embraced chaos and destruction, they ended
themselves. The silver hadn't saved them. It might have prolonged their existence—prolonged the survival of the tattered scraps of humanity that clung to them—but it hadn't
saved them.

Voluntary self-annihilation, Molly thought, was her
happy ending, the brightest future she had to look forward
to. Her bad ending would be to permit herself to become a
dark god like Baanraak. To taste the death of a world and
find sustenance and addiction there, and to begin to work for
the deaths of other worlds to feed her hunger.

And every time she died, she would take one step closer
to that fate—to becoming what Baanraak was. Already she

found his view of the universe and his place in it understandable. She did not approve of him or agree with him, but
she could see how he had come to be what he was. She could
even find a place in herself that pitied him for all he had suffered. Eventually she would look at him and find that their
common ground outweighed everything she shared with the
people she once loved. Love and compassion fallen away,
hunger all that drove her, she would finally and truly be lost.

The presence—the contamination—of silver had not
stopped Baanraak from being the worst and most dreaded of
all the monstrous dark gods. In fact, it might have con-
tributed to his success—that tiny push toward order, that tiny
taste of life that clung with silver might have given him an
edge the dark gods who wore pure gold did not share. It
might have given him layers to which they had no access. It
might have *made* him the fiercest of the dark gods.

She did not let herself think about what she was doing.
Baanraak had finally landed, and was settling himself onto a
sun-warmed rock at some distance from her. She marked the
spot and disengaged carefully from his mind. He was seeking silence—mostly as a precursor to sleep, but she did not
want him to find her out. That would destroy her element of
surprise.

Molly pulled mind and body back together. She became
aware of her body again, of the grass tickling the back of her
neck, of her breath rushing through her lungs again and her
heart quickening. She lay atop the huge mound for a moment, staring up at the sky, noticing that evening was already coming. Then she rose and ran down the Fael Faen
into the city to one stone arch she had walked through with
Baanraak.

She ran because she could not know how long what she
needed to do would take her. She had never done it before.

Lauren was the master gateweaver—the one who could
find a path into Hell and back, should she so choose; the one
who could track a whisper across worlds and make a path
that would get her to the recipient ahead of the message.
Molly had no such skill. But Lauren had patiently taught her

the basic techniques of weaving a simple gate, one that could take her from one point to another on a single world, in a single universe. The two of them had practiced endlessly, until with focus, Molly could get herself from one point to another on Oria without damaging herself or anyone or anything else.

Molly had been an interesting failure at moving between worlds, though. Lauren was determined that she would learn, but they were going to need more time; Molly could open and use existing gates, but when she tried to create her own, she got lost, and the gates meandered not just through space but through time. She opened gates into the past and the future, into sideways universes and places at off angles that neither she nor Lauren could even comprehend. Lauren had been both impressed and appalled. "You're the equivalent of a pitcher with a one-hundred-and-ten-mile-per-hour fastball and a wild arm; if you don't learn how to control your aim, you're going to kill someone."

Molly didn't need to move between the worlds at the moment, though. And her slow pitch—her stay-on-my-own-world gate—would be accurate enough for what she needed.

She took the dagger at her hip—the one she'd worn since the day a traitor in Copper House had nearly murdered Lauren right in front of her—and held it with both hands palm-up and a bit apart. She willed it to change, and in her hands it became a full sword, double-edged and razor-sharp, with a point designed for thrusting. She then willed poison onto the tip; a brutally powerful, fast-acting neurotoxin that would spread through her victim's bloodstream and paralyze both voluntary and involuntary muscles in an instant, killing him. She would have to be careful with the blade, but going after Baanraak, she would make sure her tools were the deadliest she could manage. She'd already died more than once to him. No more. This would be the last day of his existence.

Molly considered expanding the dagger sheath to hold the blade, but decided against it. She would not be sheathing the weapon in its current form. She and the sword would go through the gate and kill Baanraak in a single motion. Then she would butcher him and gather up his resurrection rings, for like her, he wore his embedded in his body. When she had carved her way through his corpse and located them all, she would burn his body and destroy the rings . . . and then she would return to Copper House and Seolar and the place where she was both wanted and loved.

Molly smiled a little at that thought. She had someone who loved her. And she was still hanging on to enough of her memories of being human, of having a soul, that knowing that mattered to her.

Images of everything that could go wrong flashed in front of her—the gate opening in the wrong spot, or too loudly; Baanraak being awake and ready for her; Baanraak having already moved on. She shook off the worries and took a deep breath. A lot of things could go wrong, but she would simply make sure that they didn't. Sword in hand, she rested her fingers on the sun-warmed stone of the arch.

She looked through the arch and unfocused her eyes, so that she stared not at what lay before her but at Baanraak lying on his rock. She felt with mind and heart for the tug of the place between worlds, for the energy that connected and fed all of existence. For a long moment, nothing happened, and she felt a taste of panic and of foolishness at trying to summon the road of gods for her own use.

But then she felt the first faint, crisp snap as she connected, and power flowed toward her. She focused her attention on the unbroken passageway created by the arch, and drew in her mind the image of a child's bubble wand being dipped into bubble solution. In her mind's eye, she lifted the wand from the liquid and found an unbroken circle of iridescent film shimmering inside the bubble ring; in the real world, the soft, hypnotic green fire of the place between worlds burned in an equally thin film across the archway. Molly looked into that fire. For a moment she could see the ruins on the other side of the arch, but as she relaxed her mind and her body, she drew an ever-sharper picture of the tall, worn rock that rose above the treetops in a vast wilderness of trees, and the rrôn asleep on the highest point of that rock, wings settled, nose draped across rump, long tail wrapped all the way around him in a fashion she found disturbingly catlike. Asleep and viewed at a distance, Baanraak was almost . . . beautiful.

Molly did not pursue that thought. Instead she moved her view around until she was looking at the juncture where his long, sinuous neck joined his body. That would be the perfect place to strike, she thought. She was bound to hit arteries that would spread the poison quickly, and with luck she'd slice vital organs on that first thrust, too. She wanted him dead quickly, because in a fight between the two of them, he had all the advantages—size, strength, built-in weapons designed by evolution to make him a nightmare predator, and tens or hundreds of thousands of years in which to perfect their use.

Another deep breath.

Time to go. The first part—killing him—would go quickly. The second part—making sure that this time he stayed dead—would be disgusting and time-consuming, and she didn't relish it. But when she was done, the universe would be free from Baanraak.

She lifted the sword to the exact spot where she would run it into him, pressed the fingers of her free hand against the fire of the gate, and for just an instant created in her mind the image of holding up the bubble wand and blowing a bubble straight to Baanraak. It was a childish image . . . but she felt the gate open for her, if unwillingly. She stepped into it, and the energy of the universe flowed into and around her—discordant and disturbing, alive and vibrant and resonant with the flow of an eternity that did not belong to her, singing of an immortality that excluded dead, made monstrosities like her. She did not belong in the universe, the green fire sang— she had no place in it, no business being what she was, no right to draw breath. She was not welcome, not welcome, not welcome, not—and then she burst through on the other side, vaguely sick from her passage, and landed exactly where she'd intended to, sword drawn, and rammed the blade straight into the angle where Baanraak's neck joined his massive, muscled shoulder.

The sword drove into him as if Baanraak were no more substantial than water. Molly rammed it all the way to the hilt, twisted as she yanked it back out, and felt the spurt of hot blood gush out at her as she pulled her weapon free; she took a wild overhand swing that ripped down and through his thick, pebbled hide and into muscle, the wash of red blood ruining the rainbow shimmers of his perfect opalescent blackness.

And Baanraak roared and leapt to his feet, his head whipping around, his talons flexing, claws splayed, bellowing "You'll die for that!" in a language Molly only caught because of the magic spelled into the Vodi necklace embedded deep inside her.

He should not have been able to move at all, but he was moving just fine. He slashed at Molly, and she swung her sword, slicing off his foreleg. Any second, she thought. Any second and he'll go down. The poison will hit.

She swung at his neck, hoping to behead him, and he evaded her blow and blasted a stream of fire from gaping jaws onto the stump of his foreleg instead. Wound cauterized, he turned and grinned at her, and his gold eyes glittered.

"Cobra poison?" he whispered, and a wisp of smoke curled out of one corner of his mouth. "That would work on a human. But I'm not from your world." His grin grew broader, and Molly noticed that the gush of blood from his neck had slowed to a trickle, that the gaping slash in his shoulder was closing before her eyes. He said, "I am, of course, deeply impressed, my little tracker. You got all the way to me and struck a blow before I even knew you were here, which no one has managed to do in time out of all memory."

He laughed, and Molly felt a force lock her hands around her blade and begin twisting it around so that the point would be aimed toward her. "You're exquisite," he said. "And you and I will make *such* a pair. Once I have you trained, of course."

He shook his head sadly. "I'm going to have to kill you again, you realize. Probably a lot of times."

Molly realized that he would—that she was going to end up running herself through with her own sword because he had decided to teach her a lesson—and in that instant she visualized an explosion ripping through him, tearing him into pieces and scattering those pieces across the forest in all directions, and she *willed* it with every cell of her being.

She didn't have time to consider consequences. The explosion ripped him apart—but the force tore into her, too, and sent her flying off the rock, shredded beyond salvation, torn and shattered and dying. She had only time to think, That was stupid of me. . . .

Night Watch Control Hub, Barâd Island, Oria

Rekkathav had just managed to get away from Aril, climb into his bed-nest, and dig all the way beneath the sand when Aril's summons bored into his brain like a dagger.

Locate the keth eliminators.

That would have woken anyone up. Rekkathav scuttled from his comfortable bed, body aching from lack of sleep, head fogged, and raced to the logging sheet.

The keth eliminators. His limbs quivered just thinking about them. A triad of the most terrifying of the dark gods, they worked the frontier worlds where live magic still ran rampant and few dark gods ventured. They specialized in clearing the path for the incursion of less-skilled dark gods. They scared the piss out of Rekkathav.

He searched the logs, and found the trio ten worlds down, eliminating sentients who had gateweaver potential. Their notes complained that on Myr gateweaving was a recessive trait—so a few carriers would slip through their net. It was so much easier to control the problem on gateweaver-dominant worlds. He read in an update that they were having great success with witch-burnings. Witch-burnings. Rekkathav could think of dozens of different techniques that he would use to weed out gateweavers if he were one of the

eliminators; he wouldn't always rely on religious pogroms
and witch-hunts. Sooner or later, after all, worlds would start
realizing that the people they were eliminating were the only
ones who could save them.

But they hadn't caught on so far. And the trio did get impressive results.

He carried the sheets from his sleeping/work chamber at
the back of Aril's workroom out to the Master—he'd learned
that when the Master wanted information, he also wanted
Rekkathav handy to put to work using it. Nor was this time
any different. Aril took the sheets, studied them for a moment, then opened a gate straight through to the most recent
noted contact location. Within instants he was speaking with
one of the trio, though Rekkathav couldn't hear what he was
saying. They passed their thoughts privately, leaving Rekkathav in the dark. When they finished, though, Aril turned
to Rekkathav and said, *You will follow them. Stay out of
their way, and out of their sight. You will find out what happened to my Beithan assassin, and you will bring me a report of the trio's success. Here is your gate-ring. Guard it
well; your duty is to return to me with news.* He handed a
tiny ring to Rekkathav—the ring would expand when commanded to, but would stay very tiny to guard its stability in
the meantime. *Go in native form,* Aril added.

Rekkathav took the ring, bowed his acquiescence, and
wished fervently that he were dead. He willed himself to human form—soft, bipedal, vulnerable, weak—and stared
through the holed center of the ring until the Master's gate
felt him calling it and came to him. He slipped the ring on
his finger then, and the ring expanded to engulf all of him.

He raced through the tunnel of green fire; through the Infinite Song his people, scattered after the death of their
world, had sung of and yearned for; and for a moment he felt
guilty. He had what his people had yearned for. And he
was—or would eventually be—one of the people drinking
all the life out of it.

But he'd never seen his own world; it had been dead long
before a recruiter for the Night Watch had discovered his tal-

ents with magic and his total lack of moral compass and had suggested he consider a new career. He'd left off going to meeting every third day to sing of the world of sand and sea, of beaches that never ended, of great surfs and the Bountiful Tide Pool. Rekkathav had gone in search of power. And look at him. Assistant to none other than the Master of the Night Watch.

Disposable assistant.

Sent to spy on a trio of keth eliminators and a Beithan assassin.

He and his tender human flesh and his severe shortage of legs stumbled out of the gate into a cypress swamp full of tea-brown water and cottonmouth snakes, and he discovered that sitting in a big sandbox singing "O, Hail, Bountiful Tide Pool, Thanks for Fishes Tender" might not have been such a bad thing after all. It had been boring. He'd thought being bored was a bad thing . . . once.

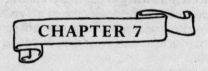

CHAPTER 7

Cat Creek, North Carolina

THE SENTINELS Were still looking at him with that expression of awe and yearning in their eyes, the name Thor shaped on their lips, when the gate opened into Cat Creek.

Heyr felt it snap wide; at the same instant, the Sentinel sitting in the mirror-gate yelped and toppled out onto the floor, blasted by flaring green fire and a push of dark energy that twisted Heyr's gut. A line of darkness edged the flare of energy in the mirror-gate. The shape of that energy slid along Heyr's nerves—dark and ugly and insatiably hungry. The gate had opened somewhere on the periphery of Cat Creek, close to town, but not in it. Like Heyr, this trouble made no secret of its arrival. He knew the shape and the signature of the things that had made that gate, and he was torn between disbelief and genuine fear. They'd come in south of town, he thought. They'd come for Lauren, and for anything that stood between her and them.

"Something big," the man thrown from the mirror said. "Something bad."

But Heyr knew the Sentinel wouldn't have the experience to know how big, or how bad. Heyr did. The keth had arrived in Cat Creek.

Mjollnir, his mighty war hammer, knew the keth and sang a warning on his hip, humming blood and death and destruction to the dark gods, hungry to fly again against the wasting of worlds. Mjollnir remembered the keth from other places, other times, from fair fields and tall cities in worlds that were now airless cinders, lost to the life they had once harbored.

Heyr knew the keth, too. They were first feeders, moving into virgin worlds and planting the first crops of death and destruction and shaping the energy of their target worlds, carving channels and beds for the river of poisoned energy that flowed from upworld. They were a long way from their chosen hunting grounds here. So they'd been sent.

Keth were worse even than the rrôn. Hot blood ran through rrôn veins, and mortal rrôn were different from rrôn dark gods. Mortal rrôn *hated* the rrôn dark gods. But the keth were cold not by the magic of their resurrection rings, but by their very natures. Insectile. Passionless. Mortal keth were different from the keth dark gods only in that they were easier to get rid of. Marginally. Heyr had loathed the keth on every world where he'd stood against them. Bloodless, relentless, free from both anger and hope, and incapable of comprehending grief or fear or loss, they knew only that they had goals, and that they would let nothing stand between them and those goals. Heyr would rather fight a swarm of rrôn alone than a single keth.

Three of them moved toward town, walking along a side road. He tried to imagine what Cat Creek's farmers and teachers and schoolkids would do if they saw keth, but then he realized it didn't matter. Any who came within reach of the keth would die—the monsters would suck the life from chance-met humans with a touch, then move on. The keth were in no hurry. Why should they be? They had no reason to think any on this world could stand against them. He'd been in seclusion for years, having given up hope. Any other true immortals who remained in spite of the pain—and Heyr knew only of Loki, who had no choice—had done the same. The keth dark gods had every reason to believe the road between them and Lauren lay clear.

They were following the trail of living magic, probably in the same fashion that Heyr had.

Heyr said, "The keth are here. Three of them. They've come to destroy Lauren and stop what she's trying to do, and we have to stop them."

Eric stared at him. "They've come to stop Lauren. Lauren, who has been sneaking behind our backs causing God only knows what sort of problem in the worldchain. Lauren, who is working with her dead-and-magically-revived sister. Lauren, whose parents were traitors, and who is supposed to be our gateweaver but who now looks like she may very well be a traitor, too. She's the one we're supposed to throw ourselves on this grenade for? Why? More importantly . . . how? We're not warriors, and the keth are gods. Magic works for them here."

Heyr said, "It works for me here, too—and for you as well, if I give you gifts. I wish I had the time to give you all of them . . ." He stared at Eric, thinking, Yes, he might do. Maybe some of these others, as well. Maybe, depending how they fought, and he'd know that in far too little time. The little bit of hope that Lauren had stirred expanded. If any of these survived the coming encounter, he might make them an offer that had not been made on this world in a thousand years. "As for why—think of this. Have the keth ever come in search of you?"

"No," Eric said.

"Of course they haven't. Because you and your little group here pose no danger to their plans. You talk about trying to hold a line. Well, you've been holding that line for hundreds of years, and the Night Watch has never deigned to come after you. Because while you *could* matter, you have chosen until now *not* to matter. None of the Sentinels has ever posed a danger to the Night Watch's plans. At best, you have slowed down their work a bit. At worst, you've kept the damage from dark magic minimized long enough that the population on the world had time to build, giving them a juicier treat when finally it falls. They don't look at you as enemies or threats. You are the subject of their occasional entertainment and common amusement. But Lauren has been weaving her connections of live magic between the worlds for only a few months, and already she has brought to this world a force unlike any that has been here for thousands of years. Because what she is doing is *working*. She is a genuine threat to the Night Watch and everything they desire."

He glared down at Eric.

"You were talking about a fight worth fighting. About being right—about fighting for home and faith and family. *This is that fight.* She's going to save this world if you can just save her. Can you see now, little man, why she is worth fighting for?"

Eric said nothing. Heyr had not expected a response, though. He pointed to Pete. "Go. Get her and the child, and drive them away from here. Drive them north. Head to the closest large town, find someplace busy and crowded, and stay there. Leave your pocket-gate behind, and anything else that links you to magic. Be, for a while, invisible. Use no gates and no magic to reach her, and none to see how we're faring here—the keth will be watching for you and her. They don't know who or where she is yet. But if she's here, it will not take them long to find her."

Pete nodded. He didn't ask questions; he just ran. Good man. He was a warrior, and Heyr hated to send him away—but Lauren would need someone strong at her side if things did not go well.

He turned to the rest of the Sentinels. A sorry lot, all of them—girls and old women, and men who'd never held a sword. If he'd had his grand idea a day or two earlier, if he'd had a week . . . But he hadn't, and the best he was going to be able to do was to hand them good weapons and hope they would hold their ground. They would run in the face of trouble, most of them.

He needed to make sure that any who stayed would fight effectively. Heyr knew he had no hope of winning against three keth by himself. He was immortal in a way they were not—he was unkillable unless they took the whole world with him, or surrounded him, used their mind commands on him, and lured him through a gate. If they outnumbered him and caught him that way, he'd be done.

But these people could at least provide a distraction to let him get the jump on the keth. The keth were dark gods, not immortals. They could be killed.

He frowned, thinking. The Æsir had always kept weapons hoards tucked away against need—spelled blades like the one he had given Lauren, weapons with which a mortal could fight a god and hope to win, or at least battle to a draw. Such weapons had not been needed on Earth for a very long time, though; Earth had been edging toward death, and most of the dark gods had moved out of the way of the pending explosion. All the really great battles were being fought on the frontiers—worlds down and away from Earth and its pending collapse. And most of the Æsir had followed the dark gods and the good fighting, and had, not inconsequently, given themselves a reprieve from the hellish, constant pain of being an immortal on a dying world.

Heyr—in his immortal aspect as Thor—loved humankind and loved Earth. When the majority of the Æsir moved on, he had gritted his teeth and stayed behind. Loki had remained behind, too, bound to the Earth as punishment for killing Balder. The last Heyr had heard, Loki was still maintaining a good hoard of up-to-date weapons. Heyr loved his war hammer, and could appreciate a well-tempered blade; Loki preferred words, but when words wouldn't do, he liked a good machine gun.

At that moment, Heyr was willing to see things Loki's way. "Give me your gate for a moment," he said to the Sentinel who had moved back into it.

The man moved out of his way, and Heyr let himself slide all the way into his Thor aspect. He pressed a hand to the surface of the mirror and concentrated on Loki, who'd been playing somewhere in Russia the last he'd heard.

And there Loki was—stirring up trouble with somebody's stockpiled warheads. Loki felt the gate open, though, and looked up, surprised, from tinkering with something electronic in a bomb casing. And when he saw who stood on the other side of the gate, a wide grin split his face.

"Thor!"

"I need to get into the Æsir hoard."

"Really? Put together a band of heroes for the last stand, have you?"

"No. We have keth. And I need to be able to work with what I have."

"Keth?" Loki dropped the screwdriver into the innards of the bomb and stood up. He turned and to someone outside of Heyr's field of vision, said, "Finish this shipment. I'll be back shortly." Then he turned to Heyr. "I'll open the hoard for you from there."

"You're coming here?"

"You have keth." Loki grinned and pressed his hands into the green fire, and Heyr stepped back, and Loki stepped through the gate into Cat Creek. "I owe the keth a bit of payback."

Like Heyr, he'd dropped his Æsir seeming for human form. Like Heyr, he hadn't bothered to alter much about his old appearance. He still looked like a fox—pointed features, sly eyes. Heyr said, "You haven't changed much."

"I *am* change," Loki said, grinning, and added, "And from the looks of things, you haven't changed at all. Tromping around in your god-suit among the mortals, and coming to me for help when things get tricky." Then his grin died a little. "Keth, eh? What the fuck are they doing here?"

"Live magic has found its way back to this world. I assume they've come to stop that at the source."

All humor dropped away from Loki, and he stood straight and grew tall, reaching back for the Æsir form he had worn for so long. "After all this time, someone has found the way to revive the worldchain?"

"Yes."

"This world might yet be saved?"

"Yes."

Loki turned without another word and put his hands flat on the surface of the mirror, and worked the gate around until he'd lined it up with a mound of dirt. He moved the gate forward so that it intersected the mound, and finally moved green fire through earth and stone and metal layers to get to open space. He reached in and started pulling things out and handing them to Heyr.

"These are good—all automatic, unlimited ammo, non-jam mechanisms. Combination spelled and mundane projectiles: No matter what the keth are carrying, something in here is bound to get through. Shields—slap 'em on your people so they'll have some protection from the incoming. I don't have any idea what the keth are fighting with these days—last I heard the biggest batch of them was eight worlds down—" He paused while he fought something big and bulky through the gate, twisting it at the last minute to make it fit and backing up so that this acquisition dropped onto the wood floor with a heavy thunk. Heyr could hear the wood floor cracking beneath it. "And I didn't think any of them *ever* came here anymore."

That was Loki. Nothing shut him up.

"Until now, they haven't had a reason."

"Live magic." Loki turned and studied the Sentinels, and looked at Heyr with the disbelief clear on his face. "By near-sighted Odin, Thor, you used to be able to pick heroes. What the hell are you doing here? Scrawny men and little girls and old ladies!"

"They're Sentinels," Heyr said.

"They could be town criers for all I care and they'd still—" His expression changed; an eyebrow flicked up and down fractionally, the eyes narrowed the tiniest bit. "Sentinels-capital-S?"

"Yes."

"Which explains why the maiden aunties over there didn't faint dead away when I came through the gate. Hello, ladies," he said. "We boys need to go kill keth now, but I'll bed any of you Thor hasn't gotten to once we get back, and those of you he has that he left disappointed." He grinned.

Heyr rammed Loki in the ribs.

"Whaaaaat?" Loki turned to him.

In a whisper, Heyr said, "I just got here yesterday."

Loki's smile turned wicked. "You just got here . . . so the whole field is ripe for the plowing?" he whispered back. "In my friend's defense," he said loudly, "I'll point out that it isn't the size of a man's hammer that matters, but what he does with it." Then he picked up a handful of weapons and shields, and started distributing them.

Heyr muttered, "That line wasn't funny in Asgard."

Loki laughed. "You never thought so, anyway."

One of the old women stepped up to Loki and said, "We're fighting, too."

Loki laughed.

She insisted. "We've fought before. Recently. A lot of our people died, but not us. We know how to use weapons like these—we've used them downworld. We won't run."

Heyr liked her. She would have made a good Valkyrie if she were younger, he thought.

Loki seemed less impressed. But he handed the woman a shield and a weapon, and watched, amusement plain on his face, as she slipped into the shield harness like a veteran. Heyr watched her, too, with less cynicism. The older ones might not be as useless as they'd looked. Jury was still out on the younger ones.

They armed quickly, and Loki said to Heyr, "Where are Tanngrísnir and Tanngnjóstr? We're going to need them to carry the big stuff."

Heyr whistled, and from far off heard the great goats bellow a reply. Disguised as his pickup truck, they would meet him in the parking lot. He and Loki grabbed the heavy box, the Sentinels picked up their weapons, and everyone headed out the door. The gate stood unguarded, but the Sentinel whose watch it had been did close the gate by tossing a pebble through it before jogging down the steps after the rest of them.

Heyr's truck spun into the parking lot on its own, spraying gravel everywhere and skidding to a stop an inch in front of him. He grinned; the goats were eager, and not too resentful of their current shape.

"Everyone in the back," he told them, and the Sentinels complied. He caught some flashes of fear, and some doubt about this whole mission as well, but these were good people led by a good man. They had a feel for what was important. He knew of battle-hardened warriors who would have stood arguing with him if presented with the same situation, who would have wasted his time in questions.

These grim-faced people just settled into the truck bed, weapons in front of them and pointed up, and watched as he and Loki loaded the big box into the back with them.

He jumped into the driver's seat, Loki took the passenger seat in the cabin, and they took off.

"What's in the box?" Heyr asked.

"Something I've been playing with. I don't know how useful it will be, but I don't think it will hurt. It's a spell I put together that dampens the energy waves of dark magic and amplifies the energy waves of live magic."

Heyr glanced over. "We won't be using it."

Loki sighed. "You have to get over this aversion of yours for progress."

"You don't know it's progress. It's untried, right? It could prove to be a disaster. It could be our undoing."

"It could. But it won't. Trust me on this."

Heyr laughed. "I cannot trust you, Brother Fox. Trust stands outside the door of the hall we share, having been beaten to a bloody pulp by your cudgel, and he will not come inside."

"Forget Balder, would you? That was then; this is now. And situations have changed. I'm chained to this damned rock forever; I have a vested interest in seeing that it survives. For Sigyn, as well as for myself. There are times when I think I could embrace death readily enough if not for her. But I want her to have her immortality, and I want to share in it with her—even if we must spend it here. She gave up so much for me. She bears this eternal pain for me, in spite of being free to leave at any time."

Heyr said, "Nonetheless, while we are allies sometimes and friends often enough, we'll stick with the weapons we know will work."

"Ragnarok still stands between us, doesn't it?"

Heyr concentrated on locating the keth, searching for them with senses attuned to their presence and their hunger. He didn't waste much thought on Loki's question. "As long as Asgard is a dead cinder, Ragnarok is not an issue. If this girl we fight to protect survives to revive Asgard and Jotunheim and Niflheim and the other upworlds, then things change. Then Ragnarok may yet come to pass. I know the Midgard Serpent still exists, but he and I will not again share a world until my hall is restored to me, and the branches and roots of the world tree do not wither and die."

"And yet, I would that you trusted me—that you knew we stood on the same side."

"We don't. Or at least, we won't. Not at the end."

They looked at each other, friends who shared a long past and, somewhere very far off, a dark future.

Heyr added, "And if we succeed in stopping these keth— if we succeed in stopping the Night Watch here and eventually holding them off long enough to reverse the dying of this world—we both take one step back to our own foretold dooms."

Loki nodded. "And yet, I find myself wondering often if that doom, like other dooms, might not be rewritten. If the future the hag saw was, perhaps, only the shadowing of frontworlds or sideworlds, and not a true telling of the coming events of our own."

Heyr felt his truck slowing down of its own accord. Tanngrísnir and Tanngnjóstr felt the presence of the keth ahead. They would stop far enough in front of their path to permit Heyr to deploy his warriors. He touched gloved fingertips to Mjollnir, which shivered eagerly at his hip, and said, "And if you could rewrite your own future by betraying mine— though we are friends—I do not doubt for a moment that you would do it."

He felt Loki's eyes on him as he jumped out of the cab, and saw the other old god watching through the back window as he went to the Sentinels. "We will circle around behind them and take them by surprise, Loki and I. Our powers here are not as great as they once were, yet thanks to your Lauren they are greater than they have been. You will remain behind, and from the distance fire at them, providing a distraction. Keep up a steady fire. You won't be likely to kill them or even do them much harm with the weapons you have, but if you can let us flank them, we can take them."

"You're going to be up there with them," one of the women said. "If we fire at them, we fire at you."

Thor appreciated the concern. "The weapons are spelled to hit only creatures bound by dark magic. . . ." And then his voice trailed off. The weapons hoards of the old gods had always been treated that way, yet Loki had always had a foot in both camps. Loki's mistress, Angrboda, a creature from Asgard's downworld with whom Loki had fathered three children, had become one of the dark gods when Loki had refused to leave Sigyn for her. And even Odin had declared Loki's love for his mistress and his children as great as the love he felt for his loyal wife. Perhaps these weapons would not destroy dark gods at all; perhaps they would only do damage to the living—to old gods, and those who helped them.

But no. Heyr took a deep breath. If this planet died, Loki died with it. He was bound here, cursed here until the way was found to break the curse—and according to the hag, the curse would hold until Ragnarok itself. No matter where his future loyalties might lay, Loki could gain no benefit from the dying of this world.

Heyr took a deep breath and said, "You may fire straight at both of us if you get a shot at the keth behind us by doing it. Your bullets will not harm us."

Loki got out of the truck. "Very good, Thunder Boy. Worked your way through that one at last. I could see it grinding its way through your brain—a tedious process for sure. And yet you did finally find your way to the right answer." He went to the back, slung one of his own stockpiled weapons on his shoulder, and said, "Your wits have gotten a bit quicker since last I saw you."

Heyr didn't take offense. He knew that next to Loki, he was no genius. He shrugged. "You're using one of those?"

"Words don't move the keth," Loki told him. "They don't use them and don't need them. They're immune to poetry and prose alike. And they don't get jokes—for that sin alone, the fuckers have to die."

Heyr looked at Loki and grinned. "At least you have your priorities."

The humans were on the ground, looking uncertain. Loki said, "You deploy half of them in a fan to one side of your chariot and I'll deploy the other half. They don't know what to do."

"Quickly," Heyr agreed. "Then you and I will run forward and out to either side of them. We'll flank them and attack inward."

Loki said, "You think we'll get the benefit of surprise?"

Heyr shrugged. "Perhaps. We've done nothing yet to alert them—there were already gates here, and we've used only what existed."

Loki nodded. "Nonetheless, we'd be wise, perhaps, to assume they'll be ready."

"Wise," Heyr agreed. And carefully, quietly, from all the corners around, he began to summon the storms.

Cat Creek, North Carolina

I'm getting too old for this, June Bug thought. I don't care so much if I win anymore. It's getting easier to think about dying—about walking away from all of this and leaving the younger folks to chase after it.

Maybe today.

Belly down in the tall grass, waiting, she didn't have much trouble thinking that on the other side of all this fear and pain, nearly everyone she'd ever loved waited. Her parents. Aunts and uncles. Sister, nephew, friends. The two women she would have risked everything for, that she would have loved if she'd dared.

But the earth smelled of autumn coming, and the air was sweet and good in her lungs. On either side of her waited people who depended on her, needed her, cared about her. She wasn't all that old. She wasn't all that tired.

So.

Maybe not today, either. She still had a lot on this side of eternity, too.

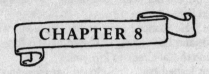

CHAPTER 8

Cat Creek, North Carolina

LAUREN SAW PETE running across the lawn before he had time to ring the doorbell. She should have been asleep, but she could not sleep. Dread filled her; something had rippled through the gate in the house, and the energy of that ripple had yanked her into wakefulness from sound sleep, still so weary she almost couldn't stand on her feet. She paced the floor around the bed where Jake slept with Heyr's blade in her hand, fretting and waiting.

She dared not leave Jake alone in the room, whether sleeping or awake, even for a minute, so at the sight of Pete, she picked her son up with some difficulty, wrapped both arms around the still-sleeping child, and clutching the sword, hurried through the house and down the stairs.

Pete didn't waste time on greetings. "We have to get out of here now," he said.

Lauren didn't ask—"Why?" would wait until they were safer. She nodded and handed Jake to Pete. She grabbed her house keys and her bag, and barefooted, dressed in the over-sized black T-shirt and black sweatpants that had belonged to Brian, she ran out the door after him. She took time to lock the front door, but didn't worry about anything else.

They jumped into Lauren's van, which had the car seat for Jake already in place. Pete took the driver's seat and was already backing them out of the drive while Lauren fastened Jake in.

She slipped the blade into its sheath once she climbed to the front of the car; only then, with the doors locked and her seat belt on, did her heart stop racing. "What's happening?" she asked Pete.

"A lot." He glanced over at her. His skin was pale and bleached, and he looked as scared as she felt. "First, keth have come to Cat Creek to kill you."

Lauren leaned back and closed her eyes and swallowed. She knew of the keth only by reputation. The reputation, however, was that even the rrôn were terrified of the keth. And she knew and feared the rrôn. "I see. What else?"

"Heyr is one of the old gods."

"I'd suspected as much."

"One of the well-known old gods."

She turned a bit and looked at him. A tiny smile touched the corner of his mouth.

"Oh? Which one?"

"Thor."

Lauren digested that for a bit. Thor. Well . . . she wasn't that conversant with Norse mythology, but she did recall that Thor had always been one of the good guys where people were concerned. She sat there, considering. Yes, if she'd been paying a bit better attention, she might have recognized him when he pulled her and Jake and Pete out of certain death on that downworld.

Of course, how often did people really consider the possibility that they were meeting Thor?

"He's going to arm the Sentinels and lead them into battle against the keth."

Lauren shook her head, and Pete must have caught the disgust she was feeling, for he said, "Wha-a-a-at?" It was a pretty good Nathan Lane impression; at another time she would have laughed.

"My life used to make sense. It didn't have gates or goroths or magic or visitations from dragons or . . . whatever the hell the keth were in our mythology—I'm sure they were in there—or Thor and magic battles, for God's sake."

"But that was only because you didn't see any of this—
not because it wasn't there. Is it better to know? Or not to
know?" Pete accelerated to pass a car on the two-lane road
to Fayetteville, and for the first time Lauren realized how
far above the speed limit he was driving. "Speaking for myself, I'd rather know. I'd rather be able to see the danger and
do something than walk around thinking that everything is
fine, and be helpless and unprepared against whatever is
coming."

They drove for a few minutes, and Pete suddenly slowed
down to legal speeds. "There's usually a guy with a radar
gun up ahead," he said. He glanced in the rearview mirror,
then back at the road. "What about Jake? You two could
have been just like everyone else, dumb and happy; you
could have enjoyed him and not worried about anything, and
one day the world would have just gone up in smoke around
you. Though, probably there would be clues before that happened—wars and disease and horror—and *then* it would
have gone up in smoke around you, and you would have
been helpless. This way, you're doing something." He
sighed. "Hell, this way, you're the one person who's doing
something that's actually working. If you weren't, the keth
wouldn't be coming after you."

"I'm glad I'm making a difference. I still wish someone
else was doing it. I wish I could be happy and ignorant of the
danger and just have fun watching Jake grow up, and other
people could take all the risks and have monsters trying to
kill them. And that wonderful, mythical 'someone else'
would save everything." She turned and looked out the window at the countryside rolling past. Trees crowded up close
to the road on her side—a forest of young wood, scrub oak
and dogwood and a lot of tall pines, the occasional scattered
sycamore; she had always enjoyed being the passenger in a
car, looking out the window and daydreaming. She hadn't
been a passenger in quite some time. It was comforting to let
someone else drive; she just wished she could let someone
else do all the other things that she was doing. "I spent most

of my life wanting adventures, and magic, and wonder—and as soon as I get them, all I can do is wonder what the *hell* I was thinking."

"I'm sure you weren't thinking about being the bull's-eye in a game of let's-destroy-the-planet. And I know you want things to be normal. I wish you could have a normal life; I wish someone else could save the worldchain and that you could just be a mom with a nice little kid. It would . . . it would make a lot of things easier."

Lauren kept staring out the window, pretending that she didn't get what he meant. He was talking about the two of them—or rather, the continuation of there not being any two of them, in spite of the fact that they were so clearly attracted to each other.

After a while, when she didn't say anything, he sighed. "We could be really good together, Lauren."

"I know we could."

"Then what's the problem?"

Lauren looked over at Pete. She could still feel Brian's arms wrapped around her when he told her good-bye in that place that could have been Heaven or the Summerland but that was, whatever it was, the final destination and resting place of most souls. She could still see Brian's eyes when he told her to go on and get on with her life. When he told her that he would be waiting for her in the afterlife, but that in the meantime she could love again. That there was no jealousy in Heaven. She believed him, believed what he said was both true and right. And it didn't change anything. She could care about Pete, she could like him, she could want him, she could think he was sexy and that he'd probably be great in bed—but the second a stray yearning for Pete crossed her mind, she felt that she was being unfaithful to Brian.

She looked sadly at Pete. "I'm having a hard time letting go," she said.

"I know. But it's been what—three years?"

"Almost. Or three months, depending on how you look at

it." Her trip down the River of the Dead was far too fresh in her mind.

"I'd rather look at it as three years," Pete said.

Lauren smiled a little. "Except that three months ago he held me in his arms and told me good-bye and to get on with my life and that he'd be there waiting for me when I got back. I can still feel his tears on the back of my neck."

Pete sighed.

"You know how many times I told him almost the same thing as he was getting on a plane to go off to serve his country? I don't. But a lot. I said, 'Go ahead. What you're doing matters. I love you, and I'll always love you. And I'll be here when you get back.'" Lauren leaned her face against the window and stared down at the pavement sliding by beneath the van. The painted line wobbled and jiggled in a hypnotic fashion as it streamed past.

"I have to let go. I know I do. But I was happy once. I had someone who loved me, and someone I loved, and I never took it for granted. There was not a single day that we were together that I regretted him—not when we were fighting, not when we were mad at each other, not when he had to be away on duty. I never regretted him. I only regret that I lost him. That's it." She clenched her hands into tight fists and swallowed against the tears that still came too easily. "How do I move on to something new with someone else when all that I want is what I already had?"

"I don't know," Pete said. "I'll try to help you find out if you want, but I don't have any answers. I've never had one special person I wanted to keep. I don't know how you get past that."

"Not ever?"

"I've never let myself think in terms of forever. My life has not offered a lot of stability or a lot of security. So my relationships already had an exit clearly marked before I went in. I knew it, the women involved knew it—"

"Did they?"

"Well, most of them." She could hear embarrassment in

his voice. "I did a few things I regret. I've never been a play-boy. But I wasn't always completely honest, either."

Lauren smiled a little and watched the road roll by. Per-haps he hadn't been, nor was he completely honest with her. She wondered again what he was hiding from everyone in the Sentinels, including her. He was one of the good guys; she knew it, and she had already bet her life on it more than once. She could feel his goodness in her bones. But what-ever he was hiding was big.

She sat up straight and turned to look at him. "Why don't you tell me your big secret—the one you've been keeping from me and Eric and everyone else."

He looked over at her, and she saw shock in his eyes, and behind that shock, a faint edge of fear.

"Now is the perfect time," she said. "We know they aren't watching the gates; they aren't watching us at all. We're out of viewing range of anyone but June Bug and maybe May-hem, but even then, they have bigger problems right now than us. I don't think any of the rest of them suspect; if they did, they would have been all over you about it before now. And I promise that I won't tell them. But I need to know."

He looked at the road, and she could see his doubts and worries and yearning crossing his face. He wanted to tell her, he was afraid to tell her, and there was something else, too. Perhaps he wasn't allowed to tell her.

Lauren glanced back at Jake. "Jake's still asleep, too," she said. "Right now is about as good as it's ever going to get."

Pete took a deep breath. "This is life and death," he said. "If I tell you this, and you betray me, I'm dead."

She'd figured the thing he was hiding was that big. "I swear I won't tell anyone. But you and I are fighting to save worlds together. Even if our relationship is never anything more than that, I still need to know what you're hiding. And why."

He nodded. "Yes. You do. You need to know that you can trust me. I think you already do trust me."

"With my life."

"Yeah. The feeling is mutual, you know."

"I know."

He smiled a little. "I'm a special agent with the FBI. I've been undercover for quite a few years, first in England because we got a very hot lead there, and then back to Cat Creek, which was where the lead took me."

"Investigating . . . what? Drugs? Organized crime?"

"Aliens."

"Oh, dear."

"The things I'm going to tell you are classified Top Secret, and if you didn't already know the truth behind all of them, I couldn't tell you. But you know much more than the FBI does. So . . ."

Lauren said, "They ran across some upworld stuff, huh?"

"Oh, yeah. The Roswell incident was real—on July 4, 1947, an alien craft crash-landed outside of Roswell, New Mexico. There's been a lot of speculation about it—the military hadn't had nearly as much experience in covering up alien encounters as they have now. So they were sloppy. They do a much, much slicker job today, believe me."

"I'm sure." Lauren laughed.

"Working on the reasonable theory that the craft they found was of extraterrestrial origin, and designed for space flight, they took it, hid it and the bodies they recovered from it, and spent a long time studying everything. The information they acquired aided our own science and military development efforts. We made huge leaps in vehicle and armament technologies."

Lauren frowned a bit, considering that. "So the crash was probably a dark god plant."

Pete looked startled. "A what?"

"An information plant engineered to look like an accident by the dark gods. Their objective is to bring our world closer to its own destruction. Dropping usable advanced technology in a convenient location and in a conspicuous fashion would be the perfect Trojan horse. How could the military *not* take it in and study it? And the Soviet military programs no doubt benefited from some similar 'alien accident' that gave them access to more advanced technology."

He said, "You do paranoia really well, you know that? Your theory could almost make sense."

Lauren grinned. *This* ground she'd been over on more than one occasion. Brian had been a conspiracy theory buff; she knew major details of some of the theories he'd thought most likely to hold some truth. The Roswell incident had been at the top of his list. She told Pete, "It's a simple application of Occam's razor—*One should not increase, beyond what is necessary, the number of entities required to explain anything.* Or, more plainly, the simplest explanation is usually the truest. We know upworlders move through here regularly and have for some time. We know the dark gods are out to get us, and that they're doing it by feeding us technology and baiting us to fight each other. So if we posit the dark gods as the source of the Roswell crash, we have to make no wild-ass guesses about how the crash might have occurred. That gets an Occam score of zero—the best there is." She turned in her seat to look straight at him, and said, "Now look at the aliens-from-space theory. The closest star to us is four light-years away, more or less. Right?"

"Right."

"So we're looking at the use of either wormhole technology, or faster-than-light travel, or some other really amazing scientific discovery that hasn't shown up on our radar yet, because if it were a slow ship, it would have had to be a lot bigger to hold all the supplies and the generations of pilots."

Pete considered that for a minute. "I might have a simple explanation that would still let it be extraterrestrials. How about just flying the thing from there to here with a gate?"

Lauren shook her head. "I don't think that can be done. I don't think there's a way to get a fix on a distant planet to create a gate from one to the other." She felt her cheeks grow hot and said, "I'm embarrassed to admit this, but I was going to get a moon rock for Jake. I thought it would be kind of neat to have one, and I figured that it would be easy enough to get. After all, you can just look right up and see the moon. Straight shot at your target."

"Makes sense."

"You'd think so." Lauren sighed. "I waited for a night with clear skies and a full moon, and fixed a little mirror in the window, big enough for my hand to go through and pull back a nice-sized rock, and I looked at the moon, to see exactly the spot I was shooting for, and when I had it, I tried to make a gate."

Pete looked bemused. "I'm guessing it didn't work."

"I didn't even come close. In the mirror, I couldn't get the moon to hold still long enough to see it, much less fix on it. The closer I took my image to the surface, the faster it raced past. I could no more have opened a gate on the moon than I could have walked there on foot."

"Moving bodies problem," Pete said thoughtfully, in a voice that suggested he was talking more to himself than to her.

"What?"

"What? Oh. What you were doing—it's like when you look through a fixed telescope at a distant object, the object will move out of the telescope's range. To keep the object in range, the telescope has to rotate to compensate for the movement of the Earth. But that doesn't even begin to describe all the movements in the relationship. The object moves in relationship to Earth. It also moves through space. And the finer the focus you need, the more those different sets of movement are going to mess you up."

"That's the problem then. Gates are fixed points, with a fixed path between them."

"And there is no way to have two fixed points and a fixed path with objects that are all moving relative to each other and relative to their suns and relative to their galaxies and relative to all of space."

"So the Roswell aliens didn't get here from another planet by gate," Lauren said, grinning a little. "By the way, thank you. I hadn't actually thought through why that didn't work."

Pete said, "Then why do the gates through to all the worlds you can reach work?"

Lauren said, "That's easy. They're all this world. They aren't just fixed in relationship to each other. They *are* each other. Top floor, middle floor, bottom floor, basement of the same house. The stairs might not work too well during earthquakes and tornadoes, but the rest of the time they're fine."

"Oria's day is longer than Earth's. On some of the down-worlds, the day is shorter. Some of them have weird orbits. So they're still moving in different ways relative to each other."

Lauren shook her head. "They're the same planet. The differences are like . . . weather. Rainy day, sunny day, hurricane, blizzard—they're all external, and if you're inside, you can still use the stairs." She leaned her head back on the seat and rested her arms on the armrests. "Anyway, back to your aliens—the bodies-in-motion problem is one point against the space-aliens-in-Roswell theory. You *have* to posit interstellar travel."

"Right."

"The second theory against is visibility. Why would aliens be coming from as close as four light-years away, or as far as a million light-years away, to here? It's like having international travelers choose Cat Creek as their vacation destination. It just isn't going to happen. People might drop off on their way through Cat Creek, though, so even that analogy doesn't really work. Our galaxy is small, it's isolated in space, and our planet is way out on one of the arms, isolated even in our own galaxy. This planet is literally in the middle of nowhere. *No one* is going to look at this as a reasonable destination, or even as a convenient stop-off on the way to somewhere else." She gave him a wry little smile. "So that's two points against the theory of space aliens."

"It was probably a plant," he agreed. "I just hate thinking of things in terms of conspiracy."

Lauren looked at him and shook her head, and spread her hands wide. "Pete . . . I've reached the point where I think conspiracy is all there is. Look at where we are. At what we're doing. Every bizarre theory, crackpot delusion, and old myth I ever heard of is turning out to be true. Not true in the 'Well, the ancients turned their most favorite citizens into gods, so they really did exist—sort of' brand of true, either. We have ghosts in the kitchen, monsters in the bedroom, aliens all over the place, gods and dragons and *probably* elves, and doors that open up out of nowhere and swallow passersby, and magic, and secret cabals dedicated to good and to evil, and a coming Armageddon, and it's all been there all along, right under our noses . . ." She ran out of steam and sat there staring at him, and she sighed heavily.

"And what's next?" He nodded and smiled at her, looking like he understood. "Spontaneous human combustion, and gnomes in the garden and pixies in the milk, no doubt."

She closed her eyes. "Probably. It's the Grand Unified Field Conspiracy Theory—everything you ever scoffed at is true, and they really *are* all out to get you."

"At least it's not random. It all fits—it all has the same background explanation, no matter how strange the foreground may look. It's something you can make sense of, and once you know why—*why* these things are happening, *why* these people and creatures are involved—you can start working on how—how to stop them, how to beat them, how to fix things." He reached over and patted her knee. "And you've done that, Lauren. You figured it out. You put the pieces together and figured out the *how* that people who aren't even human have been looking for since maybe before our world was even born." He slowed down again as they headed into Raeford.

"Not that long. I don't think the oldest rrôn are older than about ten . . . maybe fifteen thousand years. Which is old, but not billions of years old. And the rrôn were around when the first worlds died."

"Still. People have been trying to save things for a very long time. You're the first one who succeeded."

Lauren looked back out the window again. "I wish that were true."

"Of course it's true. If it weren't true, the worldchain wouldn't still be dying."

Lauren pressed her cheek against the glass and stared down at the road running beneath her, and remembered being a kid and feeling safe. "That's not actually the only explanation," she said. "Think Occam's razor. What's the simplest explanation for why no one has ever managed to fix things?"

She could feel him looking at her, but he didn't say anything.

After a while she said, "They might have just killed all the ones who figured it out before."

CHAPTER 9

Cat Creek

ERIC LAY ON HIS BELLY in the tall grass to one side of the road, weapon braced on a fallen log, finger on the trigger. His mouth was dry, his palms were sweating, and his gut churned and twisted. He could feel them coming—he could feel the weight of magic in the air and the sick dread of the kids to either side of him, who had trained for a lot of emergency situations before they became Sentinels, but not for shooting dark gods.

The Sentinels had made a point of avoiding all nonhumans, both upworlders and downworlders. They'd had an isolationist policy, because that had seemed to make the most sense. The dark gods only came gunning for people who directly involved themselves in dark god business. And since the Sentinels had never done that, they were left alone to police human magic misuse and to hold back the tide of devastation that was rolling toward them.

Eric shifted a little as the tree root digging itself into his hipbone finally caught his attention.

The Sentinels had prided themselves on being so secretive, on always keeping themselves and their activities below the radar of the enemies they fought. But they hadn't been a secret to the gods, old or dark. They'd simply been too ineffective to bother about. The first time someone did something that actually threatened the dark gods' goals, they reacted fast enough. And kept reacting when their first shot missed.

To his right, Betty Kay sneezed, muffling it pretty well, but probably not well enough. To his left, Raymond Smetty squirmed and fidgeted with his weapon and glanced up at the truck, pulled off to the side of the road beside his position. The hair on Eric's arms stood up. Who'd put Smetty closest to the truck? And the keys were still in it, weren't they? Thor and Loki had been positioning people, telling them where to fire and when . . . but who had decided Smetty, the Sentinel Eric marked as the least dedicated, the least reliable, and the most likely to bolt in the face of real trouble, needed to be right next to the means by which he might bolt? Who had done that?

Eric ran the last quarter of an hour back in his mind and saw what he'd feared to see. It had been Loki. Loki, grinning, leaning close to Raymond Smetty's ear and whispering something that made Smetty smile.

Loki was a troublemaker, a trickster, a deceiver. Loki played games with people because he could, because it amused him to do so.

Eric wanted to wave Smetty over to him, tell him to change places. But there wasn't time. The keth moved into view, coming over the rise.

He would have known them anywhere—he'd spent time pretending to be one, but he could see that he'd been a poor imitation. They were . . . majestic.

Slender as reeds, twice as tall as a man, they moved forward with inhuman grace, gazellelike. Two of the three had hair red as flame. The third was golden. The hair, braided into a million tiny braids, floated around them as if it was alive. Medusas, he thought, who could turn a man to stone with a single gaze. They had strangely beautiful faces—enormous almond eyes black as jet, tiny rosebud mouths, nearly invisible noses. They wore beautiful, complex gowns, gauzy and brilliantly colored and patterned, that lifted and swirled, cloudlike, in the faintest of breezes.

Compared with them, Thor and Loki were lumpish and

gnomish and crude. Compared to them, he was even less. He was shameful. Hideous. Something that should be hidden— that should be destroyed.

He started, slowly, to turn his weapon around, to point it toward himself. He didn't deserve to live. He was ashamed of himself, ashamed for breathing air and eating food, for poisoning the world with his existence.

Eric had the muzzle against his chest. Was fumbling with his shoe, to get it off so that he could pull the trigger with his toe, when he caught movement to his left and saw Raymond Smetty leap up and hit something in the back of the truck.

The box, he thought dully. The one that Loki brought, that Thor didn't want.

And then his mind cleared, and he realized what he had almost done—what the keth had almost pushed him to, so smoothly and easily that he hadn't even felt their knives slide beneath his skin. He turned the weapon in the right direction, lined them up in his sights, and began to fire.

Around him, the other Sentinels did the same. Even Smetty—Smetty, who Eric guessed had been Loki's choice for least likely to listen to Thor and Eric, who represented authority, and who was most likely to do something simply because he thought he shouldn't.

The Sentinels hit the keth. He could see blood spatter, could see the impact of the bullets and whatever else he and the other Sentinels were sending at the dark gods. But the keth did not fall. Fire sprang up around them, dark and swirling— reverse-image rainbows—and fire erupted from them, hard fast arcs that hit every one of the Sentinels' positions.

Eric thought he was dead. Closed his eyes against the blinding explosion of light around him. Heard the silence, and pulled the trigger hard, willing the keth dead even though on Earth his will held no magic, and opened his eyes to find a glow surrounding him. The shield Loki had brought. It worked. He wasn't dead yet, and neither were his people. Firing started again from all around him.

The keth moved closer, not splitting up or getting off the road. That, he thought, was hubris—to be so sure of victory that they did not act defensively. Or maybe it was Loki's box, doing something to them that kept them from thinking clearly. The rules had changed, the playing field had evened out, the instant Smetty had switched on the box. . . .

Right. They were coming for the box, because if they could turn that off, he and the other Sentinels would fall to them.

They fired and the bullets hit, but the keth weren't falling. They kept coming. They were healing their own wounds as fast as he and the other Sentinels made them, and though their once-beautiful robes were blood-soaked and cut to ribbons, the keth bore no permanent harm.

Everything he and the other Sentinels could do was not enough. *Die, you bastards—DIE!* he thought. But they didn't.

Then the bright morning sky went black in an instant, and thunder rumbled and lightning crashed, blinding, deafening, hitting the keth, binding them to the road, and the sharp breath of ozone and the stink of burning flesh filled the air. Heyr stepped onto the road behind them, clearly revealed as Thor, with his hair flying in the sudden wind and with his hammer in his hand. He sang, louder than the constant crashing of the thunder—a warrior's song in the language of another place, another time—and unholy joy lit his eyes and shone from his face. He threw Mjollnir, the war hammer, and the head of one of the keth exploded; the lightning incinerated the dark god in an instant. Though it was too bright to watch—though the whole thing burned itself into his retinas and Eric thought he would be blinded as well as deafened once this was done—he could not look away.

Heyr-Thor's war hammer flew back into his gloved hand, and he threw it again, and the second keth fell, exploded, and was incinerated. A second catch, a third throw, a third death.

The lightning stopped. The constant bombardment of the thunder stopped. Eric could see only the flashes of retinal afterburn; he could hear nothing at all. He lay in pouring rain, blind and deaf, blinking rain out of his face, wondering if he dared stand up until his vision cleared.

He heard before he saw—heard faint voices that became louder, calling names. "Eric?" "Betty Kay?" "Darlene?" "I'm here—Darlene, that is." "June Bug?" "Mayhem?" "George?" "Louisa?" "Raymond?"

"I'm here!" Eric shouted.

He heard George Mercer's drawled "Here," and June Bug's voice, and Mayhem's. And after a moment Raymond and Louisa called out, too. But not Betty Kay.

Then vision returned, though the world looked bleached out and pale to him, and ghostly afterimages of the three burning dark gods clouded everything.

The others were standing up with their weapons pointed down or resting on their shoulders; all of them were looking around.

"Nothing from Betty Kay," June Bug said.

She'd been on the left flank, right up against the woods. Eric had thought that the safest place to put her—she'd never been in a fight, and he guessed that of all of them, she would be the one most likely to panic.

Heyr and Loki were at the truck, arguing about the box. Raymond Smetty stood next to Loki and a little behind him, looking defiant. Eric could see everyone else. But not Betty Kay. And he remembered the first attack of the keth, the subtle mind manipulation, and he knew what he was going to find.

He took off for Betty Kay's position at a run, praying that he was wrong and that he'd find her alive, and knowing that he wouldn't.

He found the place where she'd hidden, the tall grass beaten down flat. But of her, no sign. Not her weapon, not any blood, no body.

She'd run. He could understand that. She'd fled before the keth got there. She was a kid, she was too tender to be a Sentinel, she'd washed out. But he could understand that. Not everyone could go into battle. Many soldiers were found after battles with their weapons unfired—and no one was going to mistake Betty Kay for a soldier. She could go back home to Ohio to be somebody's nice wife, Eric thought.

They would have to blank out her memories of the Sentinels, but the Sentinels had been using that spell for a long time. It meant she got to live.

He looked into the woods, wondering how far she'd gotten. Maybe she was already back at the Daisies and Dahlias. Maybe she was already home and packing.

"Betty Kay!" Mayhem shouted, and Eric turned around.

She was standing up out of the grass right next to the place where the three dark gods had fallen. The weapon, casually held against her hip, pointed down—Good girl, he thought—and she was rubbing her eyes.

"Betty Kay!" he yelled, but she didn't jump or turn or give any sign that she'd heard.

If she'd been there, she'd been right in the heart of it. Center of the storm, up next to the lightning and the thunder. She might have taken an indirect hit from the lightning as it bled off into the ground.

She looked around, still not hearing the people yelling at her, and stepped out into the road. From the pavement, she started picking things up. He saw a glimmer, a dull, lovely gleam. Gold.

Eric hurried to her side, touched her shoulder. She looked up at him and grinned, and on her face he saw the same wild joy he'd seen when Heyr-Thor strode into battle.

"WE GOT THE BASTARDS!" she shouted.

He put a finger to his lips. "I can hear you."

"I CAN'T HEAR YOU!" She held out what she'd found, and he stared.

Gold jewelry—beautiful hinged gold bands meant to be locked through skin. Piercing rings. Resurrection rings. The immortality of the three keth—memories that might run back ten thousand years or more, lay gleaming in her hand.

And they were poison. He stood staring at them for a long time, feeling their pull, their call. Wrap one around his wrist or clamp it through his skin and he would never die. He would claim knowledge and memories of worlds that no longer existed, of times before men built their first cities. He would be a god. He reached out to touch one of the bands, and the greasy feel of it and a horrible, blinding hunger rocked him.

"WE HAVE TO DESTROY THEM!" he yelled.

Betty Kay cringed. "Not so loud," she shouted, but softer than before.

So her hearing was coming back.

The other Sentinels clustered around them, and the two old gods as well.

"I'll take those off your hands," Loki said, and reached for the resurrection rings, but Betty Kay pulled them back. Instead, she flashed a smile at Heyr-Thor that was pure come-on—a smile unlike anything that Eric had ever seen on her face, and said, "You were . . . magnificent. Here."

And she handed the rings to him.

Loki stood there, hand still out, looking from Betty Kay to Heyr-Thor and back, and said, "Let me do something useful. I'll dispose of the rings."

Heyr-Thor hefted them in one hand, and Pete could see him sizing Loki up. After a moment, Heyr-Thor shook his head. "I've got it."

"All of this, and you still don't trust me."

"You are brother, friend, and comrade, and yet I know that in the end you will betray me, and all of us. I know where you will stand in the end days," Heyr-Thor said.

Loki's voice was a growl. "Have you ever thought your actions now might play some part in where I stand in the end days?" He studied all of them. "Don't call on me again, Thor. Not in your direst need, not in your deepest desperation. My ears are deaf to your pleas. For now at least, I will not stand against you and yours. But I will no longer stand for you, either." And then he pointed to the road and drew an arch out of it—a black asphalt vine that whipped up from the pavement in a loop—and when it was tall enough to permit him passage, he summoned green fire and vanished. The gate he'd created blinked out behind him, but the arch in the pavement remained.

Heyr-Thor stood staring at the gate, frowning. After a moment, he tapped the arch with his war hammer and it crumbled into dust.

Eric, with Loki's dark-god gun slung over his shoulder, shivered a little. That hadn't gone as well as it might have.

Heyr-Thor, however, seemed unperturbed. He put the resurrection rings on the ground. "Stand back."

He hefted his war hammer and measured the distance between him and his targets. All the Sentinels backed away.

Mjollnir slammed into the bands, and the pavement where they lay exploded into a cloud of black dust and a long, piercing scream. Eric, not back far enough, got a face full of asphalt. He felt the tiny shards go into his eyelids, his cheeks, his nose and lips. Great. Road rash the quick and easy way. He would be pulling bits of tar out of his skin for weeks, probably.

"That was all three?" Eric asked.

"All three," Heyr-Thor agreed. "All broken, but none yet sufficiently destroyed." He went over to the crater in the road and pulled out a fused, flattened tangle of gold. Eric saw similar patterns during the summer, when snakes got run over by cars.

"These have to be melted down," Heyr-Thor said. "Melted down, the gold poured into a mold and left to cool. Then ground to powder and the powder poured into moving water. This gold can never be used again. It is tainted, and if it is not ground and scattered, it will call to evil those who are willing to listen, and subvert even those who are not. This gold has been poisoned by the keth, who are the vilest of the dark gods—at least the ones we know."

Eric looked at the flattened metal bands. "I'll take care of it," he said.

Heyr-Thor told him, "It isn't the work for one man. In the dark, the gold will call to you. It will twist you. Let all of us work on it together; we must destroy it quickly and get free of it. It will work on us as much as it works on you."

Eric said, "Let's get off the road and back to the watch room. We have work yet to do."

Heyr nodded. "We should be doing it, and quickly. The keth won't be the last the Night Watch sends here."

Kerras

Lights swirled, sparkled, erupted across the dark side of Kerras, through the ice-layered chasms, deep in the dead abysses. Lights, pale blue and white, green and gold and pink; they crawled through the airless cold, slippery and liquid, stirring the ghosts with the rebound magic that had birthed them, pouring upworld, released from a battle that had seen the deaths of three dark gods, and that was witnessing their destruction.

Change. They were all change. Movement where there had been none before, energy reborn in a depleted land. The lights burrowed into the dead world, deep below the surface. They were potential waiting for a trigger. But the trigger had not yet come.

Cat Creek, North Carolina

Rekkathav had found a good location to watch the battle. And he had seen the whole thing. He had discovered that he would be going back as the bearer of bad tidings, no matter what had happened to the Beithan assassin. Having seen the unthinkable disaster with the keth, he started getting little nervous twitches and chills all over his tender, alien skin every time he considered the likely fate of the lone Beithan.

Aril, keth Master of the Night Watch, was not a creature who took bad news well. He would not be . . . pleasant.

He'd wiped out ten fieldmasters for his last bit of bad news. Now Rekkathav was going to go tell him that all three of his hand-picked keth were dead, destroyed, gone forever. That Thor was back in business. That the immortal had enough live magic in hand to fight effectively, and that he'd put together what looked like a team.

Yes. Rekkathav was going to go tell Aril all of that, with nothing to leaven the load. And he was going to visit the terminal box in short order.

Well, he didn't actually know what had happened to the Beithan, did he? And he had firm orders to find out. Thank the eternities for literal interpretation of orders.

Rekkathav was going to be very thorough in finding out about the Beithan. Very thorough, and if necessary, very slow. It was going to take him exactly as long to find the Beithan, he decided, as it took him to find enough good news to save his miserable life.

Cross Creek Mall, Fayetteville, North Carolina

Pete, sitting in the Cross Creek Mall's tiny food court with Lauren and a now-very-awake Jake, felt his beeper go off. He took the call at a pay phone—still the best way not to be tracked by anyone who might be watching—and got the good news.

He patted Lauren on the shoulder. "We can go home."

"We can?" Lauren looked at him. "They beat the keth? Who's dead?"

"Just the keth, from what I hear. We have to go back. You need to get some sleep. I'll stay with you to stand guard while you sleep, just in case. And then you're going to have to go talk to them."

"They don't want to hear anything I might have to say about this, Pete."

"Maybe they didn't before. I'm betting that they do now, though. They have to see that you must be doing something big and powerful if it's getting the attention of the Night Watch."

"Actually," Lauren said, standing and taking Jake's hand, "they don't have to see anything except that I'm causing them problems they never had before. These are not flexible people, Pete. They're men and women who have been part of this hereditary order since they were very young. They were taught that there was One True Way, and they believe it, and what I'm doing challenges everything they have worked for and believed in their whole lives."

Pete wanted to pull her into his arms and hold her and assure her that everything would be fine, that they would see her side of things, and that if they didn't he'd stand between her and hell itself. But he didn't. He just gave her what he hoped was a reassuring smile, and said, "Give them a chance. I have your back if things don't go well. So does Heyr."

The ride back to Cat Creek was uneventful. Lauren slept, Jake sang and looked out the window and talked to Pete—or, when Pete wasn't talking, to an invisible friend.

Pete bet the invisible friend gave Lauren the creeps. How did one go about telling whether the kid was talking to nothing or talking to a downworlder who'd come to visit? Cold spots, maybe, but the van still had decent air-conditioning, so in this case, that wouldn't be the tip-off.

He took them home, tucked Lauren onto the couch, set him and Jake up across the hall in the dining room playing cars. And when Lauren was asleep, he called June Bug.

"It went well enough," June Bug told him. "One of the children has a bad case of buck fever now and wants to run right back out and do it all again."

"Raymond."

"Raymond is still all the ass he ever was, even though I think he did save us. But no. Not Raymond. Betty Kay."

Pete considered that for a moment, then laughed. "The quiet ones can surprise you. I wouldn't have picked her for the role."

"Nor I. But she's all fired up and hanging around Heyr like a cat in heat, wanting to go hunt more dark gods and gods-know-what all else. I see a lot of unhappiness coming there."

Pete tried to imagine Betty Kay doing anything like a cat in heat, and couldn't get the picture to focus. He let it go, and said, "I need to talk to you. Later, though."

"That'll be fine. I'll be in the library all day and probably most of the evening. I'm doing a bit of research."

"I'll stop by later, then."

Cat Creek, North Carolina

It was late when Pete left Lauren, and he left her with Heyr standing guard, which should have given him some comfort but which instead made him terribly nervous.

June Bug was in the back room with the doors all locked. He had to tap on the window to get her attention.

"So what has gone wrong in your world, Pete?" she asked by way of greeting.

"And hello to you, too."

"Don't chitchat me, boy. You wouldn't have come to talk to me if you didn't have a problem, and one, at that, that you figured I might be able to help you fix."

"That's a hell of a way to look at things."

"Maybe, but you've never come by to talk to me before. So. What's wrong?"

"Lauren."

"Who does not love you the way you love her."

Pete gave June Bug an exasperated look. "How did you know that?"

"You keep some of your secrets better than others. That one you're not doing too well with."

Pete felt his heart drop into his shoes.

June Bug laughed. "I've been around, boy. I've been watching people for a long lifetime. And I've kept a few secrets of my own. I know the signs." She waved him to a seat filled with books. "Put them on the floor, sit, and talk to me."

"What secrets?" Pete asked.

"If I told you, they wouldn't *be* secrets, would they?" She smiled a little. She'd been attractive in her day, he guessed. She still had good bones, kind eyes, and hair that was mostly brown. She'd aged well. She carried herself with certainty— she knew who she was and had come to peace with that. Which was more than he had done. He still lived in the middle of turmoil and endless, agonizing self-doubt.

She seemed always a little sad, but he'd heard the stories of the man she'd loved—the one who had left her when she was young. He'd heard from the other Sentinels how she had never loved again. He thought that was hard to imagine, and that she had chosen to carry her sorrow far too long. But then, Lauren wasn't giving up on her grief any too quickly, either.

Which was why he was here.

He took a deep breath. "I want to talk to you about Lauren."

"I figured as much."

"But I want to do it in a roundabout way—I want to know why you never loved anyone else after that man left you when you were young."

June Bug burst out laughing.

"What?"

"Well, you're direct. But why the hell would you want to know that?"

"Because if I can figure out why you hung on to someone who was gone, and to a relationship that was just a memory, maybe I can use that to figure out how to help Lauren let go."

June Bug sighed and moved things around on her desk. "And now I can lie to you or I can give you a bit of my secret, and chance your guessing the rest."

Pete sat very still, waiting.

"I can't help you, Pete," she said after another minute. "Not because I don't want to, but because the stories you've heard about me and my one long-lost love are lies. I made them up to cover a truth I didn't want to admit. That I still don't want to admit."

"What truth?" he asked when she was silent too long.

"That I spent most of my life in love with someone—but someone I couldn't have."

"Married?"

"Yes, happily married. And with family. And had I admitted the truth, this person would not have understood. The truth would have ended our friendship. And I was willing to take friendship over nothing."

"You could have said something. Taken a chance."

"No. First, trying to break up a family is a vile thing. And second, sometimes you know what the answer is going to be. And . . ." Her voice faltered. She shrugged, and managed a sad little smile, and he could see her eyes go bright with tears. "They're dead now, anyway, so it doesn't matter."

Something about the way she'd phrased things suddenly pinged on him. *This person.* And *they*, used incorrectly—when June Bug was always careful to get her words right. Pronoun game, he realized, and went for the wild guess. "What was her name?"

June Bug laughed again. "As I said, give you a bit and you get it all. Marian Hotchkiss."

"*Lauren's* mother?"

"Yes."

Pete rubbed his temples. "And people say small towns are boring."

"Not the people who pay attention."

"No. Probably not. So . . . you loved Lauren's mother, who never knew how you felt. But now she's been dead for a long time. And you've never loved again."

"I didn't say that."

"Who else, then?"

"It's too embarrassing to admit."

Pete ran possibilities through his mind, and the obvious answer popped up. "Lauren. Marian's daughter."

June Bug paled a little, but in her eyes Pete saw relief. So not Lauren. But he'd still been close. If they'd been playing Battleship, he would have only missed by one square. June Bug said, "I think we need to discuss your problem for a while. Or perhaps I need to get back to my research."

"We *are* discussing my problem. This talk of ours is helping a great deal. I'm seeing that Lauren could care about me as much as I could care about her and never let me know."

"Or she could be carrying a torch for her dead husband. You can't discount that and you can't ignore it. Some women really do only love once."

"I'd rather not consider that possibility."

"You'll spare yourself a world of hurt if you keep it in mind."

"Probably. You spare yourself any hurt over Molly?"

June Bug's eyes narrowed, and she looked dangerous for a moment. "She was too young for me—but she looked and sounded exactly like Marian. Exactly. I know why she did now, but it didn't help then. In any case, you're too perceptive by half. I think perhaps I need to look a little more closely into the other secrets you're keeping."

"Maybe not," Pete said. "I'll keep your secrets if you'll keep mine."

"I'm not going to promise anything right now. As long as you don't pose a danger to the Sentinels, I'll let whatever you have buried in your closet stay there."

"I don't pose a danger to the Sentinels. We're both on the same side—me and the Sentinels," he said, and he meant it. And he tried not to think too hard about the FBI, which did pose a danger to June Bug and her secret society and its goals.

"Sides are tricky things," June Bug said. "They can shift suddenly. I don't want to suddenly discover that you're one of the bad guys."

"Not going to happen."

The conversation moved on. They talked for a while about the old gods, and about the keth, about the gold of the resurrection rings, about Lauren's bringing magic back to Earth, and about Molly.

"You've seen her?"

"Yes."

"How is she?"

Pete sighed. "Different. She looks different, and there's this aura of darkness around her that wasn't there before. I can still see a lot of the person she was before she died. But there's something else there now, too. Something dark and strange and frightening."

"Death changes people," June Bug said, her voice a whisper.

Which, Pete thought, pretty well summed up not only June Bug's problem, but his. And Lauren's. And, for that matter, Molly's.

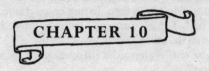

CHAPTER 10

Night Watch Control Hub, Barâd Island, Oria

REKKATHAV KNEW HOW TO WORK HARD, and he had worked harder in the last half day than he'd ever worked before in his life. And the work had paid off, to the point that he dared to go home and face the Master of the Night Watch with some hope that his head would still be attached to his body when he'd told his tale.

He bowed low before Aril. "I have the information you required—both bad news and good news."

Well . . . ?

"Bad news first."

I'll have all of it together, the keth said, and went for his mind with the ruthlessness that had made him Master.

But Rekkathav was still a truly living creature—never resurrected, with the breath of his birth still in him and his soul still bound to his flesh. Aril could suggest to him. He could compel to a certain extent. But so long as Rekkathav was braced and shielded with his soul standing guard over his thoughts, Aril could not rip into Rekkathav with the same ruthlessness he had employed on Vanak. Rekkathav was capable of keeping secrets—as long as he didn't try to keep them too long.

"Bad news first," Rekkathav said, hanging on to his plan like grim death. Or grim life, in his case.

He told Aril about the return of the immortals, about their

team of mortals, about the deaths of the keth and the Beithan, and about the destruction of their resurrection rings.

Aril sat frozen, disbelieving. He stared into Rekkathav's eyes with that cold death-hunger that was as close as he ever came to genuine fury. The whisper in Rekkathav's mind was gentle.

Rekkathav didn't relax. "I found the source of the magic. The source is incredibly vulnerable."

The death-hunger in the Master's eyes did not lessen. *I could do as much.*

"I did more. I also found out about the source's protector. I could not locate the protector, but I can tell you how to find her, and what she is."

Tell me.

Rekkathav told everything he had found out about the purely mortal Lauren and her child, and about Molly, who was both dark god and dark god hunter. He noted that Molly could be connected with the disappearance of the Night Watch team stationed in the Orian technical development center down in Fyre, as well as some solo disappearances, and was probably responsible for more.

And this is your good *news?*

"The good news is that there are only two of them. And you only have to kill one to win. Our enemies have no backup, no second system in place ready to carry on if anything happens to their mortal. She's it. She's a freak. A fluke. And she's tender. Wait until they've relaxed, until they think this business with the keth gave you pause, and then go in with an all-out assault—everything we can throw at them. Be prepared to take some losses from the two immortals and don't get sidetracked by anything they throw at your people, then pump the whole of our force against that one mortal target on her home planet with not the first bit of her own magic to protect herself, and she'll die. We'll pay something for it—maybe even a lot. But they'll pay everything."

Aril watched Rekkathav for a long time without giving

any response at all. Then he asked, *How long a wait would you suggest?*

"Two weeks minimum. Maybe a month. No attempts at all during that time, then a hundred gates simultaneously and everything we have poured in on top of her in one rush."

Aril nodded. *A sound plan. You surprise me. I thought you had more of a secretarial spirit.* He paused, and tipped his head to one side so that his hair, floating around his head in a thousand braids like living snakes, coiled and slithered. The effect always gave Rekkathav the creeps, and this time was no different.

You may put the team together and lead the charge. I believe—he smiled just a little, and his gaze never left Rekkathav—*that initiative should be rewarded.*

The Master of the Night Watch dismissed Rekkathav from his presence with the flick of a finger.

Rekkathav scuttled back to his own chambers, keeping his thoughts tucked close. He was still alive. Still alive—but the Master might as well have signed his death warrant. *Him* lead the charge against immortals and well-armed mortals; him, who had read every battle history and tactical treatise he could find, but who had never been in so much as a mating duel.

He studied the heavy gold band clamped into his hide. The band that had promised immortality, that had promised that he would stand among the masters of eternity, that had made him one with the dark gods of the Night Watch. It had felt like his own pair of wings when they'd first clamped it on him.

Now it felt like shackles.

The Wilds of Southern Oria

Molly woke in leaves and dirt, and this time she remembered where she was and knew what had happened to her. Dead again. She stood and looked up, and up, to the top of the rock where she and Baanraak had fought. She could go up there, see if he was still there, if he had resurrected more slowly than she, so that she might take another shot at destroying him.

She stood naked in a forest a long way from her home. But she did not need to remain in that state. She closed her eyes and willed the magic of Oria into her body, and summoned hunter's clothes—comfortable jeans and sturdy walking shoes and a good, stretchy knit shirt. She visualized that dagger that Seolar had given her, the one with which she had once killed herself to save her existence, and brought it and the sheath and belt to hand, and found her weapon covered with dried blood and much the worse for wear.

A touch of her hand, a focused command, and the dagger was both clean and self-cleaning, sharp and self-sharpening. A weapon worthy of a hunter. She looked up toward the top of the rock again and judged distances. Two hundred feet, perhaps. Maybe a little more. She could get there in the blink of an eye. But what would she find when she got there? She felt for Baanraak's thoughts, but could find no sign of them. She tried to recall the memory of his flesh, which she had both touched and, when she hid within his mind, worn. She could not bring it back, either. He might be lying atop the rock, halfway through his resurrection and helpless. He might be all the way through, and blocking her attempts to locate him.

She floated up the rock face, hoping it would not be the latter. She had no wish to confront him when he knew she was coming—he had size and age and experience and built-in weaponry all in his favor, and if he also had warning of her arrival, she would have no chance. But she could not ignore the possibility that his resurrection rings might be lying atop the rock, waiting for her to pick them up. She could end his pursuit of her for good.

But atop the rock there was nothing but a single black scale. She picked it up. It shimmered in the palm of her hand—about the size of her thumbnail, iridescent, translucent, too beautiful to be part of such an evil creature. It was Baanraak's—she could feel what he had been when she touched it, but she could not feel him. She shoved it into her pocket, frowning. He'd resurrected and gone, or something else had beaten her to the rings.

Then from down in the forest she felt what she'd been seeking. Baanraak's mind, fogged and bewildered, crawling back to consciousness. But still vulnerable.

The explosion. He'd been blown clear of the rock like she had—he'd resurrected in the forest.

Molly didn't waste time pondering alternatives—she ran to the edge, jumped in the direction of the waking mind she felt, and let herself drop in free fall, pretending she had a parachute strapped to her back again, holding her arms and legs out and controlling the direction of her fall. She visualized a cushion that would slow her fall, but did not put it into place until the last instant, when she'd broken through an opening in the canopy of trees and could see Baanraak below her, one wing flopping, legs twitching, neck outstretched. He wasn't quite finished resurrecting, she realized, and blew the cushion spell into place beneath her, over him. She whipped out her dagger as her spell brought her in for a smooth landing, changed it into a sword in the blink of an eye, put weight behind the blow she aimed at the joining of his huge head and serpentine neck, willed the sword through him in one smooth blow.

She'd learned from experience—she kept out of Baanraak's way as his body thrashed in its death throes. When the thrashing and the twitching stopped, she willed him to flames and burned him to ash, and when it was done, dug through the ash until she'd located two heavy gold rings.

She held them in her hand for a long moment, feeling the greasy darkness of them, the weight that came from the taint of death magic heavier than the gold that bound it.

She could not destroy the resurrection rings with magic alone—she already knew that. She did not wish to take them with her because already they called to her, their magic mingling with everything that she was to twist her farther toward destruction. So she created a kiln, spinning it upward out of local bedrock, and summoned the ingredients to build a hot enough fire, and used magic to light the wood. The fire was not magical, though, merely hot. She put the rings into it and let the gold run down and collect in a small square mold. While it melted, the hellish magics coiled around her so tightly she almost couldn't breathe; she could feel Baanraak's touch, his hunger, his power, and she wanted them. Nor were they beyond her grasp. Not yet.

She clenched her teeth until her jaws ached and shivered at Baanraak's invisible touch. To fight the call of the magic while she waited, she created the grinding apparatus she would need later, and when the gold had melted, used more magic to cool and harden it. Used the grinder to rasp the bar down to gold dust, and felt the spells weaken as she did. She put the gold dust in a bag and willed herself to a river she knew of that fell straight down the side of the mountain into the sea. She stood on a boulder beside the crashing, racing water, bag of gold in hand.

"We're done," she said to the shadows of Baanraak that remained. "We're done, and it's over."

She poured the gold into whitewater. She felt the last of the magic leave her, and watched the powder gleam and sparkle as it poured away from her. Beautiful. Achingly beautiful. And finally gone.

She pulled the scale out of her pocket and stared at it. Baanraak was gone. This tiny thing was all that remained of him. She should be rejoicing. So why did the hollowness inside her feel worse?

She needed to go home.

She held the scale over the water, thinking to toss it away—but at the last moment she could not. She spun a little stainless steel chain out of air and magic, not a magic metal or a binding metal like silver or gold, but a simple metal that would let her keep the little scale with her. She edged it with a delicate stainless steel frame, and held it up when she was done to watch the dark rainbows move within it, and then she donned the necklace she'd created. A trophy, she told herself. A tangible symbol of her triumph over her first great enemy.

Molly stood atop the cliff with spray from the falls cold and sharp as needles against her skin, touching the rrôn scale at her throat, and tried to think of anything else that she might do to put off the inevitable. But she had to go back. She had to let Seolar know where she had been for the last . . . well, she did not know how long she'd been gone. For the last days, then, or maybe weeks.

She had to face him. Hollower inside, with the darkness at her core spreading outward, with her feelings for him numbed and with the knowledge that she was being ripped away a little at a time, like an onion stripped of successive layers until nothing remained but the memory that an onion had once been there.

She was diminished; the darkness had spread. And this would keep happening, because even with Baanraak dead, Molly could not give up and stop hunting the Night Watch, the other dark gods. If she quit, the result would be the same as if Lauren just quit. The worldchain would fail, and her world and Oria and everything she had ever loved would die—and even though the ability to love faded inside her with each death, and she lost more and more of her passion, she still . . . remembered. She remembered caring.

She stared out at the sea that sprawled before her, glittering like a vast sapphire. It was beautiful, and alive, and already forces worked knowingly toward its destruction and the destruction of the rest of Oria as well. This world, like Earth, would die without her help. All the beauty before her would pass away, while she would go on, knowing all the while that she could have been the difference.

Molly turned her face to the north, lifted her chin, and gathered her resolve. She would face him. She would find a way to talk to him. She had to, for both their sakes.

The Wilds of Southern Oria—and a Band of Hunter's Gold

Baanraak woke, hungry, with late afternoon sunlight in his eyes. He looked up at the trees overhead, at the vast natural rock tower that rose over the forest to his right. He sniffed the air, felt for life. Nothing edible moved anywhere near him—something had scared off all the game. The air stank of dark magic and of the destruction of dark magic. A dark god had died nearby, and not long ago.

He should hunt for Molly, but at the moment his hunger was all-consuming. He would find her without difficulty, he decided. And then he would destroy her for what she had done to him. Everything had become clear to him—he couldn't imagine why he'd had such a struggle deciding on his path of action.

He looked up through the trees, found a clearing, and leapt into the air. He headed south.

The Wilds of Southern Oria—and a Band of Master's Gold

. . . and Baanraak woke, hungry, with the sun creeping down the far edge of the sky. He looked up at the trees overhead, at the vast natural rock tower that rose over the forest to his left. He sniffed the air and caught the stink of dark magic and the death of a dark god some time earlier, but fresh enough to be worrisome.

He breathed, deep and slow, feeling the life fill him again, feeling the rush of blood through his veins, the power in his muscles, the flex of talon and wing.

The world had become clear to him; the choices lay before him, obvious and logical. He could remember his confusion before Molly blew him into bits, but he could not understand why he had been confused.

He had become annoyed with the Night Watch, with the ineptitude of its leadership, with its pathetic cultivation of

unripe downworlds and its sloppy harvesting of prime
worlds. But he had no need to be annoyed; he had walked
away from the Mastery. It was time to go back.

He would eat first, and then he would pursue his new
destiny.

He looked up through the trees, found a clearing, and
leapt into the air. He headed west.

The Wilds of Southern Oria—and a Band of Beginner's Gold

. . . and Baanraak woke, hungry, to early twilight. He
sniffed the air and found the faint stink of the destruction of
dark magic. Someone had slaughtered a dark god a while
ago, though the scent had cooled and would be gone for certain
by morning.

He knew how he had come to be where he was. He knew
who he was. But he felt incomplete, as if the vast stretches of
who he was had been erased. He knew that he had known
more, but he did not know what he had known, only that he
was a vessel that had once been full but was now nearly empty.

Game moved through the forest, however, and his hunger
chased other thoughts from his mind. He tucked his wings in
tight and stepped lightly along the path toward his dinner.

The Wilds of Southern Oria—and a Band of Silver and Gold

. . . and Baanraak woke, hungry, in darkness and cold, with
the stars glittering in a cloudless sky. There would be frost
before morning. But the clear sky did not confer clear
thoughts, nor did the sharp cold offer the sharpness of irrefutable
logic. The weight of doubt and the sprawling tangle
of choices that made little sense or less sense or no sense
at all lay before him, and he closed his eyes against them and
despaired.

Copper House, Ballahara, Nuue, Oria

Molly stepped out of the gate she'd created and into the safe room in the subbasement of Copper House. She locked down the gate-mirror she'd used to come in, rekeying it to accept only her magic or Lauren's. She showered in the modern shower that Lauren had created there when she was stuck in the subbasement running a small war to rescue Molly. Molly let herself enjoy the endless hot water and great pressure—hot showers were not among the luxuries Oria had yet discovered—and when she had finished and dried herself with a wonderful, thick, soft bath towel the size of a carpet, she created for herself a simple court gown. Green silk with a fitted bodice and a floor-length skirt. She did not worry herself with overskirts or underlayers or the trappings of insignia; on Oria she was an old god, and the rules of court hierarchy did not apply to her. She was above them.

She wanted to look nice, but she wanted, also, to look like one apart. She dried her hair with the focusing of her will, and twisted it quickly into a simple braid that hung down the middle of her back nearly to her knees. On her feet, she put shoes with good traction and good support, covered in green silk to make them look acceptable. Goddess in green sneakers, she thought—but a goddess who could fight and run if she needed to.

She strapped her dagger around her hips and surveyed herself in the mirror. She tested the skirt to make sure that it did not bind her movement, and checked that she could tuck the material quickly out of her way at need. Satisfied, she turned away from the mirrors. She'd do. She needed to get going, though, before she lost her nerve.

She moved through the subbasement, noticing that it was insufficiently guarded—she'd need to let Seolar know about that. And up the ramps, and into the main hallways of the vast house, where suddenly the veyâr were everywhere, and excited to see her, and clearly anxious to know what had happened to her. But she sought Seolar. Everything else would wait. She told that to the people who greeted her with such plain relief, and watched them fade out of her way, bowing.

Seolar, when she finally found him, was in his day office, meeting with veyâr from the village. When she stepped to the door he rose and excused himself, telling them he would have to meet with them again on the morrow.

They rose and left, and she stepped into the office.

Seolar came to her and wrapped his arms around her. She could see the anguish in his eyes, and feel it in his body. "A week, and you did not come. What happened?"

"I went for a walk," she said.

"For a *week*?"

"No. I found a nest of Night Watch. Was killed destroying them. Resurrected, went to talk to my sister, took a walk. The walk only lasted a few hours, but during it I found Baanraak, and caught him off guard. So I followed him, and when the time was right, I killed him."

Seolar leaned back to look her full in the face, hope clear and bright in his eyes. "The monster who hunts you and who killed you—he is dead? Destroyed?"

Molly took a deep breath. "He killed me in the process of my killing him. The last days, I've been . . . coming back. I woke up some distance from here, shortly before he resurrected. I killed him again, this time when he was weak and helpless. I destroyed both of his resurrection rings. He's gone for good."

"But in the process I have lost a little more of you." Seolar pushed away from her, and when he was free of her embrace, turned his back to her. "We have lost a little more of us."

"We have," Molly said.

"Do you still love me?"

"Yes," Molly said. But already she did not mean, when she said it, what he meant when he said the same thing. She cared about him—cared what happened to him, wanted him to be happy, wanted him to find joy. Her passion, though, was gone. Her excitement about *them*, her breathless anticipation of the next moment when the two of them could steal time together alone—all gone. Nothing she could do would bring them back. "I still love you," she said.

"How many more deaths until you don't, beloved? How much more of this until you look at me one day and I mean no more to you than the chair I sit upon or the floor I stand on? How much longer do we have?" His voice broke, and he walked to his bookcase and rested his face against the volumes there.

"I don't know. I can feel that there is less of me, but I cannot begin to tell you where I am less or where I am unchanged. I sense my . . . my diminishment. But it's a vague thing, not measurable, not steady. I cannot look at what I've lost and say, 'I'll only be able to die ten more times before I'm not me anymore.' It doesn't work that way."

"Well, *I'm* dying from the dread. Each time this happens, I die a little more."

She walked over to him and put a hand on his shoulder and turned him around. "Do you still love me?"

"With all my heart and soul. Otherwise it would not matter to me that you are going away from me and that one day you will be here but will no longer be you. And that day will come in my lifetime, I think. Because you are not being careful." He gripped her shoulders. "You are not staying clear of trouble."

"If the universe is to live, Seo, I cannot. I am not what you thought I was, nor what I'd come to hope I was. I am not the healer of all things good." She pulled his hands from her shoulders and clasped them, and held them. She stared into his bottomless black eyes and said, "I am, instead, the destroyer of evil. But evil has teeth, and sometimes I'm going to fail. Sometimes I am going to die. For the worldchain to survive, I must. No one else can do what I can do. No one else can find the Night Watch by feel, can annihilate them without spawning awful rebound magic that would bounce upworld and smash innocents; no one else can do all that and die in the process and come back to do it again. No one else. If I give up, if I fail, no one else will step in to take my place."

"Does that matter? The world above us is poised to die. I have heard from many that there is little about it worth saving. So. Let it die. Bring those you love, and those they love, and come here. Stay with me. Be safe. Heal the veyâr, do as the other Vodian did, be careful of yourself and cherish the love we share."

"I cannot do that."

He shoved her hands away from him and shouted, "*Why not?* The other Vodian did. They healed the sick and kept the dark gods from our doors—"

"They sold you down the river a piece at a time, making concessions that cost you your lands and your people and that will cost you the very existence of the veyâr if you stay on that path. You cannot negotiate with those whose only wish is to see you dead. All you can do is destroy them first. And that is what I intend to do."

"And there are thousands, perhaps tens of thousands, of them, and only one of you."

"There are less of them now than there were a week ago. There will be less of them in two weeks than there are today. I have eternity, and they are not infinite. I will come to the end of them, Seolar. And the veyâr will live, and thrive, and expand again. And the worldchain will revive." She did not tell him of the darkness within her, of her growing yearning toward all the flavors of destruction, of her doubts about her role. She was uncertain—but he would have read her uncertainty as a sign that she could walk away from what she was doing and hide with him in Copper House. About that path she had no doubts whatsoever; she would not be hiding out of the way of things.

He spoke with a voice ragged with pain. "If you would continue on this path of yours, then, kill me. Here . . . now . . . quickly. You will be doing me a kindness. For I would rather die right now sure of your love than a piece at a time watching you fade away." He met her eyes—she realized he meant every word he'd just said.

Molly pulled him into her arms and held him and stroked his head. "I'm sorry," she whispered. "I'm so sorry—that I am not the person you hoped I would be, that times are so dark and so hard. That you and I . . ."

A chill passed over her then. She felt, as if from a distance, that her heart was breaking. But she was standing a little apart from that pain. And she realized that once she would have wept. That she should be crying. That she wanted to cry, as he was crying, for the death of dreams and hopes and desire. For the death of love.

But she had no tears. And even her horror at realizing how much of herself she had already lost was not enough to bring them.

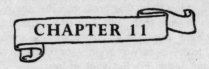

CHAPTER 11

**Hendricks, Tucker County, West Virginia—
Baanraak of Silver and Gold**

BAANRAAK LOOKED NORTH at the tiny town and inhaled, long and deep, wondering if this had been the right direction to take. The magic was nearby—live magic, downworld magic shifted upworld, the source of the Night Watch's discomfort and his amusement. But its source still lay southward, just a bit farther. He was close to locating the first and smallest of Lauren's siphons, but already he could tell it wasn't as small as he'd hoped. It was pumping out a lot of magic. More than he would have expected.

Molly's sister had done something strong here, something scary. He'd thought two people taking on the whole of the Night Watch had been ludicrous—but Molly was a terrifying creature, and would be even more awe-inspiring when she came into her full power. She wasn't even close yet. And the sister came from that same stock—ferocious and strong and passionate. He could feel the passion in the magic that surrounded him. He could taste the sister, and that taste shook him to his core. He tasted love, love that moved even him, fierce and certain that it could change a world or a worldchain.

Love was the spell she had cast, Baanraak realized. Love born of loss, and hope, and fear, and determination to survive. Love of life itself, love of the world and the creatures that lived on it and in it. Love of blue skies and thunderheads and the sweet smell of rain on the grass; love of bright lights and city streets and the people who walked through every day oblivious to the wonder of their own existence—and love of those who knew, and who cherished every breath.

Every bit of this came through in the magic that he breathed in, clear as pictures, sharp as edged steel. The magic urged him to hang on, to keep fighting for good, to *live* with everything in him, to share love through action. To protect, to preserve, to defend.

He was a dead thing animated, a creature without love or passion or compassion . . . or hope . . . and still the power of this plea shook him, and ripped into him with invisible talons, and dragged him weeping to his knees who had not wept in an eon, nor wanted to.

It was not the human form he had taken that was doing this. Flesh he could cast aside or remake at will—his flesh was under his control. It could not be his soul that this plea—this command—reached, for he had no soul. Millennia dead, he had been for millennia free of the pain of grief and tears. This was betrayal by silver yet again—betrayal of the Baanraak he had known for all of his existence by the Baanraak that had hidden within him, waiting for something to bring him forth. He *felt* the silver now, felt it burying its talons deep in his heart and blood. It was as if the silver had been sleeping, but was now awake and fighting everything he had been to remake him into something new. Something he feared and did not desire.

Sobbing, Baanraak pulled himself to his feet. He shuddered, and blocked the magic away from himself as best he could, but it had wormed its way inside him and had filled empty places with itself. Nature, which abhorred a vacuum, had never found the vacuum within him. But a few careless moments in the presence of one human's magic had done something that a millennia with Nature could not.

He only wished he could tell what that something was.

He turned his back on the little town of Hendricks and headed south on WV 72, walking on the berm, watching out for cars. There were a few, but not many. He was heading into the heart of the magic.

He would not taste it again, he promised himself. He did not dare. But this would be, he thought, his best hope of a good hiding place. Everyone knew live magic could not feed the dark gods. So this would be the last place anyone would look for him.

He needed time to think. To re-figure. His encounter with Molly, which had ended with him dead but not destroyed, had shaken him badly. He didn't know how she'd beaten him. He'd had her. But then she'd done something and he'd found himself in the forest, some little time later, rebuilt of humus and moss and rock, sun and water, and with some of his resurrection rings missing. The main one, the traitorous one that carried the silver channel in its vile heart, still animated him. But of the others he had found no sign. They were lesser rings, made only in supplement to his main one, or stolen from enemies he'd admired—and he'd added them to his wearable trove of immortality simply as a form of backup. He would not be lost without them, but he did not like the fact that he had lost them. And he did not like the fact that he did not know what had become of them.

He walked for a mile, and then another, and then off to his right he saw a trail sign. He turned onto the trail, feeling the magic becoming stronger with every step.

Here, the magic had had plenty of time to start soaking into the ground, the trees, and the water. Before long, uncanny things would begin happening in the wilderness near Hendricks. Hikers on the Otter Creek trail would have some fairy sightings, though they probably would not report them—people had gotten wary of reporting things like fairies. But before long the wee folk would be all over the area. They were like mosquitoes that way; give them running water, appropriate terrain, and live magic, and not even DDT would get rid of them.

He glanced up at the canopy of green over his head—summer leaves on their last legs before autumn came. It was a beautiful place. And it felt alive now. Any world's natives were by nature almost blind to their own world's magic, but the stuff Molly's sister had brought in here had an unmistakable flavor. People would notice, even if they didn't know what they were noticing. This area would get a reputation with the New Agers, and even though the area had bears along with its deer and its pheasants and its pretty rhododendrons, they'd start coming in search of the magic. And here they would actually find it.

Hikers walking along this path would be imbued with that same ferocious love that Baanraak felt, and they would be moved. They would become . . . heroic. Self-sacrificing. Men and women who had never before thought of anyone but themselves would start taking chances to protect others. This was going to be a dangerous stretch of woods—it was going to change people's lives.

The surviving flora and fauna of Earth's magical ecology would find their way here, too. Baanraak wondered how many of the wee folk and the weyrd folk had managed to hang on this long on this planet with things so bad. The pookas, the black dogs, the werewolves and whisperers—in spite of all their strength, they were delicate creatures. When the magic started going, most of them had died off. If any survived, this place would be a little bit of heaven to them— if they could just get here. And their being here would add to the magic, make the place stronger.

Eventually, the trees would wake up, he thought, and start guarding the place themselves. Wouldn't the tree-huggers be surprised when the trees hugged back. And wouldn't let go. These were all second-growth trees—they'd never known rich magic and wouldn't know how to handle themselves. They'd be wild or stupid unless someone trained them. Still, that would be a long time from now.

And then, hiking deeper into the forest, Baanraak caught one of the trees watching him. His skin twitched, and inwardly he swore. There was already an old god here, then, using this magic, accelerating the area's recovery. In no other way could the trees have woken up so fast. And these were canny—they had given no sign to him of what they were as he'd walked forward. So they had been trained already. If he had not been thinking about trees, he would not have noticed them watching him. If he had not stopped and stared when he caught the tree watching, he would have been fine, perhaps. But now his cover was blown. He would have to leave; trees were not taken in by form. They could see him for what he really was, and they would tell the old god. Killing the old god wouldn't help his situation, either. He wanted to keep a low profile, *not* draw attention to his presence. If Molly and her sister had enlisted old gods in the effort to restore this world, those old gods would be watching out for each other. If the trees had been quick about it—and he could hear their leaves rustling and their branches rattling even as he stood there—the odds were that the old gods, and perhaps even Molly, already knew he was here.

And the only thing he wanted—the *only* thing—was to stay out of sight for a while in a place where no one would think to look for him.

He turned and started out of the forest, back toward Hendricks. He could find a mirror there, make a gate. Go someplace else. He'd thought Molly would not look for him on Earth, but now he needed someplace even more unlikely than Earth.

He was careful not to think until he was well clear of the forest, well free of the watching trees. He was careful not to think until he'd found a public rest room with a big mirror at a gas station. He would have to make himself smaller to fit through it. But now he had the means—he only needed the destination.

And he thought of Kerras, upworld, dead and dark and burned and frozen. He could hide there while he thought. While he reassessed and planned and figured. He'd make a bubble for himself, a bit of air, a bit of warmth. He'd be fine. And no one would look for him on Kerras—the gods both old and dark had abandoned that world.

Rr'garn's Cliff, Oria—Baanraak of Master's Gold

Baanraak, free of doubt and despair since this last resurrection, slipped through the air silently; he circled the spot where Rr'garn, head of Oria's rrôn contingent of the Night Watch, curled atop his cliff. Rr'garn wasn't asleep, for the dark gods did not sleep. But he was resting his eyes, and trotting through his busy, noisy little mind all the triumphs he planned for himself when he overthrew Aril and became Master of the Night Watch. The destruction of the keth, the elevation of the rrôn, the shaming of Trrtrag, who as his second in command showed too much ability and not enough obeisance.

Ahh. Thank you, Rr'garn. I had forgotten about Trrtrag.

Baanraak listened further, still circling, and was pleased to find that Trrtrag actually kept watch, not assuming that he was big enough or fearsome enough to be immune from attack. His mind was quiet—not quiet enough, but Baanraak found something workable in him. He might make something of Trrtrag. Rr'garn was worthless.

I have need of you, Baanraak whispered into Trrtrag's mind. He felt the other rrôn start inside, but that inner surprise did not result in any outward movement. Good. Trrtrag's hunting instincts remained keen.

Who are you?

Baanraak didn't choose to give that bit of information yet. Instead, he said, *Still your mind and release your own thoughts—and let Rr'garn's thoughts flow into you.*

Trrtrag, curious, maintained his watch but managed to comply. Baanraak found the moment that Trrtrag discovered his way into Rr'garn's fantasies amusing; Trrtrag was not amused.

I have come to claim what is mine, Baanraak said. *I choose you as my second.*

If I destroy that double-crossing bastard, I can be first, Trrtrag noted, reasonably enough, considering the circumstances.

Baanraak circled overhead, patient. Patience was, in the right time and the right situation, a wonderful virtue. *If you then survive me,* he said.

And who are you, that I should fear you?

Baanraak.

Second will be fine, Trrtrag assured him with not even a second's hesitation.

Baanraak spiraled in. *Be ready.*

He dropped on top of Rr'garn without making a single sound, and slashed Rr'garn's head off with one clean swipe of talons and a neat rip-and-twist.

Trrtrag, in the darkness at the south end of the cliff, jumped at the sight of Rr'garn's head flying past him, and twisted around.

"Call in the wing," Baanraak told him, making himself visible for the first time. "We're taking back the Mastery."

Trrtrag tipped back his head and bellowed the long, deep, booming call of summons. After far too long, Baanraak started hearing wingbeats in the night—too loud, too slow, too sloppy. Rr'garn might have dreamed of taking the Mastery, but he had no idea how to hone his troops, or how to inspire them, or how to use them. He mistook noise and presence for threat.

Baanraak knew better. He faded back to invisibility and kept to the back of Trrtrag's mind. *Let them come in. Let them see that Rr'garn is dead. Be ready.*

I'm ready, Trrtrag assured him.

He might be. He wasn't the pompous, boasting fool Rr'garn had been. But then, why had he satisfied himself with the second's place? Did he lack ambition? Was he loyal? Either of those would be a benefit to Baanraak. Or was he simply lazy?

The rrôn straggled in, one and two at a time. They had not been far away but had felt no reason to hurry.

As they came, they saw Rr'garn. They eyed Trrtrag, and one asked, "Are you declaring yourself, then?" and another simply laughed and muttered, "Well, that's a step in the right direction."

One, though, turned to Trrtrag and without word or warning leapt on him, jaws gaping, claws extended. Baanraak had been following the noisy thoughts, and knew before the fool jumped what he would do and how he would do it. Trrtrag responded with satisfactory speed and viciousness, but

Baanraak did not wish to have Trrtrag make the kill. Instead, he moved in and neatly slaughtered the ambitious rrôn.

With his example made, he let them see him for the first time. "I am Baanraak," he said, and froze all of them in place. "You are *my* wing now. We fly for the Hub tomorrow—between now and then, you'll start learning my way of doing things." He nodded to Trrtrag. "Destroy their rings."

He felt their fear deepen. He knew of some of the dark gods who disciplined by death. He was not one of them. Those who failed him in any significant way failed permanently. In Rr'garn he had found nothing worth saving. In the second rrôn he'd killed, he had found treachery and a scheming personality that did not suit him. These others had an opportunity to prove their worth—but the same opportunity would be before them daily for as long as they served him. He rewarded excellence as well as he punished failure, however. That—well . . . that they would get to see on the morrow.

Cat Creek, North Carolina

"We have to do something about you," Heyr said.

Lauren looked up at him, standing on her porch waiting for her to let him in the door. He'd saved her life. She didn't trust him. What did that say about her?

Warily, she invited him back in. Jake grinned at him, which was something. Jake didn't like strangers.

"It's pretty late for a visit," she told Heyr.

"I've been watching over you most of the day. I figured I'd come and talk to you when you got back up."

She headed back to the kitchen with Jake dawdling behind her to smile up at Heyr. That was *so* unlike Jake.

"I'm making Jake and me a late dinner. If you want something to eat, I'll add extra for you."

"Thank you. That would be just fine." Heyr took a seat at the table in one of her old chairs, and the chair creaked when he sat down. Lauren hoped he didn't see her wince.

She sliced fresh broccoli, then cubed potatoes and carrots, and diced two onions. She dropped a couple of bouillon cubes into the water at the bottom of the steamer, and put all the vegetables in the top. Then she went over to sit down at the table with Heyr.

He was eyeing her strangely. "Where's the rest of the meal?"

"There's a nice loaf of Italian bread in the oven, brushed with olive oil and fresh crushed garlic and a little salt. It's heating up now—you won't be able to smell it for a few minutes, though."

"I wasn't talking about bread. Where's the rest of the *meal*?"

"That's it—steamed vegetables, garlic bread, maybe a little vegan ice cream for dessert. Why?"

"There's no meat in that meal."

"Nor will there be. When I have a choice, I don't eat meat."

He looked at her. "I'm a Viking god, dear. A *warrior*. I eat meat and bread, and I drink beer. Vegetables are for farm animals."

She rested her chin on a hand and said, "That doesn't work with me, Heyr. I know what you are because I'm the same thing. You aren't a Viking god. You're a guy from up-world. What you might be underneath the human skin, I don't know—"

"I'm as human as you are."

"Doesn't matter. If you liked the Viking lifestyle, that's fine, but I'm not a Viking. I don't have any meat in the house, and I'm not going to get some tonight. It makes the place smell. Sorry."

"You're a warrior. Your son is a warrior—already he has the warrior's eye and the warrior's heart. A warrior's blood needs meat."

Jake looked at Heyr and corrected him. "I'm a superhero."

Heyr grinned at him. "Same thing, kid."

Lauren sighed. "I'm not having this discussion again. Move on. Why are you here?"

Heyr started to argue with her, but Lauren narrowed her eyes and he backed off. "Because . . . by Freya's eyes, you're lovely when you're angry. You are as fierce and as fair as any Valkyrie. I thought it when I fought the rrôn beside you, but . . . oh, Lauren."

He stared into her eyes, and Lauren felt heat rising to her cheeks. She could not look away—she had never looked into eyes like those. She could see pictures—the two of them naked, touching, moving together.

No, she thought, but just telling herself no didn't help. She could feel a tension in the air between them, an almost supernatural electricity. She could envision the two of them in bed, hot and sweaty and hungry—

Lauren blinked and caught her breath. "Stop it," she said. "Turn off the lust magic right now or I'm kicking you out the door, and whatever you actually came here to tell me can just go to hell, and you with it."

He looked shocked. "You could tell?"

She raised an eyebrow in query.

"That I was using magic on you . . . you could tell?" He frowned. "Betty Kay couldn't tell. Neither could Louisa."

Lauren's eyebrows shot up. "Betty Kay . . . *and* Louisa? You've . . . ummm . . ."

"Yes," he said, and grinned a little. "Quite a few times. It . . . eases various pains. Mine, theirs, the Sentinels'. Louisa, for example, is half the harridan she was. Her I consider a public service. Betty Kay is"—his eyes sparkled— "surprised. And Darlene *will* be."

He frowned again. "But you could tell."

Lauren hadn't actually noticed the magic. But she knew she didn't have any desire to go to bed with Heyr. "I could tell."

He looked pensive. "That's never happened to me before."

She resisted the urge to tell him, "It happens to everyone sooner or later." She would have found it funny, but she wasn't sure he would. Instead, she said, "Forget it. Why did you really come here?"

She might as well not have said anything. "Women have always found me irresistible."

"Well, yes . . . when you *cheat*."

"No, no. Nothing of the sort. I have never forced anyone or tricked anyone. I only give the smallest suggestion that I would like to be with them. I let them know I'm thinking what they're thinking."

"And you've never been turned down before."

"Never so quickly, or with so much vehemence. Never by someone who realized what I was doing."

"Yes, well. I'm as interested in your sex life as I am in your dietary preferences, which is to say, I'm not. Why are you here?"

"I intend to live with you. Which is why it would have worked better if you and I shared a . . . passion."

Lauren leaned back in her chair and stared at him. And she burst out laughing. "You intend to *live with me*? Just like that!"

"Not because I am so drawn to you, but because you need me."

"Heyr, I'm not sleeping with you, and I'm not living with you—though if you thought I was going to take you in, I could see why you made an issue about what I cooked for dinner. I don't know what you have running through that head of yours, but you need to take it outside and walk it on a leash, boy."

But Heyr looked determined. "You can't let the Sentinels stand watch over you. Not as they are now. Later . . . maybe. We'll see. But right now, they haven't the skills and they haven't the magic to protect you from whatever the Night Watch will throw at you and your son. But I do. And you cannot be allowed to die. Yours is the magic that has started bringing life back to this world. And this world *must* be saved."

Lauren sat and studied him. "I agree with you. But . . . I have to ask this. Why are you making your stand here? You've seen a lot of other worlds die, right?"

Heyr nodded.

"So why dig in and fight for this one? You've always been known as a champion of mankind—but the other Æsir aren't. Why are you so gung-ho on Earth and humans?"

He sighed. "Because I believe this is the last of the human worlds."

Lauren tipped her head. "The human *worlds*? Plural?"

Heyr nodded. "As I told you, I'm human. As human as you are. I have not taken a strange form to fit in here. I put on the guise of Thor when I must command, but"—he spread his arms wide—"this is me. I can father human children without magic—and have done so many times. My Earth children, and the Earth children of the other Æsir, and the other human upworlders still have some facility with magic. But they are purely human. They do not have to struggle to figure out where they fit in this world, as your sister must here or in her other world of Oria. They belong here." He looked at her, and his eyes were sad and haunted. "This is the last place I can find that I could call home. The other Æsir believe that farther down the line there will be other human worlds. I do not."

"Why?" Lauren found that she was interested in spite of herself.

"Because many worlds up the chain, where I was born, there was a cluster of human worlds. My world was Opfann, also called Asgard. Right below it on the chain was Lopei, and below that was Middling Ground. All three were human worlds—so when the dark gods destroyed Opfann and those of us who could escape moved to Lopei, everything was very much the same. We fit in, though we had power. We belonged . . . and when the dark gods took Lopei, Middling Ground was the same. Human. We had never felt any need to explore farther down the chain. We thought the dark gods were demons of some sort—aberrations—and that all worlds were human worlds. But then the next world was M'war, and it was not human—not by any stretch of the imagination. So we took what we could and began a downward trek. Four worlds down from Middling Ground, we found Tripwoll, which was human. But now we had seen that we were not alone, and that the dark gods were not aberrations. So some of us hunted farther downworld, to see where we might find more of our people."

The oven alarm went off, and Lauren remembered that her dinner was cooking. She jumped up and pulled the garlic bread from the oven, then checked the vegetables—they'd gotten a bit softer than she preferred, but they weren't yet mushy.

She quickly put the food onto plates and served it. She and Jake dug in, and Heyr looked at his meal of vegetables and bread and a big glass of water, and sighed. But he ate.

Lauren settled back into her seat. "So what did you find?"

"The next human world was Raven. Eleven worlds down from Tripwoll."

"And beyond that?"

"Here. Nineteen worlds down from Tripwoll."

Lauren closed her eyes. "One, one, one, four, eleven, nineteen. Is that a mathematical sequence? Has anyone looked at it that way to see if they could predict the recurrence of human worlds farther down the line?"

He gave her a quick, approving grin. "We did, eventually, but it wasn't the first thing we thought of. The one you note, by the way, is one of the two possible sequences. The other sequence is one, two, three, seven, eighteen, thirty-seven—which is each world's position relative to Opfann, the first known human world."

Lauren ate and thought. After a minute, she said, "The fact that there *is* a first known human world makes it pretty likely that there would be a last one as well."

"It does, and that is the conclusion I finally came to. That this world is humanity's last stand, and if we lose it, we lose not just our entire species but everything humankind has done. Art and architecture, science and music, literature and humor, history and law. It stops here. Which is why I've stopped here. I will not leave Earth—if this planet falls, I go with it. Loki is the same, though for other reasons. He's simply trapped here, though being trapped without choice has created a degree of loyalty in him that no amount of reason ever managed."

Lauren considered that. "I'd never even imagined that

there had ever been other human worlds. Does this mean there are other rrôn worlds? Other keth worlds?"

"Not that I know of. But they might have had many worlds of their own up the chain." Heyr shrugged. "I could go to Oria. The veyâr at least have a human sense of passion and an interest in the arts and sciences. They're comprehensible. But . . . I have no wish to live out the rest of eternity wrapped in alien flesh. Here—here I can have a home and a woman and good honest work, wearing my own skin. I can go about my business day to day without wondering if anyone has noticed that I'm not quite right. I do not have to worry that I have somehow betrayed myself, or that my neighbors, grown suspicious of me and what I am, will creep into my house at night to try to kill me."

"I suppose that depends on your neighborhood as much as anything, but I do understand."

"Perhaps you understand intellectually. But I have arisen each morning to look in the mirror and see the face of a stranger looking back at me. I have lived on worlds not my own. The call of 'same' becomes very strong, Lauren. We begin to cry out for people like us. We want to understand and be understood, to know that we belong. And this is the last world where we belong."

Lauren tried to imagine looking into a mirror and having something green with horns look back at her. She tried to imagine having to make Jake over into a veyâr replica, or a goroth replica, or . . . something else. She closed her eyes and bit her lip. "I see."

"Do you? Then you have to let me stay with you. I hope to convince others to share my burden—to join me as immortals and as gods, but the weight I carry has proven too much for almost all of the old gods. It is heavy beyond all reason, and it may be that I alone can stand against the horrors that will come for you. You have to let me protect you. You're alone, you and your boy. The biggest and worst nightmares in the universe are coming after you, and even though we beat them today, they're going to keep coming.

Without me, they'll eventually get to you. And then you will die, and Earth, which is the last repository for all of humankind through all the ages, will come to an end. And some little smattering of humankind will flee downworld, lost, refugees forever after with only memories of what they once had."

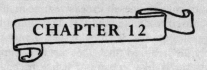

CHAPTER 12

Kerras—Baanraak of Silver and Gold

BAANRAAK ARRIVED ON the dark side of Kerras in the cold—the bitter, vile, airless cold. He'd expected to have to struggle to find enough live magic on the planet to form a pocket of atmosphere around his body that he could keep warm and full of oxygen. Instead, the magic he needed was right there, rich and live and plentiful. It caused him physical pain to use it, though—it was clearly *hers*, the sister's. He knew her name if he thought about it—Molly had thought of her sister. Lauren. Yes. Lauren with one child, and the power to reshape a worldchain. Lauren had found a way to place a magic siphon on Kerras. And Baanraak was going to be dependent on it as long as he was here.

He closed his eyes and breathed the layer of air that surrounded him, and made it warm. It was already sweet, irrevocably tainted by the magical energy that had transformed it.

But he liked sweet air. He liked sun-warmed rocks, too, and the sound of tall grasses rustling in the breeze, and the sight of Vraish wildlife—eons extinct but never far from his memory. On this airless, icebound rock he now found enough magic that he could create a little pocket of his long-gone world. He could give himself a gift no other dark god had experienced—the luxury of going home, if only in a little way and for a little while.

He would have to use live magic to do it, and that would cause him a great deal of pain. But, by the Egg, it would be better than lying on a frozen rock surrounded by nothing but ice and snow and howling winds.

Baanraak closed his eyes. Some things one had to do without permitting oneself excessive time to think—if he allowed himself to think about this, he would find reasons to talk himself out of it. It probably was a very bad idea. But suddenly he realized that the air that surrounded him smelled exactly like Vraish air, which he had not smelled since he'd fled his world at its destruction, certain that he would not miss it. And the feeling of homesickness overwhelmed him.

Just a little pocket, he thought, and inhaled the burning magic deeply. He fought the pain, and when he could move past it, Baanraak, with his eyes tightly closed, breathed out a pocket of air and warmth. He did not permit himself to look, for the eyes could be deceived and the art destroyed.

He inhaled. Held the magic through agonizing pain. Exhaled, expanding the sphere of warmth and atmosphere, shaping it, controlling the live magic with the same skill and precision that he controlled death magic. The techniques were the same; only the materials and the results differed.

Through a dozen breaths, he brought the magic into himself and shaped it outward, expanding his bubble until it was large enough that he would be able to fly, if only a little, and to hunt, if only a little, and to swim in a charming, if very small, lake.

With his eyes still tightly closed, Baanraak began to shape. A night breeze. The rustling of tall grass. The lapping of a lake at its shores. The sound of ceyrji—little night insects—buzzing and chuckling. The low hoots and grunts of a herd of felka, his preferred prey. The scents of lizards and birds and little saurids, the chitters and rustlings. And beneath his four feet, the wonderful rightness of the land as it spread away from him in all directions, transforming.

The place felt right—right in a way that nothing had since his world died.

But he was not done yet.

He pressed his body flat to the ground and breathed in the

magic once more, paying close attention this time to where it came from. It bubbled up from deep within the earth, its source hidden from even his closest study. Very well, then. If he could not find the source, he would create a scavenger to sweep up the magic as it was released. He wouldn't need the source that way. He didn't feel like doing maintenance work to keep this little pocket of his alive. If he was going for illusion, he decided he would have the whole illusion, and be able to spend this time in his world simply basking on his rock and eating tasty things. He had no wish to be reminded of the artificiality of his little hideaway by its constant need for upkeep. So he set his scavenger to funnel all the magic he could get from Lauren's siphon into his little domain, and set that magic to maintain the place in working condition.

When he was done, he lay for a while on his belly, waiting for the searing pain caused by handling live magic to subside. The stillness felt good, and the sounds of the place were like being held by his mother in the nest, when she had wrapped herself around him and they had wound necks and tails in loving embrace.

Warmth touched his right wing tip, and he raised his head and looked. The sun was coming up over the eastern horizon, between the rocks from his family's outcropping, reflected in his family's lake. The grass waved, a herd of felka strolled in front of him, as yet unhunted and unwary, and just overhead, a pair of mating black-drops looped and rolled.

The air smelled right, the sky looked right, the land felt right, and suddenly it was all too much for him.

This was what he and the rest of the dark gods had lost. Had given up voluntarily. No, not even that. Had destroyed willfully. This little pocket of home brought back to him the spire cities of the rrôn carved from whole mountains, and the great vast plains filled with game—husbanded, cherished, and harvested with care and reverence. The halls of records, in which were kept tablets of the epic song cycles of the rrôn. The holy caverns that wound deep into the belly of the earth.

Tears again filled his eyes, but he blinked them back. Instead, he stood up, launched himself into the air, and flew to the top of his rock.

That proved to be a mistake. Flat on his belly on the ground, his little world looked and felt complete. But from the high vantage of the rocks, he could see its edges, carved out of sheets of snow and airless rock. And it only showed him that he was not home. It only dug truth's talons deeper into him, that he would never be home again.

He took a deep breath, and the air that filled his lungs smelled so sweet, but it burned of her. Of Lauren, the sister.

Baanraak wondered if any of the surviving live rrôn— those that had eschewed the immortality of dark godhood for life and parenthood and the continuation of the species— remembered any of the song cycles. He didn't imagine that they did. Why would they? The world they celebrated was millennia dead, along with everything on it.

He remembered, though.

He dug his talons into the rock, anchoring himself, and began booming his wings, remembering the rhythms of the Cycle of the Hunt. He began chanting softly the list of the sacred game.

> *Felka, khroga, grorvash, rrogvall,*
> *Magwe, muurrhag, droovna, harrnak,*
> *Durgakar, goforhar, togi,*
> *Rradernak, formino, baghak . . .*

Closing his eyes, he could make it all feel real again. He could recall the voices of the chanters, the crooners, and the murmurers, all winding together in and out of each other to the beat of the steady booming of the wings of the hundred rrôn crouched upon their singing rocks as the sun rose, and again as the sun set, with necks upraised and eyes closed, lost in the hypnotic bliss of the chant. Gripping that rock, chanting the old chants, the dust of lost worlds and the stains of alien places and alien civilizations and alien people fell away from him, and he was, for a moment, wild again. Rrôn without taint and without compromise. The living hunter of live food, the hot-blooded drake rrôn lusting after the lithe young broodies.

He chanted through the dozen lines of the List of Choice Herd Beasts and the three dozen lines of the List of Choice Solitary Game Beasts, and because no one had sung the full Cycle of the Hunt in long ages, and it would be disrespectful to sing only the short Choice lists—once known simply as the Daily Devotion—he continued with the full cycle: the List of Game Fishes; the List of Flying Game; the tedious but necessary List of Inedibles; and the sometimes whimsical List of Lesser Creatures, with its staccato beat and its famed Insults to the Parasites stanzas. The Cycle of the Hunt was both prayer and celebration, and he performed it with full reverence, though he longed for the backup of the full chorus—the crooners carrying the cycle's ancient melody, the murmurers providing commentary on the best way to hunt each category of beasts, with asides on famous hunting accidents and blunders.

When he was finished, he opened his eyes and bowed to the sun, for this was tradition, and the final reverence of the morning. And then he launched from his rocky perch like an arrow and plummeted into the heart of the herd, and killed the first felka in time out of memory.

He ate it with gratitude and reverence, right where he'd dropped it, surrounded by the ghosts of his ancestors and his world, and full of guilt at his role in their demise.

When he was finished, he flew to the edge of the little oasis he'd created and pushed through the shield that held it together, into the harsh and unprotected glare of Kerras.

I'm sorry, he told the world. I'm sorry for what we did to you. We were wrong. I was wrong.

He did not feel forgiveness. All he felt was the screaming of the dead, frozen into the bleak, airless terrain.

Night Watch Control Hub, Barâd Island, Oria—Baanraak of Master's Gold

First light of dawn. Someone had redesigned the Hub. Baanraak, circling high above it, studying the extra gates, the convenience paths, and the way that new construction blocked a few degrees of visibility in one key watchtower, had to grin. The keth were a frightening crew—powerful, smart, and telepathic. They had done a good job of improving their security against magic; Baanraak could not see a way to open a gate into any part of the structure save the gate center in the Hub. And the keth had an arsenal trained on each gate; unwanted guests coming in that way would die before their bodies moved free of the fire road.

But the keth had grown complacent in maintaining their purely physical defenses. Baanraak could mark more than a dozen areas around the Hub that he would never have permitted to exist in their current state, because they provided excellent cover for enemies.

He marked these locations and linked the markers to his massed troops.

At that moment, Aril entertained a handful of Orian heads of state from the factionalized territories that lay around the Hub. The breakfast was nothing of great import; Baanraak guessed Aril held something similar for different heads of state on a regular basis. He was using flock management to govern his subject races—he gave the leaders a few minor concessions and they kept all their subjects pacified and malleable. Baanraak approved.

The keth Master, however, was running the Hub on a skeleton crew. Half a dozen rebchyks, minor dark gods whose people had originated on Agrabaa, six worlds above Oria, made a show at the front gate. The rebchyks were big and bulky and fearsome-looking. But they weren't particularly bright, they'd never grasped telepathy, and they had mastered only the rudiments of magic and none of the fine points. They were lucky to have made it through the world gates when their planet died. They were in place to look impressive for the mortals who had to march between their crossed pikes.

The secondary gates to the Hub were locked but unguarded. All the towers save the front two lay empty. And the people who would have been available for the Hub's defense most of the time had been shifted upworld to Earth as the Night Watch moved closer toward its countdown for a world harvest—always an intensive operation. Those who remained either operated the Hub itself or stayed close to the breakfast party to help the Master keep up the appearance of a crowded, vital power base.

Impressing the rubes was easy. So was keeping the well-intentioned in line. But Aril had forgotten that the Hub sat inside a massive fortress for a reason: Not everyone who might want to come inside was either well-intentioned or a rube.

Baanraak, probing the Master's surface thoughts, found this oversight understandable. In the several hundred years Aril had held the position of Master of the Night Watch, he had never faced a challenge against his Mastery.

Aril had made an understandable mistake. But it was still a mistake. Baanraak intended to make the keth pay for it.

Baanraak's wing—forty-six rrôn in all—hung well back. He gave his wingleaders concise instructions on where they were to land and which paths they were to follow. He placed tiny magical tracking tags on the few keth dark gods he wanted to have eliminated and linked these tags to the minds of his followers along with entry points, assigning five rrôn to each keth target, leaving twenty-six rrôn plus himself to pay a visit to Aril at his breakfast.

Though he could have the mechanics of the takeover complete before Aril even knew he was under attack, Baanraak would not be able to claim the Mastery simply by overwhelming the current regime. Challenges for the Mastery required more ceremony than that. Baanraak would have to fulfill the covenants of challenge to win the acknowledgment of all the dark gods; to do that, he had to defeat Aril publicly in the Hub arena.

He bent light around him and faded to invisibility. *At my count*, he told his wingleaders, and plummeted toward his target—and his destiny.

Copper House, Ballahara, Nuue, Oria

Molly lay in the bed beside Seolar and watched him until he woke. He woke beautifully—a little twitch, a graceful stretch, and a yawn—and turned to her with a smile so full of love it felt like a knife through her heart.

"You slept well?" he asked.

"Certainly," she lied. She had not slept since her first death—a proof of her inhuman condition that she kept far from him.

"I dreamed of you," he told her. "And of a solution that I think would save you, though I know it is selfish of me."

Molly didn't want to hear him continue, but she asked anyway. "What did you dream, my love?"

"That you turned away from hunting down monsters and began doing the same work as your sister—bringing worlds back to life. It would go faster with two of you, and you would not be constantly in the path of the dark gods."

He said it with such hope. He still dared to hope, in spite of everything he knew and everything he dreaded, and his hope was going to crush him and rip him apart, because he would not let himself see her as she truly was.

Molly shook her head. "The magic Lauren does is based in emotion—and I suspect that she is drawing parts of it directly from her soul. I can't even stand to touch the energies she's moving, Seo. They burn me. I'm . . . like antimatter. I could not do what she's doing. I'm not sure anyone else could. These links she's making are as much who she is as what she's doing—and no one else has been where she's been."

"To death and back? You have."

"No. Not in the same way, I haven't. And that isn't even it, though I think it's a part of it. She . . . she stepped right into the heart of the universe, Seo. She—for lack of a better way to say it, she looked in God's eye. And it marked her. It hurts me to get too close to her, or to Jake, either. It didn't before she followed Jake through Hell and back, but since then, I can see things in her that I couldn't see before. She's changed. She's unique."

"Then you have to keep her safe. Stay with her, or keep her here with you. Stop chasing those nightmares."

"I can't. If I spend my time as Lauren's bodyguard, I give up everything I'm supposed to be accomplishing. Her job is to create, Seo. Mine is to destroy."

"That isn't what you love," he said, stroking her hair. "You healed. You made everything better—you touched my people, our people, and made them whole. Walk away from the cycles of death, my beloved, before it's too late. Your parents cannot have meant for you to die over and over again. No parents could be so cruel. This thing you're doing—it can't have been their plan."

Molly said, "They didn't know me when they planned it. I was . . . theoretical. I was someone who could wear the necklace and wield the necessary magic to do a job—I wasn't yet someone with a mind or a heart." She turned away from him. "Or a soul. I don't want to talk about this anymore, Seo. It's too hard and too ugly and it hurts too much. If I ever had dreams, they're gone. I can't go back to them, I can't fix them, I can't have them."

"You can find new dreams," he said, but she smiled and shook her head.

"I don't sleep, Seo. All dreamers sometimes sleep."

He was still for a moment, looking into her eyes. "I thought that was the case. That I never woke before you . . . Well. I didn't mean *that* kind of dream."

"I know. And I was being flippant—but it just points out a truth that neither one of us has been willing to face. I'm not who I was—I'm not the woman you loved, the one who died that first time. I can't be her, no matter how much I wish I could. I'm really nothing more than a tool to get a job done—and the job is terrible, so I am terrible, too, because anything that was not terrible would break." She did not remind him that he'd had a hand in making her the thing that she was. He already knew that, and she did not want to hurt him any more than she had to.

But she turned and saw the tears in his eyes, and that cut her. Not that he cried, but that he could cry, while she could not.

"I love you," he whispered.

"Show me, then," she said. "Love me as if I were the woman I was when we met."

He did—and she pretended to love him back, to give him that, at least. He was a skilled lover, and if her emotions had been stripped away, physical sensation remained. She did not have to pretend too much, and at the end, for a few moments, she did not have to pretend at all.

But then it was over, and he lay spent and smiling on the soft sheets beside her, and she smiled and said the things that lovers say, and meant them not at all.

"You look tired," she told him, and he laughed.

"I just woke up."

"You still look tired."

He rolled onto his side and draped an arm over her. "I haven't been sleeping well. I worry about you when you're not here. And you were gone a long time this time. I slept hardly at all while you were away."

Molly kissed her fingertip and pressed it to his lips. "Then close your eyes and let me hold you. Sleep again. The world will wait—your imal and all its business will not collapse if just once you let the sun rise to the middle of the sky before you get out of bed. Just this once."

He smiled and, trusting, rolled over and spooned against her and relaxed.

For just an instant it was there again—her love. It filled her, and the power of it hit her so hard it almost took her breath away. Her love for him filled her up like sunlight from the inside, warming and exciting and comforting her. Her eyes filled with tears as she felt—and as she fought to hold on to—the feeling. Maybe it wasn't hopeless after all.

Maybe she didn't have to lose everything. She felt human. Whole.

And then it was gone, as if her love were a bulb that had brightened one final time before it burned out. Molly lay there with her arms around Seolar, and she could feel a tear on her right cheek, and she could not understand why it was there. She could remember. But she could not comprehend.

He was asleep.

She worked her right arm out from under him carefully, so as not to wake him, and quickly found a robe and put it on. She slipped out of the bedchamber into the anteroom. The guards were there, of course. They were always there.

She nodded to the three of them.

"Vodi," they said, and bowed.

She pointed to the one she knew vaguely and said, "Fetch Birra, and have him meet me in the workroom. Tell him this is on my order as Vodi. Have him bring silver with him from the treasury—pure silver, unworked."

The guard nodded and ran from the room. Molly turned away from the other two. She could not look at them knowing what she was going to do to their imallin. She could not meet their eyes.

She found paper, envelope, and sealing wax on the little escritoire in the anteroom, sat down, and began to write.

I love you, Seo. I love you with everything in me—but everything in me is fading, and I cannot bear to face the day when I look at your face and remember what we once had, and feel nothing. I cannot stay here. While I still care about you— while we still share the pain of our parting—I have to leave.

I know love still awaits you, Seo. But not with me. Find happiness, and know that your world and your people will be as safe as I can make them. It's time for me to do my duty. You have done yours all your life, and for that you deserve a better reward than I can be.

And perhaps Lauren is right, and someday I will find my way back to being real. Perhaps I can create my own soul. But not if our worlds die and I have done nothing to stop it. I don't know if God or gods could love a destroyer, but duty does not permit such questions. Duty demands only that we fulfill it or fail. I do not intend to fail.

Wear the ring I leave for you. Never take it off. This is my promise to you, that no matter where I am, a part of me will always be with you, and I will always watch over you, and if it is within my power to do so, I will keep you safe.

Good-bye, Seo. We will not meet again, I think. Or if we do, I will be someone else. I'm sorry. Whatever happens, I will always know that once I loved, and was loved in return. Without you, love would have passed me by.

Molly

She sat in the chair for a moment, wondering if perhaps it might be better to say nothing, to just leave and not come back. But then he would not know. He would be left wondering about her and worrying needlessly. He would lose sleep; fear would wear him away. He was a good man; he deserved far better than that.

She placed her note in the sand tray and scattered sand across it to dry the ink. When she was sure it would not blur to unreadability, she took it out, folded it, placed it in an envelope, and sealed the envelope with wax, using her thumb to mark the seal.

She thought about handing the envelope to one of the guards, but she did not want Seo to have to read what she had written in front of anyone. So she held her breath and slipped back into the room just long enough to leave the note on the bed beside him.

She looked at him lying there, asleep and for the moment at peace. Then she looked at the marks of herself—the person she had been—scattered around the room. The twelve-string guitar hung on the wall by the backless, armless guitar stool; the tab paper; the oil painting half finished on the easel over next to the balcony; her clothing, neatly folded.

She was not just walking away from Seolar. She was walking away from herself, too. From the woman who had found a measure of happiness in Oria that she had not even been able to imagine in her own world. From the woman who loved to play guitar and write songs, loved to paint, loved to read. From the woman who had *loved*. From the woman who had dreamed.

Duty called and Molly responded, knowing that she might never find that other woman again.

Copper House

Birra waited for Molly outside the door of the safe room, a large bar of silver in one hand. He handed it to her and said, "I'm pleased to see you again, Vodi. We worried greatly while you were gone." Which was Birra's way of saying "Where the hell were you and why weren't you here?"

Molly took the silver without a word and brushed past him into the safe room and out of the influence of copper, which bound her away from magic. She felt the power of the universe flowing into her again, and she took a deep breath.

"Vodi?"

"Things are not good," she told Birra. He was Seolar's second in command, a veyâr of honor and forthrightness. She had known him from the beginning of her contact with the veyâr, and she respected him. More, she trusted him to do what had to be done.

She lay the bar of silver on the floor and sat cross-legged before it, and rested her fingertips on it. It burned her when she touched it—she was bound to life through gold, and silver was gold's antithesis. But silver channeled through the core of the broken Vodi necklace that coiled inside of her. She thought she would be able to tolerate the contact. She poured her magic and her will into the silver, fashioning from a small part of it two rings, both of them heavy and smooth and featureless. One she created to fit Seolar's hand; one she created to fit her own.

She held them together and stared through their centers, and spun a simple binding between them. Lauren would have been able to do something bigger, better, more useful. Lauren would have been able to fashion the rings in such a way that she could hear and see everything the other wearer was doing, Molly thought. Molly had no such talent with gateweaving, which was what she was using to bind the rings—and the very nature of silver limited what it would permit her to do. She could only bind the rings with a rudimentary spell that would allow her to connect with Seolar. To find him, wherever he was. As long as she could find him, though, she could open a small gate between the two of them—one big enough that she could check on him.

She could have used gold for the rings—she would have been able to work more comfortably with gold, and she would have been able to wear gold without pain. But the chaotic nature of gold would have eventually subverted the nature of the rings, and at the moment when she most needed to find him, they would work against her and betray her. So she would suffer silver and its constraints.

She rose and handed the bar of silver and the ring she'd made for Seolar to Birra. "Put the ring on the envelope and press it into the seal. I've explained everything to him."

Birra took the ring and stared at her with bottomless eyes. "You're leaving."

"Things are getting bad, Birra. I . . . have to be elsewhere."

"Why?"

She smiled at him and stared into his eyes, letting the hollowness inside her show through. "I'm not a good person to be around right now, Birra. And that is only going to get worse." She rested a hand on his shoulder, a familiarity that would not have been tolerable had she been a true part of the veyâr world she inhabited, but useful to her for emphasizing how different she was from what he was, and by extension, how different she was from Seolar, for whom Birra would have moved the world. She dropped her voice low and narrowed her eyes and said, "Make him understand that he's better off without me. Help him get over me. If you have to, find him someone who can love him the way he deserves to be loved. I charge you with that."

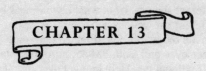

CHAPTER 13

Night Watch Control Hub, Barâd Island, Oria

AT HIS POST BEHIND and to the right of Aril, Rekkathav was wishing the breakfast would end so that he might go back to his sandbox and sleep, when rrôn exploded into the long hall through the doors at the end.

The armed guards standing at attention along the walls died together and all at once, engulfed in flame, screaming. The guests at the table screamed, too, and dove beneath it— Rekkathav could see them huddling together, clinging to each other when they had been bickering only the instant before about trade rights and treaties.

The great hall had always seemed ludicrously outsized to Rekkathav, until more than two dozen rrôn lined the walls to either side of the long banquet table. Then he realized to whose scale it had been built—the rrôn clearly belonged there. One of the intruders, blood-red with black wings, black legs and talons, and a black face, said, "We are come to stand witness to the challenge for Mastery."

It had happened faster than Rekkathav could have believed; in just a few breaths, the guards were dead, and Aril sat under the aim of two dozen and more weapons. The Master of the Night Watch rose to his feet, filled with a cold, mad hunger for the deaths of all those before him, and pulled into himself magic to cast a spell against everyone in the room— planning, Rekkathav realized, to destroy everyone there save himself alone.

But then a rrôn, black as the guts of the earth itself, yet iridescent and shimmering as if he were encrusted with jewels everywhere sunlight touched him, strode into the long hall, wings half unfurled, rilles straight out around his face like giant, glittering fans.

"Don't try that, Aril," he said. "There are traditions to be followed. A ritual to be played out. You cannot win this by cheating; you can only face me in the arena, with your second behind you and mine behind me. Your most powerful supporters are all dead; I saw to that before we came in here. Mine, however, will swear their allegiance to you if you successfully defend your title against me."

Who are you that I cannot read you, that I could not sense you? Who are you to come here this way, to challenge me, Aril, under whose Mastery the Night Watch prospers?

"I'm Baanraak," the black rrôn said, and Rekkathav could not suppress his own hiss of dismay. Even he, newly banded, still alive, a dark god only in name until he should survive his first death and reincarnation—even *he* had heard of Baanraak.

Aril seemed to have heard of a different Baanraak than Rekkathav had, however, for his tone was condescending. *The quitter? Ah. I see how you have survived so long now— you're very good at sneaking and hiding yourself and skulking in shadows. Unfortunately, those talents won't be worth much in the arena. Come—let us go and get this over with so I can get back to my breakfast with my subjects before the meal is completely ruined.*

Rekkathav wondered if Aril thought his confidence would unnerve his opponent. Baanraak didn't seem unnerved. He simply laughed. "Oh, let's," he said. "Breakfast is a fine idea; I haven't had keth in some years now, and you lads are *so* very tasty."

Aril turned to Rekkathav. *You are my second. We'll go to the arena now.*

He stepped away from the table and walked down the long row of rrôn. Rekkathav skittered behind him, his many knees quaking. Beneath the table, the regional lords and masters of the many local realms shivered in silence. But the room was full of rrôn dark gods, headed up by the past Master who had been a creature of myth and nightmare for centuries. It was as if the Tide-Eater, the monstrosity used to frighten children among his people, had suddenly crashed through the door with all the adults still in the room.

The ranks of the rrôn folded in behind Aril and Rekkathav as they marched to the door. The beasts dwarfed the two of them, stalking along to either side—a silent, deadly escort. Baanraak stepped out into the High Hall of Masters and waited, and when Aril came even with him, the ranks of the rrôn parted to let him into their midst. He walked beside Aril. Baanraak was observing the ritual of challenge in every way—except, perhaps, in killing off Aril's staff of dark-lord masters first. Rekkathav could certainly see the advantage in doing such a thing—from a tactical standpoint, if not from the personal one that made him an almost certain next target—but he wasn't aware of any other Masters who had purged the Hub staff before taking office. History said that sort of thing usually came afterwards.

History also said that the losers' seconds received the hero's choice once the challenge itself had been resolved; they could die by their own hand, in which event their resurrection rings might be tossed into a random gate, sending them to banishment, or they could die at the hand of the champion, in which case they were destroyed.

Rekkathav, still on his first life, did not find either outcome acceptable.

Pray I win, then, Aril told him.

They marched down the High Hall of Masters to the arena doors at the south end. Two more rrôn held the massive doors open, and inside, Rekkathav could see even more rrôn, lined along the back and sides of the huge domed room, waiting silently.

In the arena, there would be Aril. There would be him. And there would be a wall of rrôn. Aril would have no supporters present because they were all dead. He would have no one save Rekkathav to validate his claim of Mastery should he defeat the massive, ancient Baanraak in a fight. And should Aril win—and Rekkathav would wager on the Master over the would-be usurper for sheer skill and viciousness—why then would the rrôn, who already controlled the Hub, relinquish that control and hand it back to Aril?

You're thinking along the right lines, another voice said inside his head, and Rekkathav realized that Baanraak spoke to him. *The question you've so far failed to ask, however, is "How do I get out of this alive?" Because there is a way.*

Rekkathav waited, not daring to ask what it might be.

Walk away from him now, Baanraak said. *Declare your loyalty to me, and I'll let you live. Your Master won't survive—I can assure both of you of that. He'll not be around to grant you any rewards—or punish you for any disloyalties.*

Rekkathav had always thought himself a coward. He'd hoped that by the time he was ready to become the new Master of the Night Watch, some uncertain but surely very distant number of years ahead, he would have found a way to counteract his cowardice. Or that at least he would have gathered sufficient power over those who were brave that his own weakness might not be an issue. But marching onto the cold stone floor of the arena, hearing the clicking of claws and talons echoing from the hard surfaces all around him, he found one mad streak of courage in him. He said aloud, "I will not leave the Master to stand alone."

He didn't know where that had come from. But it seemed to him the right decision.

The Master looked sidelong at Rekkathav, but kept his thoughts to himself.

They took their places in the arena—Aril and Rekkathav in the gold end, Baanraak and the red rrôn with the black points in the white end. Rekkathav's job was to put a shield in place around Aril and hold it until the count. Baanraak's second would do the same thing for Baanraak.

Rekkathav was good at shields. He knew he could keep a strong, solid shield around Aril; could keep him safe until the end of the count. Then Aril would be on his own, and Aril would make his casts, deciding both Rekkathav's fate and his own. Rekkathav drew in energy—still using live energy because he could not yet handle the magic of death without pain. He took a deep breath; this would probably be his last day for that. If he survived at all past this day, it would almost certainly be as one of the dark gods—and odds were that he would not survive at all.

He stopped his thoughts from chasing farther down that path. Instead, he watched the rrôn who walked out into the center of the floor. Rekkathav felt sick inside—excitement and nerves and fear all twisted around in his gut until he feared his stomach would evert out of sheer tension, spewing its contents everywhere and causing him public humiliation. He'd discovered that other species found his people's tendency to flip the entire stomach out between the hard mouthparts when stressed disgusting; and Rekkathav knew that if he died, he didn't want to die humiliated.

So he clamped his mouthparts tight and braced himself and held the live energy while the rrôn in the center of the arena bowed to Aril, and then to Baanraak, and said, "This official decree of challenge having been made by Baanraak of the rrôn, past Master of the Night Watch, against Aril of the keth, current Master of the Night Watch, and duly attended by witnesses who are informed and aware of their duties as witnesses and who have declared their willingness to carry these duties out when the challenge has been decided, and which is duly seconded by seconds chosen by the Challenger and Defender without duress or coercion, and with the full knowledge and consent of the seconds to fulfill their duties, I now present the rules and rituals of the challenge.

"Challenger and Defender will stay within their shields until the drop of the gold ball into the center of the drop-cup; at its clear ringing, seconds will drop shields and move into the seconds' waiting area, which is to the left of each—"

Rekkathav looked quickly left. In the smooth stone floor, covered on his half with gold leaf, he saw a broad square of red stone—polished marble, perhaps, but of a peculiarly bloody hue.

"—and at the instant that the shields drop, Challenger and

Defender are free to attack in any and all manners of their choosing, save only that they may not use any weapon which does not originate from their bodies or their minds."

The rrôn had daggerlike teeth and talons and vast bulk, and the keth was slender and blunt of tooth and with the most delicate of claws at the ends of his finger pads. To Rekkathav, this seemed terribly unfair.

"To assure that Challenger and Defender both follow these rules, both will fight naked of all clothing."

Which meant nothing to Baanraak, of course; he wore nothing but his skin anyway. Rekkathav had never seen the Master in anything less than his full robes, however.

Aril shrugged and shed the floating robes; without him to animate them, the silks crumpled into a brightly colored puddle on the floor. The Master stood naked before them all—tall and stretched and smooth, sexless, almost featureless, terribly pale, soft-looking and ill-defined. He began to glow, filling up with an ugly, dirty light as muddy as the light that chased ahead of deadly storms. His braids floated in a nimbus around him, that same light running along them and crackling between them as if Aril had filled himself with lightning. He smiled a little, but that was just a twisting of his mouth, a grimace without any real meaning. Rekkathav, whose face was incapable of expression, had learned that while Aril's face was more mobile than his own, the Master's twistings and flexings of his facial features could be ignored as irrelevant. What lay inside of Aril was always the same—always deadly cold and sharp as edged steel, always layered and full of twists and deceptions.

The light show unnerved Rekkathav, but it didn't seem to be of interest to any of the rrôn. The speaker in the center of the arena continued with his reading of the rules, unfazed, and Rekkathav stared at his Master and lost the voice of the rrôn until suddenly he heard the words, ". . . and if both Challenger and Defender shall fall dead, the challenge will fall to the seconds, who will hold their places while the deaths of both are adjudged by the witnesses, and if both Defender and Challenger are found to be truly dead, then at the sound of the drop of the gold ball into the drop-cup they shall step unshielded into the center of the arena and immediately and without second pick up the attack, with the survivor made Master."

On the other side of the arena, the red-and-black rrôn looked Rekkathav in the eye and grinned, showing all his teeth, and winked.

Without warning, Rekkathav's stomach everted, its contents spewing everywhere. It dangled between his mouthparts, bright pink and soft and bulbous, and the rrôn all exploded with laughter.

"A fine Master he'll make," one laughed, and another roared, "At least we've seen his secret weapon now," and they all laughed again.

Rekkathav would have sunk into the floor and died right then of shame, but circumstances were likely to put him out of his misery soon enough. Instead, he willed the mess off the gleaming gold floor and swallowed hard to get his stomach back inside. He did not look at Aril; he could feel the Master's distaste, and that was bad enough.

The rrôn finished reading the rules, and Rekkathav pretended that the rest of this debacle did not exist, that nothing in the world existed save the voice of the rrôn in the center of the arena and his Master and the pending sound of a huge ball of solid gold dropping into a metal cup large enough to shelter a rrôn. Rekkathav cast the shield when he heard that rrôn say "And shields up." When the gold ball dropped into the cup with a sharp, clear ringing that could likely be heard everywhere in the Hub, and perhaps beyond, Rekkathav dropped the shield and skittered hell-bent for his blood-red stone square and its implied safety.

The battle in the center of the arena was the stuff of nightmares for a dreamer far more twisted than Rekkathav. Fire and blood rained down, and lightning crashed and thunder roared, and monsters appeared out of nowhere only to dissolve into nothing; winds tore in all directions, screaming; the stone floor grew heads and mouths and terrible teeth; darkness fell, so deep it was blindness, only to be torn away by light like the surface of the sun, and searing heat, with that chased by blizzards, and the blizzards scattered by explosions, and the explosions washed away by torrential rain.

And then it all stopped.

Silence, and Rekkathav found himself curled in a ball on the floor with his legs wrapped over his head in a position of defense. He peeked through the shield of his many legs and found the room held Aril, standing, bloodied and torn but still clearly alive, on one side. And nothing on the other, save a gleam of gold on the floor.

The rrôn that filled the stands crouched in silence, stunned. Baanraak's second whipped his head from side to side, looking for Baanraak, with his wings flat against his back and his rilles pulled tight to his neck. He looked . . . terrified.

Rekkathav unfolded. Dared to put legs on the floor. Dared to push himself to standing. No sign of Baanraak, no feel of Baanraak. Aril seemed surprised. Cautious. Rekkathav could sense him feeling around the room with his mind, trying to figure out what had happened.

He kept returning to the gold on the floor. A resurrection ring, Rekkathav thought. Aril, still Master of the Night Watch, summoned his robes and donned them again with a flick of a finger. The light around him died and the robes billowed out, seemingly alive; Rekkathav wondered if there was some connection. Aril walked to the center of the floor and said, "I have won. I'll have your allegiance now."

And the rrôn in the center said, "No one saw you kill Baanraak—not even you saw it happen. It is your duty to destroy your Challenger in a manner that can be witnessed, in a manner that permits the witnesses to determine that the Challenger is dead. You have not done this. Therefore, the battle is not over, and you must face Trrtrag, Baanraak's second."

Behind Aril, a voice said, "That won't be necessary," and light unfolded itself from around Baanraak in time for the assembly to see him reach down, jaws gaping, and rip Aril's head off. Baanraak spit the head out, and it bounced and then rolled across the floor to hit the drop-cup, which tolled softly—The sound of my doom, Rekkathav thought. The end of my life, and the sound of my doom. Baanraak lifted his eyes to the stands and said, "Any of you not see that?"

And the rrôn laughed.

Rekkathav forced himself to leave his place along the wall, all pretense of hope gone. Stiff-legged, he headed for the center of the room, for Baanraak and the rrôn who had read the rules and dropped the gold ball. It seemed to Rekkathav that all the air was gone from the vast room and that at the same time gravity had tripled; he could barely find the strength to lift one leg after the other. And yet he did. He got himself to the center of the room, and then he managed to stand there, and he looked up at the rrôn and he waited for his fate.

Baanraak looked down at him. He turned back to his witnesses and said, "Go, then. Spread the news—Baanraak has reclaimed the Mastery and the rrôn have returned to the Hub." The rrôn witnesses cheered and slipped from the stands and galloped from the room.

When they were gone, Baanraak turned to Rekkathav and said, "Still standing under your own power, I see." He rested a single talon against Rekkathav's neck and said, "You're ringed—I can feel the magic of your resurrection ring coursing through you—but you have not even had your first death yet. Aril made a mockery of the challenge by taking you as his second. What did you do for him?"

"I was his liaison. I kept track of operatives in the field, logged missions, read his decrees sometimes, researched in the vaults."

"You were his . . . secretary?"

"In a manner of speaking."

"Have you ever fought in a battle?"

"No."

Baanraak cocked his head to one side and grinned, and Rekkathav could see blood still smeared across his face. "Do you want to die today?"

"No."

"You didn't turn your back on your Master when given

the opportunity. You didn't cower when facing your fate. Are you loyal to the dead, that you would follow him to oblivion—or would you be loyal to me if I gave you the chance?"

In Rekkathav, a coil of hope stirred. "I would serve you faithfully and honestly."

"We'll see. Convince me of your worth today, apart from your most impressive puking. You amuse me, but the role of jester may not suit your considerable ambition."

Baanraak's Enclave, Kerras—Baanraak of Silver and Gold

Baanraak erupted from the lake, a grand fish clamped between his jaws, and flung rainbow droplets in all directions. He shot into the air, wings cupping and paddling him upward, swallowed the fish down whole, and dove back in again in one sweet, sinuous movement.

He'd had to enlarge the lake twice—once for swimming and a second time for fishing. To do that, he'd had to expand his hideout considerably. But he'd wanted to do that anyway, because he didn't like lying on his rock while he sunned and seeing beyond the edge of his little domain to the hell beyond. It ruined the illusion.

So he'd spread things out a bit. Not so much that anyone would notice. His hideout was no more than a hundred miles in diameter—a nothing, a tidbit when compared to the whole of a planet. He'd shielded the magic so that it didn't leave much of a sign, too, though the fact that Kerras *had* live magic again was eventually going to catch the attention of the Night Watch.

When it did, they would return and destroy it again.

He didn't waste a lot of time thinking about that. He'd created this place only as a temporary haven, and he was taking the time to enjoy it while it existed. He didn't like thinking about its eventual destruction, but he would resign himself to the inevitable.

Gliding beneath the surface of the lake, looking for a big,

tasty finny grey-rock to round out his snack, he thought that
if he could keep his little world intact, he might be willing to
hide there for a hundred years. Or a thousand. He'd fixed it
up beautifully. He'd fringed the perimeter with forests full
of the trees he remembered from his childhood, and filled
his forests with some of the wildlife he best recalled. He
kept being surprised—finding things he didn't know he'd
created in the corners of his domain. Insects and birds too
small to even eat, and a few mammals—mammals had
never gotten much of a foothold on Vraish, but there had
been a few varieties, and he kept discovering that he'd
willed more into being than he realized when he made his
hideaway.

Baanraak found the finny grey-rock, one of the tastiest of
the Vraish cold-water lake fish, deep beneath the surface,
where the water would be only a few degrees above freezing
all year round. Wings tucked flat against his body to cut the
drag, tail whipping to propel him forward, Baanraak glided
down toward it, neck coiled back.

The fish realized its danger before he reached it, and
darted away—but he extended his neck with one powerful
thrust and caught it between his teeth. He angled back to the
surface—the sun overhead was a spot of gold surrounded by
black and rich blue-green. The world above him brightened
as he shot toward the surface, until it shimmered with its rippled reflections. And then Baanraak burst free again.

He wanted someone to share this world with. Someone
who would love it, who would revel in it. But of all the rrôn
who had become dark gods—the only rrôn who would remember this place as home—he could not think of a single
one who would see it as anything but something else to be
destroyed for a quick surge of power.

And Baanraak didn't know any live rrôn anymore. They
had moved on and found other homes—and this place would
be meaningless to them. They would not understand the
smells, the tastes, the weight of the air, or the sounds. This
place would not be home to them. To their children and
grandchildren if they settled here, certainly—but never to

them. The first generation in a new land became perpetual strangers, forever torn between memory and reality. Baanraak had been such a stranger for longer than humans had been human.

Baanraak landed on his rock and crunched his fish, savoring the taste of this one. It was big enough to require more than one swallow—man-size, but far less bony, and better designed for the gullet. Like everything else, it tasted as wonderful as he remembered.

He was living in a fantasy. He knew that, but he didn't care. Perhaps this was the first sign of senility, or of madness. He didn't care about that, either. After long wandering, he was home.

This place would be better if it had families here—drakes and jennies soaring through the air with their still-flightless sprats shrieking up at them for food or attention; and singers on the high places at dawn and dusk; and craftsmen carving the spire-cities from mountains; and warriors sparring in the dusty areas, battling for play when they were not battling for real. It would be better if it encompassed the whole of this world.

It would be better if it would survive.

He closed his eyes against sudden pain.

He found himself with something he wanted to keep, something he cherished. He did not want to see this place destroyed. He wanted to fight for it. He wanted to save it. And the two creatures who might help him were the two in all the universes who most wanted to see him annihilated, Lauren Dane and Molly McColl.

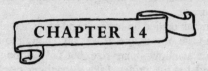

CHAPTER 14

Daisies and Dahlias, Cat Creek, North Carolina

"THIS IS AN UNOFFICIAL HEARING of the Cat Creek Sentinels. We are questioning Lauren Dane as part of our fact-finding mission before we determine whether or not formal charges of treason should be brought against her in this body or carried up to the Council of Sentinels. Because this is a fact-finding mission, no areas of questioning can be marked off-limits, and no evidence can be ruled out or removed from consideration." Eric MacAvery looked down at Lauren and said, "That means for this inquiry we will not be leaving your parents and the fact that they were found guilty of treason by the High Council out of the evidence. If we bring formal charges against you, a member of the High Council will take your side as your advocate, and may rule that what your parents did has no bearing on what you're doing. But for now, we're looking at everything."

Lauren nodded. She sat with her back to the wall, with Eric and the gate-mirror to her left and the map table to her right. They'd given her one of the few metal folding chairs, instead of one of the wooden ones; she had the chair that sat unevenly on the floor, one leg shorter than the others so that it rocked slightly every time she shifted. And, like all metal folding chairs, it had been designed for maximum discomfort. Behind her was a floor mirror she'd brought with her—her version of a presentation screen. For the moment, it reflected the room and the people in it, and nothing more.

Jake had been on her lap, but even before everyone arrived he'd grown restless. Now he sat on the floor beside her, mostly under the table, drawing on a small stack of the Sentinels' vector-charting and mapping paper with a blue ballpoint pen she'd had in her bag.

The Sentinels sat in two rows facing her. They mostly looked grim. June Bug Tate and her sister, Louisa; George Mercer; and Darlene Fullbright had the front row. Terry Mayhew, Betty Kay Nye, Raymond Smetty, and Pete had the back row.

Heyr sat in the gate-mirror, keeping track of movement between the worlds for the duration.

Pete had wanted to sit in the front with her. Eric had refused the request. Heyr had told her that he would level the town and reduce the Cat Creek Sentinels to their component atoms before he would let them charge her with treason or pass a death sentence on her, and she found that she believed him. Heyr had informed the Sentinels that he was watching the gate during their inquest. They had not been happy about it, but they'd had to concede that he was the 600-pound gorilla. If he wanted to watch the gate, none of them could do anything to stop him.

Eric asked Lauren, "Do you have any questions before we begin?"

"Yes," Lauren said. She didn't say anything else.

Eric waited for a moment, then said, "Well?"

"Have you looked into any of this before my arrival, or is questioning me your first step?"

"Questioning you is our first step," Eric said.

"No, it isn't," June Bug said. "I've done some work on this on my own time. I'll have results to present at the appropriate moment."

Lauren glanced at Eric and caught a faint expression of irritation on his face, quickly erased. Well, he couldn't be seen to be partial, could he? She suspected that he wanted her and Jake removed from town—at the very least banished to a city, where they would not be able to make gates work. She thought he was a good man, but he had little tolerance for people who worked outside the confines of authority. He saw the universe full of clear-cut good guys and bad guys— the good guys followed the law and listened to authority, and the bad guys didn't.

And when he'd been attracted to her, Lauren hadn't wanted him; and she was working way outside of any authority's supervision or approval; and her parents had been judged traitors by the Sentinels. The fact that she had saved his life once—that wasn't going to be allowed to figure into his equation. The fact that her parents had been working outside of their mandate, though—*that* he'd hang on to. There were times when Lauren found it easy not to like Eric very much.

Eric cleared his throat. "I'm opening the floor for questions," he said.

Raymond Smetty, arms crossed and eyes narrowed, had the first one. "Your actions are responsible for almost getting all of us killed yesterday—yours and your sister's, and I notice that she isn't here. How can you say you're doing something good when you're like to get us all killed?" To Eric he said, "We already know she's guilty. Why are we even wasting time with this?"

Lauren stood up. The chair was killing her butt anyway, and the feeling of having Eric standing above her was getting on her nerves.

"I'm going to show you," she said. She put a hand on the mirror and began to feel for the live magic now pouring into Earth. She wanted proof that what she had already done had mattered. She said, "Working between this world and a number of downworlds, I've created live magic siphons that pull live magic up to us from the worlds below us. I have that magic anchored to low-population regions for now, and have managed to locate old gods who were hiding or simply living on various downworlds, but who wanted to get involved in bringing the worldchain back. They are stationed around these siphons I've made, and they're using the energy that is coming in to do magic."

She took a deep breath. "Live magic hasn't worked well here for a long time."

"Barely at all," Heyr interrupted. "The old gods have found themselves relegated to near-mortal status here by the scarcity of live energy—meanwhile, the dark gods have become more and more powerful. With nothing to work with, the old gods become targets and leave, and magic dies further. Magic breeds magic as like breeds like."

"You're an old god," Eric said, sounding peeved.

"I'm an immortal," Heyr told him. "The difference is immense."

Lauren took her presentation back. She found what she wanted in Porth yr Ogof, in Fforest Fawr, Wales, in the siphon that she'd buried under a cave. Live energy had first permeated the cave, making a nice home for the old god who'd agreed to live there and work with the magic.

"Which old god?" Eric wanted to know.

"Tam Lin. He knew the area and was happy to go back."

"Tam Lin? Population start rising there yet?" Heyr asked. His expression, when Lauren turned to look at him, was droll.

"There are a lot of . . . er . . . wee folk in the area now. Some fairies."

"I meant the human population."

"Why?"

"Tam Lin was big on fertility. Seeded his place with wild roses, waited for pretty maidens to come along and pick them, then weaseled a lay in exchange for his stolen property. He's like your sister, you know."

"Like her? I don't think so—Molly hasn't been seducing young women to the best of my knowledge."

"Like her the other way—he's half of this world, half of one well up the line. He has a lot of magic in him, but this place really is his home."

"I didn't know that."

"He wouldn't tell you. He always preferred to keep his origins mysterious. But I'd bet a third of the Celts in the region can attribute their second sight to a great-great-great-

great-great-grandmother's dalliance in the middle of Tam Lin's roses."

Lauren sighed. There weren't any hiring forms for old gods, and references were hard to come by. And the old gods weren't exactly standing in line waiting to help her. She had to hunt them out and beg them for their assistance.

She looked back to her mirror. In it, everyone could see a couple of wee folk as they ran across a rock with something they'd "borrowed," no doubt. They'd be into the milk again in a few years, as the magic spread into populated areas. People were going to have to relearn the old ways—the things they had brushed off for years as superstition were once again going to be very real.

"Wee folk," she said, and linked to the next siphon, the one in West Virginia.

A white deer strolled through the forest, a tiny, slender woman—not human—dressed in green sitting astride him.

"Hey!" Heyr said. "A wood elf! I thought they'd died out."

"They're making a comeback," Lauren said. "They're a bit rarer than the spotted owl and the snail darter, and equally as endangered. But I think they'll make it . . . if I can keep doing what I'm doing."

Lauren said, "The Nunnehi are back, too. They're the old gods who inhabited the Blue Ridge Mountains even before the Cherokee. And there's more." She lay a hand on the surface of the glass and found her siphon in Georgia. She'd linked it beneath the lakebed, under the long south arm of Blue Ridge Lake, outside of Blue Ridge, Georgia.

"Mermaids?" Pete blurted.

Lauren turned and looked. There were, in fact, three mermaids playing along the bank. She'd linked into the strongest magic in the section; she hadn't been sure what any of them were going to see.

"I thought mermaids were a saltwater thing," Betty Kay Nye said, but Lauren had to give her credit—Betty Kay was looking puzzled because they weren't where she would have expected them. Which implied that at some level Betty Kay had been expecting them. Which made Betty Kay much more interesting than Lauren would have imagined.

Eric turned to her. "How many more places like this are there?"

"I've done twenty-three siphons so far."

"And you have an old god stationed at each one, using magic to create magical things?"

"No. I've managed to find five old gods so far who were willing to work with me. Three of them insisted on staying in one place. Tam Lin was one of those."

"Technically—from your perspective, anyway—he isn't precisely an old god," Heyr said, proving to be a bit of a stickler about terminology, but Lauren waved that off.

"He can do the work. Anyway . . . two of the old gods are moving from place to place among the unclaimed territories, working with magic as it builds up, then moving on. I need more help, but old gods make themselves hard to find—and they're good at it."

"If they weren't, most of them would be dead," Heyr said.

Lauren said, "This is about more than just here, and it's about more than just us." Hand on glass, she reached farther. She followed her lines and threads upward, where the magic turned ugly and foul, where all she could feel was death and destruction and horror and pain, and on the other side of the glass she could feel Kerras, and her connection to it. Eyes closed, seeking the one clear thread that was hers, the one bit of live magic, she said, "This is also about restoring our worldchain. Bringing the upworlds back to life so that we are not the next world to die. It's about stopping the Night Watch—even destroying the Night Watch—so that those worlds can live." She felt her connection, the live magic brighter and stronger than she had expected, and looked into the faces in the chairs. "This is Kerras," she said. "There's nothing to see here yet, because I have not yet found an old god who would dare the wrath of the Night Watch to go there and use the magic, but even in its raw form, the magic comes back to us down the chain."

"What are you *talking* about?" June Bug asked. She was the Sentinel Lauren thought she would be most likely to win over, but June Bug looked annoyed.

"I created a live magic siphon on Kerras. The same sort of connection that I've created from the downworlds to Earth—well, I created one to our first upworld. I can go higher, too, but it's hard right now. I can't skip a world."

"That's not what I mean," June Bug said. "If that's Kerras and you haven't found an upworlder to move in and use the magic, why are you showing us images of a field and a lake and dinosaurs. What *are* you showing us?"

Lauren turned and stared at the image beneath her hand. She looked, not at a blackened cinder covered with patches of ice, but at a world full of life and beauty. It was no world she had ever seen—tall grasses, vibrant blue-green so rich they looked fake; a herd of little striped dinosaurish grass-eaters moving across the plain; a great gleaming lake, blue with a black center, deep and as clear as good crystal; huge insects, small birds, ancient-looking trees. And on a tall rock, asleep with nose on rump and wings tucked in tight, lay a huge creature, opalescent black, that looked very much like a dragon. Or a rrôn.

Lauren backed out fast, the image in the glass receding until the live world on Kerras began to show edges, and then receded to a perfect circle, and then to a glowing dot on the black cinder. The only rrôn she had ever encountered were dark gods. The dark gods would not have created a live spot on Kerras—but she had to assume that an old-god rrôn would be as dangerous as a dark-god rrôn. At least if disturbed.

She turned to look at the Sentinels. "I don't know who—or what—that was. I do not want to wake it."

"You got a volunteer," Pete said. He gave her an encouraging little grin.

Lauren was less sure. "I got something that was going to Kerras anyway, and that found live magic when it got there and decided to use it."

"A dark god would have destroyed your siphon."

Lauren nodded. "Or would have tried, anyway. I made

them tough and I hid them well. But I'm not saying a dark god found the magic. I'm just saying that whatever found it and is using it isn't necessarily . . . good. I was looking for an old god who would restore Kerras as it had been—same terrain, same wildlife, same everything. We have to give the world back to the surviving Kerrans."

Eric said, "That would seem to be the Kerrans' problem, wouldn't it?"

"Why?" Lauren said. "They could no more rebuild their world with magic than we could rebuild ours. The rules haven't changed—this isn't some new sort of magic. What I'm having to do is find old gods with an altruistic streak—those willing to work on a world not their own, knowing that even if they revive worlds, incurring terrible danger as they do, we may never be able to revive their worlds. It's not been an easy task."

"There are other options," Heyr muttered.

And Raymond said, "There are. We have all the proof we need that Lauren is working against the orders of the Council and the Sentinels' rules. We have sure proof that she's a traitor. So I say we're done—that we vote to charge her, and we lock her up, and we send her to be tried by the Council."

"There's *life* on Kerras," Lauren said. "It might not be the right kind of life, but I suspect that can be fixed. Right now, though, for the first time since Kerras went up in flames, Earth is getting a natural flow of live energy coming to us from our upworld. It may not be much yet, but it's there, and it's real, and it will add to everything I'm bringing in the hard way from downworld. Only I don't have to do anything to get it here."

Most of them looked at her differently than they had before. Lauren would guess that June Bug would be firmly on her side. Louisa—no. Nothing Lauren could do would change Louisa's mind about her. The same went for Raymond, whose distaste for her was blatant enough to be unmissable, even by the most oblivious. George looked like he might be won over. Darlene looked like she'd swallowed a lemon. Terry . . . well, if Terry would ever stop staring at Betty Kay's breasts, Lauren might be able to guess which way he would go. Betty Kay seemed excited. Pete didn't count—she already knew where he stood, and so did everyone else.

She had to turn to look at Eric. His face gave away nothing—but then, it almost never did.

She stood there looking at him for what seemed like a very long time.

"Do you have anything else you want to show us?" Eric asked.

"No."

"Do you have anything else you need to say about this, then, before we resume our questions?"

Lauren took a deep breath. "Yes. My parents died for this. This was their work, their idea, their struggle. If you decide that I'm not a traitor to the Sentinels and their goals for doing this, then I want an acknowledgment that my mother and father weren't traitors, either. That the Sentinels were wrong when they killed them."

"Any formal declaration of that sort would have to come through the Council," Eric said. "And I'm not sure how the Council is going to feel about this, no matter what we decide."

"I'm not asking to have them formally cleared. I'm asking you people in this room right now to acknowledge that if what I'm doing is right, then what they were doing was right, too. I don't care about the Council. But your father, Eric, was directly involved in my parents' deaths. Some of the rest of your relatives were, too. It matters to me that their names are cleared, at least among the people I work with."

Lauren heard Raymond mutter, "It won't be an issue." But he didn't say it loudly, and none of the other Sentinels seemed to notice.

Eric nodded after a moment. "We'll keep it in mind," he said. He turned to the Sentinels. "The floor is reopened for questions."

She hadn't won them over yet—she could see that in their eyes. But she thought she had a fighting chance.

White Hold, Ayem, Oria

Molly stepped through a mirror into the High Palace in White Hold in the middle of delicate negotiations. She knew precisely how delicate the situation was because she'd been spying on the negotiators for quite some time. The Tradona people of White Hold were about to make a deal with a devil they did not know. But Molly knew him—if she did not know him personally, at least she knew what he was.

She stepped through green fire into a room of white marble, sword already drawn, and with one swing cut off the head of the creature sitting across the table from The Bright, who was the official voice of the Tradona people in White Hold. The Bright leapt from his chair, screeching—a small, furry creature with a mad thing's monkey howl—as blood spattered him and his desk, and began to sizzle on the paper.

The body in the chair toppled to the floor to join the head, while The Bright backed into a corner and, still screeching, tried to disappear into a solid marble wall—without success.

Molly waited for a moment, and the body, which had in life been disguised to look like one of the faolshe—the gray-skinned, knuckle-dragging fourth major native sentient species of Oria—seemed to melt.

The thing on the floor was nothing from Oria, a fact that was becoming clear to the panicked Speaker for the People. The corpse twisted and changed, unfolding as it did, until it was nearly seven feet tall, and massively muscled.

"Dark god," Molly said to The Bright, pointing her blade at the corpse. "You were about to sign a deal that would have traded your people's lives for mechanical contrivances."

"I've known him for years," The Bright whispered, his eyes huge and round.

"Not as well as you thought you did. You've already signed away a great deal to him, haven't you?"

"He was . . . clever. He created things—a globe that lights with the pulling of a chain, with its fire enclosed so that it does not create a burning threat. A very fine steam engine with which we could create conveyances that would travel faster than horses on land, and faster than sail-powered ships in the sea. A mechanical thresher that would tirelessly separate wheat from chaff, sparing our people to do other and better things." He looked frightened. "These things are evil?"

Molly looked at him and took a deep breath. "No. Technology isn't evil. It isn't good, either. It just is—like fire. You can use fire to warm yourself or burn your house down." She knelt on the floor and held her hands over the body of the dark god, using magic to search for resurrection rings. She hated this part of her duty. Though, if she chose to be honest with herself, she didn't care much for any part of her duty. Killing things, burning the bodies, destroying the resurrection rings, trying not to die. It wasn't the sort of job description that would get a lot of applicants.

At that moment, The Bright's guards, a bit slow in responding, burst through the doors and drew their swords. Molly looked at them, said "You're late," and turned back to the dark god, which was of a type she'd never seen before.

"Stand down," The Bright told them. "The Vodi has already taken care of the problem." The guards looked at her again and nearly impaled each other getting their swords back into their sheaths. Drawing steel against the Vodi was a definite social faux pas, though if they had actually come at her with weapons drawn, they would have been the only ones to get hurt. The Bright asked Molly, "Why did that thing pretend to be my ally? The dark gods don't need us. They can take whatever they want without trade."

Molly studied him. "You're more useful to the dark gods if your population is growing, if your civilization is getting more complex, and if your technology is improving right along with it. The better you are able to wage war, the more you serve their needs." She gave him a sad little smile.

"But a steam engine is not a weapon of war, and neither is a thresher."

Molly sat back on her heels and looked over at him. "At a time of need, if you were being attacked by sea, do you think you could find a way to adapt that steam engine to power a weapon that would give you an advantage?"

The Bright came out of the corner and walked over to her, his fur and his elaborate robes spattered with the blood of an enemy that wanted to see not just him, but his whole world, dead.

"Of course we could," he said. "Techniques learned in the construction of one mechanical contrivance can easily be adapted to suit the purposes of a dozen or a hundred unrelated contrivances. That was why I was willing to pay so dearly for the working model of Ride-Slowly Son of Falling-in-Battle's steam engine. I intended that our artificers take the thing apart and determine the method of its working."

"Right. And that's why the dark gods prefer to work with you over the veyâr, for example. Or the goroths. You and your people are always looking for the better way."

"And *that* is a bad thing?"

Again she shook her head. "It's just a thing. Like technology. Like fire. Looking for the better way creates change, and every change is an opportunity that opposing forces can exploit. The veyâr don't change, so to the dark gods they're useless except as sources of land and bodies. Your people—you change. They can work with people like you."

"Which makes me and my people . . . evil." He looked distressed.

Molly reached into the body of the dark god, her fingers glowing with the fire of the universe, and pulled out one resurrection ring, and then another, and then a third. The gold gleamed in her hand, shedding the dark god's blood across the floor; the stink of the corpse and the fresh memory of his guts on her hands made Molly want to throw up.

Molly closed her eyes against the nausea and breathed shallowly through her mouth for a moment. When she was sure she had herself under control, she stood and said to the guards, "You may burn the body now."

They bowed to her and hurried forward to drag away the pieces of the corpse. Molly waited until they were gone, then turned back to The Bright. "You're very hung up on the whole good/bad thing, aren't you?"

"Hung up?"

Molly heard the words in his language but his meaning in English—the magic that permitted her to understand down-worlders and make herself understood to them, no matter what language they spoke, had faltered at its one sticking point. The Bright had no concept of a hang-up—a personal obsession that carried negative connotations—so her words had been rendered to him literally. And, taken literally, they made no sense.

She sighed. "You see the world as divided between those things which are good and those things which are bad."

"That is because that is how the world is," The Bright said. "I am the Speaker of my people, the Master of White Hold, the City of Light. I am The Bright—the personifica-tion of all that walks under sunlight. It is my duty to find for my people all that is good in the light and bring it to them, and to identify all that is evil beneath the light, and make an end to it. For this I was born, for this I have lived. You met my two counterparts once—The Dark and The Deep. They hold the other two great cities of the Tradona people, and they are as I am—The Deep is Speaker for the seafaring Tradona, the Dark for those who delve the deep places of Oria and work beneath the stars. If we do not divine that which is good and that which is evil, we have failed our duty and our people." He hung his head. "As I have failed my people."

"You didn't fail anybody," Molly said. She cleaned her blade and resheathed it, then stood there for a moment look-ing at The Bright. "You three didn't like me very much when we first met," she said. "You doubted that I could be the true Vodi."

"I remember. I was clearly mistaken."

"You weren't. If a Vodi is someone good, someone who comes to heal and nurture and comfort, then I am no Vodi."

He looked at her. "You wear the Vodi necklace."

"I know that."

"But you claim you are not the Vodi. Then what are you?"

"I'm a hunter. A killer. A destroyer." She sighed. "I am the death of Death, in a small way. I hunt the dark gods and destroy them, and make sure they cannot come back. I am a useful tool, made in the same fashion as the monsters I hunt."

"But you are good. And they are evil."

She smiled a little. "That was the point I was trying to make. Evil and good are not in things, but in the way things are used. People—of whatever sort—are not innately evil or good; they choose to do evil things or good things, and so mark themselves as good or evil people. But any evil creature can choose at any time to do a kindness, and any good creature can commit an evil act."

"This is not the way I have learned to see the world."

"I know. I was just telling you this because . . . well . . . don't stop looking for the better way. Don't shun technology, don't hide from progress. I know you have the power to take the whole of the Tradona people back to a city lit only by fire, to vehicles powered only by horses, to grain threshed only by hand." Molly walked over to him and knelt down on one knee so the two of them were eye to eye. "And I saw in you a sudden desire to shun the things you have sought out. But don't. Don't walk away from things that can be used for good just because they can also be used for evil. Just be wary. Not everyone who calls you friend is a friend. The greatest enemies you face feed off death and destruction—and they don't care if you win or lose, so long as someone dies in the process."

One of the guards came back in. "The body is burning. Will you wish to watch?"

"No," she said. "I have what I need. I must . . . keep moving."

She left The Bright standing in his meeting hall, lost in thought. She walked alone through winding passageways and down stairs and out of the round, white stone city of White Hold.

I'm doing my job, she told herself. I'm moving on. This is

my life now—the whole of my life. Hunt, kill, destroy. It's better this way. Seolar will do better if he does not have to watch me fade, and I will be able to fade in peace, without being constantly reminded that I'm losing myself—that I was once so much more than I am.

The resurrection rings of the dark god jangled softly in her pocket with each step she took, and purred against her hip. They called to her with songs of decadence and lust and orgiastic feeding. She could hear the song they sang as clearly as she heard the call of the darkness itself. She could clean them. Claim them for herself. Become stronger and more dangerous.

She walked faster, forcing herself to ignore the seduction of that call.

"It's better this way," she muttered.

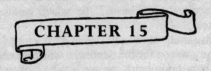

CHAPTER 15

Daisies and Dahlias Florist, Cat Creek

ERIC SAID, "If there are no further questions, Lauren, you and Jake need to leave the room for a moment."

Pete looked at Heyr—one of them needed to go with Lauren to make sure she was safe, and one needed to stay and try to influence the voting. Heyr caught his look and stepped out of the mirror, and shut the gate all the way down behind him.

"We'll need to have that open," Eric said, and Heyr grinned a little.

"I know. And once you've voted, either your gateweaver or I will rebuild the gate for you." Heyr didn't point out that the only two people around who were capable of rebuilding the gate were him and Lauren, or that he was firmly in Lauren's corner. He didn't need to. It was subtle pressure, and Pete liked it.

The Sentinels needed Lauren—they needed her a lot more than she needed them, but he figured she needed them pretty badly, too.

"I don't think Pete should be in here, since he's involved in this and has been working with her," Raymond said. Pete spent a few seconds fantasizing about doing a little FBI background investigation on Raymond, maybe having his colleagues go through Raymond's personal life with a microscope and a pair of tweezers, just to see what fell out.

But Eric said, "Pete stays. I'm not sure if he votes, but he stays."

Small triumphs.

"Are you calling for a vote?" June Bug asked.

Eric shrugged. "Do any of you have any comments—that we haven't already heard?" he asked, looking straight at Raymond.

Louisa said, "He's only saying what a lot of us are thinking. She's wrong for the Sentinels, whatever else we decide, and at barest minimum she needs to be sent away."

Eric said, "We'll find out how many of us are thinking that in a moment, Louisa. Don't try to make your opinion seem like the only one."

Betty Kay looked at Eric, her hands clasped on her lap. "I'd really like to hear what you think. You're the only one who hasn't said anything."

"Hasn't been my place to say anything." Eric propped himself on the corner of the heavy oak table. "But since you asked, here are the issues as I see them. Lauren is and has been working far outside the Sentinel mandate. I can't deny it, you can't deny it, and she didn't try to deny it. So that's one point against her." He raised a finger. "She's doing something damned risky, something that is going to put Cat Creek right in the crosshairs of forces we're not big enough to fight, and the things on the other end of the gun are nasty. That's two." He raised a second finger. "The Cat Creek Sentinels are only semiautonomous, and in instances where anything really big is going on, we're supposed to make sure the Council knows what we're facing—and I think it's a safe bet that the Council is going to be scared shitless of this, pardon my French." He nodded to Darlene, who, along with her aversion to smoking, had a tendency to play vocabulary police and get offended in the presence of profanity.

Darlene, Pete thought, desperately needed to get laid. And probably never would if she kept being such a bitch.

"So if we involved ourselves in this," Eric continued, "it would have to be in a nonsanctioned manner. Frankly, I cannot recall the last time an entire group went rogue or received censure." He sighed. "So that's three against, and that last one is big."

"How do you know the Council won't be thrilled to find life on Kerras?" Pete asked.

"I don't. But the Council has never, to my knowledge, voted in favor of innovation. The entire purpose of the Sentinels has been to prevent change, to hold the line, to keep things stable."

Pete said, "An exclusively defensive military campaign is by its very nature a losing campaign. If you cannot retake territory, you cannot win the war."

Raymond leaned around to sneer at him. "Thank you, General Patton. But as Eric has pointed out, we have a job to do. *This* is not our job. I think the issue is as simple and obvious as that—and I think Eric has outlined perfectly the reasons why we cannot participate in this. I'm voting with him."

"I wasn't finished yet," Eric said, voice mild.

Raymond froze like a deer in headlights. It was fun to see.

"Those are my three points against Lauren and what she's doing. Here are my points in favor"—he looked from Raymond to Louisa and back to Raymond, and then scanned the rest of the Sentinels—"and yes, I do have points in favor."

"First of those is that what Lauren is doing is working. You saw life on Kerras. You saw magic working here. At present all of the live magic coming in is limited to tiny areas in unpopulated regions, but it's spreading out. For the first time in thousands of years—or maybe longer—things are getting better instead of worse. And we can point a finger to the exact reason, to the exact source, of the improvement, and that is Lauren. So, one in favor of Lauren. She's doing something that is making a difference." He raised a finger on his other hand. "Next, she had every reason to keep this to herself and distrust all of us, and at the same time, every reason to take the chance she was taking. If one of you knew how to save our world and everyone on it, including your child, wouldn't you? I would, or at least I like to think I would. And if you thought the people who should be helping and protecting you would instead find a way to have you killed for what you were doing, wouldn't you hide your actions from them? I would. So, that's two in favor of her." He paused and raised another finger. "Actually, that makes three. I understand that she chose to act. *And* I understand why she hid her actions." He looked at his hands, three fingers raised on each one.

A tie, Pete thought. A singularly unhelpful tie.

And then Eric took a deep breath. "Finally, the question of Sentinel involvement in what she's doing." He let his breath out and shook his head. "She's going to bring trouble wherever she is. But I don't think we should take the NIMBY approach to this."

"NIMBY?" Pete asked.

"Acronym. Not In My Back Yard. Usually refers to corporations looking to build power plants, landfills, recycling centers, prisons, and group homes." Eric leaned back and studied all the Sentinels again. "All things that people need, and know they need, but that they'd rather shove off on someone else. I think sending her away would be the wrong thing to do. I think leaving her to do her work alone would *also* be the wrong thing to do. I think we need to say to ourselves, 'If not me, then who? If not now, then when?'" He stood again, and hooked his thumbs into the pockets of his uniform pants. "This is our moment, I think. Today, with war all around us, and with a winning strategy before us for the first time, we have been called to serve. And we can either fight or we can run." His voice went quiet. "I'm a Southerner," he said. "Running doesn't sit well with me."

"So, Sheriff," Louisa said, "you're in favor of taking the Cat Creek Sentinels rogue?"

Eric winced a little at the way she phrased the question, but said, "I don't see that we have any other choice. Just as when Lauren decided to do what she's doing, I don't see that she had any other choice. We must do what is right. We must."

"Then you're not going to call for a vote? You're just going to tell us that we're going to do this?" Louisa asked.

Pete liked that idea, but Eric shook his head.

"No. If we do this, we must all do it, and we must all agree to it. We cannot have any in the group that we cannot trust to stand behind us—because if we do this, all we're going to have is each other."

"Then you don't even have to vote," Raymond said. "Because nothing you can say will convince me that sneaking around behind the Council or going rogue is the right thing to do. It isn't, and I know it, and in your gut every single one of you knows it."

"Not even to save this world and everyone on it, Raymond?"

Raymond crossed his arms over his chest. "If that's what's at stake, you'll be able to take this before the full Council."

"We can't risk that," George said suddenly. Everyone turned to look at him.

"We can't?" Eric looked surprised and interested.

"If the Council decides in her favor, fine. But if the Council decides against her, there is no one else who can do what she's doing. At least not that we know of."

Darlene hadn't said much, either. Now she spoke up as well. "This isn't something a committee could replace or correct if it made a mistake. They couldn't just plug someone else into her job to make everything better. They can't be given the opportunity to make a mistake, because if they make a mistake, they can't fix it."

"So we get to make the mistake instead," Raymond said. "I can't believe you people. This is simple. This is wrong versus right, and you're trying to make it into something else. And you, Darlene. I thought you and I had already agreed to vote against Lauren on this."

Darlene said, "Healthy magic is coming through to us from Kerras for the first time since the Cuban Missile Crisis. There's *life* on Kerras again."

Raymond gave Darlene a murderous look. "And in a day or two the Night Watch will discover that and wipe it out. And they'll come here, too, and kill you and me and everyone else in this town on their way to get to Lauren."

Eric studied Raymond. "You're not going to see reason on this? You're not going to see why this is important?"

"I already see reason," Raymond said. "Either banish her or have her killed and be done with it. The Sentinels don't need her. We can do what this world needs, just like we always have. We don't need rogues, or traitors, or the children of traitors."

"And Pete?"

"He's a traitor. He helped her. He's known what she's been up to all along. That's—what? Aiding and abetting? Accessory?"

"Those are criminal justice terms," Eric said. "They don't apply within the Sentinels." He stood before them, thinking, one arm crossed over his stomach, elbow of the other resting on it, head down, forehead cupped in hand.

Pete felt sick. Eric was looking for unanimity, and he wasn't going to get it. Which meant the vote would have to go against Lauren. He'd been sure it wouldn't—he'd been sure these idiots would see reason. That's why he'd convinced her to come before them and present her case—and he'd been wrong.

And the start of it all had been so small. Heyr had said only one innocent thing. He'd mentioned Molly in the present tense—a tiny slip, and one he hadn't even realized *was* a slip.

One slip. Pete wondered if anyone, ever, had betrayed so much with a word.

The truth will out. Old saying, painfully correct. Whether you wanted it or not, truth would at last find its way into the light.

Eric looked up. "There is no need to call a vote. We know in advance that we will not reach a consensus, and for an issue of this magnitude, consensus must be reached."

Raymond said, "You know in advance that you won't get consensus in her favor. But you might get consensus against her. Why don't you take the vote anyway?"

"Because I *do* know that I won't get a consensus against her. Because even if I were the only one voting in her favor, I would still vote in her favor. Therefore, there can be no agreement on this issue, and the decision on what we do about her falls to me. Without consensus, I will not take the

Sentinels rogue. I will not force someone who disagrees with what we would be doing to serve. So . . . we cannot help her."

Pete started to stand, to protest. His fists were clenched, his arms rigid.

Eric said, "Sit down, Pete. The Sentinels cannot help her, and I am sorry about that, and I am deeply ashamed that we will not. I am ashamed that we are taking the cowards' road. But . . . if we are forced to stand on the cowards' road, we will not march on it. I will not send her away, I will not report what she is doing to the Council, and our official position on all of this is that she is our gateweaver and none of us knows of anything that she is doing that falls outside of her mandate. *None of us,*" he repeated, and he looked at each of the Sentinels in turn. "Because what she is doing matters, and I will not take the route of Not In My Back Yard. She will stay here; we will deal with the consequences of her being here. And, just to make myself *very* clear, the one of you who reports her to the Council betrays all of us. No matter where you are, no matter what you are doing, no matter when you decide to pass the information on. And if you are considering betraying all of us, I will state that we in the Cat Creek Sentinels are good people. But we are not nice people. We will protect our own without qualm or hesitation."

"So you're saying that you're going to do nothing," Raymond said. His face had gone an ugly, beefy red.

"I'm saying that I'm going to do nothing. And that *you* are going to do nothing. You need to be clear about that distinction, Raymond." Eric looked at Pete. "Call her in. She needs to hear the decision."

Pete felt sick. He rose and walked out the door, down the back stairs of the old house, past the worktable covered with lace and pins and ribbons and green foamy florist stuff, out the back door. Heyr and Lauren stood there, talking. Heyr had Jake on his shoulders.

"They're ready for you," Pete said, and his voice gave away too much. Lauren's eyes went wide, and she turned pale.

"They won't live to turn you in to the Council," Heyr said.

Lauren said nothing. She walked past Pete, up the stairs. Heyr, carrying Jake, followed her, and Pete brought up the rear.

He walked into the room to find her already at the front, facing Eric.

"We will not help you," Eric said. "To help you, I would have had to get a unanimous vote, and I didn't get one. We will not make any move against you, either, however—you'll stay here, you'll be our gateweaver, and none of us knows anything about your extracurricular activities. We will deal with the fallout of what you're doing as if it were a normal result of what we do. No one will turn you in."

Lauren looked surprised. "So—I'm not going to be banished or reported to the Council."

"No, you aren't."

"I'm still the Cat Creek gateweaver."

"Right."

"But with . . . the other thing . . . I'm on my own."

"Right."

Lauren nodded. "All right. I'm no worse off than I was before, anyway. I can live with that." She turned, took Jake from Heyr, and walked out of the room and down the stairs without another word. Heyr hurried after her, clearly unwilling to have her out of his sight for any length of time at all.

Eric's cell phone rang. He answered it, muttered something, and said, "Pete, emergency. You're coming with me." Then he glanced at the mirror, where a gate should be but was not. "June Bug, you're supposed to have the current watch, right?"

"I am."

"Then go get her and get that gate reopened. The rest of you are free to go."

"What do we have?" Pete asked Eric.

"Shots fired. We need to hurry. Neighbors are in an uproar."

The two of them ran down the stairs, out into the graveled parking lot. "Ride with me," Eric said.

Usually they went in separate cars. But Pete nodded and jumped into the passenger seat in Eric's squad car.

They pulled out with lights flashing but no siren, and Eric headed them north.

"That meeting was bullshit," Eric said.

"You need to get rid of Raymond Smetty and Louisa Tate," Pete said. "I think you brought everyone else around."

"Can't. Our troublemakers already know about Lauren. We have to keep them where we can see them. But that's not what I meant. I mean that the meeting was just for show, just to convince Raymond and Louisa that the Cat Creek Sentinels aren't going to involve themselves in this. It'll keep them quiet and out of the way."

The back of Pete's neck started to itch. "That wasn't real?"

"Nope. June Bug came to me when she started tracking live magic from Kerras last night. She backtraced it, found the live spot on the world, and realized it was part of Lauren's work. The rest of us are already on board—we'll do whatever Lauren needs us to do. Which is what June Bug is on the way over to tell Lauren and Heyr right now. But that old saying about keeping your friends close and your enemies closer is true. I didn't want Raymond covering my back if things got bad. But I couldn't let him leave town, either. This was the only solution I could come up with."

Pete felt better. Suddenly he wasn't carrying the whole planet on his shoulders anymore. He exhaled, and turned to Eric. "Good. That's good. So—what about this shooting?"

"There's no shooting. We're taking the back way, and we're going to get a couple of boxes of Krispy Kremes for the station. I just needed to talk with you while I had a good idea of where everyone else was and what they were doing."

Pete was definitely in the mood for a few Krispy Kremes.

Cat Creek

"So y'all are really going to help me." Lauren sat at the kitchen table watching Jake pick at the steamed vegetables he'd previously loved, and trying to adjust to what June Bug had told her.

June Bug leaned back in her chair. "We knew going in that we would. My sister is a problem—as she has been most of her time in the Sentinels. But with the Sentinels, the only way out is to have someone wipe your memory or to die. Since both of those are . . . last-ditch solutions, we find ways around problems. We always have. At least Louisa isn't malicious."

"Like Raymond, you mean."

"I'm not sure that—long term, anyway—Raymond is a problem we can work around. But none of us right now is willing to deal with the Enigma Sentinels. His parents are still alive and still fully active, and it would be difficult to send their son back to them in Enigma with everything about the Cat Greek Sentinels removed from his mind, along with any random memories that didn't get out of the way."

"They sent him to us because they couldn't deal with him. I'm guessing they're hoping we'll do what they didn't have the nerve to."

"You might be right. We've discussed that possibility, Eric and George and I. And while we all agreed it was likely, we also agreed that the price we pay if we're wrong is more than we want to deal with right now. The lower we keep our profile, the more useful we'll be to you. If we end up crawling with Council members, we're going to be tied up pretending everything is normal—and time is something we don't have enough of to waste that way."

Lauren rested her elbows on the table and said, "So—where do we go from here?"

"That's up to you. We'll cover for you, of course—let us know when you need to be gone, and Eric or I or George or Mayhem will always have an excuse for where you are and what you're doing, and we'll be sure we can back it up. We'll make sure it looks like you're always on Sentinel business so that neither Raymond nor Louisa can give any sort of accurate information if they decide to go over our heads. We'll lie for you. If you want us along, we'll travel downworld with you and set up gun emplacements and guard your back—Betty Kay still has the worst case of buck fever after taking out those keth, and she's just itching to get her hands on a gun again. You'll have a hard time keeping her away."

Lauren shook her head and smiled a little. "Perky little Betty Kay, florist, unicorn lover . . . trigger-happy warrior. Who knew?"

"People will surprise you."

Lauren leaned back in her chair and stretched her legs out in front of her and played with her ponytail. "Some of them will." She sighed. "I'd like to say, 'Gee, it's so sweet of y'all to be willing to help out, but if you'll just pretend you didn't see anything, I'll be fine.'"

June Bug waited, then laughed. "But that's not what you're going to say."

"No, it isn't. I need an armed team to follow me in every time I go downworld. Heyr will be there, and Pete will usually be there, but you know how fast things can go to worms."

"I do," June Bug said. "And speaking about something that has nothing to do with worms . . ."

"All right."

"How are you and Pete doing?"

Lauren smiled a little. "I don't know where we're going with that. It's my fault—I want him, and I feel guilty for wanting him, and I'm doing a fine job of making both of us miserable."

"I'm not the one to give advice about romance."

"I never understood why you never found anyone. You could have."

June Bug sighed deeply. "In ten or fifteen years, people will be saying the same things about you, you know. 'She had chances. Why didn't she find someone? She didn't have to be alone.' I was there when Brian spoke to you through Jake—it's not the sort of thing you could tell most people, but you already know you had someone once. And somewhere you have him still."

"He told me to move on."

"But you can't."

"I don't seem to be able to."

"Mama, I hate broccoli," Jake said suddenly. "I want cookies for supper."

Lauren stared at her son, who'd been remarkably quiet, and burst out laughing. "Eat four more bites and I'll let you have some cookies."

"Four is yuck."

"Four." Lauren took Jake's fork from him and scooted food around on the plate, separating the bites he needed to eat off to one side. "Eat those. And then you can have some cookies."

He narrowed his eyes and tipped his head to one side. "Four cookies?"

"We'll see. Eat." Lauren looked at June Bug. "Not a big plus to any adult relationship. I keep him with me. Right with me. All the time. I never let him out of my sight or out of arm's reach; I don't dare."

"You do what you have to do. Pete would be willing to work around the problems, I think, and Jake is a wonderful little boy—"

"Yes," Jake interrupted. "I *am* a wonderful boy. And modest, too."

"I was just about to say that," June Bug said to him.

"Eat your broccoli," Lauren told her son, and to June Bug said, "Unfortunately, I've already mentioned his modesty to him," Lauren said. "Which is why he says that. He just fails to get the proper note of facetiousness in his voice when he does it."

"Kids are immune to irony." June Bug leaned forward and looked at Lauren earnestly. "From an old lady to a young one, I'm going to give you some unwanted advice. The time goes faster than you think it ever could, and all the things you promise yourself you're going to do tomorrow pass you by. Opportunities not taken haunt you—I think that's why old people don't sleep, Lauren. The ghosts of all the chances we failed to take whisper in our minds until we could no more sleep than be young again. If you make a mistake, you can look back on it and at least say, 'I learned something from that. I tried. I failed, but I tried.' If you don't even try, all you can do is wonder. It might have been a mistake, but it also might have been the best thing that ever happened to you, and you can never know because the chance is gone, and it won't be back."

"You think I should take a chance with Pete."

"I think you should know that when you get old, you will regret every single thing you wanted but were afraid to try a million times more than you regret any mistakes you made in trying." June Bug stared down at her hands, flexing them, frowning a little. "I have lived a coward's life, Lauren, afraid of my dreams. Some things I wanted I couldn't pursue because that pursuit would have hurt other people. I don't regret doing the right thing. But some chances I didn't take just because I was afraid. And now I'm one of those old people, haunted by ghosts of what might have been, and I have no memories of what was to silence them."

Lauren sat, staring at her hands.

June Bug said, "If you have dreams you want to pursue, the time to pursue them is now. There is no perfect time, and there is no better time. There is only the time you lose while you're making excuses."

CHAPTER 16

Herb's Steakhouse, Bennettsville, South Carolina

THE SENTINELS—minus Raymond and Louisa—met in Bennettsville at Heyr's request. Heyr had picked a steakhouse on the north side of town, a big, rambling place with red-and-white-checked tablecloths and baked potatoes the size of footballs and steaks that sizzled so loudly as they traveled from the kitchen to the tables that Lauren almost ordered one.

But she'd eaten already, and Jake was falling asleep on her lap, and somehow she didn't think this gathering was really about the steaks.

It was about protecting her, maybe. Heyr had been close-mouthed and strange ever since June Bug's announcement that the Sentinels were going to back her.

The rest were eating—chewing absentmindedly on steaks that deserved better, sipping at beers slowly growing warm. In their eyes, Lauren could see worry, the recognition that each person at the table had stepped beyond the comparatively safe harbor that was the Sentinels—that with a single word, a single choice, they had moved into vast unknown reaches.

Here there be dragons, Lauren thought. And they're coming to get us.

It wasn't a happy prospect.

Pete looked at her and then at his plate. Eric stared at his fork as if it were the scepter of a king. June Bug played with the keys on her keychain. Betty Kay stared at Heyr with naked lust, and Mayhem stared at Betty Kay with an identical expression.

So not everyone was consumed by dread. Lauren found herself smiling just a little.

And then Heyr cleared his throat, and fear dropped into her stomach like a ball of hot lead, and her arms tightened around Jake.

"I have a proposition for you," Heyr said. "It isn't a happy one, it isn't a pleasant one—but if you accept my offer you'll be able to stand against the Night Watch, and maybe win. And you won't die doing it."

"Not dying is good," Pete said. "I'm all in favor of that."

Eric looked at him sidelong and said, "I'd be inclined to agree. But I'm sure there's an old saying somewhere about being wary of gods bearing gifts."

"It's not a gift," Heyr said. "Unless you want to look at it as a gift from you to your world and your friends and families—and to each other. It's a sacrifice."

June Bug said, "We're back on familiar territory, then. All my life it's been 'Do this for the good of everyone else. Be a Sentinel, go along with the Council, offer up your life to service—the world needs you.' I wouldn't know what to make of a gift. But I know all about sacrifices."

Around the table, a few soft chuckles.

Heyr smiled sadly. "Perhaps. But I'm asking you to make the ultimate sacrifice."

"You want us to die?" Betty Kay asked. "Like . . . in the line of duty?"

Heyr shook his head. "I want you to live." At the bewildered expressions he got from that remark, he added, "Sometimes dying is easier. *Usually* dying is easier. And I'm asking that you don't. That you stand and fight beside me."

Eric shook his head and started to laugh. "Sure. No problem, Heyr, old boy. We'll just live. And the Night Watch—what? The Night Watch is just going to fade into the background because we decide to live? Is it that easy?"

"It's that easy, and it's that hard. I can make each one of

you immortal in this world. I can make you all gods in this world. But there's a price."

"We've seen the price of immortality," Lauren said. "Soullessness, endless dying and returning, loss of self and humanity . . . a growing hunger for death and evil." She couldn't understand how he could even bring this up. *He* didn't trust Molly—how could he think that making more Mollys would help the Sentinels' situation, or save the world?

Heyr raised a hand to stop her. "I'm not suggesting you join the Night Watch or the legion of death-eaters. There's another way."

They were all looking at him, waiting—not really wanting to hear what he had to say, because it wasn't going to be good, but needing to hear because he had offered them a bit of hope.

Save your friends, save your families, save your world. Jake's weight against Lauren was all the reason she needed to hear him out. The monsters were coming for her, and Heyr said, *You can live.*

"I can take you upworld. To Kerras at first, later farther up the line. I can . . . fit you to the upworld so that it becomes your homeworld. I can make you old gods here. And you— when you become old gods, you can make yourselves immortal. You cannot die so long as your world lives."

"So now would be a bad time to be an immortal on Earth," Eric said.

Heyr nodded. "The worst. Except that if no one steps up and chooses this path, I don't think there's going to be another time. This is our last stand."

Mayhem shrugged. "But . . . what you're saying is that we can be gods in our own world. We can live forever. And we can be the heroes who come riding in at the last minute and save everything. I may be stupid, but I don't see the sacrificing part of this."

Lauren looked at him, and remembered talking to Molly, and thought, *No, you wouldn't.*

Heyr shrugged. "If it were all good, Loki and I wouldn't be the last of the Æsir still here."

Lauren stroked Jake's hair and felt him shift in her lap, snuggling closer. She pressed her face into his hair and breathed in. He smelled of shampoo and autumn leaves, sunshine and warmth. He'd always smelled like that. She would have known him blindfolded. She thought about Jake, about immortality. The problem with immortality wasn't going to be watching friends and family grow old and die in the blink of an eye, then; the Æsir had already been through that. They'd stayed immortal—and then something else had changed, and they'd moved on.

"To become immortal, you have to take on the life force of the world you inhabit," Heyr said. "You feel what your world feels. You feel what the people of your world feel. ALL of them. You bear the foulness of the torturer and the pain of the tortured. You share in birth and in death, in every triumph, and in every tragedy." He closed his eyes, and for a moment he looked pale to Lauren, and almost fragile. He took a slow, deep breath. "You learn to block out a lot of it after a while—to dim it down. But this world is so full of the poisons of the Night Watch and so near its own death that after you've done the very best you can do, once you've blocked out almost everything, what remains is still terrible. At first, though, you aren't going to be able to get enough of a hold on the pain to block any of it, so it will all come in, and it's bad enough that it would kill you if you could die. But you can't—so you live in it, and through it. If there is a hell, it's the first days or weeks of immortality, when the whole pain of this world sits on your shoulders, when you are every person on the planet crying out for help at the same time that you are every monster on the planet drawing pleasure from his victim's pain, when you would give anything to make it all stop."

"But you can't, can you?" Eric asked. "The change is permanent. Irreversible."

"No," Heyr said. "Quitting is the easiest thing in the

world. It's easier to reverse immortality than it is to grab
onto it. You just let go of your hold on the life of the world.
If you do, you'll stay an old god, but you'll be a mortal one.
Being an old god is all the pleasure, none of the pain. But the
Night Watch can kill old gods, and they seek them out at
every opportunity and kill every one they find, to prevent old
gods from getting any ideas about standing against them.
Which is why old gods stay out of the way and don't make
any waves. A lot of them thought they were going to be heroes once upon a time. They thought they were going to
grasp immortality and stand against the fall of life—but it's
hard to stand, and on dying worlds it just keeps getting
harder. Immortality is hard, quitting is easy—but the only
people who are going to be able to stand against the Night
Watch and win are the ones who stay."

"How do you get through it?" June Bug asked.

Heyr gave her a big grin. "You laugh and drink and boast
and fight and fuck. It all eases the pain, at least for a little
while. You stand with your fellow heroes, your fellow gods,
and raise up your bands of warriors, and draw your line in
the dirt and tell the Night Watch, 'This line you shall not
cross.'" He stared at his bottle of beer, the smile dying away,
and he took a long, hard drink. His voice dropped, until he
seemed to be speaking to himself. "And worlds fall anyway,
because death is so much easier than life, and destruction is
so much easier than creation, and the wide, smooth path
beckons to so many more than the narrow, hard one." He
looked up at all of them, and shook off the mood. "But now
Lauren is doing what no one has ever been able to do before.
She's reversing the death of worlds—and that means that being an immortal and standing against the Night Watch is not
a doomed exercise in ethics anymore. It has meaning. We
can fight, and we can win."

The catch to being immortal would have to be something
like that, Lauren thought. Living inside the nightmare of the
world. She considered her magic, her gateweaving, the way
she bound upworlds to downworlds and linked them all by
her love. And she wondered if she would be able to love her

world and the people on it if she knew them too well. If she were privy to the thoughts of not just the evil people but also the good ones. Because even good people hid darkness within themselves. If the pain and evil of the world filled her, would she still be able to love it enough to save it?

And what of Jake? She couldn't become immortal if he wasn't. And even if she could make him immortal—and from what Heyr said, it sounded like something that each person had to do for himself—how could she do that to a child? How could she fill him with every horror on the planet? He'd get all the good, too—but Heyr hadn't spent a lot of time talking about all the good in the world, had he?

Lauren looked at the other Sentinels, wondering what they would say.

Pete cleared his throat. "I don't know about the rest of you, but I want to be able to fight. I want to have a chance of winning." He looked at Lauren. "I have something worth fighting for." He turned to Heyr. "I'm in."

"The first of the new Æsir," Heyr said, and raised his beer to him.

"And the second," Eric said, and shrugged. "In for a penny, in for a pound. I can't stand on the sacrifices of my ancestors and the blood they spilled fighting for home and family and freedom and survival and not offer myself up when the need arises. I love my country. I love my world. The things you love, you fight for."

"I'm in, too." Betty Kay nodded at Eric. "I have a chance to make a difference when it really counts. I'm afraid, and I may not be strong enough—but I won't know unless I do it."

Heyr nodded. "You're stronger than you think you are."

And Betty Kay gave him a grin that was both happy and fierce. "That's what I'm counting on."

Darlene stared at her hands, and June Bug chewed on a thumbnail, and George had pulled an old slide rule out of his briefcase and was fiddling with it, his eyes unfocused. Lauren understood their ambivalence. Basically, Heyr had told them all, You can be a god and you can save your world—but it's going to suck.

Not a real strong sales pitch, that.

Mayhem sighed. "I have the awful feeling that this is a huge mistake. I hate pain. I'm a complete wuss. But I can't *not* do it."

Darlene gave him a sidelong look and said, "I was counting on you to chicken out—if you did, I could."

Heyr looked from Mayhem to Darlene and said, "If you don't want to do this, don't. Nothing you do will ever be harder, or hurt worse."

But Darlene said, "Like Mayhem, I just can't *not* do it. It matters too much."

George dropped his slide rule back into his briefcase, and closed the briefcase, and looked up at all of them, and Lauren realized that tears were dripping down his cheeks. "I have a wife I love. I have kids I love. I thought I'd lost them when the flu came through, but they made it. I dodged one bullet, and that may be the only lucky break I get. I have to do this for them—to protect them, to give them a world to live in. But doing it, I'm going to lose them. I'm going to watch them get old and die and leave this life without me, and I'll tell you right now I don't know that I *can* do that. I might fight with you for a while and then quit. Put down the gloves, tear up my ticket, and . . ." He looked down again. "I'm sorry. I should be stronger. But I'm not."

"This is not an obligation to any of you," Eric said. "When I told you we might have to take our fight into the mouth of Hell, I didn't intend that we should take up residence there. Now . . . well . . . you are already heroes. You have already given your lives over to the service of humanity. You have already sacrificed."

June Bug sighed. "I'm old. I'm tired. I want to carry the pain of the world on my shoulders about as much as I want to know what all of y'all think when you wake up in the morning, which is not at all. And I want to live forever in this skin even less than that." She closed her eyes, and for a moment she looked ancient. "What I want most in all the world is just to reach the natural end of my days and go wherever the people I loved have gone. I miss them." Then she pulled her shoulders back and lifted her chin and looked at all of them. "This can't be about me or about what I want. I'll serve because I can. I'll deal with forever because that's what I have to do to serve."

And that left Lauren alone among them—the sole holdout against immortality.

They were turning to look at her, expectant.

She wanted to tell them yes—she wanted to be the hero with her sword unsheathed, charging headlong against the enemy arrayed before her, heedless of her own danger. But she could not. "I don't know that I can carry the weight of immortality as Heyr describes it and still do what I must do," she said. "I owe much of the magic that is pulling the worlds back together to an idealism I don't think I could sustain if I saw everything about everyone. I'm not sure I'd be able to love what is best in everyone if I were constantly drowning in their worst."

Heyr was nodding as if he understood. "I thought that might be the case. I would prefer knowing that the Night Watch couldn't touch you, but if I have to choose between you at risk and fighting them effectively, and you safe but with your magic destroyed, I have to choose you at risk. I'll protect you to the best of my ability, imperfect though that is. We're in this together."

He reached a hand across the table, and Lauren scooted closer to the table without waking Jake, and clasped it. Pete put his hand atop the two of theirs—and then George and Mayhem and June Bug and Betty Kay and Darlene and Eric did the same.

"To the new Æsir," Heyr said softly.

"To the new Sentinels," June Bug added.

"To the stands we take, and the line we hold," Eric said.

And Lauren said, "To the things worth fighting for—life and love, home and family, friends and freedom."

Baanraak's Demesne, Kerras, to Research Triangle Park, Raleigh, North Carolina— Baanraak of Silver and Gold

Baanraak finished chanting the long version of the Salute to the Sun at Close of Day just as the sun, dull red against a sky of pinks and purples, dropped below the horizon. Baanraak bowed, and held the bow out of respect.

In darkness he rose, and inhaled the sweet air into his lungs, and listened to the sounds of life in the world he had made, and he knew, suddenly and with certainty, that Molly would be coming for him soon. She would seek him out because of the bonds they shared—the bond of hunters, the bonds of silver and gold, the bond of shared pain. And of shared nightmares. She walked through his dreams, wielding her sword, seeking his life. And he walked through her nightmares, aware of her sleeping, wanting to make her understand him. Or he wanted to make her *into* him. His desires still churned in him, muddy and confused. It had been long since he'd desired anything, and now he desired much, most of which could only exist at the expense of his other desires.

There had never been anyone—anything—like Baanraak before. In the history of his universe and his worldchain, he had been unique, though he had not recognized his uniqueness for what it was until he discovered Molly and saw in his reflection how different he was from the others he'd mistaken for brethren.

He would get to Molly through Lauren, talk to her through Lauren. He could not approach her directly—she would attempt to kill him, and at least one of them would die again. Maybe both of them. He needed an intercessor. He needed Lauren. It was time. He stood with wings outstretched, reveling for one final moment in the shape of his flesh, in the way he belonged in this world of his making. Then he closed his eyes and dug talons into the rock and drew into his body the power that would twist his form, shrinking himself into the rough approximation of a human.

He did not worry about the details—he would provide himself with those when he reached Earth. For the moment, he wanted only to displace as much body mass as he could and to approximate general shape, so that when he found the identity he wanted, he could take it with minimal loss of time. He could not just compress his true mass into the necessary size—this disguise needed to be perfect, and perfect meant not leaving footprints four inches deep when walking across lawns, or collapsing chairs when sitting in them.

The pain devoured Baanraak—he shifted and re-formed every cell in his body, stripping away everything not essential, literally ripping himself apart, cell from cell, and the fire tore him and clawed him until he collapsed on the rock in a heap. He trembled and panted, while the fire raged through his flesh.

The pain became bearable again and he stood up—a roughly human thing, with two crude arms with workable hands and two crude legs with stump feet, a torso, a lumpish head, and rudimentary eyes, with his resurrection ring buried all the way inside him.

When the pain ebbed to the point where Baanraak could think again, he got to his feet. He was small and weak, no longer simply a rrôn disguised, with mass and power at his call. Amputated in every direction, wingless and tailless and short-necked and small-bodied not just in appearance but in fact, raw and fresh, his flesh sought matter that it could absorb, that he might rebuild himself. He had to fight against his body's ache to return to its true form. He stilled himself. He had done this before—the Night Watch all did it when working in secret, in places where they had to not just pass as human but be human. It had been a long time, but he was no stranger to flesh other than his own.

He stilled himself. In this time spent in his own little domain, he had abandoned discipline. He had let himself play, and had fallen into the habits of childhood, and had lived for a time in a fantasy. No more. He was Baanraak, at whose name the very Night Watch trembled.

He was Baanraak, who drank the death of worlds.

He was Baanraak. And he was going hunting.

He shook off the feeling of weakness that assailed this new flesh. He embraced the pain and accepted it; pain had made him, and pain would in the end give him those things he sought. He ran the live fire through himself, letting it bite himself, and created for himself a man-size mirror, silver-backed, square and sturdy. He set it in a stone frame and melded the frame into the living rock of his perch. When he did not need it anymore, he would destroy it. But it would be convenient to have a waiting gate into which he could slip at need.

He rested his fingers against the glass and sent his mind spinning through the void, searching for one very specific man: young, single, attractive, rich, powerful, admired, corrupt . . . and conveniently located. He found that man in Hahlen Geoffrey Nottingham, well-diversified tech entrepreneur and billionaire with his main offices in Research Triangle Park in Raleigh, North Carolina. Nottingham was working late. He had everything Baanraak needed conveniently at hand.

Baanraak waited until Nottingham's secretary, also working late, and at that instant discussing some task with her boss, went back to her own office. Then Baanraak stepped through the gate right in front of Nottingham's office door, closed the door, and locked it.

He turned, and Nottingham stared at him, frozen with shock and disbelief and horror for just one instant. Of course—Baanraak didn't look human. He looked like a mass of raw pink flesh on a two-legged armature. Nottingham took in a breath to scream, and in the split second before he did, Baanraak reached into Nottingham's mind and silenced him.

No, he said into his prey's thoughts. *Neither that nor the buzzer to call her.* He locked Nottingham's muscles.

He walked across the office, many-windowed, plush-carpeted, and vast, around the fine teak-and-ebony desk, to the man in his silk suit and his club tie, and reached out lumpish fingers and settled them over Nottingham's face.

He took his time. Baanraak absorbed Nottingham's memories: names and details of friends and associates, knowledge of places, links to accounts and passwords, connections to business deals, and dirty little secrets. At the same time, he absorbed Nottingham's cellular information—body composition, blood type, bone structure, skin composition, finger and retinal patterns, hair structure and composition and growth patterns. When he was done, he wore a perfect overlay of Nottingham; he knew everything Nottingham knew, could do Nottingham's business without missing a step if he chose, could not be discovered as a fraud by any means available to normal human beings. He was Nottingham—if Nottingham had been a god. Silver and gold still marked him, of course; immortality marked him. But he could hide those marks from most of those who could read them. He could pass among even the most cautious of old gods, the most paranoid of dark gods. Further, he could pass in a high enough circle that he was basically free to do as he chose, surrounded by people whose job it was to cover for him and make him look good.

"My problem now being," he said in Nottingham's refined, upscale Charleston Battery accent, "that I don't need two of us."

Nottingham's eyes bulged, and again he tried to scream, but Baanraak didn't let him.

"Your screaming would pose problems for me."

Baanraak stood naked beside Nottingham's desk, and stroked Nottingham's cheek with a finger. "You've been very good at being a very bad boy. You're about to get even better at it. Your friends will be astonished. But you won't be around to enjoy it."

Nottingham's body ignited with a dark fire, an absence of light that flickered through him while he writhed and fought—but silently. Silently. Baanraak didn't like noise, especially with the secretary in the other room.

A hand rattled the doorknob, and Baanraak said, loudly enough that the sound would carry through the door, "I understand, Jim. I'll have to rearrange my schedule, but Susan's still here. I can put her on it right away. I'll drive down tonight, meet with you first thing in the morning." He paused and smiled at Nottingham, who—wide awake and fully aware—was suffering being ripped atom from atom in hellish agony and dead silence. After letting the pause draw out in his pretend phone conversation, Baanraak said, "I can be out the door in fifteen minutes, I suppose, if you want to get together yet tonight. You know how long it will take me to get there. . . . No. I'll drive myself. I'd rather have my own car available, and I'd rather leave everyone else out of this for now." Another artful pause. "That'll be fine. I'll meet you there as soon as I can make it."

Nottingham, nearly burned through by Baanraak's death-fire, faded. Baanraak could devour his death energy, could feed on fresh dying, fresh anguish, could . . . could . . . and should not let such a treat go to waste. A little taste of the death of worlds, but fresh and intimate, no more filling than a doughnut freshly made, but for the instant it lay on the palate, just as satisfying.

Instead, he let the death slip past him, uncaught, untasted. Then, disgusted with himself, Baanraak sped up the dissolution of Nottingham's flesh, and the body vanished in a blink, leaving all the clothes untouched.

Baanraak put them on, rage growing within him. Poisoned by silver, he had let slip a taste of death honed to perfect sweetness by horror and pain and disbelief; he had not fed on his natural food when he hungered for it to the point of aching.

Poisoned by silver. And he thought to capture Molly and make her his heir, when he should destroy her. She had wakened the silver that had been dormant—or at least easy to ignore—through long ages of worlds now dead and lost. He had walked unscathed, untouched, unscarred, through hell after toppling hell, and had not ached for his own lost world or any lost world, nor grieved for the lost dead, nor taken hurt from pain, until Molly.

Silver. The metal of order, the universe's guard against the undead, and a brand, a white-hot poker now shoved into his flesh and left there to constantly burn and smoke.

He closed his eyes and dropped gently into the still place within him, the place beyond breath and scent and sensation, where he became mind without body, where he became reason without distraction.

In that place, he looked at Molly. He wanted her companionship because alone through all the worlds she was the one creature like him that he had found. And he wanted her destruction, because if she were gone he would see no mirror of himself, and he could once again live within the stillness he had wrought for himself without the intrusion of the worlds and all their noise. The scales balanced and gave him no direction.

Within his silence, he looked at himself. He wanted to be Baanraak as he had ever been. And that should have been simple enough—it should have clearly marked out his path for him. Except that he had just rediscovered what he had long forgotten: that he had been Baanraak mortal before he had been Baanraak eternal, and that the living silver yearned for Baanraak mortal with a power that equaled the cold hunger of gold for Baanraak eternal.

No direction. He had no direction. He was a compass in a place with two norths, torn from pole to pole, whipping wildly in this new and terrible shift in the fundament of his universe, he who had once been steady and unwavering and unshakable.

The world was riven, the poles tossed and torn. But he would find Lauren, and through her acquire Molly, and with Molly in his possession he would know what to do. With her in his possession the two of them would line up, either attracted or repelled, and he would know then which path to follow.

Baanraak breathed and came back to the world, and the office, and the moment. Time to move.

He picked up his briefcase, checked to be sure the cell phone, car keys, PDA, and other essentials were in place, and went into his secretary's office.

"What's wrong?" she said.

"Don't ask. What you don't know you can't be drawn

into. I'm not sure how long I'll be gone this time. Put Larry on the Triex deal, reschedule my appointments so that the senior partners handle them, call each of them tonight and say, 'Ruby Bowman vetoed the merger.' You have that?"

She was a good secretary—she did not ask what or why. She wrote his instructions down—but not the line about Ruby Bowman, which was a code phrase that meant, essentially, "The shit has hit the fan; hide all evidence and put everything illicit on hold. Pretend to be legit until this blows over." That phrase would forestall any searches for him by the partners when he didn't reappear. The partners would assume he'd gone to Brazil or Argentina, that he was in hiding, and that he'd resurface when things had cooled down.

In the meantime, Baanraak would be free to move around with unlimited access to Nottingham's money, his persona, his power, and his very fine car. He didn't have to worry about flimsy cover stories or fake IDs—he was exactly who he said he was, and could prove it in any way that might be required.

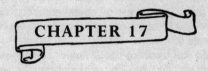

CHAPTER 17

Rockingham, North Carolina

RAYMOND SMETTY turned to Louisa Tate. "Still a chance to back out now," he said.

She shook her head.

"You're sure we shouldn't call the Fayetteville office?" he said.

"Charlotte oversees all one hundred counties in the state. If we call Fayetteville, we're going to end up having to talk to Charlotte eventually anyway, and we're going to lose time. We need them out of here." Louisa snorted, exasperated, and said, "I did the research, boy."

"All right," he said. Now that the two of them were here, he'd lost faith in the idea. He wasn't sure if he could carry this off without screwing it up, and he was sorely tempted to hand the whole thing off to Louisa, who'd gotten on the Internet and rounded up the information for them anyway. But it had been his idea. It was a *good* idea, dammit.

He took a deep breath. "Hand me the stuff."

She handed him a thin sheaf of paper, stapled together at the top left corner. The pages were printouts of the Charlotte FBI website. He flipped through them until he found the one he wanted:

Charlotte Office—FBI
Special Agent in Charge: Fred Buchanan
Assistant Special Agent in Charge: Loren Hammersmith

Law Enforcement Training Coordinator: Dave Boehm
InfraGard Coordinator: Patty Dawson

And below that a list of phone numbers. He called the main one and listened to the phone ring on the other end, his heart in his throat.

I could still back out now. I could. I could just walk away from this and do what Eric said and stay the hell out of the whole thing—

And then, "FBI, Charlotte office, this is Gracie MacDeel. How may I help you?"

Raymond sputtered and stuttered, and finally got out, "I'd like to report a m-m-murder. There's a body of a . . . a foreigner . . . in a barrel in Cat Creek, North Carolina, and I know who killed him and who put the body there."

A faint pause. "All right. Have you reported this to local law enforcement?"

"I can't," Raymond said. "One of the people who put it there *is* local law enforcement. I say anything, I'm dead. The killer's name is Pete Stark, and he's the deputy sheriff in Cat Creek."

"Pete . . . Stark. Cat Creek. Okay." He heard a pencil scribbling across paper, and the woman said, "Hold, please."

He held, suddenly needing to take a leak, wishing to hell he could have thought of some other way of getting rid of Lauren and Pete and maybe Eric that didn't involve him and conversations with the FBI, which had seemed like a real good idea until he was standing at the pay phone with Louisa staring at him with those bugged-out fish eyes of hers.

"This is Fred Buchanan," a guy said on the other end of the line, and Raymond wanted to drop the phone. This guy's voice was not kidding around—had probably never kidded around about anything ever—and Raymond could close his eyes and get what he figured was a pretty good picture of him. Fred Buchanan was, from the sound of his voice, about eight feet tall, and weighed three hundred pounds, all of it muscle, and he ate small children for breakfast. Raymond's balls crawled into his belly to hide, and Raymond would have given anything right then to have had the 'nads to drop the phone and run. But he was transfixed by the voice, which said, "You found Pete Stark, did you? Can you describe him for me?"

Raymond swallowed around a tongue turned to sand in a mouth dry as Hell itself, and said, "Uh, yessir. He's about thirty years old, about six feet tall, I reckon. Light hair cut short, light eyes. He's a right big fellah."

"Scars?"

"Nossir. Not that I've seen." He put a hand over the mouthpiece. "Pete Stark have any scars?"

Louisa shrugged. "Not that I've seen. Lauren might know. You remember to tell him about Lauren now, too."

Raymond nodded. He was a Sentinel. He should not be intimidated by some mere lackey of the FBI. He shouldn't. He took a deep breath, acknowledging that he was intimidated, and said, "No scars that we've seen, sir."

"Sounds like someone we've been looking for now for quite some time," the FBI agent said. "He's dangerous if he's our guy." A pause. "He know you?"

"Yessir," Raymond said, giving Louise a frantic look.

"All right. That's not good. He's dangerous. Very dangerous."

"Well, yeah," Raymond said, feeling sick but justified. Didn't it figure that Pete Stark was wanted by the FBI? Didn't that just beat all?

"I'll come down there," the guy said. "You can show me where he's hiding out, where the body is, point out his accomplices—"

Raymond stopped him fast. "We can't meet with you in Cat Creek. We didn't even dare use a phone in Cat Creek. It's . . . it's just not safe."

A pause. "Then come to Charlotte. Meet with me here in the office, and I'll make sure the two of you stay safe."

Charlotte. A trip into the big city would work, Raymond thought. He and Louisa could take off for a day, drive over, talk with this man. He covered the mouthpiece and said, "He wants us to meet him in Charlotte. Pete's wanted. We'll be doing the Sentinels a favor."

Louisa thought about it for just a second, then nodded. "Find out when."

"Today?"

"No. I have watch, and I never ask to get out of watch. Can't change that now. Tomorrow?"

Raymond asked the FBI agent, "Tomorrow? Y'all open on Saturday?"

"The office is open Monday through Friday for walk-ins, but I'll be there tomorrow. So I'll see you first thing in the morning," the agent told them. "You know your way around town enough to find the place?"

Raymond didn't know his way around Rockingham yet, much less Charlotte. But Louisa had lived in the area all her life, and they had the Internet for maps, and he was getting an itchy feeling between his shoulder blades. He wanted to get off the phone.

He quickly gave the agent his name, and then Louisa's, and said they'd find the place and they'd be there by ten in the morning.

When he hung up the phone, he was sweating. He turned to Louisa and said, "We have to pull this off without anyone knowing we're involved. If the Sentinels ever find out we pointed the FBI at any of our own people, we're dead."

Louisa shrugged. "Once they find out what Pete and Lauren and . . . Molly"— she spat the name—"have been doing, they won't care how the FBI got involved. Don't worry about us. We'll watch our backs until this is over, and then we'll be heroes."

Cat Creek, North Carolina

Pete sat on Lauren's porch swing beside her, watching Jake stack Legos into complex and unrecognizable shapes. "Are you sure you won't reconsider Heyr's offer of immortality?" he asked her. Wrapped inside of that perfectly reasonable request, delivered in an almost casual tone of voice, was Pete's ice-cold utter terror that she was going to get herself killed at any minute, and that he was going to be right with her and still be helpless to save her.

"It comes down to where I draw magic from. . . ." She looked down at Jake. "A lot of it is love. A lot of it is fear. Almost all of it is raw emotion—not remembered emotion, but what I'm feeling right at the moment when I create the links between the worlds. In a way, those links are me—and if I was safe, and if I didn't have to fear for myself, I don't know that I could make them."

Pete looked into her eyes and brushed her cheek with his thumb. "I can feel that love when you make the siphons. I can feel the strength and the passion in you." He took a deep breath, deciding to ask a question that had been crawling around in the back of his mind since the dinner with Heyr and the rest of the would-be immortals. "Is loving . . . someone else . . . sort of like that, too? Do you think that if you fell in love again you wouldn't be able to give as much of yourself to rebuilding the magic?"

She studied him for a long moment, and a smile started, and without any warning she wrapped her arms around his neck and kissed him full on the lips—a deep, hard, passionate kiss that sent his blood surging and made his heart race in his chest like a caged cheetah. Before he could respond, she pulled away, and said, "I don't think that at all. And though I hadn't thought of it until you asked that question, more love in my life could only be a good thing. I think." She frowned a little, and he waited for the guilt to show up in her eyes. But it didn't.

Lauren bit her lip. "I'm going to have to do some thinking, Pete. I'm definitely going to have to think this through—but . . ." Her voice trailed off, and she shrugged. "I don't know."

Pete nodded, afraid to hope anymore, but still feeling that kiss on his lips. "It comes down to this. You do what you have to do to get through this. I'll do everything I can to back you up. I'm here for you. I'm going to make sure that I'm always here for you." I love you, he thought, but *that* was something he didn't dare say. Not yet.

She reached out and took his hand. "Thank you."

He gave her hand a gentle squeeze. "Heyr wants to start taking us through to Kerras as soon as possible, to . . . transform us. He wants you and Jake with us, so that he can make sure you're safe."

Lauren nodded. "I'll go with you when you do your transformation." She grinned a little. "Even if I didn't have to, I'd still go."

Pete looked at his watch and sighed. "I'm due in at work in forty-five minutes. I guess I ought to go home and change."

Lauren nodded. "I'll see you later."

"You'll be all right?"

"Heyr's around."

"He would be," Pete said, feeling ungracious. Heyr could keep Lauren safe, and he couldn't—yet. But that didn't mean he had to be happy about the old god's hanging around. Heyr made no pretense of his interest in Lauren—just as he made no pretense of his interest in Betty Kay, or in Darlene. . . . Pete didn't like the direction his thoughts were taking. He and Lauren stood, and he gave her a quick hug, and waited while she and Jake went into the house. And then he left.

He was scheduled to become an immortal after his shift. For just a moment—until he considered the implications—that struck him as funny.

Somewhere Far Downworld—Baanraak of Beginner's Gold

Baanraak sprawled on a broad, hot rock beneath a blazing desert sun, miserable. Something was wrong with him. He felt shattered. Broken.

He knew that he knew how to fade himself. Knew that he knew how to become invisible to the prey he wanted to spy on, because he could remember wrapping light around himself and vanishing from all knowing. He could remember glorious stillness, silence of the mind and of the body. He knew he held within himself not just the mastery of his own thoughts, but also mastery over thoughts of other dark gods.

But he could not make anything work. He could not find his silence, he could not fade from sight, and he could not make sense of what had happened to him. It was as if a part of him had gone missing. As if *most* of him had gone missing.

He'd felt like this since returning to life.

He didn't think that was coincidence. She had done it to him—whatever had happened was her fault. She had thought to destroy him, and evidently even as she'd tried that she had planned to render him toothless if she failed.

But he was not toothless. Damaged, yes—but not so damaged that his mind was muddled about what he should do in response. Whatever she'd done to him had given him back his clarity and his decisiveness, even if it had laid waste to his hunting skills.

He could not understand why he had once wanted to possess her; what bizarre turns had his mind taken to even touch on such idiocy? They had nothing in common—he felt no more kinship with her than he felt with any meal. Perhaps, then, he had been broken before, and whatever she had done to him had cured him. Because at last he knew exactly what he had to do with Molly the Vodi. He had to find her, kill her, and destroy her resurrection ring.

When she was dead and dust, and when he knew she would not return, then he would come back to this quiet downworld. Here he would make his way back to the place where silence lay. He would relearn all that he had lost. He would recapture light and wrap it around himself as a shield, would find the inroads to the minds of the dark gods, would become once again the Baanraak who made the living weep and the dark gods shiver. She would not conquer him. Her magic would fail her, and she would fall, and he would continue.

He uncurled from his rock and unfurled his wings. Time to go hunting.

Cat Creek to Kerras

Saturday morning, with Cat Creek gray on gray, bleak, leaves falling, the trunks of trees soaked black and the roads shining black with wet, and no spots of color to erase the grimness of the day. Rain dripped and sprayed and gusted, and the wet cold chilled Lauren straight through to the bone. The heroes met in the shed behind her house, in her father's old workshop. She'd set up a gate for them, and Heyr had tested it, and the two of them had confirmed that the rrôn creator of the live spot on Kerras was gone.

Eric said, "We don't have anyone watching the gates. Louisa took off last night after her shift to visit a sick cousin, and I couldn't reach that idiot Raymond. So we need to do this quickly, so that nothing happens to the gates while we're gone. But"—he grinned a little—"the upside is that if we're quick about it, our two biggest thorns aren't going to suspect anything."

Heyr said, "It won't take long." He gave each Sentinel a careful look. "Remember—you can back out of this at any time. You're going to have to hang on to that thought. Memorize it now, because after today thinking will be hard and painful for quite some time." He sighed. "I'd take you one at a time, and slowly over the course of weeks, to let each of you adjust to the changes before I altered the next one of you. But we don't have a year to do this. I don't think we have long at all. Weeks. Maybe days. I've been through the end of worlds before, and it feels like the Night Watch is working toward closing this one out. So . . . if we're going to fight them here, for this last human world"—he took a deep breath—"we do it now."

And that was it. Lauren scooped Jake into her arms and the Sentinels started stepping through the gate, one after the other, and when they were through, she moved in with Heyr right behind her.

They were going to create the immortals of a new mythology. Marching off to save the world on a crappy, miserable day; unheralded, unappreciated, unsung. If they failed, no one would ever know. But if they succeeded . . . no one would ever know.

With that thought possessing her, she soared through infinity and eternity and came out the other side to a world that had, the last time she'd floated ghostlike across its surface, been nothing but cold and darkness—ice and stone and airless hell.

Now it was Earth's Jurassic Period with six-limbed dinosaurs, and in its odd, alien fashion it sang to her. She felt the love in the place, and she was moved. Whoever had created it had poured passion and hope and desire into it, and had given birth to a tiny, perfect gem.

They all stood atop the rock where they had seen the rrôn sleeping, for a moment just looking around at the artwork someone had created out of nothing. The sun looked warm, breezes blew, insects hummed through the tall grass, birds were everywhere, and below the rock, beasts of all sizes grazed or napped around a shimmering lake that was sapphire-blue at the shores, darkening to bottomless black in the center. The water was so clear that Lauren could see fish swimming beneath the surface, and either the water magnified their sizes or they were big enough to make a lunch of her and Jake.

It didn't look like a safe world for people. But it was impossibly beautiful.

Pretty dinosaurs, Jake told her. He spoke into her mind. None of the Sentinels had solid form—they were wraiths, or muses, or ghosts, animated shadows. Heyr was the only solid one among them, the only one Lauren couldn't see right through. She couldn't smell the air or feel the sun's warmth. She wasn't complete enough to do that. But she wanted to.

Then Heyr turned to Pete and said, "Ready?" and Lauren could hear the faint whisper that was Pete's shout.

"Do it."

Heyr reached out a hand, and it moved through Pete. He backed out a little, and suddenly Pete started to fill with light from the inside out—the light so bright and beautiful it

stunned Lauren and warmed her at the same time. She had
seen light like that once before—at the moment when, fighting to keep her son, she challenged the administrators of
Hell and looked into the face of the eternal *I am*.

That light was life and love made manifest. It was wondrous. And she yearned for it—yearned for its touch and its
power and its comfort. Before her eyes, Pete became as radiant as the brightest star, a creature of impossible beauty. Jake
reached for Pete, and Lauren understood completely. She
wanted to go to him, too, and fill herself with everything that
he was.

Then the light faded and Pete was Pete again—but now
solid, standing firmly on the rock beside Heyr. He looked
down at himself and touched his shirt, his pants, his arms
and hands. Patted his face. "That's it?" He looked at Heyr. "I
feel great," he said. "But . . . normal."

"You are normal here. When we get back to Earth, you'll
be an old god. And when you reach into the world's life and
bind yourself to it, you'll become an immortal. Then . . .
then it hurts. It's real pain, Pete. I didn't exaggerate to make
it seem worse than it is. You'll be as vulnerable as the world
you bind yourself to. And you'll be vulnerable the second
you unbind yourself to go between the worlds to another
world; and to be immortal there, you have to bind yourself to
that world for as long as you're there, even if it's only for a
few minutes. If you don't, you'll end up some dark god's
lunch. This isn't easy; it isn't like the immortality of the
Night Watch, which requires no thought and no effort and is
always with them. It's both better and worse. You can't be
killed as long as your world lives. But they're trying to kill
your world, and are close to doing it."

"I know that. I understand. And I'm ready to do what I
have to do."

Heyr nodded. "Then who's next?"

Lauren watched him fill them all up, changing them all. *I
could have that. I could have it for me, and for Jake. We
could feel that light again—we could take it into ourselves.*

She didn't slip, though. She didn't let herself give in to the temptation. She held fast while the people she knew became old gods and left her behind. She was doing the right thing.

She was almost certain she was doing the right thing.

Kerras to Cat Creek

Heyr reached out, and Pete felt the power of Kerras's life energy and Heyr's magic fill him and change him—it was fresh and vibrant and alive and full of love, and it resonated with Lauren's presence, with her touch. This world was her gift as much as it was the gift of whoever had created the place. And the embracing, trusting, hopeful love he felt vibrating through him was the thing she was afraid she would lose.

If she lost it, that would be an unthinkable tragedy.

Maybe—maybe she was right not to accept immortality. Weight settled into him, and Pete began to need to breathe, began to fight gravity again, with the fullness of bone and muscle and blood. He could feel himself becoming a man in this place, instead of a ghost.

It didn't take long, and then the magic faded out of him and he felt . . . normal. And bereft. He wanted to feel that light within him forever. But it wasn't just the light—it was the person who had shaped the light in this place. He looked at the wraith-shape of Lauren holding Jake. It was her love. He wanted that love for himself. He wanted *her*.

And that was why he was doing this, wasn't it? Deep down, beneath the nobility of saving the world from destruction, wasn't there some part of him that was still in sixth grade, wanting Celie McDermott to notice him and taking her bookbag and teasing her so she would?

He wanted to think he was deeper than that. But the cynical part of him whispered, "Look, buddy. You're just like every other male on the planet—you'd figure out a way to walk on water if you thought it'd get you laid."

He watched Heyr change the other Sentinels, and that was amazing—but it wasn't what he'd hoped for. He'd wanted something that would make him feel like he always imag-

ined Odin and Thor and Freya and Loki and the rest of the
gods of Asgard felt. Or, for that matter, Zeus and Aphrodite
and the gods of Olympus. He wanted to feel like he could
stand against anything—like he could pick the world up on
his shoulders and move it to safety. And he wanted to feel
that the people fighting with him could do the same. Instead,
he just felt like a man. Nothing special.

Then Heyr cocked an eye skyward at big birds that were
beginning to cluster, and said, "Time to go home."

When they returned to the cold and the rain and the drea-
riness of Cat Creek's crummy day, Pete still didn't feel
much different. The cold didn't seem as biting as it had
when he left, but that he could attribute to the day's warming
up a bit as easily as he could blame it on his new status as
one of Earth's old gods.

Lauren and Jake and Heyr were last through the gate. Pete
felt better as soon as he saw Lauren in solid form again.

"You're all right?" Heyr asked Lauren.

"I'm all right," she agreed. "It was hard watching everyone else and knowing I wouldn't be joining you . . . but I'm
fine." She kissed Jake on the top of the head. "*We're* fine."

"Good," Heyr said. "Then you need to leave. Head into
the house, make sure you have your knife with you, keep
Jake close. I'll be in as soon as I can, and while I'm out here,
I'll keep my feelers open for any trouble. But I can't leave
these folks vulnerable, and you don't want Jake to be here
for what happens next. Just be careful."

Lauren looked like she wanted to argue. But after starting
to say something and then stopping herself in mid-breath,
she just nodded. "I'll see all of you when you're finished."

When she was gone, Heyr turned to face them all, and he
wasn't smiling anymore.

"Now it gets hard. Right now, you are old gods here,"
Heyr said. "But you are not immortal. Immortality is a burden you have to pick up for yourself. I can tell you how to do
it, but I can't do it for you. And I can't help you if it proves
to be more than you can take. All I can tell you is that you

can let go, go back to being what you are right now, and we can either change you back to what you were before, or you can run downworld far enough that the Night Watch won't look for you."

Pete and Eric exchanged grim looks. Eric said, "I hired temp coverage from Laurinburg for a couple of days. We can both do this right now so long as at least one of us is able to function by Tuesday."

The others were nodding. "Three-day weekend," Terry said. "For me, it's now or not until much later."

"There isn't going to be a good time for me," Betty Kay said. "I just put a message on the machine saying I was sick and referring everyone to Scott's. It'll cost the shop some business, but . . . I'm not really here for the business anyway, fun though it is."

"We're ready," June Bug said. "What do we have to do?"

"The first time, it's easiest if you lie flat on the ground. Face up or face down doesn't matter. Naked is best, but so long as you have bare skin in contact with the ground you'll be able to find the world pulse. Your will is your word here now—what you say will be, as if you were on any of your downworlds." He sighed. "Come on outside. It's easier if I show you."

Darlene said, "It's . . . raining out there."

Pete found Heyr's reaction to that genuinely funny. Heyr told her, "First rule of immortality. Sometimes you get wet."

Everyone else laughed, and after a moment even Darlene managed a little chuckle.

They followed Heyr out to Lauren's backyard, with the thick centipede grass turned brown for the coming winter, with the soft faraway hissing of the tires of cars driving down wet streets far from where they stood, with the echo of the voices of kids unseen playing in the rain. It was cold out, and dreary. But not unbearable.

Heyr sat on the wet grass. "It doesn't matter where you lie down—just find yourself a place where your fingers can push through the grass down to dirt. You want to have a clear contact with the ground."

Pete dropped to the ground and sprawled on his back. Eric and George and Terry and June Bug did the same. Both Darlene and Betty Kay hesitated, looking at each other with shared expressions of distaste. And then Betty Kay sighed and sat down on the wet grass, and sighed again and lay down. After a moment, Darlene muttered "Whatever," and followed suit.

The hard, sharp blades of centipede grass dug into Pete's neck. He pressed his hands palm down on the lawn, burrowing the tips of his fingers down to dirt. "Got it," he said. The others announced their readiness.

Heyr said, "Close your eyes and exhale until your lungs are as empty as you can make them, and when you inhale, don't just breathe in air. Breathe in the life of the world. Pull it up through your fingertips and the back of your head, through the backs of your legs, through your shoulders, through your loins. See yourself planted like a tree, with roots made of air—very important that you see the roots made of air, or we're going to have to cut you loose and start over—drinking in your nourishment from the planet and breathing out magic the way trees breathe out oxygen."

Pete started forcing the air from his lungs.

Heyr added, "And don't panic when what comes in hurts. It hurts a lot—but the pain won't kill you. Just let it come."

How bad could it be? Really? With his lungs empty to the point of aching, Pete closed his eyes and tried to feel roots of air digging into the ground, pulling in sustenance. The life of the planet, he thought. Green growing things, and animals in forests, and fish in the water. Good stuff. He pulled—and the first sharp blades of pain slid beneath his skin. Don't block it, he told himself. Don't block it. Let it come.

Birth and death. Treachery and betrayal. Poison poured into the air, into the water, into the ground. The movement of tanks and submarines and missiles and troops, war blood-red and angry as open wounds, cities torn and people slaughtered. Forests living and breathing, forests uprooted. Storms tearing across the surface of the planet, volcanoes heaving up the guts of the world in violent spasms, earthquakes ripping the planet and its people flesh from bone.

Birth—babies, human and not, all moving into the world, welcome or unwelcome but alive. Alive. The thin threads of life gave him something to hang on to, something to cling to. The massive outpouring of death was railroad spikes driven into his flesh, into his blood, into his soul until he wanted to scream—or die.

Pete gritted his teeth and the sweat poured from his face and the drizzling rain became cooling, soothing, but not enough—not nearly enough—while the clashing fury of the world in its turmoil, spasming in its death throes, screamed in his head. He was the murderer of a child, and he was the child; he was the rapist in the alley and the rapist's victim; he was every boy on his belly in the dirt with an M-16 in his hands, thinking of home and girl, and he was them when the mortars blew them apart. He was the penitent praying, "Who am I that Thou art mindful of me?" and the angry man praying, "Let them suffer, the perverted bastards—and when they've suffered on Earth, let them burn in Hell forever." And he was the powerful liars in high places, scheming for profit and dealing the death of the world with contracts, and he was the trees falling and the wildlife burning in fires and he was burning and freezing to death, and the babble of six billion voices roared in his head with every voice different and every pain unique.

He sobbed, writhed, choked on bile, arched against the in-rushing torture, fighting to break free from something that wrapped him like an airless cocoon and would not let him breathe or let him go.

A thunderclap in his head shook him just a little—just enough to wedge a familiar voice to the front of his overwhelmed mind. ". . . wall, Pete. You have to build a wall. When you feel it, you can't let yourself feel it all. See a wall around you—thin, because the pain is your immortality. You have to have the pain. But you can fill the wall with insulation. Like cotton batting, or pillows. Something that breathes, but that will keep the noise down . . ."

The voice faded out in a red wash of horror—the slaughter of innocents by a despot, somewhere. He had to stop it. He had to save them.

The thunderclap again. ". . . because I can't do this for you . . . make the fucking wall or you're going to be an immortal vegetable . . . or this is going to take you and you'll lose your grip on immortality and die. Right here, right now."

Die. Yes. Dying sounded good.

But no. He had to protect Lauren.

He fought to hang on to an inch of space in his own mind, and he wrapped a wall around that inch. Pete pictured cotton, loose the way he'd pull it from the boll, saw himself shoving handfuls of raw cotton with the seeds and all into the rifts in that tiny wall where the horror poured in. At first it was like trying to hold back the ocean with a cotton swab. But he discovered that he didn't have to concentrate on one rent at a time; he could stand in the center of the storm that assaulted him and make himself the eye of his own counterstorm. He created a blizzard of white that poured out from him in all directions, raging against the horrors that were to become a part of him, and slowly the onslaught slowed, and the roar of the world's anguish dulled and faded, and he expanded the space he occupied until he could hear what was going on around him again, and think his own thoughts again.

The pain, though—the pain still ate at him from the inside out. Men with sharp knives cutting through him like POWs digging their way to freedom, buzzards tearing at his flesh, agony that he could not find the way to mute or remove.

"It's bad, isn't it?" Heyr said.

Pete opened his eyes and sat up slowly. The others were already sitting—they looked like corpses propped up, and Pete could only imagine that he looked as bad or worse. "*This* is what you feel?" he rasped through gritted teeth.

Heyr nodded. "Maybe a little less than what you're feeling. But that's pretty much it. It's been this way for the last hundred years or so, though it's been getting worse for thousands. Be glad you weren't Loki back in the day—the Æsir punished him for the death of Balder by taking away his ability to block out the pain of the world. For long he was bound here and spread open to all the horrors of this place, forced to suffer the growing anguish and the spreading death. And if it wasn't as bad then as it is now, it was bad enough. He suffered like that for a thousand years before one of the Æsir had pity on him and freed him. Loki—Loki has reason to hate the Æsir, even though he brought much of his pain on himself through thoughtlessness and through treachery. Odin still has hope for him. I see some good in him myself. But that was a great and terrible torture they put on him."

"How do we bear it?" Darlene asked. She sat forward, arms wrapped tight against her chest, rocking. Her eyes weren't focused; her skin was as gray as the day.

"I cannot tell each of you how to bear it. I can only tell you that I bear it because it matters that I live, and it matters that I fight—though in these last years I have been mostly deaf to those who called upon me. The world was dying, and I with it. I dulled the noise as best I could, and hid myself away with work and a woman, and I—even I—prayed for salvation or deliverance, and thought none would come. Odin once said:

> Hard is the earth that deals death for life
> When the soil is gone
> And the harrow breaks.

Heyr stood up. "I suffered. If you stand as one of the new Æsir, you too will suffer. You will hear the cries of those who need you and you will not answer, because not even gods such as we are can be everywhere for everyone. Once we were many, and we answered the cries of those in need. But now most of the true immortals have moved on. The pain here is too great, the need is too great, and the magic . . . the magic was dying, and even such as I—who love Humankind—lost hope."

The pain washed through Pete, and he tasted death sharper than bile, and he was not sure that he was strong enough to stand. Running would be sad, but it wouldn't hurt this way.

George staggered to his feet and leaned one hand against the nearest tree. Tears ran down his cheeks. "I can't do this," he said, his words echoing Pete's thoughts. "I won't abandon you all, but there are things in my head right now that I can't live with. There are pictures in here that I can't see and still stay sane. I need to go back to being just a man." He hung his head. "I thought I could be a hero. But it isn't in me."

"If you aren't running, you're a hero," Heyr told him. "We'll need one of our own to watch Raymond and Louisa, to make sure that they stay well away from what we're doing. We would have had to find someone like you, George, if we hadn't had you. I'll take you to Kerras and change you back as soon as I know who else needs to go. In the meantime, shake off the pain. Pull your roots back in and release the Earth." He turned to the rest of them. "Who else needs to go back? There's no shame in it, people—gods who held their immortality for tens of thousands of years have fled this world because it was too much for them. It's better to live a sane man than a mad immortal."

"Will it always be like this?" Betty Kay asked.

Heyr laughed a little. "That's why *Lauren* matters. The pain isn't as bad as it was. The despair is . . . less. She is healing the wounds, leaching out the poison, bringing back the life that should have been here all along."

"If she dies," Pete said, "everything is lost."

"So we surround her with a wall of us, and we keep her safe." Heyr breathed out softly, a small, tired sigh. "I want her to be a diamond," he said after a moment. "Hard and durable and fierce—as close to indestructible as anything *can* be. But I think she's an opal instead—the softest of the gemstones, fragile and beautiful and full of a fire that rough handling would destroy. That too much pain and horror would destroy. She's the only one of her kind. Maybe she can teach someone else to do what she does, but I don't think so. I think it's simply who she is that creates the magic that unbreaks the worldchain."

They were all finding their way to their feet. Pete stood,

too, feeling shaky and at the verge of vomiting, and he said, "How long until I can think straight—until I'll be anything like myself again?"

"Hours or days. It depends on you." Heyr smiled. "And no matter how terrible you feel, you are still a god now. One of the immortals. You may want to die, but nothing can kill you without killing the whole world with you."

"Does it get easier?"

"For the last few thousand years, it's only gotten harder." Heyr shrugged. "If Lauren and Molly and we Æsir can beat them, it'll get easier. If Lauren can bring the worldchain back from death, everyone will want to be immortal again." He grinned a little. "And the halls of the heroes will once again fill up with gods, and drinking and wenching and merriment and the tales of great feats will fill the world. Right now, we're a lonely little band, and our tales are mostly tragedies."

Heyr took Pete aside and whispered, "About you and Lauren. You love her, and you want her to love you. But if she never accepts immortality, then your immortality will be a wall between the two of you that will just get thicker and higher and harder over time. I've done it. It's hell. And it's a hell that gets away from you over time, with the gap between you and her starting as nothing and becoming impassable within a span of years that will feel like the space between two quick breaths. You can contemplate it now, but in a minute it'll be over—she'll be old and dying and you'll be just as you are right now. And whether she ever comes to love you or not, she'll still be gone, and you will watch her go."

"You've lost someone you loved."

"I'm immortal. I've lost a lot of someones I loved. It doesn't get easier."

"You should have saved them."

Heyr's eyes narrowed and his grin grew feral. "Try it. Try to give her immortality. Now that you know what it costs, now that you're wearing it in your own skin and bones, try to give her forever."

And Pete thought about doing this to Lauren—making her feel like this just so he could keep her—and he couldn't. She didn't want this, and nothing in him would force it on her.

Heyr was watching his eyes. "Right. You got it. Now . . . just keep it in mind. Because for you, this is hard. But it's going to get harder."

CHAPTER 18

Wold Mountain, Oria

Molly woke in a little tent to the sound of a steady, driving rain. The air was cold enough that she could see her breath, and the warmth and softness of her sleeping bag cradled her and embraced her, offering her the promise of womblike comfort and wonderful peace if only she would stay. She sighed and lay staring up at the top of the tent, knowing that she had to stop putting off the inevitable.

If she was going to be a dark avenger and fulfill the purpose of her existence, she had to go back to Earth. The Night Watch was focusing its activities there, and she could not hide in Oria, hunting down Oria's problems, when her first world needed her more. She'd discovered a whole nest of the Night Watch in Washington, D.C.—a group of lobbyists with a stranglehold on the men and women who made policy. Dark gods with poisonous intent, all of them—corporate demons, monsters in silk suits who plotted the destruction of her world over brunch and delivered death with canapés and cocktails and campaign contributions funneled through Swiss banks and offshore accounts.

If she wasn't going to fulfill her purpose . . .

That was another issue entirely. She lay inside the heads of the Night Watch as she hunted them, seeing through their eyes, sensing through their bodies everything that came to them. She could feel the aching emptiness of their lives, but she could also taste death as they tasted it—as a heady rush of power that filled the emptiness for a little while. Hunting, she lived inside a banquet spread before her in addictive bounty, and she had as yet tasted nothing for herself.

But she wanted to. She hungered, and every time she died she came back emptier and hungrier, and the banquet grew richer before her eyes, and more compelling.

She hungered, and her hunger had grown as keen as a good knife. Meanwhile, her desire to be a good girl and fight on the side of truth and justice had tattered with her other human feelings, and had worn thin in places, and she *knew* that she could be one of the Night Watch. Her kinship with them resonated every time she touched one of them, and underscored the fact that in the presence of the living she felt only pain and more pain, and a vague but distasteful shame in the fact of her own existence. The Night Watch was her natural direction, and joining it was her choice to make. She did not have to follow her predecessors among the Vodi into madness and eventual oblivion. She could experience ecstasy. She could rip her life from death itself and grow powerful beyond her own wildest imaginings. She could drink the blood of worlds and walk Baanraak's path, and eventually rule a universe.

She slid out of the sleeping bag and let the cold seep into her flesh. She breathed deeply, feeling the cold burn her lungs, shivering as she exhaled and her breath frosted into swirling plumes.

What did she owe the world?

What did she owe Lauren?

She didn't know. She rested her chin on her knees and wrapped her arms around her legs. It would all just get darker for her—she had no hope anymore. Every death would simply take her closer to the point where she had to either succumb to the call of the Night Watch or destroy herself. There was no third path. She had no doubts anymore why the other Vodi had destroyed themselves. They'd looked into their own futures and they had seen the nightmare that she saw waiting in her own. And they had been strong enough to destroy themselves rather than betray everything they had once held dear.

She had to admire that. Before, Molly had thought her predecessors cowards who had taken the easy way out. But they'd had the same banquet of slaughter and pain and torture and death spread before them that she could see spread before her, and they had chosen to destroy themselves rather than partake.

How much longer was she going to be able to hold out? There would come a time when she no longer cared. When she would not be able to see why she had fought so hard against the coming darkness. The shards of that future already cut into her, and soon enough they would break through.

Perhaps this would be her last chance to avoid becoming the monster that lived inside of her. Perhaps she needed to destroy herself now. Maybe even tomorrow would be too late.

She needed to talk to Lauren. Not that Lauren would understand, but Lauren had a right to know that Molly was going to have to go away. And Lauren—Lauren was fighting right on the front lines, and she deserved more than a note telling her that Molly had gone and wouldn't be back.

Death or oblivion—hell of a choice.

Molly willed breakfast into being—pan-fried potatoes and slabs of country ham; and eggs, scrambled and larded through with New York sharp cheddar cheese and sautéed onions and red and green peppers; a stack of buttermilk pancakes with real butter and real maple syrup; a pitcher of coffee, hot and black; and for dessert, a bar of Dove chocolate. The condemned woman's last meal, she told herself. Her last grasp at being human before making her choice. She sat shivering and naked in the cold because feeling the cold was feeling *something*, and she devoured her feast.

And when she was done, she erased her campsite with a word, and dug a small cave in the side of the mountain out of the living rock, and at the back of the little cave created for herself a mirror. And into the mirror she wove a gate—a link into Lauren's mirror in the foyer of her house in Cat Creek. She looked through it and saw that the way was clear. She dressed herself in jeans and sneakers and a T-shirt, all black, and took a deep breath.

She stepped into the gate and into the green fire that burned her—that did not welcome her but instead reminded her of everything she had lost and could never have again—and she pushed through that eternity into Lauren's foyer. Into the world of her birth. Into the world that had once been steeped in the pain and sickness and despair of strangers.

And she felt nothing.

Cat Creek, North Carolina

Molly walked into the kitchen, and Lauren almost dropped the plate she was washing. Jake, running in circles in the kitchen—yelling "Look, Mama. Look, Mama. Look at me!"—stopped running, stopped yelling, and tore over to his mother to cling to her leg.

Cold blew into the room with Molly, physical cold—outdoor air that clung to her and smelled of rain and pines and winter coming—and something else. Something more frightening. Like an unscheduled eclipse of the sun.

"I finally decided to come back," Molly said by way of greeting.

"First time since . . ." Lauren faltered.

"Since I died here. Yes. Stepping through the gate into your foyer again could have been distressing, I suppose. But it wasn't."

Molly looked exactly the way she had on Oria. That was a problem. "You didn't change when you came through the mirror," Lauren told her.

"Change?"

"You still look mostly Orian—hair, eyes, bone structure, height, weight . . ."

Molly looked down at herself. "Well, shit. That's not going to work." She looked at Lauren with eyes that reflected no warmth, no emotion, nothing. "Right back. Let me see if I can fix this here or if I have to go back."

Lauren felt relief when Molly left the room, and dismay that she would feel that way on seeing her sister leave. Or that she could find it in herself to hope Molly would just go on to whatever else she'd planned to do and not come back.

But just when Lauren thought her unvoiced wish might come true, Molly, looking human, if not as she had once looked, stepped back into the kitchen. "Couldn't fix it here. I had to go to Oria. It doesn't matter anyway." She shrugged. "It's not the big problem. We need to talk."

Lauren's stomach flipped. "Heyr can help you get full magic here, if that's what you need to do . . . things; he's already made most of the other Sentinels into old gods—immortals."

Molly arched an eyebrow. "Interesting. Doesn't have anything to do with me, but it's good to know. That you won't be alone, anyway."

Lauren picked Jake up and held him close. "Why would I be alone, Molly?"

"I left Seolar. I thought you should know, since you're likely to have to deal with some of the fallout. I'd meant to guard him—to watch over him. I told him I would. But . . . it isn't going to work out even that well."

Lauren waited, saying nothing, feeling the cold around Molly as a chill in her heart.

Molly's mouth twisted into something that was probably intended to be a smile. "You see it in me, don't you?"

"See what?"

"The monster beneath the skin. The thing that's just waiting for the last of *me* to die so it can come out and . . . wallow in death." She closed her eyes, and Lauren saw a flicker of emotion pass across Molly's face. Eyes closed, voice soft, Molly said, "It's almost here." She looked up at Lauren. "And the bad thing is, I'm almost past caring. Almost."

Lauren looked at Molly and wanted to cry. She cuddled Jake and said, "Oh, God, I'm so sorry, Molly."

Molly shrugged. "That's the thing. I'm not. This is

like . . . it's like . . . alcoholism, maybe, or Alzheimer's—the biggest symptom is that the worse you get the less you care that it's killing you."

Lauren remembered the Molly she had first met only a handful of months before—a woman with her whole life ahead of her, with joy in her eyes and hope in her heart for a future she wanted, who held on to the belief that she had something worth fighting for.

Mere months, and that was all gone. In its place, what remained of Molly? Some notion of duty, come at emotionlessly and out of cold logic? Some shreds of the woman she had once been, perhaps, but the Molly who sat before her bore little resemblance to the woman she had once been.

"I have a decision to make. No good choices offered, but—but before I decide anything, I wanted to ask you something," Molly said, and Lauren realized they'd been standing there looking at each other without saying anything for an uncomfortably long time.

"Make her go away," Jake whispered in her ear, and Lauren could feel his heart pounding against her, and could feel his muscles trembling as he clung to her.

She stood, rocking him, stroking his hair, and she told Molly, "Sure. Ask away." And she thought, *What the hell are you, that you're scaring my kid like this?*

"When you talked to . . . the mind of the universe . . . the creative force . . ." Molly shrugged and laughed a little, and for that instant she looked and sounded like her old self. "*God* . . . he really mentioned me? Not my soul, already elsewhere and doing fine, but *me*."

"Yes," Lauren said. "He said you had the chance to be a person if you chose to be, that you could create your own soul." She sighed. "He didn't tell me how or give me any clues. He said that there were people who had souls who chose to throw them away, but that you could grow one. Not get one back, but grow one."

Molly nibbled her bottom lip and stared at the floor. She looked young and vulnerable. And then she straightened and the vulnerability fell away, and the emptiness in her eyes made her look a hundred years old. "Doesn't seem too likely," she said. "I'm losing ground faster than I ever thought possible. When I discovered what was happening to me, I believed it would take years for me to lose myself. I really believed that I would be able to hang on to Seolar and my feelings for him at least through his lifetime." She looked up at Lauren. "I thought I would care about you, about what we were doing. . . ." She shook her head and went back to staring at the floor. "I don't. I don't even care about hunting the Night Watch. It's an amusing mental exercise, something to fill up the time. You'd be amazed at how much time there is when you don't sleep and you won't die—at least, not permanently. Lots of hours, Lauren." Molly looked out the back window. "You know what's funny?"

"What?"

"When I first stopped sleeping, after I came back the first time, I told myself that at least I had all sorts of time to paint and write songs, learn some new pieces on the guitar—lots of time." Molly shook her head. "I never realized that I would lose all of those things, too. I haven't forgotten how to draw, or how to rhyme words, or how to find the notes on the guitar. But painting and poetry and music are all emotion-driven. You can have technical skills, but if you can't look at the world and wonder, and if you can't feel pain, or loss, or hope, or love, all art dies." She looked sidelong at Lauren. "So I have all the time in the world and nothing to fill it with but eating and killing. I don't see my growing a new soul out of it, that's for sure."

Lauren sat there, aching for what Molly had lost, and also what she had lost in Molly.

Then Heyr slammed through the kitchen door, and Lauren jumped and clutched Jake, who screamed, and saw that Heyr's war hammer was in his hand and he was getting ready to throw it.

"My sister!" Lauren shrieked, and Heyr froze.

Molly and Heyr squared off against each other, and Heyr said, "This is a dark god."

"She's my sister."

"Perhaps she is a dark god wearing your sister's skin."

"She's my sister."

Lauren could see the muscles in Heyr's arms bunching and flexing. "I need to touch her," he said.

Molly hooked her thumbs into her pockets and lifted her chin. "If you do, I'll make sure you regret it."

Heyr shook his head. "I swear on Odin's eye and my own soul I will not harm you so long as you do not attempt harm against those who are mine." He nodded at Lauren and Jake, and Lauren was tempted to protest the "mine" designation, but kept her mouth shut instead. "I will touch only your forehead, and only for a moment. You are not what you first seem to be, but I do not know what you are."

Molly studied Heyr. It felt like watching two big dogs squaring off, sniffing each other to decide if they should rip each other apart or come to a truce.

Molly nodded. "You may touch me." She stepped within his reach, her eyes on the hammer, still in his hand, and he noticed and slid it into the loop in his belt, and it looked like a normal claw hammer again.

Heyr rested two fingers on Molly's forehead and half closed his eyes and breathed through his mouth, panting a little. Almost immediately, his brow beaded with sweat and his skin grayed. Lauren could see the muscles in his shoulders tighten; cords stood out on his neck. He held the pose, though, for what could only have been a minute or two, but felt like a week.

And then he pulled away, and still gray and sweating, walked without a word to Lauren's kitchen table, and pulled out a chair and dropped into it. He propped his elbows on the table and buried his face in his hands. He said nothing.

Lauren looked at Molly, bewildered, and found an expression of clear curiosity in her sister's eyes. Both of them shrugged at each other at the same time, and Lauren turned to the old god.

"Heyr? Are you all right?"

Heyr raised a trembling index finger—a "One minute" gesture—and sat there until Lauren said, "Do you need a glass of water? Something for a headache? Anything?"

Heyr dropped his hands to the table and looked from her to Molly with blue eyes washed gray. "I don't know how you bear it," he told Molly. "I carry the weight of the world, and I have for time uncounted, and yet I do not know how you can find the strength to breathe."

Molly cocked her head. "Bear what?"

"The weight of that thing inside of you. I've touched the resurrection rings of many a dark god, in my father's hall before the fall of Asgard when I was a child, as a mortal man, and as I am now." He nodded toward Molly. "But not like that one. A tale I offer, if you would accept it—for it speaks to both what you are and, perhaps, to where you will go."

"I have time for a short story, I suppose." Molly walked to the table and took a seat, and Lauren, with Jake still clinging to her, settled into the chair beside Heyr's, on the side opposite her sister.

Heyr said, "Thank you." He took a deep breath, and looking directly at Molly, began. "I was as you once were—in my own world I was born half a god. My father Odin came from upworld and found my mother, who was of Asgard, and took her as his goddess, and raised her to hold in Asgard the powers of the gods. And he taught her the path to immortality, so that they should have each other forever. But I was born before he did that, and so in Asgard I was for a little while mortal and only half a god. Yet because I was the son of a god, I was bigger and stronger than the men of Asgard, and because I was *me*, I yearned for the fight. A dark god, one of the giants of Jotunheim and my enemy, came one night into my father's hall to kill me while I slept. And though I was not yet a god, or immortal, I ripped his gold band from him and slew him with my hammer, Mjollnir, and with the strength of my belt, Megingjard, which doubled my power, and when he was dead I lifted the gold he had worn from the ground—and it no longer was bound to him. It was free, and it wanted a wearer, and it sang to me. It reveled in death and destruction, and it begged me to wear it and let it bind itself to me, that I might forever embrace the battle it sought, and that I might feed its hunger as it fed mine."

He sighed. "I will not lie—I yearned for it as many yearn for the power of gold and listen to the song that spelled gold can sing. I knew I had within me that which would make me great. I was little more than a boy, but already I had fought as a man, and I could sing the songs of men. To fight forever and to feel the mad rush always within my veins . . ."

He said, "I knew it was wrong. I knew it was a thing of great evil, and so, though I suffered mightily, I at last put it aside without donning it. Then my father came and took it and destroyed it, and that day, because he knew what I had re- sisted and knew that I was his true son, he gave me the pow- ers of a god in my own world, and named me with the god-name Thor, which name I bore through all the kennings of men, until I came to the last days of this world and believed I should die here. When I felt the powers of godhood falling away from me I took back my child-name, my mortal name."

Lauren said, "I wondered why you called yourself Heyr."

"I had chosen to die with this world when I could not save it rather than to go on, and did not wish to wear a god's name to my death. It seemed like . . . hubris. When I know this world will live, I will take back my god-name." He smiled a little looking at Lauren and Jake, but then he turned to Molly, and the smile fell away. His color had returned to his face, and his eyes seemed bluer, but he still looked shaken.

"You stand on the sharp edge of a knife blade," he told Molly. "On one side, you fight for what is right even though rightness no longer matters to you. Deep within you is a core of goodness that has not yet been destroyed—that is bound not to trinkets nor to the silver that marks you, but to some- thing within you that repeated deaths have not touched. On the surface, you are a dark god. Beneath the surface lies something else, and in that something else there may be hope, if you choose to pursue it. I can feel this—that you are who you say you are, that you have done much to fight the evil that besets us. You have been a hero, and still you walk that path. But the pathway has narrowed, and a cold wind blows through you, and on the other side of the blade lies the call that I once felt—the call to death and destruction, to the power that comes from oblivion. And you falter."

Molly studied him with steady eyes, emerald green and cold as winter. "I feel the call," she said. "It has become almost the only thing I can feel."

Heyr nodded. "It's a powerful thing. That you have not fallen to it yet and have continued to fight though you are so sorely wounded—you would have been held in high esteem in my father's house, raised to a warrior goddess, and given a place at his table. That you have not drunk of death, when it calls to you so strongly that I can feel the call through you and can once again taste that hunger . . . for that, I would welcome you into my hall and name you hero and call you sister and friend. I could make you a true god here. I could show you the path to immortality, though no dark god has ever been a true immortal." Heyr looked bleak. "But you have begun to listen to the darkness, and to creep toward it— to hold your hands over it as if warming them at a fire. And then you pull away and think of oblivion, and see only those two directions, as if you believe yourself at the point of the knife, where you must jump, and where only darkness lies to either side."

"Yes," Molly said. "That is why I came here today. I can't hold on any longer. I have to choose—oblivion's short fall, or death's long one."

"I see a third way in you, though its voice has faded."

"I see no third choice. I don't have the strength to fight anymore."

"I think I could give you strength, though it would bring its own pain with it. But if I gave you the strength you need and then you decided to step away from the thin, hard path you now walk, in you I would have created the worst of all possible enemies for us. In my long life, I have known two others who fill my heart with the dread I feel in your presence, and one I have slain but failed to kill, and the other will one day kill me. The latter is the Midgard serpent, a dark god of great strength and great cunning who moves through the worlds, waiting for the end days. The former . . . *you* know. His mark is upon you."

Molly said, "Baanraak."

Heyr nodded. "Who is a son of the Midgard serpent, and nearly his equal in cunning and evil and power." Heyr said, "And you have killed Baanraak, hunted him down when he did not wish to be found and killed him, which not even I have done. Perhaps you could destroy the Midgard serpent and change the ends of days. If you turn against us, I fear you." Heyr shrugged. "If I am honest, I must confess I fear you now."

"You're better off letting me destroy myself. In oblivion there's nothing for me, and at least nothing bad for you."

Lauren had been listening quietly, but now she shook her head. "Without you, the world ends."

"The me that could fight is almost all gone, Lauren. Without me, you're no worse off than you are right now. With me . . ." She made a face. "I'm not betting on me. I've seen the odds, and the smart money is all going the other way."

Heyr said, "Lauren is right, though—you bring things to this that none of the immortals have. You can find the dark gods anywhere—you can feel them where they hide, which I cannot do. You could hunt the dark gods like no old god ever could. If you could just find your way out of this . . . this place you're in . . . if you could only find it within yourself to fight with us . . ."

"I can barely find myself, Heyr. One more death and anything within me that gives a shit about Lauren or this world or anything but feeding that screaming maw that has opened up inside of me may be gone. I've never been a quitter. Never. But I'm just about to the end of me, and the thing that's going to be left when I'm gone isn't a quitter, either. It just isn't anything you'd want to save. And if I don't walk away from this now . . . No. Let's be blunt. If I don't get the damned Vodi necklace out of me and get myself killed or kill myself while I'm not wearing it, I may not get another chance. And then the thing you fear is going to be all that's left." Molly turned and looked at Lauren. "Mostly, I just came to say good-bye."

Fearing her words, fearing Molly, fearing for Jake, Lauren reached across the table and took her sister's hand. "Don't quit yet. Hang on to it as an option if you have to, but don't quit yet."

CHAPTER 19

Upworld to Cat Creek—Baanraak of Beginner's Gold

BAANRAAK SNIFFED HIS WAY up the worldchain, hunting for Molly. By sheer force of will he gained some control of his anger, enough that he could think about the steps he needed to take to find her. It took him one full world to figure out that he was bound to her by shared blood—for surely when he exploded he had gotten his blood on her. And she had gotten her blood on him more than once. He could call on the connections woven by this blood to find her.

It took him a second world to figure out how to shield himself well enough that locals did not notice him. He could not bend light, he could not summon invisibility, and the inner silence he had once so prized eluded him. But with a shield, at least he might hope to get close to her in moments when she was distracted, and so destroy her.

By the time he reached Earth, he did not feel so helpless or so vulnerable, but he still could not understand why he was so crippled or what she had done to him to cause him such terrible damage. Never before had he felt so . . . fragmented.

Blood called to blood, and she wore his beneath her skin. He felt the faint tug that connected them for the first time on Earth. He stood in a cold place, with snow blowing around him in fierce gales, and darkness that felt like it would last half a season, and turned his nose to the south. Yes. She waited for him in the south.

Baanraak spun a gate and stepped through it, and on the other side found tall, thin pines and rolling sand hills and humans with weapons, dressed in mottled green-and-brown clothes as if to offer some little disguise. He was hungry, so when they turned their weapons against him, screaming in rage and terror, he stopped up their weapons with a spell, then ate them. Humans were dreadfully unsatisfying as a meal, but better than nothing, he supposed.

Then, with his stomachs full of lumpish bone ends and a great weariness fallen upon him, he found a good sand hillock and settled himself atop it and shielded himself. He could rest and watch all that passed him and refine his sense of where Molly was, and what she was doing, and what stood between him and her. When he was sure he would not step into a trap, he would go and gather her in.

FBI Office, Charlotte, North Carolina

Raymond and Louisa found the place just short of eleven in the morning, after swearing with frustration and looping in circles on one-way streets and ending up in residential neighborhoods. But that was all right. The guy was there, and when they knocked on the door, he came and opened it for them, and he didn't look anything like the way he'd sounded.

He was lean and not much more than about six feet tall, and he wore his hair in a buzz cut, and he had a kind face. Raymond figured he outweighed the guy by about forty pounds, and he was younger, too. Bad knee or not, he figured he could take the FBI agent if he had to.

"Fred Buchanan," the guy said, holding out his hand, and they shook, and Raymond said, "Raymond Smetty," and Louisa said, "Pleased to meet you. I'm Louisa Tate," and they all walked through an empty open office where the desks were all clean, into a private office with a door. Fred showed the two of them to chairs, then took a seat opposite them behind his desk.

Fred had on a white button-down shirt, and had the

sleeves rolled up, and he looked sort of like an accountant, Raymond thought. Not a G-man, that was for damn-all sure. And what sort of big-shot FBI guy would be named Fred, anyway? Raymond had a basset hound named Fred when he was a kid. The dog and the guy had the same eyes.

Raymond relaxed.

Fred picked up a manila envelope and pulled out a couple of photos—one was of a group of people walking down one of those cobblestone streets in some European city with fancy stone buildings and pigeons all over the place. The other was two guys standing and talking in a park—could have been anywhere, pretty much. Raymond took the pigeon-and-street picture; Louisa took the other one.

"Recognize anyone in those pictures?" Fred asked.

Raymond studied faces. A couple of rough-looking men, a gorgeous woman, and—though he was younger and thinner and his hair was black and he had a mustache—Pete. Pete with a dangerous look on his face that Raymond had never seen when the deputy sat in the sheriff's office with his feet up on the sheriff's desk reading. "Yeah," he said, handing the picture back. "The one with the mustache is Pete, but he doesn't look like that now."

Fred nodded.

Louisa looked at the picture in her hands and said, "The one on the right. With the gun."

"That's him," Fred said. "And you say he killed someone and shoved the body in a barrel."

Louisa and Raymond both nodded.

Fred pulled out a topographical map of Cat Creek. "Show me where he stays, where we can find him, where we can find the body—anything else you have. And tell us who he's working for now."

Between the two of them, Louisa and Raymond implicated not just Pete, but also Lauren, Eric, and even June Bug.

Fred took it all in, got the details, was thankful and grateful to the point that Raymond felt like a hero by the time he and Louisa were ready to go.

And then they got up to leave and Fred stood and said, "You aren't going to be able to go back there, not for a while. I don't want to see either one of you end up diced into little pieces. I don't dare let you go back there yet."

Raymond felt his stomach drop. "We don't have a choice," he said. "We're going to have to go back. We don't dare leave." He was thinking of the Sentinels, and of how badly they took unexplained absences. He was thinking of how this whole business ceased to be a clever operation if he and Louisa couldn't get back to Cat Creek in a timely fashion and act like nothing had happened. Because while Pete's being some kind of whacked-out international killer scared him, it didn't scare him half as much as having the Sentinels realize what he'd done and come after him. The Sentinels' reach was a hell of a lot longer than the FBI's—and unlike the FBI, the Sentinels were bound by neither the laws of their country nor the watchful eyes of human rights groups like the ACLU and Amnesty International. If *they* came after him or Louisa, nobody was going to get a chance to call a lawyer or finagle bunches of appeals.

And then there were four big guys at the door, guys who looked the way Raymond thought FBI agents would look. Bigger than him, and tougher, with cold eyes and cold expressions.

Fred was smiling, saying, "We're going to put the two of you up at our expense for a few days, to make sure our witnesses survive long enough for us to gather up Pete and his cronies." And he and Louisa were hustled off in opposite directions, into separate cars, and he was scared.

But not as scared as he got when the two FBI guys took him into his room in a seedy hotel out away from everything, and there wasn't a mirror anywhere in the place. Then, when it was too late for him to do a damn thing about it, he realized that he'd run to the wrong people.

FBI Headquarters, Charlotte, NC

Fred Buchanan ripped a corner off a piece of notepaper and scrawled a quick note on it.

> Louisa Tate and Raymond Smetty tried to turn you and a few of your contacts in. Both under protective custody, separated, rooms with no mirrors. Don't know what's going on down there, but watch your back.
>
> Fred

He handed it to Wylie Blake, one of the guys who'd worked with Pete before, and said, "Get this down to the Hot Zone without anyone seeing you. Including Pete if you can help it. And then get back here fast as you can."

Wylie nodded. "Sure, boss. Couple hours down, couple hours back. I'll take care of it now."

That would have to be good enough. Fred hoped that all the traitors had come forward at once; he wasn't sure how much help the office would be if Pete got himself into real trouble down in Cat Creek. Fred didn't know if even Pete was altogether up on what it was he was hooked into down there. Fred had good people available, but against aliens and a technology that looked very much like magic . . .

Fred sighed. Aliens interested him. He was happy to be in charge of the hottest region in one of the most interesting cases the Bureau had ever worked. But he wanted to start seeing where everything fit, and instead, Pete's portion of the case kept getting weirder and scarier. Fred found himself wondering if all the pieces would ever fall into place.

He hoped Pete had a better handle on Cat Creek's goings on than he did.

Raleigh to Cat Creek—Baanraak of Silver and Gold

Baanraak, driving his black Mercedes Benz CL600 Coupe DE, slid into Cat Creek quietly but not unnoticed. The car alone would make invisibility impossible, but that was fine. He didn't want to be unnoticed. He simply wanted to be misidentified.

He had not hurried his trip from Raleigh. He'd meandered, taking back roads and stopping from time to time to look around, to get a feel for the region and to mark the territories of old gods and Night Watch and Sentinels and other irritants. They were, most of them, bright and sharp and shiny against the dull background noise of mortal, mundane humanity. The Sentinels marked themselves with their standing gates and their laughably vigilant, unblinking stares into the between. Toothless and handcuffed by crippling rules, the whole lot of them. They might have been a threat to the plans of the Night Watch, but the Night Watch under Baanraak's leadership had infiltrated their Council long ages past, and guaranteed that the Sentinels would serve no greater purpose than to clean up messes made by third parties and keep their world on its rails until it was ripe enough to be tasty. The Night Watch certainly could have been dangerous, but its current members hadn't taken the time or effort to mask themselves against each other. Unopposed by any real threat for time out of mind, they'd fallen into the complacency of top-of-the-chain predators, and their noisy minds and extravagant feeding and sharp-edged use of the world's dark magic screamed to Baanraak. He would have no surprises from any of them.

Even the old gods, timid and few and perpetually in hiding, hid only from the Night Watch. They kept small enough and silent enough to hide from those with minds and magic noisier than their own. To Baanraak, master of stillness, they might as well have been dancing and screaming, silhouetted against a level horizon.

Reaching Cat Creek, he knew what lay at his back. A handful of Sentinel outposts, three timorous old gods, a

dozen dark gods of the Night Watch. And one disturbing
patch of ground in the sand hills out by the Fort Bragg reser-
vation where he'd thought he sensed something, but on careful inspection had discovered nothing but some odd echoes
of his own mind. That bad patch bothered him, but not
enough to stop him entirely. It wasn't an issue unless it made
itself an issue, he decided—and if it made itself an issue,
nothing in the universe existed more capable than he to deal
with it.

So he was comfortable that he had control of what lay behind him.

What lay in front of him, however, was another matter.
Lauren he located without too much trouble. She was not
noisy—mortal and for the moment out of the touch of the
between, she would not have stood out at all from other mortals except for that strange echo of immortal love and hope
that clung to her—the fingerprint of her brush with the soul
of the infinite, a power beyond his scope or reach or knowing. Her child bore that same faint, pure light. But she would
have been easy enough to locate had she been no one special. For she had protectors. She was bounded round with
old gods, which in this world were already rare as peacocks
on an arctic snowfield. But the old gods surrounding her
were not upworld mortals stretching out their mortal years
with self-serving magic and timorousness, but true immortals. Pain-bearers, Baanraak had always called them. And
those he had thought long gone from Earth.

Unlike the general run of old gods, the pain-bearers were
dangerous, even to him. He could not kill them, could not
harm them, could not even slow them down unless he could
draw them into gates and so break their links to their
binding-world. The death of their binding-world would put a
quick enough end to them, but destroying Earth was outside
the scope of Baanraak's current mission, even had he the
time or the means or the interest to accomplish it.

One of these pain-bearers Baanraak knew. He and Thor
had crossed paths twice, on other worlds and in days long
past. A newly immortal Thor had once nearly bested Baan-

raak in a head-to-head fight long before Baanraak had become the Master of the Night Watch. At the time, Baanraak had been a dark god still in the forging and did not know that in a straight fight a true immortal had the advantage over one such as he. Thor had been, in fact, the last creature to successfully kill Baanraak's body—until Molly. Baanraak's mentor, Fherghass, had not wished to see all his work on Baanraak go to waste. He'd inserted himself into the fight, and had taken great personal risks to prevent Thor from pillaging Baanraak's corpse or capturing his resurrection rings.

On their second meeting, after Baanraak had destroyed Fherghass and taken Mastery of the Night Watch for himself, Baanraak nearly bested Thor, catching the old god as he came through a gate, before Thor had a chance to bind himself to the world he'd just reached. Thor's skill with magic and weapons had not been enough to spare him grievous injury, though unfortunately he had lived. And here he was, and he was one third of the portcullis that stood between Baanraak and what he wanted.

Thor was not as strong as he had been on their first meeting. This world didn't have enough live magic in it to feed the monster *that* Thor had been. But he was still a power to be reckoned with. And unless he walked to another world and Baanraak got to his destination first, Baanraak couldn't touch him. And did not want to try.

The others felt familiar to Baanraak, but could not have been. They were immortals newly made, still sickened by pain, weak with the full weight of the dying of their world. Unlike Thor, they had not yet learned to drink life from pure springs—they had not found their way to one of the wells where Lauren had brought live magic. They watered from the river of the world, and the river of the world was poison to living things.

Yet—weak and newly hatched and still naïve—even they were untouchable. Baanraak snarled.

And then there was the object of Baanraak's desire and the author of his pain. Molly.

Molly, whom he wished to possess, whom he yearned to

destroy. He tasted her in the air only as the faintest shimmer, her power damped down as low as he kept his own. In all the worlds, Molly alone would be able to see him coming and perhaps read his intent and waylay him. In this world, Molly had only faint magic born of her dual heritage. But Thor at that moment debated the merits of changing her.

And it was when Baanraak strip-mined Thor's thoughts for the means by which Thor intended to change Molly that he discovered his little demesne on Kerras had been discovered. And not just discovered but invaded.

Most of the Sentinels in Cat Creek had been to his hiding place; most of them had become gods there. The only one who had not was Molly. If she went there—if Thor did as he considered and took her—she would know the place, and she would know its creator. His work would betray him, and he would not be there to give her an explanation or to show her how to see what he had done. She would see it through other filters than his, and she would make of it something over which he had no influence and no control. And he discovered that he could not even begin to imagine what she would think.

He discovered himself clenching the steering wheel of the car with hands white-knuckled and aching from the strain. He released them.

He needed a diversion.

Fast.

Cat Creek, North Carolina

Pete lay in the bed, restless, unable to sleep, unable to think, ravaged by pain no drug could touch. In his head, voices screamed for rescue, and he could not save them. Villains dealt horror and death, and he could not stop them. The world slipped a little closer to oblivion, and he could not pull it back or even stand in its way to keep it from sliding. At that moment he could do nothing—not even block out the sounds.

Had he been at work, he would have been worthless, but

at least he would have had something to think about besides his own distress. He wasn't sick. He wasn't likely to ever be sick in the normal sense again. The fact that he wished he were dead was another matter entirely.

He reached out with his mind and touched Lauren, yearning for comfort and something to hang on to. She was reading, with Jake curled up on her lap. They were singing nursery rhymes out of a big red book. He smiled and closed his eyes and let himself drift into her, past the surface. He opened himself to her, letting her drown out the six billion other voices by concentrating on her alone.

And he found things he wished he'd never seen. Her and Brian, meeting in a library when they both reached for the same Theodore Sturgeon novel on the shelf.

Them fighting—the fights had been amazing. No violence against each other, but doors and clothes hampers and plastic-wrapped bacon hadn't fared well. And them making up after the fights; that was even harder to bear. They had been something wonderful; they had experienced a love that Pete couldn't even imagine. He hadn't realized until that instant how much of the magic that Lauren wove was shaped by Brian's touch, and by her yearning for him. Pete could feel the shape of Brian still inside Lauren's heart, and he could feel, for the first time, her ocean-deep love for him. And for the first time he could understand why she clung to Brian's memory. He absorbed her anguish and her agony at losing Brian as if it were his own.

And Pete saw himself through her eyes, and through her heart, and he realized that he was no Brian and never could be. Lauren and Brian had been painted in primary colors and vibrant, thick brush strokes. They had shaken the world with their love. Nothing about what the two of them shared had been thin or shallow or pale. If Brian had lived longer, perhaps the love they had shared would have mellowed a bit, or faded at the edges. But Brian hadn't lived longer, and when he died he'd ignored Heaven to stay with her and eventually to give a part of his soul to save their child—and how the hell could anyone compete with that?

Pete could see that Lauren cared about him. But Pete was a watercolor kind of guy, done with nice detail in faded washes and quiet colors. Lauren was edging sideways toward thinking that she might love him, that she might need him, that she might find a place in her heart and her life for him. But she could not conceive of Pete's being anything but secondary to the love and the life she had lost. And seeing what she had lost from the inside, neither could he.

He pulled away from her. Better the impersonal agony of six billion strangers than the clear, honest, and painfully unflattering reflection of him as seen through the eyes of the woman he wanted to love.

Pete sat up. He had to move, had to do something. The noise in his head was unbearable; the pain in his body screamed for a cure, a fix, some sort of ease. And he had nothing to offer but movement. He changed into jeans and sneakers and went walking. He hooked his thumbs in his pockets and plodded forward, with no direction and no goal.

The streets of Cat Creek, quiet even on weekdays, were empty. The cold and the drizzle had everyone inside—the tiny town might have been abandoned save for voices that carried into the street through poorly insulated walls. The smell of burning wood as people used their fireplaces to take off the chill seemed cozy—but he was looking at Cat Creek through new eyes. He'd never thought of the town as a particularly peaceful place; his time in the Sheriff's Department had disabused him of any illusions of that sort. But he hadn't realized the quiet pain behind the doors—heartache and loss and loneliness and rage and betrayal that never made it to the surface. That had never reached him.

He ambled past fine old houses and those that had once been fine, along streets where the old oaks formed arches across the road and blocked out the sky, and he tried to keep it all out. Heyr had told him to look for the good, for everything that was live and healthy and strong, and to draw from that. Pete was having a hard time finding that healthy power. But he kept looking.

"Bit nasty for a walk," someone said, and Pete turned. A

man sat in shadow on the steps of one of the old houses. The red tip of a cigarette glowed in the grayness of the shadowed eaves and the day.

"It is," Pete agreed, stopping. "Bit nasty for anything, really."

The man shrugged. "Not for thinking, I guess. Woman trouble—that seems to be available in all sorts of weather."

Pete laughed a little. *"Paisan!"*

"Ah. A fellow sufferer. Want a seat? A smoke?"

Pete took the offered seat on the steps, out of the rain. "Don't smoke," he said.

"You'll live longer that way," the man said.

Pete snorted. "Maybe I ought to take it up, then." He turned to study the man—someone he didn't know. That happened from time to time. Following the virulent magic-spawned flu that had killed more than a tenth of Cat Creek's population, and millions worldwide, there'd been a lot of houses on the market in Cat Creek, which lowered their value, and the recession had pushed values even lower, and interest rates were down. So suddenly new families were finding the Cat Creek bargains and moving in.

Pete held out a hand. "Pete Stark."

"Hahlen Nottingham," the man said, shaking hands. "Call me Hal."

Pete stared out from under the eaves. The front porch was comfortable, the company of Hal was oddly soothing, and for a while he just sat there, watching the rain and feeling the cold without being inconvenienced by it—and catching the occasional scent of Hal's tobacco, which was smooth and laced with a hint of . . . cherries? Not a typical cigarette smell.

Hal seemed content to just sit, too. The silence was companionable, not awkward, and when Hal finally spoke, that wasn't awkward, either.

"So after looking for longer than I can even describe, I found the perfect woman for me," Hal said, finishing his cigarette and dropping the butt on the worn step and grinding it out with his heel. "Only she doesn't see it that way. She's dark and light all rolled into one. She fits me. And part of the time she's pulled to me as much as I'm pulled to her, and part of the time she can't stand the sight of me." He shook his head. "I've twisted myself up over this until I don't know if I'm coming or going."

Pete grinned at him. "Neither at the moment, if that helps."

Hal managed a thin chuckle.

"I'm sorry," Pete said. "I shouldn't joke. And I'm the last guy in the world to offer suggestions, but I'm definitely sorry."

"So what's your story?" Hal asked.

"She's a widow. He was a better guy than I'll ever be."

"Tells you that a lot, does she?"

"Never said it once. He really *was* a better guy than I'll ever be. She's finally starting to realize that I'm there, but I'm not him and never will be, and that's pretty plain to both of us. It was always pretty plain to her." Pete shrugged. "So she approaches, she retreats, she approaches, she retreats. She likes me, she wants me, she feels guilty for wanting me, and she goes away."

Hal laughed. "That sounds like a fun game. Mine's more along the lines of she wants me, she hates me, she wants to kill me. Also great fun. I see everything I ever hoped to find in her eyes. I can feel how perfect she is in her mind. She's smart, she's talented . . . she's dangerous." He sat there for a second, and said, "I have a real thing for dangerous women."

"That might not end happily," Pete said. "I've watched the forensics guys picking bone fragments out of residential walls more times than I care to think about."

Hal gave a noncommittal grunt.

Pete could have taken that as Hal's changing the subject, but he didn't. He could have bowed out, too, and resumed his solitary slog. But he found Hal easy to talk to. Soothing. Hal didn't add any weight to Pete's thoughts, and sitting there talking to him, Pete realized that Hal almost seemed to buffer the screaming masses. He wrapped silence around himself like a blanket . . . and he seemed willing to share the blanket. So Pete said, "How dangerous is she?"

Hal laughed. "You want a beer?"

"I'd love a beer."

"I don't have any. But if you know a place where we can get some, I'm buying."

Pete thought for a minute. "Nice place? Ratty place?"

"Close place with good beer."

"All right. Long as you don't mind driving to South Carolina, I know a place that'll do."

"I'll get my car."

CHAPTER 20

Fort Bragg, North Carolina—Baanraak of Beginner's Gold

BAANRAAK ROSE FROM his vantage point atop the sand hill, and stretched one wing at a time, and arched his back. Darkness came, and it favored him. He inhaled, mouth partly open, and tasted the dangers that stood between him and his objectives, and found them considerable but not impassable. Old gods guarded her, but he had dealt with old gods before. He fought for stillness, but it still eluded him, so he satisfied himself with a shield and blended himself with the world as best he could.

Then, heart pounding with desire and fury, gut tight with nerves, he caught the air with his wings and bunched like a cat and leapt upward, launching himself toward Molly. Toward resolution.

Night Watch Control Hub, Barâd Island, Oria

Rekkathav, finally finished calling in all the deployed teams from Earth, approached the new Master of the Night Watch and bowed. His stomach twitched nervously, and he dreaded shaming himself again, which did not improve his odds of avoiding doing that very thing. "The agents to Earth are all gathered in the arena as you requested, Master Baanraak."

The rrôn grinned at Rekkathav, and Rekkathav cringed inwardly. Working for Baanraak the rrôn was worse than working for Aril the keth had ever been, he thought. The keth knew no loyalty, valued no one but himself, and destroyed those around him out of capriciousness as often as out of need. Yet in the entire time Rekkathav had worked for Aril, he'd never gotten the impression that the Master was studying him and imagining how he would taste with a keg of wine and some greens on the side. Every time Baanraak looked at him, Rekkathav felt like an appetizer.

"You're tracking the woman I showed you?" Baanraak asked.

"Yes, Master."

"I have to go to the arena. I may have to . . . reassign . . . some of our agents. There is, after all, a question of loyalty. While I'm gone, don't lose sight of her. She's the key to many things." He headed for the door, then turned around. "Where is she now?"

"She has traveled to Earth," Rekkathav said. "She's visiting with her sister and surrounded by an entire nest of immortals."

Baanraak paused, looking thoughtful. "Immortals. On Earth. Fancy that. Can you identify any of them?"

Rekkathav swallowed hard to keep his stomach down. He'd already studied the records, anticipating this very question—and he loathed passing on his findings. "The main one with whom we must concern ourselves is Thor," he said weakly.

But Baanraak didn't respond as Aril would have. Instead, he simply arched an eyerille. "She's made quite the art of falling in with bad company." He sighed. "I'll deal with it later—this isn't the sort of situation that is likely to improve on its own, but I really do have other things to attend to first. Keep track of her until I get back."

"Very well, Master Baanraak."

Baanraak left, and Rekkathav had just enough time to exhale with relief when the new Master poked his head back into Rekkathav's observation room. "By the way," Baanraak said, "I don't see you with wine and a salad at all. You're more of a beer snack."

Cat Creek

Molly stood on Lauren's back porch. The house was a homely thing—broad wraparound porches and old gingerbread in need of repainting and wood stairs worn smooth by the tread of generations of feet. It was the sort of place she had yearned for as a child, and as a young woman. It was the sort of place that had once said "Home" to her. But nothing said "Home" to her anymore.

She touched the ring on her right hand, feeling the connection with Seolar, knowing that he was alive. Safe. She opened the pinhole gate that linked her to him just enough that she could see him for a moment. He was working—bent over a document of some sort, scratching across it with a quill-tipped pen, dipping the pen into an inkwell. He looked haggard—lines in his previously unlined face, grief in his eyes and the set of his shoulders. She had done that to him. She was poison. She returned the gate to its pinhole size and twisted at the ring. Lauren could wear it. Lauren could watch over him, make sure he stayed safe. Molly would not be breaking her word to him so long as she made sure he was not abandoned. It wouldn't matter if she was not the one to stand guard over him.

Behind her, the back door opened. Lauren came out and stood beside her, and together they watched twilight shuttering the world around them. Lauren said, "How are you?" and Molly just laughed.

"I think once you've died as many times as I have, not even the prissiest minister ought to consider one suicide to end it all a mortal sin. That's how I am."

Lauren's eyes were dark with worry. "Heyr thinks there's hope."

"Heyr's on the outside looking in. And even he doesn't know how I bear it—and I have to tell you, while he was looking me over, I got a taste of what he's been dealing with for the past half an eternity. I truly can't understand why he hasn't quit."

"Take him up on his offer to make you an old god here," Lauren said. "Maybe it will make things better for you." She sounded so hopeful—so caring. But that was Lauren—the one whose assignment included living and keeping her soul. The one who got to save the world by loving it. The one who got to feel love, and not just remember what it had once been like. Lauren's parents hadn't consigned *her* even before her conception to an eternity of soulless torture and an undead existence as Molly's parents had. Molly was surprised to discover she could still feel bitterness. Everything else had washed away, but bitterness remained.

Didn't it just figure?

And then she felt a faint stirring in the air, a darkness moving both toward her and away from her. Tugged by instinct, she put her hand to the rrôn scale on the little chain around her neck. She slipped the chain over her head and held the scale firmly in one hand, and she could feel Baanraak. Not shadows of what Baanraak had been—not memories of Baanraak. Baanraak living, when she had killed him, when she had destroyed his resurrection rings, when she had ground them to powder and poured them into running water to scatter the gold. She could feel the invisible thread spun between the two of them catch fire. She could feel him. On this world. Close. Impossible, but he lived.

"Molly?" Lauren said in a loud voice.

Molly started, and looked away from the scale.

"What?"

"You just said 'Baanraak.' Why?"

"He's here."

"You said you destroyed him." Lauren paled and whispered "Jake," and turned toward the house, where Jake and Heyr waited. Then she put a hand on Molly's arm. "Here, Earth?"

"Here, Cat Creek." Molly tried to get a fix on Baanraak, but couldn't. He was so close. So very close, but he'd found a way to scatter his traces so that she couldn't pin-point him. Even using the link of his scale, she couldn't break through whatever magic he was using. She felt fresh traces of him all around her—strongest in front of her and behind her—but she could not find one single point that she could mark and say "That's where he is right now." He had always been subtle. He had grown even more so since their last meeting.

Heyr appeared, holding Jake, and said, "You're sure it's Baanraak?"

"Yes," Molly said. "No . . ." She closed her eyes, trying to find the clear picture, the clear intent, but Baanraak, not completely still, not completely hidden, nonetheless left her casting north, then south, then north again, and the shadows she chased refused to resolve into a clear picture. What magic had he discovered that would let him do this?

"He's coming for me," she said after a moment. "And for Lauren. He's done something to make it harder for me to track him—I can't get a clear fix on him even though he's moving and not fully shielded."

"What's he doing?"

"He's . . ." She shrugged. "He seems to have echoed him-self. I read him north of here and south of here."

"But you can't tell which is the real Baanraak and which is the echo?"

"No. Both traces are faint—he's always careful."

"Are both heading in this direction?"

"No. One is coming straight for us, and one is heading away."

Heyr said, "I think it would be a good idea, then, to as-sume that the shadow coming toward us conceals the real Baanraak, and the one moving away is the decoy."

"For the sake of protecting ourselves, yes," Lauren said. "We have to figure he's coming for us." She looked at Heyr. "I have my knife, but I want one of the good guns."

"Upstairs, in my closet. Stacked along the wall. Spelled, of course—Jake won't be able to touch them. But you will."

Lauren ran upstairs. Molly turned to Heyr. "There's

something wrong with this. Tracking Baanraak, it isn't like I'm looking at the same image twice. It's two different images. You've been working with magic a lot longer than I have; do you know how he's doing this?"

Heyr looked at her. "I didn't know how he was doing two identical images. I cannot even begin to imagine what he's doing if the images are different."

Molly said, "Summon the Sentinels. And guard all of us for a few minutes. I need silence for this." She walked past him into the house, and through the kitchen and the hall and past the gate-mirror and the foyer and into the living room, were she lay down on the couch. Eyes closed, body relaxed, she began stilling herself—slowing breath and heartbeat and thought until she became mind without body, suspended, aware, and receptive. She could not send her mind searching in two directions, though, so first she chose the north, the image that moved toward her and Lauren.

She brushed Baanraak, moving slowly and carefully. Molly did not push, did not force anything. She let herself seep into him, not judging, not reacting, simply lying there still and open.

Hunger. She felt it, hard and hot, a sharper and more violent form of the constant ache that filled her. Baanraak wanted to feed, but solid food would not do. He hungered for death, for the high that came from drinking destruction. He'd fed recently, she realized—and feeding had rekindled the hunger, the ache, the addiction to death that the dark gods all shared, even those who had never tasted it. His hunger sharpened her own hunger just by contact, and she realized that staying too close to him for too long would be dangerous, even if he didn't notice her. But she didn't back out yet.

He was hunting—her; Lauren and Jake. He'd escaped his confusion, had come to a decision. He was no longer torn between keeping her and destroying her; he wanted her gone. Well enough. He became easier to deal with when his goals were simpler.

He was angry at what she had done to him. He was angry

that he had lost some of his abilities. He wore the shield that she had penetrated because he could not become still inside anymore. He could not become invisible anymore. He blamed her. And he intended to destroy her because of what she had done to him, and then he intended to devour her death, because he was hungry. And then he wanted to destroy the old gods around her, and Lauren and Jake, and drink their deaths, too.

Molly experienced a faint shock at this revelation, and pulled out of him before that shock could betray her presence.

For just an instant she permitted herself to wonder what the hell was going on.

The scale in her hand was Baanraak's scale. The memories in his mind were his. The personality was his. But he didn't know that the old gods around her, including Thor, were immortals. He didn't know, in spite of the fact that he had fought Thor. Twice.

Molly couldn't make sense of this. She had found Baanraak on her first try, but what she had known to be true didn't fit the reality of the moment.

She cast her mind toward the shadow he had created, hoping that if she could find it, she would at least be able to get some sense of what he planned.

And she found, not a decoy, not a trick, but . . . Baanraak. Wearing different skin, a different face, but beneath a convincing exterior possessed of the same mind she knew. Weighted by doubts, scarred by a startling and unexpected sense of loss, but in full possession of the skills and talents and treacheries of uncounted thousands of years of existence.

Her blood went to ice in her veins, and she shuddered.

No. This second creature could not also be Baanraak.

But it was.

Cat Creek

Heyr closed his eyes and winnowed out the background noise of the world, seeking the individual members of the Cat Creek Sentinels. He hoped to find one or two who might stand against the dark god that was coming, but the news wasn't good.

He could pull George out of the gate where he was keeping watch, but George was mortal and purely human, and Heyr didn't want to use him against a dark god. He would have gladly put either Raymond Smetty or Louisa Tate into the field against Baanraak, considering *their* mortality a benefit. But they were both a long way away, and in some sort of incarceration, both feeling very betrayed. Heyr fished through their thoughts as quickly as he could, got the gist of what they'd done, and had to laugh. Bastards—he savored the realization that they were in the process of getting what they'd deserved. He thought it unlikely that they'd be any further problem to the Cat Creek Sentinels.

Heyr's immortals, though, were a problem for another reason. Of all of them, only Pete was already on his feet, and he was down in South Carolina with the shadow of Baanraak that Molly had mentioned. And a bizarre fuzz of energy surrounded Pete, blocking Heyr's attempts to reach him. Of the remainder, Eric was in the best shape, and he was rolled into a fetal position on his bed, moving only occasionally, and then only to lean over the bed to vomit into a trash can. Mayhem, Darlene, Betty Kay, June Bug—all of them were so lost in the haze of the world's horror they would be worthless for days.

The first days of immortality, when every lapse in attention let the whole weight of the world pour over the new immortal, were the worst. Had Baanraak held off for just another week, Heyr would have had a force strong enough to stand against him.

Another goddamned handful of days, and instead, Heyr was going to end up in this thing alone, with the mortal he had to save at all costs at stake and a dark god he didn't trust as his only backup.

Now he wished he hadn't pissed off Loki.

Cat Creek

Seven P.M., and Pete was feeling better. He'd discovered that he could drink prodigiously and wash drunkenness out of his system with the tiniest application of his will, leaving only a pleasant burr that dulled the edges of the pain that being in Hal's presence didn't quite alleviate.

Feeling cheery and mildly beery after he knew not how many brews, he leaned an elbow on the table and in a low voice told Hal, "It isn't just that I want to get laid, but God knows getting laid would be good. You know?"

"In theory, I know. Beyond the merely theoretical, however, I haven't screwed in so long, I've forgotten how," Hal said, laughing, and Pete laughed with him. Hal's voice was louder than Pete's, his movements broader and giddier, and the cop part of Pete noted this, and that Hal wasn't going to be driving himself home. But Hal had been matching Pete drink for drink, and Hal wasn't a god. Pete didn't believe for a minute that Hal wasn't getting laid, though, either. The guy was good-looking, had a car that Pete could only dream of, clearly had money and lots of it. Pete figured the no-sex story was just an attempt at drunken bonding—if he'd talked about having had a dozen women in the last week, he figured Hal as the kind of guy who would have claimed two dozen.

Hal took a long swig of his beer and lit up another cigarette. "My thing . . . it isn't really about sex, anyway. It's about . . ." He sat there, staring off into the distance, and the strangest look crossed his face. "You know, I don't have the faintest clue what it's about. She's a drug to me, and she is my disease and my addiction and my cure, and probably my death. And she is the first glimpse I've had in longer than I can remember of any sort of idea that something is lying on the other side of death, too." He shook his head. "And I can only conclude that I want this because I'm *stupid*."

"She's magic," Pete said, actually getting it.

Hal nodded. "More than you could know."

"So why is she not interested in you?" Pete asked.

"She is. But not in a good way."

Pete waved over the waitress and said, "Two more beers." He turned to Hal. "I'm buying now. Why isn't she?"

"Because." Hal made a face. "I'm not a nice guy. I've done some bad things in my life."

Pete didn't let his expression change or let any glimmer of his sudden interest show, but the guy with the broken heart faded into the background and the FBI agent perked up his ears. Drunken confessions were confessions nonetheless, and Hal wouldn't be the first man to solve somebody's open case over a long night of hard drinking. For the first time Pete wished he could read Hal the way he could read everyone else in the room. "She doesn't approve?"

"Some of those things I did to her," Hal said. "She's good. Not fluffy or sweet, not that sort of surface goodness that is all about appearances. But deep-down good. She's . . . I don't know how this is going to sound to you, or if it will make sense, but she loves life, even though it hurts her." Hal smiled a little. "She's a devil fighting on the side of the angels."

"And you're . . ."

"I'm finding out that I might be the same. But she knew me as a devil, and she hasn't seen the part of me that is like her. I need to show her. I need her to understand."

"Don't hold your breath," Pete said. "They hang on to the past, you know. Maybe because it's safer than the present. I don't know. But getting a woman to see you in her present can be damned near impossible."

He closed his eyes and thought of Lauren, and found that sitting in that South Carolina bar, he could touch her.

She was scared.

He hadn't planned to spy on her, but something was wrong—badly wrong—so he brushed just the surface of her thoughts.

"Baanraak," he whispered, and Hal said, "What?"

Pete opened his eyes. "How fast does that car of yours go?"

"About one-sixty on the straightaways. Why?"

"I need to get back to Cat Creek. Right now."

"Something wrong? You forget something?"

"Yes," Pete said, wishing to hell that he'd been able to get his mind around Lauren's several attempts to teach him to weave a gate. He didn't have it, he never would, and mostly he was fine with that. Gateweavers were rare and strange creatures, and he wasn't rare or strange. His mind didn't bend the way a mind needed to if it wanted to thread a path between realities. "Fuck," he muttered. "And there's that huge mirror in the bathroom, too."

Hal stood up. "A mirror. And Baanraak. And a sudden need to be someplace else in the middle of a pleasant conversation." He looked Pete in the eye, all drunkenness fallen away, and said, "I'll put a card on the table if you will."

A little chill of warning skittered down Pete's spine. "You first."

"I'm a gateweaver. If you tell me what's going on, I can make use of that big bathroom mirror. Though I will have to come pick up my car later."

"You're an old god," Pete said as the pieces fell into place. "That's the reason I can't read you. That's the reason everything is quiet around you—you're an old god, and maybe an immortal, and you have all the pain blocked out."

"I'm not an immortal," Hal said, "not a pain-eater. But . . . the gate—the hurry. What's going on?"

"They're prepping for a fight in Cat Creek. Baanraak— you know of the dark gods?"

"I know that one."

"Baanraak is on the outskirts of Cat Creek. Coming in from the north, looking to destroy Lauren and Jake and Molly. They need my help. Yours, too, if you want to give it."

Hal looked unconvinced. "*North* of Cat Creek."

"I'm reading Lauren and Heyr. Molly's there, too, but I can't get anywhere near her. She might as well be invisible."

Hal stood there for just a moment with a blank look on his face, his eyes unfocused. Then his brows knit together and he said, "Bathroom. Now."

"You feel what's going on?"

"No. I sense something I know to be impossible. That's worse."

He stood and looked past the few other drinkers and said to Hal, "Lead on."

Hal went into the bathroom. It had one stall and on the opposite wall one urinal, but Pete stayed outside to make sure no one else came in.

After just a moment, Hal opened the door. "Gate's ready. Go on."

The gate led into a room Pete didn't recognize at first. "I'm not going through there. It doesn't go into her house."

"It goes into the workroom out back. Right now going straight into her house would be a bad idea. They're all three armed, and they look like they're on a"—Hal paused, trying to find the right word—"a filed trigger."

"Hair trigger?" Pete suggested.

"Yes."

Pete nodded, and out in the hallway, someone pounded on the door. "That's enough of that, faggots! Get your asses out of there now! And then get out of my bar—we don't tolerate that shit in here!"

"Go," Hal said.

Pete climbed up on the lavatory, and crouched and squeezed into the gate, and the sounds of the world dropped away. The universe embraced him and erased the pain he carried, and silenced the six billion sorrows that seeped into his flesh and the poison of death sought and nurtured. For one timeless moment peace flowed through him. This was the universe as it should be. This was the taste of Eden. Then he stepped through the gate into Lauren's workshop.

The pain was gone. All of it. He felt light. He felt wonderful. Pete stretched and looked around, wondering if he'd landed in the wrong place, if he'd somehow ended up in a sideways Earth that lay in a healthy chain unplagued by the Night Watch.

Then he realized what had happened. He'd stepped between the worlds, and his connection to the Earth had broken. He was still an old god, but no longer immortal. The pain was waiting for him, like a heavy coat he needed to put on.

He wanted to cry. Instead, he lay on the dirt floor of the

workshop, faceup, and spread his fingers out on the cool earth and sought the life of the planet, and made it his own. The pain tore into him like starving rats caged inside him, gnawing their way out, and for a moment it was so bad it blinded him. He rolled over to his hands and knees and vomited, and tried to focus on life—the clean, pure streams of life that he and Lauren had brought into the world. He got sludge—poison-silted death, wars and corruption, evil—and then, like a pulse in a dying man, he found a single spot of pure, welling life. He pulled that to him and linked to it, and some of the pain receded. Enough that he could stand again.

Was this waiting for him every time? His head throbbed, and he crawled to his feet and rested for a moment against the wall. It couldn't be this bad every time. Heyr would never have moved anywhere by gate if it was.

Maybe you just got numb to it.

He took a slow, shaky breath and headed for the house. And then he realized that Hal hadn't come through the gate with him. Pete turned around and looked at the mirror he'd stepped through. The gate was gone. Shut tight. So Hal wasn't coming.

Well, there you go. The old gods heard the name Baanraak and fled in the opposite direction. The extra help would have been nice, but Pete realized he should have known from the look on Hal's face that he wasn't going to volunteer for the fight. Well, of course not. The mortal old gods lasted because they hid.

Pete, bound to the Earth again and again immortal, suppressed his regret. He would have liked to have Hal fighting with him. But he turned and trudged to the house, carrying a single drop of Heaven in an ocean of Hell within him.

Night Watch Control Hub, Barâd Island, Oria

Rekkathav had been watching the woman the Master wanted to have him watch. Well enough. Good enough. Watching, just watching, while she natter natter nattered. He watched, he was bored, but boredom was no great issue to him—his life for some time had fluctuated between the extremes of boredom and terror with little in between. Of the two, he preferred boredom.

Natter natter. He fidgeted, yearning for his sandbox, desperate for sleep.

And the woman and the old god started talking about Baanraak, and about Baanraak's being there.

Rekkathav's stomach quivered in his throat.

At almost the same instant, the little peripheral alarms he'd set around the house to warn him of problems went off. Boredom to terror—and this was terror. He used every tool in his arsenal, every diagnostic trick, every little spellbreaker, trying to find out what had set off the alarms, and he managed to unravel the shielding on an attacker going in hunting for the woman.

And the attacker was Baanraak.

"No," Rekkathav whimpered. "No, no, no . . ."

Baanraak was going to kill the woman. And then he was going to hold Rekkathav responsible for her death because Rekkathav hadn't informed him of the danger to her, which he had charged Rekkathav to do. Was going to use this as an excuse to devour Rekkathav with a barrel of beer.

"Runner!" Rekkathav screamed, and one of the little mortal runners popped into the room almost immediately.

"Go to the arena. Tell Baanraak the woman he bade me watch is under attack and in mortal danger. Run, damn you. Fly!"

The runner would find no Baanraak, of course. But Rekkathav could dissemble—he could claim that he had been unable to penetrate the disguise of the Master, that he had only seen a rrôn attacking, and that he had, therefore, made his best attempt to warn the Master, and more than that could surely not have been expected of him. . . .

Something else moved around the house. Something else that gave off the message that it was hunting for the woman.

This was something not trying particularly hard to hide itself, yet for all that doing a better job than the Master was doing. It was another dark god, oe wearing an exquisite second skin of manflesh and wrapped in light. Most observers—most dark gods—would have been fooled, but Rekkathav's talent, that one thing for which the dark gods had recruited him, was his ability to get to the truth of anything. He called it researching, but it was really stripping every person and every situation down to component parts, pulling out all the lies and deceptions, and discerning how those pieces that remained fit. And in this second intruder, he could read faint shadows of a deeper, real self, a core personality that lay beneath a very fine disguise and bore no relationship to it whatsoever.

Rekkathav started peeling away at the layers, carefully, cautiously—and deep within the core of the creature, he suddenly connected with its essential self.

Its essential self was Baanraak. A much more savvy, much more dangerous Baanraak—yet still Baanraak, entirely and completely.

Rekkathav swallowed his stomach and clenched his jaws tight against the terror that consumed him.

And suddenly a huge head thrust itself over his shoulder and stared at Rekkathav's displays, and a third Baanraak, an angry, bloodied Baanraak who was neither the first Baanraak to appear in Rekkathav's displays pursuing the woman, nor the second, snarled, "What the *fuck* do you want, Snacklet, and how *dare* you interrupt me in the midst of shredding traitors?"

Rekkathav, senses overwhelmed, did what any sensible creature would have done in that situation.

He fainted.

CHAPTER 21

Cat Creek

THROUGH THE WEIGHT of her own pain, June Bug could still feel the trouble heading toward Lauren and Molly over at the old Hotchkiss place. Godhood gave her an exquisite sensitivity to movements and intent around her, and though she was too weak and sick to act on anything, she was entirely capable of reading the situation that was shaping up over there.

It was bad. Because what was getting ready to happen was worse than what Lauren or Heyr expected—and what they knew was coming was bad enough.

The surprise bomb waiting to go off and destroy Lauren and Jake and any hope the world had was worse.

Molly had given up.

She was ready to die. And she was playing with a plan that would end her existence. And the means to put her plan into action had just arrived.

June Bug lay there, an old woman with an eternity she did not want stretching before her, feeling Molly's despair layered on top of her own, and she thought of Molly's mother, Marian, and how June Bug had both loved and failed Marian. She thought of the world she had fought so long to save, and she realized that she could not fight as an immortal—the chains of it bound her to the bed on which she lay. But Marian's daughter needed her—Marian's daughter, who had so much of Marian in her. Marian's daughter, on whose shoulders half of Earth's future rested.

I have the magic of a god here now, June Bug realized. *Age is a trapping I choose to wear—and Sentinels' rules be damned.*

If she were stronger, maybe she would be able to withstand the weight of immortality better. Maybe she would be able to get up and fight, do something to prevent Molly from destroying herself out of fear of what she might become. Making that kind of difference would be worth the breaking of some rules.

June Bug lay on the bed for a long moment, closing out as much of the noise as she could and filling the little spaces she cleared for herself with memories of what it had been like to be young, to wear tight supple skin and strong muscles, to breathe easily and move without pain. She led her body back through time to the place where she was once again twenty years old, and she willed her flesh to conform to that memory, focusing not on specific changes but on a total-body rejuvenation.

Pain became a fire within her, immediate and terrible and unblockable, and she lost her hold on some of the walls she'd built to ward off the pain of strangers. Like a dam crumbling, the walls came down, and the anguish of the world poured in on her again. She writhed in the bed, her body melting and twisting and changing inside and out, and a scream tore itself from her throat as she fought for some peace within the horror.

She scrabbled like a drowning woman for any bit of floating debris that she might cling to—and she found one of Lauren's siphons, pouring live magic into the Earth from someplace far down the worldchain. Someplace still full of life and hope. She latched on to that, and the thin trickle of healthy magic washed into her. It wasn't enough, but it was something. It gave her a couple of planks that she could hang on to; it helped her pull her head above water long enough to start rebuilding her walls.

With enough of her self-control regained that she could

move, she rose, and still fighting blinding pain, crept to the bedroom mirror that was her primary gate. She stared into her own eyes, and saw herself as she had once been, as she was again—a tall, plain-faced young woman with dun-brown hair and nondescript eyes, a large nose and thin lips. She sighed and muttered, "You know what? The hell with this." And in spite of the pain the change caused her, she made herself beautiful, too. It was shallow, it was vain, and she knew it. And she didn't care.

When she was finished with herself, she crawled on hands and knees and looked into the mirror again. Except for the anguish in her eyes and the tear stains on her cheeks, she looked . . . amazing. Golden-blonde hair that curled to her waist in soft ringlets; full lips; eyes the precise blue of an October sky; a pert, straight nose; and the curves of a goddess. She had become the woman of her dreams.

And, being that woman, her dreams no longer seemed so far-fetched. She no longer seemed to have so little to offer. "I could try it this time," she whispered to the stunning young woman in the mirror.

She could pursue love. She could take the chances she had been too fearful to take before. She could live the life she had never dared to live—except that Marian was dead and Molly wanted to be dead, and she could not live knowing that Molly, too, was gone from the world and she had done nothing to save her.

June Bug had a young woman's body and a goddess's beauty, but she still had an old woman's mind. A long and lonely life lay behind her, and ahead of her lay an eternity without hope of getting Marian back or finding her in the afterlife—when before June Bug had at least held deep inside her the hope that in the place beyond death she might have the courage to bare her soul and win Marian's love.

The tears slipped down her cheeks a little faster, and she collapsed again, the pain cascading over the walls she'd built to keep out the world, flattening her.

She wore a young body—but still she wasn't strong enough. Physical youth was not the cure. She could not fight like this. She curled into a fetal ball, full of failure, knowing that she was too weak even to stand for more than a moment under the weight she bore, while across Cat Creek, the hope and future of the world came under attack by monsters who had every chance of winning, and half of that future sought its own destruction.

Cat Creek

Molly turned to Heyr and said, "They're here. Outside the house." She could feel the angry Baanraak circling the house, and the faint shadow of the quiet Baanraak watching everything—the other Baanraak, the house, her.

Heyr swore. "No time to make you a god here, no time to do anything but fight. And it's just me guarding the three of you . . ."

Pete bolted onto the back porch, both feet hitting the top step with a thud that shook the kitchen—he slammed through the back door and stood panting, his back against it, locking it behind him with one hand. "You're in trouble. I got here as fast as I could."

He looked like hell.

Heyr said, "At least you're standing," but looking at Pete, Molly could only wonder how long that would be true.

Pete nodded. He turned to her. "Between you and Lauren, I heard something about . . . Baanraak?"

Molly said, "I thought I'd destroyed him. But he's here. *Two* of him are here. When I exploded him, I exploded myself as well. So I couldn't see what happened, but I think his resurrection rings must have scattered all across the forest floor in Oria. When he resurrected, I'm guessing he came back as more than one of himself. I destroyed one, and destroyed the two rings that Baanraak had in him. But . . ."

Heyr and Pete and Lauren exchanged worried looks. "Then the two that are out there might not be the only ones."

Molly shook her head.

"How many could there be?"

Molly shrugged.

"Any idea at all?" Lauren asked.

"Baanraak's old. He's had the opportunity to gather up a lot of resurrection rings and add them to his collection. The dark gods all seem to do this as they get older. He'd only be limited by the amount of gold he could carry inside him."

"He has access to magic—so that's no limit," Heyr said.

"Then . . . I guess there could be a lot more where those two came from."

"That's comforting," Pete said. He turned to Heyr. "Any sign of the other Sentinels?"

"They're too sick to move," Heyr said. "Eric can't even stand up. It'll take them days to be on their feet again. I don't know how you're standing already." He shrugged. "And as for Louisa and Raymond . . ."

"No," Lauren said. "We're better off without them."

Pete looked from Lauren to Molly and back to Lauren again, and said, "I would give anything to be with you through this, but I think I'm best in the front lines. They can't kill me even if they can hurt me. And they want the two of you dead—so we have to keep you together and safe."

Molly nodded. "We have good weapons. We can set up barricades."

Heyr leaned a hand against the wall of the house and half closed his eyes. After a moment, the walls, floors, and ceilings of the house began to glow green. "I took care of the barricades," he said, pulling his hand from the wall. The glow died away. "The house is hardened. Fireproof, windproof, and as magicproof as I can make it, though I have no doubt that there are spells and tricks I haven't discovered yet that could get through. When we close the doors behind us, only one of the four of us will be able to pass through them again. All you have to do is find a room with no windows, get in there, and bar the door behind you."

Molly said, "If the house will keep them out, why should we hide in a windowless room with the door barred?"

Heyr's voice was flat. "Because I don't know everything. Because what I don't know could kill you, and I would have you take every precaution, since I don't know which precaution will prove the valuable one."

"We'll have guns," Lauren said. "We still have Loki's weapons."

Pete muttered, "Pity we don't still have Loki."

"I've been regretting that, too," Heyr said. "I cost us a valuable ally."

Molly turned to Lauren. "I didn't think we'd just be hiding in a closed room. I thought we'd be . . . contributing. Fighting."

Lauren touched the pommel of the knife Heyr had given her, and with Jake riding on her hip, gave Molly an indecipherable look. "You can't lose any more of yourself. We can't afford for you to die again, even if you do come back. But especially if you don't. Me . . ." She shrugged. "That's obvious. Right now, though, we'll help them most if we're not easy targets." She turned to Pete and Heyr. "We'll be in the upstairs bathroom. No windows."

Heyr nodded.

Pete said, "I'd be with you if I could," and Lauren shook her head.

"Go," she said. "You're doing what you have to do." Lauren glowed with life, with the open, unsullied energy of the universe, and more than that—with the touch of the infinite. Jake had the same glow to him.

Just being close to the two of them reminded Molly of everything she wasn't. But it hurt her, too. The longer she was near Lauren, the more the life inside of Lauren burned her. It was like . . . sitting too near the sun, she decided.

She followed Lauren up the narrow back stairs into a spare bedroom, and to a very old, locked, cherrywood gun cabinet. Lauren pressed two spots on the top and side, and Molly heard a soft click, and the doors swung open to reveal an empty cabinet. "My great-great-grandfather—my father's great-grandfather—made this," Lauren said. "Woodworking ran in the family." She pressed on a central panel, and a hidden door popped forward. Behind it, Molly recognized weapons that could only have come from the old gods.

"Those'll do," Molly said.

Lauren nodded. "Loki left them. They're safe—they'll only shoot dark gods . . ." She turned to stare at Molly and her eyes went wide.

"Watch where you shoot around me, then, will you?"

Molly took the weapon Lauren handed her and followed her sister out of the room, down the hall, and into the bathroom. Jake watched her over his mother's shoulder, round-eyed and untrusting. Smart kid.

Heyr and Pete were fighting to protect what remained of Molly as much as they were fighting to protect Lauren and Jake. But what remained of Molly was so small, and so weak, and what lay underneath felt the movement of the living hunger outside the house, and ached with that same hunger, and cried out to be fed. Darkness called, even stronger when forced into a corner by the light.

Lauren's presence—and Jake's—was reminding her of everything she was not and could never be again. She took a seat on the edge of the tub, and closed her eyes while Lauren barricaded the door, and wondered how she was going to get through what was coming.

Cat Creek

For Lauren, locking the bathroom door and wedging the chair underneath the doorknob felt all wrong. She put Jake on the floor when she was done and sat on the closed toilet seat and watched Molly sitting on the tub.

Molly's proximity made her skin crawl. She didn't want to feel that way about her sister—about this woman who was her partner in fighting the evil that threatened to destroy the world. But the changes in Molly had become too clear and too perilous to ignore. Jake, too, clearly felt the danger that Molly emanated, for he clung to Lauren's knee and pressed his face against her side, pointedly not looking at Molly.

Every once in a while, Lauren could catch a flash of the

Molly she had known in her sister's eyes, but she could see the gaps now—the calculating coldness that transcended indifference and went all the way to heartlessness. Being locked in the bathroom with Molly felt like being on the wrong side of the door.

Worse, though, Lauren was just sitting there waiting for other people to save her. She understood that she and Molly were the targets of this attack. She understood that if the two of them fell, her world's chance of survival became almost zero.

But how could she sit there doing nothing? She was a gateweaver. More, she could do something no one else had ever done before—she could bring life back to her dying world. Surely she could find *something* she could do to help Heyr and Pete protect her and her son. And Molly, whatever was left of Molly.

Night Watch Control Hub, Barâd Island, Oria— Baanraak of Master's Gold

Baanraak watched the central display, trying to figure out what had so agitated Rekkathav. Initially he saw little to make him think he'd been called away from his meeting with the agents of the Night Watch to any good purpose. He saw Molly, but he would have expected to see her. She sat in a little room powerfully warded against incursions by the Night Watch. Her sister and her sister's child sat with her. They weren't doing anything, and Baanraak began to think that Rekkathav was going to serve him best, after all, as dessert.

But he caught sight of movement in one of the side displays, and after a moment he recognized Thor. His rilles went flat against his head and he caught himself growling—he bore an atavistic, bone-deep loathing for that bastard. Easy enough to be calm about his presence in the picture when Baanraak wasn't actually looking at him, wasn't it? The one with him was an immortal, too—but kitten-weak, sick and fragile and near breaking. Baanraak thought he could destroy that one without too much trouble if he could get into his head for a few moments. But still he saw nothing that would warrant calling him away from what he'd been doing.

He considered crushing Rekkathav beneath his foot.

And then he sensed something in a third display—one that appeared to hold nothing more than an image of old wooden outbuildings—and he leaned in, eyerilles drawing together, talons flexing.

There was a rrôn there, hiding, watching. Little shivers made the long trip down his spine, and the tip of his tail started to flick from side to side. Now that he knew he was there, Baanraak could make out the lines of him—he could catch stray thoughts as the other rrôn fought for the same silence that Baanraak had mastered long ago.

Interesting. He'd thought himself the only rrôn to pursue that path.

Gently, with surgical precision, he used the display gate to attach himself to that other rrôn; he eased himself into the stranger's mind, curious to discover who had finally decided to attempt to emulate him. The shock of what he found almost betrayed him.

He was inside his own mind. And worse, he was not alone in there. He felt the shape of another consciousness near him, and cautiously touched that, and discovered himself, again.

The effect was dizzying, almost sickening. He was seeing through his own eyes in three bodies, hearing his own thoughts in three minds. And while he was each of these three Baanraaks, he also was not. One of them felt young, weak, and still vulnerable, as he had been when he first became a dark god. The second had his age, his experience, his wariness and skills, but this one was scarred by silver, weakened by the emergence of a budding conscience.

He alone was Baanraak as Baanraak should be—but the presence of these others presented an opportunity. He might never have such an opportunity again.

The immortals surrounding Molly and her sister were still too weak to be effective. The attentions of the two who might provide genuine resistance were fixed on his two alter egos. And the two people who stood in the way of his plans for Earth and the worldchain sat in a cage of their own making with a child who had the smell of future trouble about him. They were armed and they were wary, but they were also vulnerable. If he could somehow draw them out of their cage . . .

Molly teetered on the brink of the long fall into dark godhood. Enough of her remained that she was still aware of all that she had lost, and still cared that she had lost it. Enough remained of her humanity that she feared the inhumanity that spread inside her—that held the majority within her now. She feared, too, the hunger for the drug of death and the desire for power that came with it. Shamed by the realization of what she was, she already yearned for oblivion.

If he could push her closer to the real self in her that longed to come out, if he could force her to embrace that hunger, he could help her find the nonexistence she wanted. She was already close—he would need only a little push to send her the rest of the way.

He studied her for a moment, and her sister, and the little boy.

The child was the key, wasn't he? She'd died for him, setting herself on this path. She bore some resentment toward him for that. Resentments could be fed. Nurtured. Prodded.

Baanraak smiled down at the just-waking Rekkathav and said, "You did well, Snacklet. I think perhaps I won't eat you today."

He left the observation room, heading for the Hub control room and for a convenient, maintained gate. His audience in the arena could wait. Only a fool would let an opportunity like this one slip between his talons, and Baanraak was no fool.

Cat Creek

"So as long as they're inside, they're safe," Pete said as he and Heyr stepped out onto the back porch.

"More or less." Heyr bound the door behind him so that it would not permit passage to any save the five of them. He would have sealed it entirely, but the chance always existed, however remote, that something would happen to break his bonds with the Earth, and that Baanraak would triumph and Heyr would die. He would not chance leaving the hope of this world caged, should that happen.

"Then we don't have to do anything but sit out here and wait for the Baanraaks to realize they can't get in and go away."

Heyr looked at Pete. The back porch light showed more than it should have—Pete's skin was an unhealthy gray, sheened with sweat in spite of the coldness of the night. Pete hadn't yet found a way to filter the little bits of live energy left on the planet so as to block out the poisons, and this wasn't something Heyr could show him. Only experience could do that—and Heyr didn't know of any way to speed experience. Pete would get it eventually, if he didn't give up first, or go mad in the interim. Heyr frowned, sympathetic with Pete's suffering, and said, "Unfortunately, this is a siege situation. Not favorable to us. We don't know how long they are prepared to stay out there, but we do know that we can't keep Lauren and Jake and Molly inside forever."

"So we have to destroy the Baanraaks."

"Yes."

"Only we can't see them."

Heyr sighed. "We have some options. We can try to make them visible. We can try to lure them out. We can shoot at where we think they are."

"We could use more people."

"We could use more *immortals*. More people would just get in the way and get themselves killed. In fact—" He waved a hand and cast a shield around Lauren's house and yard. It would hide the ungodly events that were about to erupt there from anyone on the outside. "Let's make sure we don't draw attention from the mortals." He shrugged. "We aren't going to get help from the rest of the Sentinels. You're the only one standing, and you're barely on your feet. I can't believe you're here, actually."

"I couldn't leave Lauren to get through this without me."

Heyr nodded. "Love can work miracles."

Nearby, a gate opened—softly, smoothly, making almost no ripple—and something came through. Heyr got an instant's impression of massive size, terrible power, endless intelligence, and bottomless evil. And then, as if a door had closed, nothing.

His heart sped up, and his groin tightened and his belly knotted. Without his realization that he had called it, Mjollnir was in his hand. He knew the shape of that evil, and knew how it felt to have the weight of that intelligence aimed against him. "We're going to need a miracle," he told Pete.

Pete looked at him sidelong, and his eyes narrowed. In an instant his weapon was in his hand, the safety thumbed off. "Why?"

"A third Baanraak just arrived. And this one feels like the Baanraak I remember—who once nearly killed me."

Cat Creek

One minute Molly was sitting there trying to block out the discomfort of being so close to Lauren and Jake. The next, she was hungry.

Hungry in a way she'd never been before, though. The life that radiated from her sister and her nephew suddenly smelled like food to her. *With that much life in them, think about how much death will be in them. They owe you. You died for that little bastard, and he won't even look at you now. You gave up everything for your sister—you gave up your lover and your life and your place in a world where you belonged and where you had no pain, and she doesn't trust you enough to close her eyes while you're in the same room.*

Molly's blood burned, her belly ached, her skin tingled. She had never known hunger like this. She could taste the two of them so near her. They were incapable of reacting in time to save themselves if she chose to take them. She could not use Loki's gun against them, but she still wore Seolar's dagger at her hip. She'd changed that, had turned it into a weapon worthy of a god, and even here on Earth it would have those qualities.

She sat on the tub, eyes still closed, and saw herself killing the two of them. Saw herself crouched over them, eyes closed in ecstasy, drinking death and feeling the power pour into her like a drug. Feeling herself expand, feeling her mind encompassing the whole of the universe through a gate of darkness.

She was a dark god who had not yet claimed her birthright. She clutched eternity in one hand, with the whole of this world spun out before her, naked and vulnerable and ripe for the taking. And all that stood in her way if she decided to claim what was rightfully hers were two people who owed her—who had both played a part in making her who she was. What she was.

Her hand slipped to the pommel of the dagger, and she opened her eyes, and Lauren noticed and smiled at her—a tired, worried smile. Lauren was holding Jake on her lap and rocking him back and forth, patting his back. Jake looked like he was asleep.

Molly felt a wave of revulsion at the hunger she had just felt and at the thoughts she had just entertained. How close to falling was she?

Too close. Too close by far. She might have slipped all the way off the edge right then, and taken her world and everyone in it with her. She could still feel the hunger gnawing inside of her. She was still looking at Lauren and Jake as if through two sets of eyes—the eyes that saw them as the family she'd always yearned for and had finally found, and the pair that saw them as nothing more than food to feed a hunger.

Molly took her hand off the pommel of her knife and stood. "I have to go," she said. "I can't stay in here."

She could see surprise in Lauren's eyes, but wariness, too. "What's wrong?"

"They're trying to fight blind out there." *You could have her now*, the voice in her head whispered. *You could have the life in her as your own, you could drink it down, you could fill yourself up with it.* Molly swallowed hard. "I can locate the Baanraaks for them," she said, and her hand started inching toward the pommel of her dagger again, as if of its own free will. "Stay in here. Keep the door barred. Don't open it again, except for Heyr or Pete." She shivered as she saw herself stepping downworld, changing herself into a reasonable facsimile of Pete, and coming back for Lauren and Jake. "Maybe not even them," she said, and fought her way to the door with the hunger clawing at her, stronger and more compelling every second.

She moved the chair, and through gritted teeth said, "Put this back the second I'm on the other side of the door."

She heard Lauren moving behind her, standing up while still holding Jake.

Keep going, she told herself. Keep going. Don't turn around. Don't look back.

Behind her, all she smelled was food. All she felt was food. Yet somehow she still got through that door, and pulled it shut behind her, and stood trembling on the other side. She heard Lauren push the chair under the doorknob again and kick it into place, and kick the towel that would keep it from slipping out of place, too.

She'd open it for you, her hunger said.

Molly felt tears start down her cheeks. How hard could it be to do the right thing? Almost impossible.

And it was only going to get worse.

This . . . this was what the other Vodi had felt at the end. This was the moment when they had, every single one of them, found the strength to end it. They had been strong, and she was so weak. She was so hungry.

It was only going to get worse.

She had to die—now, and for good. She could not think of a way to get the resurrection ring out of herself; it coiled inside her body, woven through her guts. Sometimes she could feel the weight of it in there, like a tumor, like a snake waiting to strike. Sometimes she could feel it purring.

She could not get it out. But one of the Baanraaks could.

She knew which one. The one who had come with a single clear intent. He had come to kill her—to destroy her. He had no doubts; he was certain. He would not falter if presented with the opportunity; he would not at the last moment change his mind.

He would rip the resurrection ring from her still-living body, and then he would kill her body, and the spell that bound her to the ring would be broken and she would be freed from the burdens and the pains of this existence. If she did not go on, if soulless, everything that she was and everything that she had known came to an abrupt halt, well, that seemed the best option she had. The best option she would ever have, now.

She forced herself down the long hall toward the stairs, and the front door, and the end of her misery.

CHAPTER 22

Cat Creek—Baanraak of Master's Gold

THAT WENT WELL, Baanraak thought, though not precisely as well as he might have hoped. Lauren and her child both still lived; had things gone ideally, both of them would be lying dead on the floor and Molly would be fleeing the house in horror at what she had done. He hadn't expected that best-of-all-possible outcomes, however. Molly still had too much of her past life clinging to her.

He shared his hunger with her again, cautiously increasing the amount that he let seep through to her. He did not want to make her aware of his own presence within the corridors of her mind. His interests were best served if she truly believed she had traveled so far along the path toward the dark gods' pure state. She had fallen far enough that his hunger stirred a genuine hunger in her—and that amused him, because it so frightened her. But she was not nearly as far gone as he had convinced her.

Ah, and she was convinced. Deliciously so. She was at that very instant launching herself toward his stupid twin-self, the one that couldn't even do a decent job of keeping himself invisible. She was going to let Stupid Baanraak have her—going to let him reach into her and rip the Vodi necklace out of her gut while she still lived, going to give herself up to him so that he might devour her and put an end to her.

Baanraak would have enjoyed doing all of that himself,

but the one who destroyed Molly was going to reveal himself to the two immortals who hunted him in the instant he tore into her. And while Stupid Baanraak didn't have the sense to stay out of the way of immortals, Baanraak the Master of the Night Watch most assuredly did. He planned to let the two immortals amuse themselves in destroying the other Baanraak, and while they did it, *he* was going to move in and take the Vodi necklace and slip quietly back to the Hub, where he could grind the thing to dust—for even though Molly would be gone for good if the necklace was removed before she was dead, the necklace could someday raise up a new Vodi, and who needed that? Baanraak preferred to cover all his bases.

Cat Creek

June Bug, sprawled on the floor in her bedroom, felt the change in Molly. She felt Molly's dull yearning for her own death suddenly become sharp and immediate. She opened herself to Molly's pain, and the girl's plan drove itself into June Bug's brain like a railroad spike.

"Oh, hell," June Bug muttered, and dragged herself to a sitting position. Molly was moving fast, and one of the two . . . no, *three* . . . Baanraaks was waiting in the front yard for her. Neither Heyr nor Pete seemed to realize what was happening; neither of them was going to get there in time to save her.

"Oh, hell," June Bug said again, and fought the pain and the weight of the world, and stood up.

Cat Creek

Through a wall of hell, Mayhem felt the end of everything coming to Cat Creek. He could see it—this darkness of death gods—blurred against a rain of war, a sleet of torture, a hurricane of genocide and starvation, and he tried to find the little thread of pure life that would give him the strength to stand and fight. He caught at it, and thought he had it, and pulled himself to his feet, heading for the mirror, and the gate; and Molly's foul hunger blindsided him and he lost the thread and went down, all the way into unconsciousness.

For Darlene, the intimations of coming battle flowed over and through her, and she could only curl tighter into a ball and close her eyes and rock herself against the pain.

Betty Kay tried. She made it to the closet where she kept what she called the god gun, crawling on hands and knees, blinking through the tears that blurred her sight. She managed to sling the gun over her shoulder, and crawled back to the mirror with it tangling between her arms and catching on her knees, but as she put a hand to her gate-mirror to push her way through, something slammed her back, and the green fire of the gate died. She gritted her teeth against the pain of the backlash, and retched, though her stomach had emptied long before. And eyes narrowed, she began crawling toward the bedroom door, determined to crawl all the way to the fight if that was the only way she could get there.

Cat Creek

Heyr drew the world's magic to him and brought his fists together with a crash that ripped thunder from the sky and slammed lightning down into the yard all around Lauren's house. He hoped the lightning would flush out one or both of the Baanraaks, but it didn't. He felt the magical surge crash all of the gates in the town, though, which was probably just as well. The magical shock wave reverberated through Cat Creek, and he felt it block both George and Betty Kay as they were getting ready to step through their gates into what would be, for both of them, certain disaster.

If he and Pete had to fight alone, that would still be better than being weighed down by the helpless and the vulnerable, and having to constantly watch out for those who couldn't keep up.

Cat Creek

Lauren breathed easier when Molly was on the other side of the door. But she was still sitting there like a damsel in distress, waiting for everyone else to go down in flames to save her. That role didn't suit Lauren. There had to be something she could do—something that would let her improve the odds for the old gods, or weaken the dark gods; something that would let her *fight*.

She stared at the floor-length oval bathroom mirror on its pretty oak stand. It was a little narrow for a mother holding a kid—but if she woke Jake up and held his hand and they stepped through sideways, and one at a time . . .

Yeah. She knew how she could help.

"Hey, kiddo," she said, and tousled Jake's hair.

He woke up just a little, just enough to open his eyes and give her a sweet, trusting smile.

She kissed the top of his head. "Come on. We're going to go do stuff." When they got where they were going, she could magic up a backpack that he could ride in, and he could go back to sleep.

She slid him off her lap and steadied him while he stood up; he clung to her hand. She led him to the mirror, and pressed her fingers to the glass and looked deep into her reflected eyes, seeking the green fire that connected her to all the layers of the universes, and all of space, and all of time.

And when she reached deep enough, she found the place she wanted. She touched it, and felt the pure power of it— she would be able to work with such a place. She spun the path between her and it, and then, still holding Jake's hand, she pressed against the mirror and the gate opened for her and she stepped through.

Cat Creek

Heyr and Pete had tracked one of their enemies to the pecan trees all the way at the back of Lauren's big lot, when something clicked softly at the back of Heyr's mind, and he froze. The front door of Lauren's house had opened.

His blood froze in his veins. All the world's hopes lay, not just in one basket, but within one egg in that basket. And the egg had just dropped and cracked.

"Run," he screamed to Pete, who turned with his weapon unslung and stared toward the house. The two of them pounded through the darkness, dodging trees and shrubs and scattered kid toys.

Heyr used magic to stretch his stride, to speed his muscles, to feel ahead. But everything that lay before him was darkness—he could no more reach within the minds of the dark gods than they could reach within his; the two sides stood separated by an unspeakable abyss, and no bridge could span it. He caught the shape of Molly, out on the porch, and the second click, as the door closed behind her and the spell respun itself. He felt one of the Baanraaks unfold and move forward with terrible, certain speed.

And then he was around the corner, in time to see the nightmare rrôn, one of Earth's mythic dragons twisted out of smoke and darkness, unveil itself beneath the yellow gleam of the porch light and reach Molly and with the delicate precision of a surgeon slice her open and rip gleaming gold and shining guts from her in a long thread.

He heard Molly's scream and felt her pain bleed into him like knives, and the world slowed down. Heyr shouted, "Stay with Molly! Don't let her die!" to Pete, and Pete staggered toward the horror on the porch, already at his breaking point, and Heyr took off in pursuit of the rrôn who had grabbed the necklace.

He threw Mjollnir, aiming for the monster's head, but the rrôn evaded the throw and kept running, cornering around the house with fierce speed and incredible grace. Heyr didn't understand why it was running instead of jumping through a gate, but he was grateful for the error. He tore off around the house in pursuit.

Cat Creek

Pete dragged himself up the stairs toward Molly, who lay gasping on the porch. She was a bloody mess, but she turned her head and stared at him and whispered, "Let me die, Pete. Please, please, let me die while I'm still me."

He put a hand on her arm and stared into her eyes. Her pain poured into him, unbearable pain, grief that in these last minutes was fully human; he couldn't carry her pain, and he didn't dare let her die. "I can't," he said.

Behind him, a voice whispered, "Ah, but you can. You will."

And something ripped into him like razors. His own pain, in its immediacy and ferocity, swallowed everything else, and he twisted as he fell to find himself looking into the eyes of Hell: a shimmering rrôn, black scales gold-tipped in the porch light, a vast grinning mouth full of teeth as long as Pete's hand, gold eyes glittering with amusement.

Pete was bound to the Earth, so he would not die. But his leg lay across the porch and his blood gushed and poured from him and the monster grinned down at him and with the splayed talons of one massive foreleg sliced across and into him, tearing him apart.

Pete tried to find the power to heal himself, to pull everything back together, but the magic he could reach and use was too sparse, too tainted. He could keep himself alive, though he did not want to, but pain was his everything.

And then green fire erupted behind the Baanraak that bent over him, and a golden-haired goddess—an avenging angel or one of Heyr's Valkyries, and yet somehow off-kilter—strode out of the mouth of Heaven wielding a sword that glowed with blinding fire and bearing a silver shield. He knew her, Pete thought, though he knew just as clearly that he had never seen her before in his life. Perhaps she was the last image dying warriors saw before they breathed their last. Or the first they saw after they died. Either way, he was okay with it. And then she tore into the rrôn, who twisted, breathing fire, and lunged at her.

The Valkyrie laughed, turned the fire back on him with her shield, and swung her sword, and the back half of the monster's tail was off. She took a step forward, and Pete realized that she was getting bigger—that she was easily as tall as the rrôn and still stretching upward, and she swung the sword again, and ripped one wing from him.

The monster screamed—rage and pain intermingled— and turned on her in his full fury, leaving Pete and Molly to bleed together.

Off-kilter. Pete kept staring at her, until he realized that the thing clenched between her teeth was not a dagger or a grenade or some other weapon. The goddess had an unlit cigar hanging out of one corner of her mouth.

And he thought, June Bug?

Cat Creek

June Bug, burning with power and free of all pain, drove at the monster with the sword she'd made for herself. This— this was what life was supposed to feel like. She shaped her will and reshaped herself, growing more powerful, more fierce, with every second. Everything she had ever wanted to do and feel as a Sentinel, everything she had denied herself because she was obedient to the dictates of the Council, everything she had yearned to feel as a human being but that she had suppressed out of fear and shame, she released and let herself experience.

Youth and strength and passion and fire and magic and love and desire and hunger, edged with fear and anger and rage, mixed and flowed and bubbled in her veins, and she charged the third Baanraak, singing death and destruction in her heart. The pain had fallen away from her the second she stepped into the gate, and now, unfettered, she was light, she was strong, she was truly a god. Free. She was free, she had eternity before her, she had broken the shackles that bound her to grief and pain and shame, and she could soar. She could fly. She could fight and save her world and experience the love she had so craved. She could truly live. *This* was what Humankind was supposed to feel. *This* was what she had been born to be.

She had come to this fight ready to die to save the people she loved, but now, with the pure sweetness of godhood in her hands, and youth light and strong in her bones, dying seemed like such a bad idea.

She drove her sword into the monster's shoulder, and had the satisfaction of his scream. She slammed it deeper, twisting as she did, and he slashed at her with teeth and fangs, but she blocked him with the silver shield, and stepped inside of his attack, and found a vulnerable spot.

June Bug hacked at his other wing, and tore halfway through it and broke the bone, and seared the cuts with the blazing silver, and heard his anguished scream.

Her heart sang. Her blood sang.

And then he snarled, "Enough."

Enough, she agreed, and turned again, intending to finish him, to end this, to move on to the next Baanraak, and then the next.

But as she turned, he vanished.

June Bug could not see him anywhere, nor could she sense his presence. She stood, blazing silver sword poised, silver shield uplifted, ready to destroy the rrôn, but she could not find him anywhere.

"Coward," she muttered.

The blow that struck her came from behind—the slash of a blade as sharp and deadly as her own, driven by the strength of an ancient god. It clove her in two, and once again she felt pain, but the pain dulled as soon as she felt it. She had time to feel regret, time to think, *Molly*. And, *Marian*.

And then the River of the Dead shifted its banks and

swept over her and its current caught at her and dragged her in, and she found that, god or no, she could not resist its pull.

The Green World

Lauren, with a backpack spun of magic on her back and Jake nestled in it, knelt in a world of lush greenery, a world in which no thinking creatures yet moved. She opened herself fully to the rich, virgin magic of the world, feeling for the very first time the power of life untainted by the poisons of the death-eaters. The power filled her, and she anchored her feet to the ground and spread her arms wide and before her spun a path through time and space and reality, reaching up and back through world after world after world, drilling deeper and deeper into the twisted, pain-ridden horror that the Night Watch and its lackeys and sympathizers had made of the upworlds.

She reached Earth at last, and burrowed into the core, as deep as she could go. She poured life into the heart of her world, then channeled a conduit of pure life straight up into Cat Creek, centering it beneath her own house, which Heyr had made impermeable to the Night Watch. She opened the conduit wide; no pinhole this time, no thumb-thin line. She fed her love, her hope for the future, her gratitude toward those willing to fight to save her, willing to bear impossible pain and the unthinkable weight of immortality bound to flesh and suffering, so that she could fight this fight. So that she could stand where she was and do what she was doing. So that she could give everything good that she had inside her and through that, push back the tide of death.

I love you, she told Brian, lost in flesh but not in her soul. I love you, she told her son, for whose sake she would never quit fighting. I love you, she told Heyr, for bringing us hope and direction and a chance to make this work. I love you, she told each of the Sentinels who had turned their backs on their traditions and beliefs and who faced censure and worse to stand beside her and fight.

I love you, she told Pete, who had turned his life upside down to fight with her—and who loved her in spite of everything. "I love you, Pete," she said, finding in this green place, in this rich world, the courage to say that for the first time, and to admit to herself that she meant it. "I love you."

Life poured through her, rushing upworld in a stream, a river, a torrent.

She stood for a moment, lost in the sheer ecstasy of that power, that life, that love. And then she bound the gate in the green world, spinning her will around it so that it would repel the dark gods and prevent them from touching the work she had done. She'd caught the shape of Heyr's magic—the warding he'd done on her house—and she used his art and his experience, shaping her will and her thoughts around this siphon in the same way that he had shaped his determination around her house, using the riches of this world's life to fuel her work, claiming sanctuary against the Night Watch through all of time and space.

Finished at last, she backed away. And felt Jake's arms tighten around her, and heard him say, "I love you, too, Mama."

She had done what she could. She hoped it would be enough.

Cat Creek and Master's Gold

Baanraak, in pain unlike anything he had ever experienced, stood over the woman to make sure she was well and truly dead, and that she did not have some *other* trick he had never seen before that might bring her back to life and let her finish what she had so effectively started.

But the two halves of her lay still in the yard, and he

stood, panting, over them, and at last was satisfied that when
he turned his back she would not pull herself together and
come after him one final time.

He stared at the sword and shield she'd carried. Purest silver, both of them. Once upon a time the heroes had known to
come after the dark gods with silver, for the dark gods could
not heal such wounds with anything but time. They'd left
aside silver in favor of things that killed quicker—machine
guns and grenades and bombs—and they had forgotten the
power that they had once held in simple weapons.

The bitch who came after him had somehow resurrected
that deadly bit of lore, whether through luck or research or
native intelligence—and worse, she had added a new twist
to old pain. The fire she had started with her blade still
burned within him, spreading, spreading, and the agony of it
would kill him before long even if the damage it was doing
did not.

He was going to die, he realized. Soon.

He snarled, infuriated by the inconvenience of it. He
needed to get to a place that would feed his resurrection
rings and at the same time prevent anyone from coming
across him or them as he came back, and he needed to do it
quickly.

He had enough time to finish off Molly, who lay on the
porch, lingering, and then he had to go.

But as he dragged himself toward the porch, something
happened that he could not understand. Life erupted all
around him. A flood of love and pure energy and magic so
powerful he could not bear it engulfed him, pouring from
the house and washing out like water burst from a dam. In
all of time, he had never felt anything like this, and for the
first time he truly understood what had arrived to stand
against the Night Watch, and he was afraid.

The torrent of life set the silver fire within him burning
brighter and harder, and he realized that if he did not flee at
that moment, he would die where he stood and leave his
body and his resurrection rings in the hands of his enemies.

With the last of his strength and will, he spun a gate to any-where, and threw himself through it.

Cat Creek with Silver and Gold

Baanraak saw his double, wounded beyond repair, fall through a gate. He could hear damned Thor in the backyard battling the other Baanraak, the foolish novice. Pete, in pieces on the porch, lay helpless. Molly's sister and her child were, for the moment, gone.

He had just enough time.

He unwrapped the darkness that had concealed him and ran to Molly's side and crouched beside her.

She opened her eyes and stared at him. Then she narrowed her eyes. "You."

"Me," he agreed, and touched her, and willed the pure energy that now poured out of this place through his own body, breathing shallowly against the terrible pain, and channeled it into her, commanding her to live. He pressed one hand hard against her breast and with all of his will tore the Vodi necklace out of the grasp of the other Baanraak, and when it appeared in his free hand, pressed it against Molly's torn belly and told her flesh to take it back.

He did not waste time with healing her—that he could do from a place of safety. From his own place. Behind him, Pete whispered, "Leave her alone, you bastard," and Baanraak, in too much pain for clever rejoinders, muttered, "Sleep, dammit," and reached around to slam Pete on the head once, knocking him unconscious with a combination of magic and simple force.

Baanraak then sketched a thin circle of ice out of the air, making it far too big because he was used to doing this trick while he was in rrôn form, and his current tiny size kept taking him by surprise. He spun a gate through that, and gathered Molly into his arms and leapt into the ring of green fire.

Behind him, the circle of ice crashed to the porch and shattered.

Baanraak's Private Quarters, Barâd Island, Oria, Wearing Master's Gold

Baanraak tumbled through the gate he'd spun, bleeding, dying, wishing against everything that he had sent others upworld to fight the immortals and the old gods rather than going himself. He sprawled on the floor with the fire of the silver sword still eating away at him, and that shivering little toady Rekkathav came skittering up to him, legs all clicking and clattering across the marble floor.

He looked up at his inherited secretary and said, "Leave this room, lock the doors, and let no one pass until I come out again."

"You're dying," Rekkathav said.

Baanraak snarled at him. "A temporary inconvenience, but I'll make sure to make it worth your while for following my command."

Rekkathav studied him, twitching and making those agitated clicks that Baanraak had discovered meant he was fighting to keep his stomach from everting. He didn't leave, though, and Baanraak blew a weak stream of fire at him and hissed, "Go."

But still Rekkathav didn't flee. Instead, he scuttled around behind Baanraak and hovered over him, inching nearer.

"What are you doing, you little freak?" Baanraak demanded.

"I can see your resurrection ring," Rekkathav said. "I can see it lying just beneath the skin, right where your wing was torn off."

Baanraak tried to raise his head to snap at the hyatvit, but he was too weak. Too near death. Fear chilled his blood. He should have gone somewhere else, somewhere where he could have died unnoticed and resurrected unseen. It had been too easy to follow the easy path back through a gate already open and waiting for him, into chambers where he had felt safe. But he didn't feel safe anymore.

"Get away from me."

"No," Rekkathav said. "No. Not going anywhere." His voice rose with excitement, and he chittered a high-pitched laugh, and rested two pairs of digging legs on Baanraak's side.

They were sharp; Baanraak had never noticed how sharp they were before. They were made for cutting, for digging, for ripping and tearing. They were weapons. He had seen the cowering, weak hyatvit, and had missed the weapons. Now his fear sharpened his pain—he was helpless, and the cringing weakling was no longer cringing.

Rekkathav, mimicking Baanraak's voice with surprising accuracy, said, "You did badly, Snacklet. I think perhaps I *will* eat you today."

Those digging claws ripped through Baanraak's skin and bones in two sharp, hard moves, and tore the resurrection ring from his still-living body. The devouring pain of his wounds, burning with silver fire, spread faster as the resurrection ring's magic left him. He discovered in that instant that the many rings he'd thought he carried within his flesh were all gone; Molly's explosion that had created the false Baanraaks had also robbed him of all his backups. He was in one blow made mortal. He was finished, Baanraak realized. This death would be his last one, and nothing would follow.

Rekkathav moved in front of Baanraak's face, clicking and chirring, and crouched so that he filled the narrowing sphere of Baanraak's fading vision.

"They won't even miss you," Rekkathav said. "I'll pass your orders on, the way I did for poor dead Aril, and I'll give the dark gods messages in your voice when I need to, and if anyone questions your whereabouts, I'll just point to one of the surviving Baanraaks and say there you are, and if they have any complaints about the way you're doing things they can take it up with you personally." He chuckled.

Baanraak felt himself fading from the edges inward. He was cold. He sighed. "They'll kill you in an hour."

Rekkathav held up the resurrection ring, its piercing bar

open for the first time in millennia, signaling that it could be donned by anyone, that its owner was gone. "I could wear this, you know. I could have all of your knowledge, all of your power, all of your secrets. I could have your form if I wanted it, could make myself into you." He hissed, and rose and turned, and Baanraak could not see him, but he could hear a sudden high-pitched whine: the grinding of gold, the destruction of the ring. And he could feel the sudden crawling darkness of the magic the ring's destruction released. "I could, but I won't. You know why? The immortals are tougher than the dark gods. And I think I'd rather live forever than die over and over and over and keep coming back." He shoved his face close to Baanraak's, so close that if Baanraak could have mustered the slightest strength he could have crushed the hyatvit's head between his jaws. Rekkathav grasped his own resurrection ring and ripped it from his hide. "Punishment from you, I'll tell them. I have to earn it back."

His laugh grew softer, or perhaps Baanraak's hearing was fading along with everything else.

"I'm already a god on this world. And now I know Thor's secret of immortality. So . . . let's see," he whispered in Baanraak's ear, "what an immortal can do to the Night Watch. Let's see how I can twist them, and how I can break them, and how I can use them, while making them believe it's all you. The name of Baanraak will one day be a thing of shame to all the dark gods." He rose and moved out of the tiny pinhole of Baanraak's dying vision, but not quite out of hearing. "Not that you'll be around to see it."

Cat Creek

Lauren, with Jake still in his backpack, stepped through the mirror and back into the bathroom. Outside, thunder tore through the trees and lightning crashed and the ground shook, so Heyr-Thor had found one enemy and was fighting. But she could not tell what else was going on.

She shut down the bathroom mirror gate, mindful of the slender possibility of enemies' tracking her from the green world and breaching Heyr's security. With the gate dismantled, she got a hand mirror and lay her fingertips on it and called the green fire one more time. She waited until she could see outside; Heyr-Thor fought one massive rrôn alone, but though Heyr was bleeding, the rrôn was nearly dead. Good. Lauren sent the image in the mirror scurrying, casting around for Molly, or for Pete.

What she saw next was a woman, astonishingly outsized, certainly once lovely, sliced in half, with one half of her all across Lauren's front yard and the other half toppled across the crushed remainder of what had once been Lauren's van.

Lauren couldn't recognize the woman, couldn't figure out how she fit into anything, but dread shivered down her spine nonetheless. She looked farther, and noticed something on her front porch, and brought her focus to bear there.

Her heart felt like it stopped beating. Pete lay there, torn to pieces. Not thinking about consequences, Lauren screamed "No!" and flung the chair away from the bathroom door and slammed open the door and raced down the hall and down the stairs and out the front door and onto the porch.

"Oh, God," she said, and dropped to her knees beside him. She had only barely realized what he might be to her, had only barely come to accept that she could love again, and she had discovered it too late.

But. His chest rose and fell, barely.

He was still breathing? She couldn't believe it—couldn't comprehend that he could be so torn, so horribly ripped apart, and that he still might live.

But she'd take the opportunities life gave her. She kicked open the front door and dragged him—or the main part of him—inside. He was too light, too light. She did not worry about going back for the arm or the leg that still lay on the porch. She pulled him through the foyer to the huge old mirror at the back, and holding on to him and begging him to just keep breathing a little longer, she opened the gate and reached downworld a short way. Just to Oria, just to the little cabin that her parents had built in the ancient forest on the edge of the veyâr realms. It was near enough that she could reach it easily, far enough that she gained the power of the old gods.

When she could see the inside of the cabin, she stepped backward into the gate, dragging Pete and hearing a sleepy "Hey!" from Jake.

The three of them tumbled through green fire, along the pathways of eternity, and though she could hear Jake clearly and feel his presence, she could feel nothing of Pete save that he still lived.

They stepped out into her parents' old bedroom, into deep cold. Winter came earlier to the ancient forest in Oria's northland, and Lauren could hear snow howling outside the windows. She crouched in the darkness, ignoring her discomfort, and willed the magic of the world through her fingertips and into Pete. She saw him whole, saw him healthy, and green fire sheened his body, and the horrible gashes in his torso closed up. An arm budded out, stretched to full length, and detailed itself; a leg regrew itself from the awful hole where his first leg had been. She pressed her hands flat against his chest and felt his heart beat stronger beneath her palms. She felt his chest rise and fall in a steadier rhythm, felt his breaths get slower and deeper.

But still he didn't open his eyes.

She tried to reach inside of him, to find any damage that might have touched his mind, but she could find nothing wrong. She crouched over him and shook him, and he didn't wake up. Tears welled in the corners of her eyes, and she swallowed them.

"Wake up, dammit," she said.

Inside Pete, she felt something click, as if a light had turned on. His eyes opened, and he whispered, "Molly," and then they focused and he looked up at her, and said, "Lauren?"

She dropped on top of him, hugging him desperately, and

heard Jake's muffled "Hey! Stop it!" as her abrupt movements tossed him around.

Pete sat up, and wrapped his arms around her, and hugged her back.

She kissed him, hungrily, desperately, searching for guarantees that she had not lost this second chance after all. He returned her kisses, tentatively at first and then with growing passion. When at last they pulled apart, he touched her cheek and said, "I'm not going to question this. Whatever changed for you, I'm just going to accept it. If what you really want is someone to talk you out of this, it's going to have to be someone else."

"Good," she told him. "Because that's not what I want at all."

Cat Creek

Heyr got the better of Baanraak at last—one blow from Mjollnir hit dead-on and crushed his skull, and he flopped to the ground, twitching. Heyr sent the thunder away and stilled the lightning after giving it the final task of blasting Baanraak's corpse to cinders. The body burned, and Heyr fed the fire with magic. In minutes he had a black pile of ash and one gleaming gold ring that lay half-buried in the pile. Heyr studied it. He recognized the style—it was Art Deco, Earth-made. He would put its creation date as 1930, but it could have been later. One new ring.

Damn.

This, then, had been a minor Baanraak; a raw, green, most-of-the-pieces-missing Baanraak.

Well, it explained the fighting style, anyway. Fierce, furious, and completely lacking in guile.

With a sigh, Heyr pocketed the ring and went around the house to see how Pete was doing.

He stopped as he rounded the corner. An enormous Valkyrie of a woman, split lengthwise, with a fine silver sword still clutched in one hand and a massive silver shield in the other, sprawled across the whole of the front yard. On the porch, an arm, a leg, and pools of blood. Footprints in the blood, and a bloody handprint on the door, and bloody drag marks that led into the house.

Heyr gripped Mjollnir and took a step toward the house, and suddenly realized that power poured out of it in a pure stream. Vast power, life rich and sweet and good enough to feed not just one immortal but an army of immortals. He anchored himself to it, and for the first time in hundreds of years, he felt more life than death, more hope than despair. He took a deep breath, and tipped his head to the heavens, and said, "By the halls of Valhalla, by the Æsir and the songs of the heroes, by all that is right and just in man, I am Thor again. And against the tide of darkness, I will *stand*."

Knowing that he might find the worst, but knowing, too, that the best had returned, if only in small measure, and that the world and Humankind had reason again to hope, he headed up the stairs and into the house.

He met Pete, with Lauren and Jake, stepping through the mirror and into the foyer.

Pete's first words were, "We haven't won yet. Baanraak took Molly."

Heyr stood in the foyer, trying to put that together. "What happened out front?"

"After you went after the Baanraak with Molly's necklace, a third Baanraak showed up as I was heading to her to heal her," Pete said. "He ripped me apart, and was going to kill her, but June Bug stepped through a gate—"

"June Bug?" Lauren and Thor asked at the same time.

"I didn't recognize her until I saw the cigar. But it was June Bug. She stepped through the gate and just started fighting—she was amazing."

"She wasn't immortal," Heyr said.

"I think that was the way she managed to stand against him. She didn't act like she had any pain, any doubt. She just waded in and tore him apart."

"She killed him?"

Pete shook his head. "I don't think so. She hurt him. But after he killed her, he was strong enough to start toward the house. He was going to kill Molly. And then something chased him off. I saw him make a gate and dive into it, and a second later the third Baanraak—the man-shaped one that I went drinking with—was up on the porch and kneeling over Molly. And he did something to me, and the next thing I knew I was in Oria, and Lauren . . . well . . ."

"I put Pete back together," Lauren said.

Thor nodded, guessing from the looks of the two of them standing there together that she had done a bit more than that.

"We have to go after Molly, then," Lauren said.

Pete said, "We have to take care of June Bug first. We can't leave her out there like that."

Thor said, "No. We'll send her to the gates of Valhalla as she deserves. As a warrior."

Baanraak's Demesne, Kerras

Molly felt the pain of the gate, and then the nothingness of being without physical form. She held up a hand, and saw it only as the faintest of shadows; she looked at the bright sunshine, the tall, vivid grass, the alien wildlife everywhere, and she wondered where Baanraak had brought her. And why.

Baanraak—a human-looking Baanraak, but still the rrôn whose mind she knew so well—stood atop a broad, flat rock. He wasn't a shadow; he was perfectly solid. Molly was with him, but not through any choice of her own. She could not move. Something was very wrong with her, but she felt no pain and no fear. She had been torn to pieces back on Earth. Was she still? Had she died? Perhaps this was some dying dream.

Then Baanraak put her down, and she realized that he had been holding her. Still she could not move. He touched her; she could see him do it though she could not feel him.

And then, in a rush, sensation returned. The warmth of the

sun on her face, the scent of the breeze, the million and one sounds of a world in motion, full of life and vibrant. And the pain. The pain returned, too, and in spite of her determination not to, she cried out.

"Wait," he said. "I had to bring you all the way here before I could heal you."

And his hands touched her again, but this time she felt them. They were gentle, and they channeled the green fire that burned her—but burned cleanly. Her wounds healed, and after a moment she could move her arms and her legs, and turn her head, and sit up on her own.

"Where are we?"

"Kerras."

"Kerras is a cinder."

"Most of it is," he agreed. "I made this place, though. I used your sister's siphon—the magic she channeled here."

Molly looked around. "It's . . . beautiful," she said. She remembered him with another face, on another day, walking with her as they talked about a city lost, its people gone, and she remembered how much pleasure she had taken from his companionship. Later that same day, she followed him and blew him into pieces, of course, and herself in the process, which rather ruined the memory.

Still, as she looked around her, she could see something of the beauty within him.

"It suits you."

He smiled a little. The smile was a lot less forbidding when he wore a human face. "It does," he said. "It is the world of my birth." He shrugged. "As I remember it, in any case."

She thought about how any contact with Lauren's magic hurt her, and she looked at the beautiful panorama of wilderness that spread around her in all directions. "How did you do it?" she asked. "How did you bear it?"

"It hurt," he admitted. "But I've borne pain before. And . . . I wanted to see my home again. I wanted to feel my own sun, smell my own air, taste the foods that I have not tasted since I was young. It mattered, so I simply did what I had to do."

She looked around her and thought about touching live magic or working with live magic. She hadn't really considered that she might be able to do anything as vast as rebuilding a world; the more of herself she stripped away, the more pain life caused her.

And yet Baanraak—this Baanraak, anyway—had changed for the better, and she thought it was this place and the fact that he had created it that had changed him. She felt the beginnings of emotion in him, and the faintest stirrings of hope. And things so rare and beautiful that she dared not even give them names. They were all buds, barely breaking the surface, certainly tender and easily trampled and destroyed.

If only Baanraak didn't have to worry about dying, he might be able to rebuild this world and somehow find his way back to being the Baanraak he would have been if the dark gods had never touched him.

He needed to be immortal, she thought, and at the same instant, she thought, *I know how to do that.*

"Have any of the dark gods ever . . . become true immortals?" she asked him.

"No," he said. "The resurrection rings wouldn't tolerate such a thing. The gold—" He looked at her, falling silent.

"We both wear gold laced with silver," she said.

He stared at her.

"Have you ever yearned for your soul?" she asked him.

He was quiet for a long time. He looked away from her, staring out over the wildlife-dotted plains. At last he said, "Of late, I have missed my mother," he said. "She died when my world died. And I know that . . . beyond . . . I would find her there, if I could only get there. But, soulless . . ." He took a deep breath, then continued. "Yes. I have longed for my soul."

"We can earn our souls," Molly said, and looking out at the world he had made, she thought she knew a way that they might do it. "We could become immortals—hang on to everything that is left of us, and rebuild on that. We could hunt down and destroy the Night Watch, because no one else could track them the way we can track them. But perhaps we could create, too. Perhaps we could be forces for life as well as for death."

He looked at her, his eyes strange and frightening.

"Or perhaps I speak too soon when I say 'we.' Maybe . . . I thought since you sought me out, since you brought me here, since you healed me . . ."

He took her hand in his. "From the first moment that our minds touched, I knew that you were a force for change. I felt something in you that gave me reason to hope—and hope is something I had turned away from long ago." He smiled a little. "Now I see where that hope might become more. Where it might become reality."

"You would fight with me? You would try this?"

"It will hurt. The pain the immortals live with is unlike anything you have ever experienced. And we would have, too, the pain of live magic, when we are at base dead things."

"I know," Molly said. "But I don't fear pain. Only oblivion."

"I'll fight with you. I'll create with you. If we do not earn our souls, it will not be because we did not try."

Molly smiled. And then she laughed softly. "What will we be, Baanraak? Will we be old gods? Will we be dark gods?"

Baanraak grinned. "We will be the gods who bring down the Night Watch. Whatever name there might be for that— that is what we'll be."

"Oh," Molly said. "We'll be heroes."

Baanraak stood up and looked out at the setting sun. "Go tell your sister that, won't you? Otherwise I fear she and that horde of immortals of hers will come after me with big guns and big magic and try to blast me into dust. And I haven't had the opportunity to be a hero in a very long time. I find I fancy the idea."

Cat Creek

In true Viking tradition, the new immortals sent June Bug out to sea in a beautiful, burning longship, arrayed in her finest clothes, bearing her silver sword and her silver shield.

The new immortals: Darlene and Betty Kay, Eric and Mayhem, and standing with them Molly the dark god, now made immortal, with pain in her eyes but an aura of hope that surrounded her, and holding her hand Baanraak—the first of the Baanraaks, and the only one to bear the burden of immortality—wearing for the moment a human seeming.

George had come, too, to see June Bug off. And so had Lauren and Jake.

They had to give her their Viking send-off on the green world Lauren had found because they were afraid of drawing attention anywhere nearer to Earth. But they would not deny her a send-off befitting a hero. When the ship sailed out of sight and even the last of the flames disappeared from view, they raised silver goblets to her, and each toasted her journey to the Hall of Heroes in silence.

Then Pete said, "May you find love waiting on the other side," and Thor said, "May you find adventures worthy of a hero." Darlene wiped at her eyes with the back of one hand and said, "I wish I'd been strong enough to do what you did. And . . . I hope they have cigars over there, and that no one minds if you smoke."

Some of the Sentinels chuckled, and Betty Kay said, "I'm going to miss her."

They stood a while longer in silence, watching the water, watching the thread of smoke on the horizon fade away to nothing.

Then Lauren kissed Pete and handed Jake to him. She walked down to the water's edge and waded in. When she was waist-deep, she took a letter that she had written to Brian, and read it out loud.

"I love you," she read. "And I will love you forever. And someday—perhaps even some day very soon—I'll rejoin you.

"You told me I was free to love again. Now I have found someone to love, and though I'm afraid, every day, of where this love might lead me and of what the future holds, still I am going to go on.

"Jake will forever hold you in his heart as his father, and I will forever hold you in my heart as my first and greatest love.

"Give me your blessing until we meet again.

"Your Laurie."

She sealed the letter in a bottle and tossed the bottle out into the waves. And then she turned back to see her friends, her supporters, the people who believed in her, standing on the shore watching her. And with them her dear friend and her new love, Pete.

Her heart skipped a beat, and she smiled at him, and he and Jake both waved to her.

She turned back to the sea, to where June Bug had vanished. I'll dare to live, she promised herself. I'll dare to love, and dare to fight, so that when I die my life will be a testament to the chances I took, and not to the chances I was afraid to take.

And she whispered, "Thank you, June Bug. Go find happiness. It's waiting there for you. I know it is."

Then she started back to shore.